"YOU HAVE THE MOST UNUSUAL WAY OF TELLING A MAN NO, LIVVY, AND YOUR TIMING IS LOUSY," HE SAID DISGUSTEDLY.

"I'm sorry," she said unsteadily.

"Are you?" His eyes were merciless as they raked her body.

"Jake, you don't understand. I—"

"Tell me something I will understand," he demanded. "Did you intend making love with me tonight? Or was it another of your little advance and retreat ploys designed to make me crazy?"

"No! You know that's not true! I—"

"How do I know that? Every time I try to touch you, you go a little berserk. Did you tease your husband, too, let him go so far and then turn him away, like you do me? Is that why he cheated on you? Why he finally divorced you?"

A CANDLELIGHT ECSTASY SUPREME

HORIZON'S GIFT

Betty Jackson

A CANDLELIGHT ECSTASY SUPREME

Published by
Dell Publishing Co., Inc.
1 Dag Hammarskjold Plaza
New York, New York 10017

Dell ® TM 681510, Dell Publishing Co., Inc.

Candlelight Ecstasy Supreme is a trademark of Dell
Publishing Co., Inc.

Candlelight Ecstasy Romance®, 1,203,540, is a registered
trademark of Dell Publishing Co., Inc.

ISBN: 0-440-13704-7

Printed in the United States of America

First printing—November 1984

To Our Readers:

Candlelight Ecstasy is delighted to announce the start of a brand-new series—Ecstasy Supremes! Now you can enjoy a romance series unlike all the others—longer and more exciting, filled with more passion, adventure, and intrigue— the stories you've been waiting for.

In months to come we look forward to presenting books by many of your favorite authors and the very finest work from new authors of romantic fiction as well. As always, we are striving to present the unique, absorbing love stories that you enjoy most—the very best love has to offer.

Breathtaking and unforgettable, Ecstasy Supremes will follow in the great romantic tradition you've come to expect *only* from Candlelight Ecstasy.

Your suggestions and comments are always welcome. Please let us hear from you.

Sincerely,

The Editors
Candlelight Romances
1 Dag Hammarskjold Plaza
New York, New York 10017

CHAPTER ONE

As the soft soles of her low-heeled leather shoes hit the middle step on the stairway, Livvy Waring heard the telephone ringing. She sped upward toward her office, the flaring hem of her cotton skirt flapping against the backs of her long, bare legs. In her arms were several folders, and she clutched them lightly to her chest as she hurried along. The aluminum can she held in one hand received a quick squeeze as the phone continued to ring, then there was a muttered imprecation and she loosened her grip when she realized the can was in danger of collapsing and sloshing its contents onto her hand. With each running step she took she could feel her dark, shoulder-length hair escaping the topknot she'd chosen in deference to the heat, and she grimaced her mild discomfort. Slightly out of breath, she rounded the doorway of her office and drew to an abrupt halt. There was no longer a need to rush.

She fixed a reproachful glare on the silent phone and muttered a softly disgruntled "Hmph!"

With her usual graceful stride Livvy moved to her pedestal desk, deposited the folders onto its dark, gleaming surface of pecan wood, and anchored them in place with the weight of the soft-drink can. Her hands swept to her hair, making swift adjustments to secure it in place. A light film of perspiration beaded her forehead, and she blotted it away with her fingertips, then positioned her wide-framed glasses more securely on the bridge of her straight, slim nose.

It was the first time she'd entered her office since the evening before, and the room was stifling and airless from being closed up overnight. She switched on the ceiling fan and opened the windows, breathing deeply of the fresh morning air. Sweet and sun-warmed and smelling faintly of dampened earth, the light breeze was perfect. Leaning farther into the windowsill, she angled her gaze skyward and sighed in appreciation.

It was one of those beautiful blue October days. After a week of nothing but overcast skies and drenching rains, it was lovely to see not a wisp of cloud disturbing the vast perfection of the sky. The sun shone brilliantly, undaunted that the first day of autumn had been officially proclaimed weeks earlier. High in the sky the golden-white globe beamed down, spreading warmth along the unfaded greens of the landscape. According to the calendar, November was just around the corner. Yet, as far as Livvy could see, no harbinger of winter had tinted the trees and grasses and shrubs to yellows and browns and oranges. In northern Texas, summer was reluctant to give up its long reign of power.

Smiling slightly at the whimsey of her thoughts, Livvy let her glance trace the fertile path of goodwill the late morning sun haloed upon the back courtyard. The heavy rains of the past week had prevented the inhabitants of Horizon House from roaming their favorite outdoor retreat. Today would be different. The rainbow path in Horizon's courtyard gleamed a bright invitation. The lush green lawn, supple and cushiony after its life-giving drink from heaven, offered a verdant enticement. The playground equipment glittered temptingly in brilliant hues of poppy-red and daisy-yellow and morning-glory blue. A gleam of pride lit Livvy's brown eyes as she surveyed the

8

familiar scene below her. She waited expectantly for it to become even brighter.

Moments later her anticipation was rewarded. The twenty-odd little members of her day-care center frolicked rambunctiously into view. Their small bodies clad in summer cottons, flying feet encased in tennis shoes and leather sandals, they laughed and shouted exuberantly, their demeanor as bright and cheerful as the day. The sun's goodwill was contagious; small souls were eager to soak up its benevolent power.

For a while longer Livvy ignored the work waiting on her desk and enjoyed the sight below her. The children skipped happily along the tiled rainbow pathway that led in an intriguing arc from the back entrance of the staid old house to the outer limits of the courtyard. There the children separated, shooting off in different directions to seek their individual pursuits. Beneath the beckoning shade of towering oaks and stately pecan trees, a rainbow-hued playhouse stood. It was flanked by sandboxes and brightly colored gym sets. A paved area in the corner of the yard offered hopscotch and tic-tac-toe designs, and, on a patch of green grass not far away, wooden learning toys were stacked.

She laughed softly as the playground became alive with activity. Her young charges were never short on energy, and she found them a delight to watch. Balls, gaily striped and constructed of foam rubber, were tossed harmlessly to and fro. Young muscles strained as small limbs played on the steel bars of the gym sets, swinging, climbing, conquering imaginary summits. Shovels and pails were wielded enthusiastically and inspired designs were molded from the rain-dampened sand. There was abundant opportunity in Horizon's courtyard for all kinds of endeavors. Livvy had planned it that way.

Strolling vigilantly among the children was one adult, the morning's guardian of the playground. Livvy's eyes crinkled with amusement. From a distance her friend and assistant, Glory Maddox, appeared scarcely old enough to supervise the playground. Her petite height made her seem considerably younger than her thirty-one years. Up close, however, Glory's maturity was in no doubt. She was five feet two and blond, her pert face topping a body that bordered on voluptuous.

Ruefully, Livvy glanced down the length of her own tall, willowly body. At five nine she weighed the same hundred and fifteen pounds that looked so sexy on her friend. On Livvy the weight looked significantly different. Granted, she had the prerequisite number of convex curves to deem her a member of womankind, but they were streamlined to a lithe, graceful slenderness that by no stretch of her imagination could be termed "sexy." A quick inventory listed small breasts, slim hips, and long legs.

Ah, well, at least I'm healthy, she decided with a smile. A no-sugar, no-caffeine diet saw to that. And the constant lifting of twenty- to forty-pound youngsters gave her supple body a tensile strength that added to her physical well-being.

"Good health and reasonable attractiveness," she summed up musingly. "Who could ask for more?"

She frowned a little, shrugging away the thought. Although the question was rhetorical, the answer would have been instinctively literal. In unguarded moments she knew exactly what she would have asked for.

"Quit your woolgathering and get to work," she muttered as she spurred herself away from the window.

Seated behind her desk, Livvy lifted the soft-drink can from the stack of folders and set it aside. Compiling the children's monthly evaluation reports wasn't a difficult task, just time-consuming. A frowning glance at her watch told her it was almost ten thirty. In just over an hour it would be lunchtime. She resolutely opened the first folder. There wasn't enough time to finish all the reports. What she failed to complete would have to go home with her that evening.

From outside came the insidious enticement of small voices lifted in laughter. A small, self-knowing grin chased away her frowning expression.

Having made a success of Horizon House in less than a year, she considered herself a capable businesswoman. The administrative side of her day-care center was seen to with care and diligence. But she knew where she'd rather be at the moment. The happy sounds from the back courtyard were invitations she found difficult to ignore.

When the phone rang a few minutes later, Livvy was writing a final notation on the fourth evaluation report. She reached for the receiver, anchoring it under her chin as she folded the completed form in half and slid it into an envelope. Already scanning the next report, she greeted the caller automatically, preoccupation making her voice flat and colorless.

"Horizon House. Olivia Waring speak—" she murmured, only to have a deep, incisive male voice stab her last syllable into oblivion.

"So you *do* answer the phone" were the first words she heard. "Yours is the eighth on a list of fifteen child-care establishments I'm contacting, Ms. Waring, and my time is limited. I need a quick rundown on Horizon House and, if it's brief, your sales pitch." There was a pause before "please" was added in brusque afterthought.

A vague frown puckered Livvy's brow. Her caller sounded like a man used to giving orders and having them obeyed. He also sounded as if his tolerance level would rival that of a three-year-old. She then decided the observation might be uncharitable to three-year-olds since they demanded, but said "please" cajolingly, not with such questionable courtesy. Livvy's pencil moved swiftly across the report form in front of her, commenting on her young charge's progress in relating with his peers.

"*Ms. Waring,* my time really is limited," the hard baritone voice reiterated, causing her nose to wrinkle in aversion to his impatient tone.

Livvy obediently responded, albeit in an abstracted monotone as she continued to write. "Horizon House is located on the city's southside at—"

"The *address* is in the *phone book.*" He sliced through her words.

His sarcasm verged on hostility, and it gained him Livvy's wary and undivided attention. Her fingers tightened around the pencil as she spent a moment identifying the restricting knot building in her stomach. Apprehension? No! *Annoyance.* She had an aversion to difficult, strong-willed men. She straightened in her chair and her chin came up a notch. Daily contact with the divergent temperaments of more than twenty children had taught her a lot of patience.

She made her voice neutrally courteous. "We have an enrollment capacity of only twenty-five children because we're—"

"Exclusive?" he supplied sardonically when she hesitated over the description of Horizon's size and staffing. The ensuing silence was pregnant with an unmistakable tension. Difficult might be too mild a description of the man. How about downright offensive? She involuntarily winced when he urged gruffly, "Go on, Ms. Waring!"

She struggled so with a rising irritation that her soft voice was reduced to a whisper. "We're open weekdays from seven A.M. until—" she tried again, but her last words were buried under his low-voiced string of profanity.

Hot color burned into Livvy's cool cheeks. The man not only had an offensive habit of interrupting, he also had a disgusting vocabulary. Her finger hovered above the disconnect button on the phone and jerked away

12

when he growled, "Someone just came in! Hold on a minute, Ms. Waring!"

On that curt order Livvy held on—tensely to the phone receiver and resolutely to her composure—her fingertips pressing into her temple. Two minutes of the man's abrasiveness had set off tiny sledgehammers in her head.

As a diversion she reached for the forgotten can of soft drink and brought it to her lips. The sugar-free, decaffeinated cola was tepid but still fizzy, and she let some of it trickle down her throat. Through the phone came muffled sounds that sped the cola to her stomach on a quick gulp of surprise. She hoped her ears were deceiving her, but as a woman's throaty contralto voiced droned on and on, Livvy realized she had become an unwitting eavesdropper to her caller's conversation with his visitor.

Her mind formed a protest, but her caller stifled the words at the tip of her tongue. His voice muffled slightly, as if he had covered the receiver with his fingers but hadn't bothered moving it away from his mouth, the man said irascibly, "Couldn't this have waited until tonight, Michelle? As you can see, I'm on the phone and I don't have the time for—"

The woman broke through his gruff reproval, her words still garbled to Livvy but her beseeching tone as clear as a bell. When the man spoke again, it was with heavy resignation. "Yes, I told you to buy something sexy. And yes, black lace will look great against red satin sheets. But this is a business office, not a bedroom, and—"

His censure didn't faze his companion. When she interrupted him the second time, Livvy sent up a silent cheer. Bully for Michelle! If anyone deserved being cut off in midsentence, it was the man on the other end of the line.

Unexpectedly, Livvy's humor asserted itself, and she fought back a persistent grin. Black lace and red satin?

13

The combination sounded like the decor of a sleazy bordello. Or was that black leather and chains? she mused. Her sense of the prurient had always been a little vague on details. In any event, the thought that her caller might need such stimulation to boost a waning libido brought a small, malicious smirk to her lips.

Her catty pleasure dimmed when she heard the man drawl cynically, "Who's disgusted? I *enjoy* spending an entire morning listening to eight chatty females trying to sell me on their exclusive little child-care centers." His short laugh was a deep bass rumble, not unpleasant to the ear. Unwillingly, Livvy felt its echo quiver along the entire length of her slender form. "No, make that seven," he amended in a voice dry with irony. "The woman from Horizon House is definitely not chatty. She's either dimwitted or indifferent, because she's yet to put two sentences together. Now, why would I—"

That was as much as Livvy heard. Her finger had obeyed the dictates of her self-respect, pressing down firmly on the disconnect button.

Amazingly, the first thing that ran through her mind was the old saw about eavesdroppers hearing only ill of themselves. Then cold outrage took over. *Put two sentences together!* When had *he* given her the chance! The man—whoever he was—could go take a flying leap off the caustic tower of his demeaning opinions! She fumed, then added aloud for good measure, "The fall will probably kill him!"

Her angry thoughts progressed no further. The phone rang under her fingertip, causing it to jerk away. Her small gasp of surprise went into the receiver still positioned at her ear.

"Ms. Waring?" questioned the male voice she had recently heard too much of.

"Yes!" she snapped.

"You hung up on me!" he accused.

"I wasn't feeling too *chatty!*"

14

There was a tense pause before he said grimly, "Michelle said you'd probably heard. Will you accept my apology?"

Would she? She didn't feel too gracious at the moment, and he certainly didn't sound very contrite. She sidestepped the issue, asking coolly, "Was there anything else you wanted to know about Horizon House?"

His understanding came in the form of a heavy sigh. "I did *offer,*" he pointed out dryly, then fired a round of questions that allowed no time for more than the cold, monosyllabic replies Livvy gave him. By the time he asked Horizon's tuition fee, she quoted it rather haughtily, fed up with his aggressively rude manner.

"Baby-sitting two small children seems to be more profitable than I'd imagined," he observed in a gratingly arid tone. "Your fee is certainly a step up from the dollar an hour teen-agers earn for the same job."

His condescension was no less nettling than his rudeness. With chilling precision, Livvy explained, "The amount is for the *care* and *supervision* of *one* child." His silence presented an opportunity to speak freely. Quickly, her stiff tone vaguely chastening, she added, "Horizon House is highly commended for its innovative concepts in Early Childhood Development, if that means anything to you. Some parents are interested in more than just a convenient place to stash their children during the day. Some want the best learning-and-growing facility available."

"Is that right?" he commented mildly, sounding oddly subdued. Unfortunately, Livvy had no time to gloat over his chastened state. In a harsh, rumbling baritone that resounded in her ear and was guaranteed to make a brave person tremble, he fired one more salvo from his arsenal of offensive repartee. "As a businessman, I've found that high commendations and high costs don't necessarily mean high quality. And I'm fast finding I'll be one of those parents who believes children's early development should be overseen by someone interested in more than

15

the size of their parents' bankbooks! You, lady, better have one hell of a setup to show me, and I suggest you be there to show it to me personally!"

After such growling, near-threatening condemnation, the dial tone in her ear sounded like the Hallelujah Chorus sung by an angel choir. It was a moment before Livvy found the presence of mind to realize he'd hung up on her. Evidently he upheld the policy of tit for tat.

Her movements jerky, she placed the phone receiver in its waiting cradle. A tired little "Whew!" whistled past her lips and she sagged back in her chair, trembling from head to toe. She felt like a battle-weary soldier after a hand-to-hand skirmish with a stronger foe. Whoever her caller was, she fervently hoped he would not find his way to Horizon House for his personally conducted tour. Meeting him face-to-face would call for full battle gear.

She jumped when the phone rang again, and her eyes flashed annoyance. If it was her obnoxious caller again, she wasn't ready for another round of his uncalled-for abuse. She considered not answering it but, on the third ring, found herself gingerly grabbing the receiver and bringing it to her ear.

"Hello?" she inquired hesitantly.

"Hi, baby," said a self-assured male voice.

"Brad?" she asked reluctantly. But she knew. Her stomach had already coiled into a remembered knot of tension. It seemed today was her lucky day.

"It's been a long time, Liv." The silky smoothness of his voice grated along her nerve endings like the screech of chalk across a blackboard.

"Yes," she managed. Eighteen months *was* a long time. She found herself wishing it could have been longer. Or that she could have had an advance warning of his call. The surprise of hearing from him had her brain functioning only enough to register the frantic signals coming from her nerve center.

"I ran into Paul and Glory last night."

"Did you?" Glory hadn't mentioned it to her. But then, both of them had been so busy all morning that there hadn't been a chance to utter more than a quick word in passing.

"When I asked about you, they both seemed reluctant to say anything. Paul finally told me about the day-care center while Glory frowned like a little prune." He laughed—that soft, relaxed laugh that at one time would have warmed her heart. She shivered, feeling cold inside and out. "I thought my mind was playing tricks on me. Glory used to be bubbly and talkative."

He said it casually, as if commenting on the changeable Texas weather. Where was the depth of feeling for meeting up with old friends? Where was the awareness or regret that his actions eighteen months ago had affected the friendship?

"Let's get together," he suggested. "I'm interested in learning more about your life on the sidelines of mother-hood."

Livvy flinched, even though the remark was typical of Brad. Anything he didn't understand or couldn't cope with, he ridiculed or rejected. Striving for an even tone, she asked, "Are you calling from Dallas?"

"I'm at the Fort Worth Hilton for a business seminar. Meet me for lunch, Liv. There's a restaurant near the hotel that does a great tempura. You always liked that. When you were pregnant with Jamie, you craved it on a regular basis."

For a moment all the old bitterness rose in her throat. *Don't mention Jamie so casually, you coward! You couldn't even meet your final responsibility to him!* In the barest whisper, she said, "No, Brad."

"Come on, baby, don't be that way. We were married for twelve years. There were times when we were perfect together. You haven't forgotten any more than I have."

His assured tone, as much as his insensitive rationale, appalled her. He remembered the perfect times. She couldn't forget the ending. After the car accident that had killed their three-year-old son, he couldn't get away from her fast enough. A Mexican divorce, for God's sake, while she was still in the hospital, while Glory and Paul made all the arrangements to bury their son. Brad had existed on the good times, the perfect times. The trauma of Jamie's death and the surgeon's pronouncement that, for her, there would be no more children, had horrified him. He had flown, gaining quick release from a wife and a marriage no longer perfect by his standards.

Livvy closed her eyes, trying to relax. "I can't leave Horizon House during the day." She wasn't even tempted. She added quietly, "And I'm really very busy right now."

"You don't need me any longer, do you, Liv."

It was a statement, not a question, and held an underlying note of challenge. As if he expected her to deny it. As if the thought of her happy and independent of him was something he refused to believe. Livvy wanted to laugh at his remarkable ability to fool himself, but her chest was constricted by the anguish of remembrance, preventing laughter, almost preventing breath.

"I can't talk anymore, Brad," she said thickly. What an understatement! All the useless, bitter words stored up for eighteen months would have to go unsaid. Speech was rapidly becoming impossible.

He hesitated, perhaps wanting to argue the point, before finally murmuring, "I'll call you again, baby."

Her mouth opened to voice a protest, to tell him no, but he was no longer on the line. For the second time that morning a man had hung up on her. Very slowly, she did the same.

The quality of the ensuing silence was tranquil, and Livvy willingly gave in to it. After removing her glasses, she laid her head on her crossed arms atop the desk. She was suddenly very, very tired, feeling completely drained of energy and emotion. *No wonder,* a mirthless little voice

18

mocked. *It isn't every day you're pitted against two male adversaries. And that last one was the killer!* Wryly agreeing with her inner voice, she felt a weak smile tremble to her lips. Two hard-fought battles back to back, and she was feeling the wounds of both. *Tonight,* she promised herself solemnly, *you treat yourself to a cool glass of wine and a long soak in the tub.* Honest to God, her muscles felt as abused as if the battles had been physical.

"Are you all right, Livvy?"

The soft query came from the door and brought Livvy's head up in surprise. She hadn't heard Glory's approach. In fact, she hadn't realized the playground squad was back inside. She fumbled for her glasses, pushing them onto her nose as her friend walked across the room carrying a tray loaded with food.

"Good grief, I've missed lunchtime!" she exclaimed distractedly, slowly rising from her chair.

"Jenny's with the children. Sit down and stop fretting."

Jenny Clarke, the college senior who worked part time at Horizon House, was a capable and enthusiastic caregiver. The children were in good hands. Better, Livvy realized in annoyance, than hers were at the moment. It was ridiculously easy to acquiesce to Glory's directive as her slender length relaxed back into the chair.

"Clear a place for this," Glory instructed quietly, inclining her head first to the tray she held and then to the cluttered desk.

She was a little lethargic, but Livvy did as bidden. She dispassionately eyed the food Glory set before her. She wasn't hungry. Around a forced, bright smile, she murmured, "Thank you, Glory. This is nice."

From the visitor's chair at the opposite side of the desk, Glory closely inspected her friend's countenance and astutely surmised that the smile was artificial and didn't extend to the brown eyes clouded with lingering disquiet. Her own features etched with concern, she confessed unhappily, "I overheard the last part of your conversation with Brad. I suppose he told you about seeing Paul and me last night." At Livvy's nod, she spread her hands wide in apology. "I'm sorry, Livvy. I should have told you this morning, but I honestly hoped he would be satisfied with the information Paul gave him. I should have known better."

"Don't worry about it. I'm in the phone book. Even if Brad hadn't learned about Horizon House, he easily could have called me at home. Besides"—her smile was wry, but more natural than her previous one had been— "they say a bad penny always turns up. Sooner or later, Brad was bound to show up."

Some of Glory's concern relaxed. "I don't suppose he offered an excuse for his rotten behavior eighteen months ago?" she ventured with more irony than interest.

Livvy carefully arranged a paper napkin across her lap. Brad had said nothing about the way he ended their marriage. His treatment of her aside, it tormented her to realize his only mention of Jamie had been the comment about her pregnant cravings. Their marriage had never been the best, but they had shared a love for Jamie. Hadn't they? Or had the depth of Brad's love for his son been measured only by pride in the tiny extension of himself?

Shaken by the thought, she answered a little vaguely. "He said something about getting together to talk over old memories." Talking to him briefly by phone had resurrected old memories. And they hurt.

"You could have told him you remembered what a louse he is," Glory suggested, not in jest. Her eyes were bright with antagonism, her cheeks rouged by indignation. "Or that you have fonder memories of your high school biology teacher who made you dissect a frog and then threatened to have you expelled when you threw up all over his science lab."

"Maybe so," Livvy murmured, smiling away both the

awful reminiscence of that long-ago high school fiasco and Glory's snide suggestions. When Brad called, she had wanted only to avoid a long conversation, not to hurl a bitter list of recriminations at him. She met Glory's angry gaze and felt a sudden lifting of spirits. "Calm down, friend," she advised, her eyes amused. "There's no reason to get into a stew. As you can see, I'm all in one piece. Brad did all the damage he could do a long time ago."

Not entirely convinced, Glory nevertheless changed the subject. Livvy's composed mien seemed to irritate her. "You're too calm," she charged disgruntledly. "And your temper is too soft. Even when you're upset or angry, you either grin and bear it or grit your teeth and count to ten. Why don't you pitch a fit and throw something? It's good for the psyche to let off steam now and then."

Livvy grinned widely as she picked up her fork. She speared a morsel of boned chicken and brought it up from her plate, countering easily, "Volatile displays and temper tantrums lead to ulcers and heart disease. I'm protecting my good health." She winked as she popped the chicken into her mouth.

Her teasing words covered a very real belief. Strong emotions were private emotions. She cried her tears where no one could see, railed against the fates when she was all alone, and controlled her anger just as Glory had charged. She survived on her composure.

The memory of her unnamed caller and his ignitable temperament popped into her head unbidden. Talk about a prime candidate for ulcers and high blood pressure! Impatience and irascibility had flowed from him as freely as water from a fountain. Once again she found herself hoping he would forget all about Horizon House.

Livvy bent her concentration to her meal. Her appetite hadn't fully returned, but she managed to put away a creditable amount, leaving only the buttermilk biscuit and a few green beans. The glass of iced pineapple juice

Glory had provided was cool and naturally sweet, and she savored it between bites.

"Men!"

Glory's abrupt exclamation jerked Livvy's attention away from her meal. Ready to nod a scornful indictment of the male sex, she checked the movement in midnod, her head thrown slightly back. There was a familiar gleam in her friend's blue eyes that warned her Glory wasn't expressing the same scorn Livvy felt. Wisely, she converted the nod into a negative shake.

"No. Absolutely not!" she stated adamantly before Glory could expand on the subject. "I don't want to get off on your favorite topic of men. No matchmaking!"

"But I've come up with a new angle!"

"Forget it."

"The least you can do is hear me out," Glory said reproachfully.

Livvy firmly squelched the desire to soften, and said, "There is positively no angle you haven't already presented to me in the last six months. Not to mention two cousins and one of Paul's co-workers," she added dryly.

Glory sighed in seeming capitulation. "Brad was the only man you were ever serious about," she commented, her tone innocuous.

Livvy's nod came slowly. That was true enough. She had married Brad right out of her tomboyish teens and had never had any real experience in dealing with other men. She eyed her friend through narrowed lids, knowing full well Glory hadn't given up the argument. Finding her best friend a mate was the blonde's pet project. Livvy asserted darkly, "I don't want to meet any more nice, marriageable men."

"Who's talking about marriage?" Glory asked with rounded, innocent eyes. "There's a whole bunch of sexy, gorgeous men out there, and a mature woman doesn't have to be seeking marriage in order to appreciate them." She held up a hand when Livvy's mouth opened to speak.

22

"There are men to have fun with, men to find companionship with, and men to enjoy a consenting adult relationship with. One of the above might put an end to your moping around your house, night after night, feeling lonely."

Livvy formed a quick and unthought-out rebuttal. "I don't mope!" she snapped, adding defensively, "And George keeps me company!"

Glory smirked. "George is a dog."

"He still keeps me company," Livvy mumbled uncomfortably. George had been a rather weak defense. Rallying swiftly, she raised one dark eyebrow in cool disdain. "Besides, I don't need a man in my life."

"You're a woman, aren't you? You're thirty-two, not eighty-two," Glory countered dryly.

Livvy was equally ironic. "Don't tell me you're seriously advocating a swinging singles life-style?"

One of Glory's shoulders moved in a nonchalant shrug. "And why not? You're single. Why not swing?"

Tongue in cheek, Livvy murmured, "Thus speaks the happily married woman whose husband took a virgin to bed on his wedding night eleven years ago."

If anything, Glory's eyes expressed renewed justification. "Exactly my point! Paul is living proof that loving, caring men still exist."

In annoyance Livvy's gaze dropped to her lap. She crumpled her napkin and tossed it onto the lunch tray. Glory had chosen a lousy day to renew her campaign. The subject of men was not Livvy's favorite topic of conversation at that moment. She brought her eyes up and steadily met her friend's gaze. "All the Pauls are married," she said. In emphasis she stabbed a finger into the middle button of her cherry-red cotton blouse. "This is one mature, single, consenting adult woman who won't grab other women's men. Anyway"—she smiled serenely —"living in the fast lane doesn't go with my sedate image of day-care center owner."

23

"You're evading the issue," Glory accused. "Refusing to acknowledge all the unmarried-male resource waiting to be tapped is the action of a coward or a celibate. That's it!" she exclaimed. She was laughing now, conceding the argument for the time being. "You intend to convert The Little Yellow House into a nunnery!"

Livvy's quick smile acknowledged the descriptive term for her small home. Located just beyond the back gate of Horizon's courtyard, it had originally been the caretaker's cottage for the main house. Painted a soft canary yellow, it was dubbed "The Little Yellow House" because of the story she told Horizon's children to allay their concern about where she lived and with whom. Appealing to their sense of fantasy, she told them she was the lady who lived with the dog and the mouse in the little yellow house. The mouse was fictional, thank the Lord, but the story was popular. Offshooting episodes provided entertainment at storytelling time.

The strident ring of the phone put an end to further discussion on the state of her love life. Livvy winced, convinced one more unpleasant telephone encounter would be her undoing. She was barely stitched together after the last two.

Her brown eyes pleading, she appealed frantically to her friend. "You take it, Glory, please? If that's Brad or . . . I'm not here. I'm busy with the children and can't be disturbed. Anything. I'm in Alaska, checking out the pipeline. I'm—"

No more excuses were necessary. Glory obligingly reached for the phone, saying a cheery "Good afternoon. Horizon House Day Care Center." As she listened to the response, her eyes brightened. "No, I'm Ms. Waring's assistant, Glory Maddox. Can I help you?"

While the caller spoke, Glory listened with rapt attention. Catching Livvy's gaze, she rolled her eyes expressively and pantomimed a lascivious panting that ended with a mouthed "Sexy man!"

Livvy dismissed the theatrics with a scowl and a contemptuous flick of her fingers. Sexy or not, she wasn't impressed.

Glory said sweetly, "There's no need to fix a special time, Mr. Masters. Horizon House is always open to visitors." Her eyes positively glowed, and she covered the receiver with her palm to whisper, "Charming!"

Livvy ignored her.

After another moment Glory said on a light laugh, "Yes, Glory is fine with me, Mr. Mas—er, Jake."

Try as she might, Livvy couldn't ignore that. Her mouth twisted in disgust and she silently added *smooth* to Glory's descriptive adjectives. Jake Masters had wasted no time reaching a first-name basis. Sexy. Charming. Smooth. Under her breath she muttered acidly, "Siss. Boom. Bah." Her opinion of Mr. Masters summed up nicely, she grinned wickedly and buffed her fingers lightly across her blouse front.

The arrested quality of Glory's "Oh?" caused her grin to slip. What was the man up to? Was he coming on to her friend? Knowing Glory's devotion to Paul Maddox, she half expected to see a disdainful "Wolf!" pucker the blonde's mouth. She saw, instead, the phone receiver being thrust in her direction.

Not bothering to lower her voice, Glory said, "Mr. Masters really should speak to you, Livvy."

Taking the receiver, Livvy pressed it tightly to her chest and whispered accusingly, "Benedict Arnold!"

Glory grinned and whispered back, "He's a doll. You'll see."

Doubting that fervently, Livvy brought the phone to her mouth, saying stiltedly, "This is Olivia Waring. How can I help you, Mr. Masters?"

"You've already helped me, Ms. Waring," Jake Masters said, his deep voice threaded with mockery. *Swell.* Glory's sexy, charming doll of a man and her own obnoxious caller were one and the same! He continued pleasantly, "Just by coming so willingly to the phone, you've shown our earlier conversations left no bad feelings."

How could his tone be so warm and charming and his words so irritatingly sarcastic? Livvy's tone was cold. "Actually, Mr. Masters, when my assistant called me to the phone I didn't realize we'd spoken before. You failed to give your name when you called earlier."

If Jake Masters was offended by the censure implied in her statement, he didn't react to it. He rejoined smoothly, "An unpardonable oversight on my part. Am I forgiven? I'd hate not to be shown through your little school because of one regrettable lapse in good manners."

One regrettable lapse? Masters was a master of understatement. Either that, or he had the conscience of a rattlesnake, Livvy thought grimly. With studied composure, and only a little malice, she said coolly, "Showing Horizon House is always a pleasure, Mr. Masters. If the interest is genuine, *anyone* is welcome."

Under his breath he muttered something low and terse that she didn't catch, but that told her Mr. Hyde was hovering very near the surface of Dr. Jekyll's personality. Then very clearly, if perhaps overpolitely, he stated, "My staff has done some quick investigating in the last hour, Ms. Waring, and apparently your little operation is physically above reproach. Your record seems to be spotless, from health inspection to admiring clientele. But I'm a very thorough man, and I don't make decisions on hearsay. My interest in viewing you is genuine enough, but so is the old saying that seeing is believing."

Livvy's fingers tightened around the telephone receiver until her knuckles showed white. Although it was commendable for parents to investigate the day-care establishments they intended to entrust with the care of their children, she didn't like the insinuation that Horizon House had anything to hide. *Seeing is believing? Count on it, Mr. Masters, count on it!*

The tautness of her voice revealed her annoyance as

she said, "I don't expect parents to make decisions on day care by phone."

"Then we agree on that much," was his immediate, ironic response.

And probably very little else, Livvy finished his unspoken thought. Aloud she said, "I'm sure a personal observation will set your mind at rest, Mr. Masters."

His "Will it?" held a current of amusement she didn't understand, but before she could respond, he was speaking again. "I aim to ensure that Mellie and Bret are placed in an atmosphere that offers more than hygienic soundness and a fee expensive enough to instill a healthy awe in socially competitive parents."

There it was again. The intimation that Horizon's tuition was outrageously high. Livvy acknowledged the innuendo with grim distaste, her hackles on the rise in defense of her business ethics. The man's opinion was way off base. While Horizon House wasn't a charity service, neither was it a huge moneymaking concern. After expenses, it cleared a modest profit. "If you consider our tuition too steep, Mr. Masters, you're free to seek out any of the state or federally funded day-care facilities in the area. They might be less expensive. I can give you the names of the more reputable ones."

A heavy sigh, perhaps disgusted, perhaps merely resigned, whispered through the line into Livvy's ear, causing her to shiver. "That won't be necessary, Ms. Waring," the man she was coming to detest said on a grim laugh. "Recently I've acquired enough information on the area's day-care facilities to be able to make my own decisions. If your little place turns out to be what's best for Mellie and Bret, I won't quibble over the cost. I'll see you in twenty minutes."

The line went dead in her ear.

Being hung up on three times in succession was enough to make any woman angry. Livvy wasn't surprised to notice her fingers were trembling as she lowered

27

the receiver to the desk phone. Moreover, her entire body was quivering with a finely suppressed outrage. Her eyes, meeting the avid interest of Glory's, were bright with incensed disbelief.

"A little difference of opinion?" Glory prompted with an expectant look.

"He hung up on me three times . . . I mean, two. He said . . . he said seeing was believing! That he'd had us investigated, that we're . . . hygienically sound!" she managed with bare coherence, her voice a tiny, scratchy whisper.

Instead of joining her outrage as Livvy expected her to do, Glory merely murmured, "My, my!" shaking her head solemnly.

"He called us baby-sitters! He insinuated that our *little* operation was intent only on making money, not on the care of the children!" When Glory still didn't become incensed, Livvy asked incredulously, "How could you have called that man a charming doll!"

Unexpectedly, Glory burst out laughing, chortling wickedly, "If you could see your expression! Attack Horizon House and the composed Livvy Waring becomes a veritable madwoman!"

"But he had no reason to attack us!"

"Darling friend, the man is a concerned parent and wants to be reassured," Glory pointed out patiently. "Once he sees Horizon House, he'll realize all his reservations are needless. He'll know that everything here is geared to making a child feel loved and secure." Her smile was strangely satisfied, as if she not only admired Jake Masters' style but also appreciated her friend's unaccustomed display of anger. She continued slyly, "He might even understand that behind the chilly exterior, you're pure hot fudge, all sweet and warm and gooey with love."

Chilly exterior? In a shaky whisper Livvy insisted, "I was polite to the man."

Her blond curls bounced as Glory nodded her head vigorously. "Distantly so," she agreed. "But don't worry. If Jake Masters is as astute as I think he is, he'll soon realize your coolness to the male gender doesn't include those under five years of age."

And with that little comment, delivered lightly but meaningfully, Glory strolled toward the door, whistling a cheerful little ditty along the way. Before she left the room, she turned back with a glance of concern. "Oh, and Livvy?"

"Yes?"

"Try to work on the volume. *You* know you're upset. *I* know you're upset. But anybody else subjected to those tiny little whispers might believe you're suffering from an acute throat disorder instead of being so angry you can barely push the words out of your mouth."

A broad, outrageous wink was the last thing Glory delivered before she sauntered out of the office, shutting the door softly behind her.

"Tiny little whispers?" echoed sibilantly into the room as Livvy felt her shoulders sag downward. Her face a study of chagrin, she cleared her throat.

It was all of thirty seconds before she bounded to her feet and sped for the door. If she was going to meet the enemy face-to-face, she would need at least two advantages. The first could be had by a quick trip to the bathroom. Every soldier knew the benefits of a good spit-and-polish. The second was a simple matter of choosing the battleground—of being able to see the enemy before he saw you. Horizon's entrance alcove sported wide double doors, glassed in to provide a view all the way to the street. Visitors could be seen from the moment they drove up to the curb.

CHAPTER TWO

Livvy entered the entrance alcove fortified by a determined air of composure. Her blouse was tucked neatly into her skirt and fresh lip gloss shone on her soft lips.

From her desk, positioned to face the wide glass doors, Glory looked up in surprise. "You needn't have come downstairs. I would have directed him to your office."

Her comments were made to a slim, straight back. Livvy had marched past the desk and taken a position in front of the doors. Over her shoulder she replied, "If I greet him as he comes in, no one can accuse me of being distantly polite."

Glory laughed and came to stand beside her. "Lillian is here," she said, referring to the retired nurse who worked at Horizon House three afternoons a week.

Livvy's gaze didn't waver from the view of the empty street. "I know," she said. "I made a quick detour by the children's area and talked to both her and Jenny. They understand I can't relieve them until after Mr. Masters leaves."

"I didn't hear any racket," Glory remarked.

Livvy smiled faintly. The little ones vied for her attention, usually vociferously. "I was careful. I caught Jenny's eye from the doorway. After I spoke to her, she sent Lillian to me."

Outside, a car pulled up to the curb and came to a slow

halt. Livvy frowned. Small and sleek, the bright green Mercedes 450 SL convertible wasn't the kind of vehicle she had expected Jake Masters to arrive in. But then, her mental imagery had conjured up something more on the lines of a Sherman tank.

"He's here, Livvy."

"I know, Glory."

The man unfolded himself from the car and stood squinting up into the early afternoon sun. Livvy quickly scanned the dark-suited figure and saw a man of lean height, with reddish-brown hair and carved masculine features. She watched his gaze shift to Horizon House and his arms come across his chest as he leaned back against his car. It was the action of a man ready to indulge in a little thoughtful perusing.

"Did you notice, Livvy, the man is quite tall."

"Glory, from your vantage point, the entire adult population is tall."

He *was* reasonably tall, Livvy conceded, judging him to be somewhere in the vicinity of six feet. And his height was proportioned by a lean, muscular strength that could be detected even from a distance. The sinew was hidden, yet somehow defined, in the dark, vested suit he wore. Livvy's fingers curled tightly into her palms. Her opponent was fit, physically as well as mentally.

"He's looking this way, but I don't think he can see us —not with the glare on the glass. What do you think, Livvy?"

"That you're right, Glory, or else neither of us would be standing here, would we?"

From the corner of her eye she caught Glory's solemn nod. Too solemn? she wondered in vague suspicion before her full attention swung back to the view at curbside.

She could almost read Jake Masters' thoughts when his hand came up to rub contemplatively along his chin and mouth. Horizon's streetside entrance was one of stability and quiet reserve, giving the place the appearance of an old established residence. Only the glass doors said otherwise, claiming it a business establishment. The immaculate front lawn, manicured by a carpet of thick grass and sculpted with the dignity of stately shrubbery and graceful English ivy, was sedately well-ordered. And Horizon's somber facade of fading red brick and dark green trim gave no hint that a child's world was housed inside. Jake Masters nodded slowly, as if coming to a doubtful conclusion, then moved away from the car. A second later he was reaching down for something on the seat.

"The man is getting something from his car. A folder, I think."

"I can see that, Glory."

Growing exasperated with Glory's unnecessary remarks breaking into her absorbed study of the visitor, Livvy threw a quick glance down to her companion. The shadow of a wicked grin hovered on Glory's features. Livvy bit her lip, struggling against her will with a similar urge. Glory was thoroughly enjoying her commentary on their guest, doing her best to heighten Livvy's awareness of the man.

"He looks about our age, Livvy. Maybe Paul's."

"Hmmm."

Paul Maddox was thirty-five. And Jake Masters did have that mature and virile look of a man in his prime. Of course, she would think of that, Livvy realized wryly, forever conscious of her own infertile condition. She watched him move away from the car and start up the walk, his hand cupped loosely around the folder. He had a long, purposeful stride, each step he took a lithe flex of broad shoulders and arms coordinated to the lean, supple movements of his hips and thighs. Such loose-limbed dexterity was natural and easy and pleasant to watch. Had it been any other man, Livvy might have enjoyed the sight.

"The man has a very masculine walk, Livvy."

"Stop drooling, Glory. The *man* is probably married."

She was remembering Michelle. If not married, then attached. She added dryly, "And if he isn't, you are."

"But you're not," Glory trilled angelically. Then the other side of her dual personality surfaced and she exclaimed softly in wicked appreciation, "If that's a daddy, I'm putting myself up for adoption!"

A funny sound came from Livvy's throat—something between a groan of despair and a sigh of resignation. For a brief second the women's eyes met, Glory's blue ones so round and innocent, Livvy's brown ones narrowed in disgusted accusation. Then both pairs of eyes snapped forward in unison; Jake Masters was halfway up the walk.

Glory's admiration of the man was easy to understand. Physically, he was a very nice specimen. What was difficult to understand, or perhaps hard to identify, were the vague, uneasy flutterings attacking the region of Livvy's stomach. How does one confront a man who was nasty and irascible one minute and almost too polite the next? She could coolly ignore his unpleasantness, she supposed, and knew without doubt that the mettle of her composure would soon be put to the test.

"Didn't I tell you he was sexy, Livvy?" Glory whispered.

"Yes, yes, Glory, you're omniscient!"

Quiet as mice, both women backed toward Glory's desk as Jake Masters bounded up the porch steps. When he reached for the pneumatic door-handle and gave it a push, Glory was standing at the near end of the desk, first in line to greet him, while Livvy, opting to bide her welcome, had positioned herself at the far end.

Over her shoulder, Glory whispered, laughing, "Now be nice, Livvy, and give the sexy man a great big smile."

There was just enough time for Livvy to retort, very quietly and very sweetly, "You're fired!" before Jake Masters walked inside the entrance alcove and dominated it with his presence.

His eyes, a shocking aqua blue in his tanned face, went

33

swiftly over both women before settling on Glory. Naturally, they would. Glory's looks usually warranted male interest. He smiled, revealing white, slightly irregular teeth, and walked forward, extending a tanned, long-fingered hand.

"Ms. Waring?"

Glory shook her head, smiling up at him as she placed her small hand in his. "Glory Maddox," she corrected. "Welcome to Horizon House, Jake."

From the opposite end of the desk Livvy covertly studied the two. Glory was beaming, her pert face full of warmth and welcome. Jake Masters' gaze, full of masculine admiration, went from the top of her blond head, down the length of her curvy body clad in a clingy pullover and snug slacks, and came to rest on her face. As if chanting the beginning words of a doxology, he muttered fervently, "Glory be!"

A sincere compliment but rather trite, Livvy thought, striving not to notice how his grin drove attractive lines down either side of his mouth. Or how, when his eyes cut briefly to her and narrowed, her spine tingled an odd warning of danger.

Glory remained unflustered. She was used to her effect on men. On a light, relaxed laugh, she said, "My father was a staunch Marine with faith in both God and country. His patriotism led him to name me after the flag, Old Glory. He felt such a stout allegiance to the Corps that Livvy and my husband, Paul, tell me to be grateful he didn't tattoo the eagle, ball, and anchor insignia on my forehead."

The nature of Jake Masters' grin altered slightly from wide appreciation to crooked acceptance, and his eyes glinted a different kind of admiration. He had understood the subtle message behind Glory's mention of Paul. He respected women who upheld their marriage vows.

Recalling his sexy black-laced and red-satin-sheeted Michelle, Livvy doubted the sincerity of his newfound respect. Flirting with Glory was hardly the action of a man who upheld fidelity in a relationship. Maybe, like Brad, he adhered to the belief that love, honor, and fidelity were rules for the female of the species. She grimaced in aversion because of her unpleasant thoughts.

Before she could erase the disapproval from her face, his aqua gaze swung her way. An element of impatience entered his expression before it became closed and impossible to read. Something flickered in his eyes as he drank in the sculptured angles of her face, her large brown eyes behind the glasses, and the dark upsweep of her hair. She drew herself erect under his regard, fighting a vague discomfort, and his gaze dropped the length of her slender body. In actual time, he studied her longer than he had Glory. Fine-boned ankles and the expanse of long, bare leg below the hem of her skirt were given a detailed scrutiny. Then, ever so slowly, the slim outline of her thighs and hips underneath her navy skirt was visually traced on an upward path that led to the barely discernible contours of her slight rib cage and small breasts beneath her red blouse. Her bones were good but starkly prominent and, as she withstood the perusal stoically, Livvy was painfully aware of the minimum of flesh covering them. If his prolonged study was a tactic to unsettle her, it was very effective. She shifted slightly, and his eyes came back to hers.

He stepped nearer. "Livvy, isn't it?" he murmured, his voice low and slightly challenging.

"Olivia," she stated with a determined aloofness, not sure she liked the affectionate shortening of her name on his lips.

A vertical cleft dented his strong chin and his mouth was firm and wide, perhaps even generous. Staring straight ahead, Livvy had a direct view of both. She sensed, rather than saw, his hand coming up, and she jerked back, her gaze flying down in alarm. His tanned hand was extended for a courteous handshake, nothing more. His low, surprised laugh acknowledged her momentary discomposure, and her chin came up a notch, her eyes flashing annoyance as they met the wicked humor of his. Her cool fingers brushed lightly against his warm ones, quickly removed themselves, and formed a tight fist hidden in the folds of her skirt.

Why, for heaven's sake, had she assumed he was going to touch her? And *why,* she thought angrily, would his touch affect her one way or another?

"I'll bet your father was in the Navy, Olivia," he said conversationally, his mouth settling into a polite smile.

Had his eyes been smiling too, she might have smiled in return. But a glimmer of something threatening lurked in their depths, and Livvy eyed him warily. "My father wasn't in any of the services, Mr. Masters."

"We've already become acquainted by phone. Don't you think you could make it Jake?"

Acquainted but not friendly, Livvy thought uneasily, but she acquiesced easily enough, saying, "My father was a college professor, Jake."

"You're married to a sailor, right?"

If this was a ploy to discover her marital status, it was an odd one. Coolly she informed him, "I'm not married."

There was something abradingly false about the way his expression suddenly lightened and he snapped his fingers, as if remembering a detail he'd forgotten. "Oh, that's right. You won't be tying the knot until the boyfriend gets back from sea duty."

Disquieting confusion tightened Livvy's expression. Anchors aweigh, my boys! The man has a fixation on the Navy! But what was he getting at? Using simple sentences any three-year-old could understand, she explained, "I'm not engaged to a sailor. I don't know any sailors. I doubt I'll ever meet any sailors."

His forefinger rubbed thoughtfully across his lips as his glance probed quickly over her length. "My mistake, then," he murmured, but his mouth quirked a little, increasing her uneasiness. "I could have sworn you were intimately acquainted with a sailor."

He seemed to be waiting for her to ask, so she did. Distrustfully. "Why?"

"It's the way you're dressed, you see, and your size," he explained with just the right touch of self-consciousness to convey reluctance to confess his mistake. But embarrassment didn't keep him from adding informatively, "And the prim, disapproving way you have of looking at a man. And the haughty chastisement you deal out over the phone." His eyes no longer veiled the dangerous glint. Stiffening under his verbal assault, Livvy watched those eyes and felt a moment of real dread. Very softly, he added, "I was positive, Olivia, that with all the little Swee' Peas under your care, there was a Popeye in the background."

He said the last so charmingly that for a full five seconds she stared at him blankly. Then she understood, perfectly, her aghast expression registering the insult. Olive Oyl—Olivia.

Apparently pleased with the results of his clever humor, Jake Masters smiled like a lazy, satisfied shark after a kill.

Somewhere in the back of Livvy's brain was the realization that her outrage had less to do with being compared to Olive Oyl's looks and personality and more to do with their circumstances being similar. Like the cartoon character, Olivia Waring claimed motherhood only through the little Swee' Peas under her care. Jake Masters didn't realize the depth of his hurtful comparison, but it scarcely mattered at the moment. Being the brunt of his cutting humor was offensive in any case.

She resisted the urge to massage her neck, settling for a tiny swallow to test the constriction in her throat. The little gulp went down. Her chin came up. Her mental count to ten had already gained her a measure of composure.

She stared at him levelly, briefly noted the skin taut over his cheekbones and the tightness around his mouth, and adopted a tone of frigid dismissal. "The *children* under my care have no complaints. Neither do their parents. But since you have so many, Mr. Masters, I suggest you look elsewhere for day care."

She brushed past him, her face brittle with tension. Not a very long battle, but at least not an unqualified defeat. The look on his face had been a small compensation for his insults. Evidently, Jake Masters wasn't used to being called on his rudeness. His expression had been utterly dumbfounded.

Through the rushing sound of blood pumping furiously to her brain, she heard the startled burst of Jake Masters' impatiently questioning voice and Glory's calmly replying one. She entered the hall, her soft-soled shoes thumping a muffled staccato on the polished hardwood floor. Maybe she would take a five-minute break to calm down. Maybe she would take a couple of aspirin for the thumping rhythm pounding at her temples. Olive Oyl, for God's sake! Lengthening strides took Livvy to the stairway.

Midway up the stairs, she heard sliding feet on the floor below her, then a hard thump. Next came a grunt of pain and muffled cursing. She whirled and saw Jake Masters ending a perilous skid on his back that catapulted him, feetfirst, against the wall, his body sprawled in haphazard fashion. Papers were strewn under him and all about the hall, and a folder—his folder, she realized dimly—was fluttering to a landing across his wide chest. As she stared at him, horror that he might be seriously injured slowly mounted. He raised his head to look at her, dazed stupefaction in his eyes. He shook his head, trying to clear it, then let it fall cautiously back to the floor.

Livvy rushed back down the stairs, knelt beside him,

and asked anxiously, "Are you hurt, Mr. Masters?" Her concern was so great she forgot she detested the man.

Through clenched teeth he rasped, "Jhe-ess."

Was that a yes? Or was he calling attention to his chest? "Could you tell me where? Perhaps you shouldn't try to move."

The agonized look he threw her said he had no intention of moving. Her concerned eyes searched his length, looking for evidence of broken bones. Everything seemed to be in proper order, his limbs extended but not at odd angles. Pushing aside the empty folder, her fingers traced lightly across his chest, finding nothing torn or bleeding or concave. Still, he seemed to be dragging air into his lungs in a shallow, painful way.

"Is it your head?"

The suggested part wagged a slow negative. Taking no chances, Livvy examined that, too. Her fingers gently probed along his temples and through the thickness of his curling chestnut hair in search for lumps.

"I can't find anything wrong, but Lillian, my employee, is a retired nurse. I'll go get her."

Exerting surprising strength for an injured man, he grabbed her arms and held her down beside him. He whispered raggedly, "Don't need . . . nurse, just . . . breath."

"But you're hurt!" Livvy whispered in agitation.

" 'M okay," he managed around a thin smile of reassurance. His fingers tightened around her upper arms, assuring that she didn't leave while he fought for the return of regular breathing. Seconds later, in answer to her continuing frown of concern, he said in a more normal tone, "Don't worry, I'm fine."

"Are you sure?"

As though the admission cost him, he said slowly, "This floor is damned slick and damned hard, but the only thing damaged is my pride."

The reluctant explanation cooled Livvy's concern.

"You'll be able to get up, then," she said flatly, relieved that he wasn't hurt, but not so relieved that she'd forgotten his recent insults.

He loosened one of her arms to smooth his fingers over the ruffled strands of his hair. Wavy and disobedient, it sprang back into disorder. Watching her closely, he said, "This time if I apologize for what I said, will you accept it?"

Why did the man always put a rider of acceptance on his apologies? It aborted forgiveness. Wanting his quick departure, knowing that she and Horizon House were better off without his presence, she stared at him. "I'll help you gather your papers before you leave."

His thick brows formed a blunt slash above eyes glinting with irritation. He caught her nape, drawing her inexorably down. His breath misted warmly over her face when he growled in husky exasperation, "Why don't you loosen up a little, Olive? I'm trying to express regret for hurting your feelings."

Was that what he was trying to do? By growling and calling her Olive? Her arched brows ascended with her skeptical thoughts. She said coolly, "My feelings aren't hurt, Mr. Masters. You can leave with a clear conscience."

The cool dismissal prompted a touch of savagery. His fingers and thumb pressed punishingly into the tendons at the back of her neck. She opened her mouth to object to the manhandling and gasped in shock as her soft lips were jerked forcefully against hard masculine ones.

For two heartbeats Livvy couldn't change the status quo. His mouth was fastened bruisingly to hers, and when her fingers pressed for release against his chest, one of his arms locked around her shoulders. Not only was he stronger than she, but her kneeling position made defensive maneuvers awkward. The pleasant scent of his aftershave assaulted her nostrils, and when the twisting pressure of his mouth suddenly changed from punishment to

40

male supplication, her senses rather than her sensibilities took up the battle. Appalled, she jerked back so forcefully that her arm and neck were blistered by the abrasive scrape of his fingers.

He rose to his elbows as she fell back on her heels. And while she stared at him with thoroughly aghast eyes, he surveyed her agitation through narrowed lids. Chests heaving, mouths panting, they both breathed as though at the end of a particularly grueling race.

She whispered furiously, "Listen, Brutus! There may not be a Popeye to protect me, but if you touch me again, I'll personally mop the floor with you!"

The threat brought a crooked grin to Jake's mouth. He drawled slowly, "Don't worry, Olive, I think you just did." Then he shook his head and muttered something low and sympathetic about Popeye's sex life, the context of which was lost under the sound of the door opening from the entrance alcove.

Glory walked sedately into the hall. "Oh, goodness, you're both still here!" she exclaimed in mild surprise before her eyes widened to saucers as it dawned on her that they were both on the floor. She glanced from one to the other. Livvy's flushed face and her fingers rubbing soothingly against a bruised arm didn't go unnoticed, nor did Jake's amused expression and the contents of his folder strewn all across the floor. But Glory seldom lost her cool. Questions and speculation were hidden beneath an easy smile. She said, "There's a phone call for you, Jake—Michelle from your office."

Showing neither guilt nor discomfort that his woman had tracked him down on the heels of his kissing another, Jake gained his feet, wincing only slightly as he straightened his back. He smiled easily at Glory. "Okay if I take it at your desk?" he asked. Receiving Glory's nodding assent, he turned to Livvy with a request. "You don't mind gathering my papers, do you, Olivia? They contain all the pertinent information on Mellie and Bret. You might study them while I'm gone." He watched her teeth grind together in vexation. His voice held a hint of grim humor when he added, "Maybe you'll change your mind about throwing me out of here. If not, then having my file together will speed me on my way."

Before Glory preceded Jake from the hall, she sent a quick, probing glance to her friend. With a flick of her fingers Livvy denied the need for concern. As the door closed softly behind them, her rigid shoulders relaxed and she breathed a heartfelt sigh.

Thank you, Michelle! Another minute with your charming husband or fellow or whatever he is, and I might have forgotten I'm a lady and gone for his jugular! On the heels of that vicious thought came the derisive jeer: *With what? Ineffectual fury and useless dismissals?* The man had the tenacity of a bulldog! After three phone confrontations and one face-to-face skirmish, he was still hanging in there! She smiled wryly. In the course of a few hours she had likened Jake Masters to a rattlesnake, a shark, and a bulldog. Was he one, or all three?

She surveyed the clutter on the hall floor with resolve. Horizon House was her territory. She decided who was welcome and she was responsible for keeping it neat and tidy. She'd do a little housecleaning—starting with the contents of Jake Masters' folder and ending with brushing him out the nearest door. She reached for the empty folder.

The papers nearest her seemed to be photocopies of birth certificates and medical records. She scooped them up with scant attention and laid them neatly in the folder. A gloss of color not far away caught her eyes and she scooted toward it, her interest piqued.

It was a photograph of a small girl. With soft pleasure Livvy smiled for the first time since Jake Masters had walked inside Horizon House. His daughter, Mellie, was a delightful pixie with bright blue eyes, straight brown hair, and perky features full of mischief and life. She laid the photograph gently inside the folder.

It stood to reason that if there was a photo of Mellie, there would also be one of Bret. Her eyes searched the floor, eager to compare sister and brother. On her knees, she went from paper to paper, inserting them into the folder until she came to the one she sought. She grinned triumphantly as she turned it faceup for perusal.

Her grin froze and her hand flew to her breast.

When it rains, it pours. The old proverb rang discordantly through her mind. Despite the beautiful October sunshine, the day had been one emotional downpour after another. The deluge of chaos created by Jake Masters and Brad Waring hadn't been nearly as overwhelming as the painful flood presently cascading into her heart.

Her fingers trembled as she traced the boy's features, lightly caressing each soft line, each rounded contour. Beautiful, adorable, Bret Masters was a blond and chubby cherub with a heartbreaking combination of innocent smile and trusting eyes. He looked enough like Jamie to be his twin.

Her hand dropped away from the photograph and formed an impotent fist in her lap. For a moment all the love, all the pain of loss, assailed her, and her eyes misted. She fought it, as she'd learned to do, blinking rapidly to dispel melancholy and the thoughts that began with "if only." Refocused, her eyes fell again to the picture of Jake Masters' son.

Something warm and unbidden began to build inside her. She refused to label it, unconsciously allowing it room to grow and to fill the emptiness. An aching curiosity formed questions. Did Bret Masters have Jamie's gruff tone when he recited his big-boy exploits? Was he, like Jamie, intelligent and quick to learn? Did he show affection as easily? Would he feel as sweet in her arms?

Realizing where her thoughts were leading, she quickly smothered them, ashamed. Bret Masters wasn't Jamie.

43

He just resembled him. It was idiocy to delve past the obvious physical likenesses. She had faced the loss of her son eighteen months ago. And for over a year she'd avoided heartache by accepting her role as caregiver to Horizon's children, loving them but detaching enough of herself to keep her sanity.

A sound behind her told her she was no longer alone, and her peripheral vision found long, trousered legs striding toward her. Her spine instinctively straightened as she slipped the photograph into the folder and closed it.

Jake stared down at her, searching her strained features. A quick frown gave his face a tough, implacable look.

"Well?" The query was peremptory.

In an automatic reflex, Livvy shook her head slightly, signifying her incomprehension of the question.

"What's your decision?"

"About what?"

He hunkered down before her, his eyes derisive when she leaned back slightly. "Don't look so pale and frightened. I seldom kiss an unwilling woman twice. I'm asking if you're going to use your dislike of me to deny Mellie and Bret the excellent benefits of your care. Do they get wiped out by the same mop that shows me the door?"

"No!" she replied, softly horrified as she clutched the folder protectively to her chest.

His narrowed glance questioned her vehemence and he said slowly, "It seems you share my belief that those two deserve every consideration."

She nodded mutely, wondering if she'd just sliced herself one big chunk of trouble and heartache or if she'd just caught the brass ring on the merry-go-round. It couldn't hurt, could it, to have Bret under her care during the day? And Mellie. She was fooling herself, and she knew it. What was more, she knew Jake Masters wouldn't take kindly to having his children under the care of a woman whose professional judgment was clouded by needs of the heart. God, for her own sanity she had to get off this emotional seesaw and tell him no.

"Mr. Masters, perhaps Horizon House isn't the best place for your children. You and I don't seem to get along and—"

He interrupted her with the same impatience he had displayed over the phone, his questions abrupt and grimly voiced. "Does their acceptance here depend on my making amends for my wrongdoings? Is that it? Or do you just make sweeping judgments? If I'm a brute, my kids will be little horrors?"

Coldly, she said, "I made the suggestion for your benefit, not mine. I never turn away children because of their parents' behavior. I love children."

"Do you?" His sudden smile dispelled any thought that he might be refuting her claim. He said wryly, "To tell you the truth, Olivia, until a few minutes ago I doubted that. But after your sincere concern for the well-being of a long-legged buffoon who'd just affronted you with his lousy humor, I'm inclined to believe you. There's compassion in you, and human warmth. And you're honest about what you feel, even when"—his mouth twisted ruefully—"it doesn't do wonders for my masculine ego. You'll find I admire truth and honesty."

Truth and honesty? Livvy felt as guilty as sin as she silently accepted the praise. She knew she should be opening her mouth, remarking on the photographs, confessing that his son was like her own. In essence, she knew she should be apprising him of all the facts and allowing him to make the choice. The man had offered an apology and a banner of truce all in one wry speech. She decided to accept both. She told herself she was tired of conflict; that, in the long run, it didn't matter because, God knew, she meant his son no harm. She told herself she didn't have to tell him her life story in order to have a polite, business relationship with him. And finally, very exhausted, she told herself she would think about his discovery of Jamie's resemblance to his son another day. And heard her inner voice jeer softly: *Rationalization like that won't make the problems go away.*

With a grave little smile, and just a touch of her normal humor, she asked, "Would you like to experience more of Horizon House than this hard hallway floor?"

Tiny fanlike lines shot toward his temples as his eyes glinted appreciation of her choice of words. He stood up, rubbed the small of his back in exaggerated misery, and offered her a hand up. She accepted gracefully but, as soon as she was standing, moved a discreet distance away from him. Politeness, not intimacy. Acquaintances, not friends. She knew the bounds, and the necessity of keeping them.

The corridor that separated the children's area of Horizon House into four large rooms was carpeted in a bright dandelion gold. Rainbow motifs against sky-blue walls added a warm and vital touch, cheerfully heralding the entrance into a child's world. As they walked along, Livvy saw Jake's quickened interest and felt a surge of pride. Seeing *was* believing.

"The Interest Centers are the two rooms at the far end of the hall. We'll visit there first," she told him. "That's where most of the indoor activity takes place. There's a reading nook, a building corner, and an art center; also areas set aside for learning toys and imaginative play. We supervise the children, but we allow them freedom to create and play on their own, as well. They learn more from experimenting than from being told what to do."

"Are the children in there now?"

Livvy's glance fell to her watch. She grimaced as she realized the time. "They're napping now, but you'll find the Interest Centers fascinating even when they're empty."

He did, inspecting each area and asking questions, some of which Livvy found appallingly uninformed, coming from a father of two children. When she explained

46

the correlation between certain toys and small- and large-muscle skills, he grinned crookedly, tapped a forefinger on the folder she held to her chest, and said, "I guess I have a lot of catching up to do." He took her elbow, guiding her out of the room. "This whole situation was thrust on me just a month ago. I haven't had a chance to do much more than iron out the legalities."

He was talking as if she were privy to details of his personal life, and Livvy was completely in the dark. A sharp mental tug told her the papers she had skipped over before finding the photographs would have supplied the information she lacked to understand his circumstances. Obviously they were more than photocopies of birth certificates and medical records. Legalities concerning children usually meant divorce and custody.

She started to venture a discreet question and was forestalled when he said, "The two times I've been around Mellie and Bret, they've either been tearing around outside or sleeping peacefully in their beds. I never gave their toys a thought."

Two times? Surely he meant two times recently. Livvy frowned pensively as she led him into the lunchroom. He moved past her, inspecting the small tables and chairs in the dining area before moving into the partitioned kitchen with its spotless chrome and Formica fixtures.

Rather starkly, she asked, "Are you married?"

In some surprise his head came out of the pantry he had opened. "Does it matter?" he asked, his expression faintly intrigued as his eyes went over her in an appraising, masculine way.

A tiny warning bell sounded in Livvy's brain, but she ignored it to ask persistently, "Are you divorced?"

One of his eyebrows lifted. He came back to her, and again took her elbow as they left the room. There was a smile in his deep voice as he explained, "The divorce happened a long time ago, but if it bothers you, I can

47

assure you that one bad experience doesn't color the way I view present relationships."

Murmuring quietly, "I see," Livvy gracefully extricated herself from his light grasp. But she didn't see, and her confused eyes clouded with her troubled thoughts. His divorce must have put a strain on his relationship with his children. Otherwise he would have seen them more than the twice he'd claimed.

"Where to now?"

"I wish I knew," she said in a vague way that brought his brows up slightly.

"Nothing left to show me before I sign on the dotted line?"

"Oh." He was talking about the tour. She smiled a little. "There's only the nap room left, but the children are resting and I'm sure you'll agree that disturbing their sleep would be pointless. Would you like to see the back courtyard?"

"Where's the nap room?"

She pointed to the door directly across from the lunchroom, and watched, her mouth parted on a soundless protest, as he calmly strode to it, quietly opened it, and stood surveying the interior of the room. Past the breadth of his back, Livvy could see the aluminum cots lining the walls, and her gaze instinctively softened, flickering over each reclining youngster.

Ranging from fetal curl to relaxed sprawl, the children were as individual in their sleeping patterns as they were when they were awake. One little fellow was arranged half on, half off his cot, a blanket trailing from the fist near his mouth to the floor at his feet. Lillian Chester sat by the door, her graying head bent over a brochure on home computers. She glanced up at Jake, smiled and nodded in answer to his low-voiced inquiry about her reading material, and went back to the study of computers. At the far end of the room Jenny Clarke was gently arranging the clothing of a female cherub who'd obviously just visited the toilet and needed help with elastic waistbands. The three-year-old siren under Jenny's capable ministrations raised brown eyes to the doorway, smiled beguilingly, and batted her eyelashes flirtatiously, completely unselfconscious in her seminudity. The fact that her bottom was almost bare was innocently forgotten. The object of her attentions grinned widely and swiftly.

He turned that same grin over his shoulder to Livvy, as if to say: *See? No harm done.* She answered it with a quick, annoyed glare, and stooped down to receive what he had failed to see coming, her arms opening in welcome.

A small, dark-haired boy had left his cot and darted toward the door, and was slipping neatly through the spread of Jake's long legs. Like a small tornado, he whirled himself right into Livvy's waiting embrace.

"Where did you go all the time?" the boy asked accusingly, referring to her prolonged absence from the children's area.

Livvy inclined her head toward Jake, who had come to stand beside them. She gave the simplest explanation. "Mr. Masters wanted to see Horizon House, David."

David's gaze slowly traveled the long length from Jake's feet to his face. To the boy, the man seemed especially tall standing above them. He asked in awe, "Does he fit in The Little Yellow House?"

Livvy's mouth twitched a little with amusement. Between Glory and the kids, her love life was a great source of interest. Planting a soft kiss on David's cheek, she whispered, "Nope. He's a daddy like your daddy."

Small hands went to her cheeks, rubbing affectionately. "At storytelling, can I sit in your lap?"

"Yes."

"Lucy and Janie, too? And Holly and Amy and Christopher and Greg? And Missy and Kim and Charlie and

Allison?" he went on in an enthusiastic list of all his closest playmates.

"I might get squashed with all of you on my lap. Maybe we'll just sit in a circle on the floor and all hold hands."

The impish light in David's eyes said he was enjoying the mental picture of Livvy under a mountain of children. Then his thoughts went quickly to another subject. "Did the mouse find the magic cleaner for your specs?"

Her fingers gently ruffled his hair. "I 'spect you'll have to wait till storytelling to find out. Now, scoot back to your cot and finish your nap."

The exuberant four-year-old threw his arms about her neck, his little fingers tangling in the hair at her nape as he kissed her smackingly on the cheek. With a shy grin at Jake, he bounded back into the nap room, gaining his cot as Lillian shut the door quietly in his wake.

The soft smile engendered by David's affection was still hovering on her face as she rose and asked Jake, "Would you like to see the back courtyard now?"

Ignoring her question, he fitted his palm snugly to the back of her neck. His fingers found loose tendrils of hair, tugging gently and doing funny little things to her nervous system. She sensed a different quality in his gaze capturing hers—a warmth that hadn't been there before. And a purposefulness.

He asked quietly, "What's The Little Yellow House?"

"My home." The pause was tense. "What are you doing?"

"Your young admirer mussed your hair, Olivia. I'm straightening it."

The lightness of his tone was at odds with the determined glint in his eyes. She wondered what he was thinking. When he edged closer, bringing both his hands into play at the back of her head, she inhaled sharply and stood as still as a statue, her nose valiantly managing to stay a millimeter away from his jaw. He worked slowly and meticulously, and when he finally moved back, there was a held-in grin hollowing his lean cheeks.

Jake inclined his head first to one side and then the other, inspecting the results of his repair work. "You're as straight as a new pin," he pronounced. "Not a hair out of place."

"Thank you!" she said stiffly.

"Anytime, Olivia, anytime," he murmured benevolently. "I admire a woman with a neat and tidy appearance."

She knew what he thought of her looks, and she wasn't about to hand him any more ammunition by bristling at his subdued baiting. Very calmly, she said, "Do you want to see the courtyard?"

"I'm sure I've taken up enough of your time. Maybe we should just skip to the part where I fill out registration forms and sign my name to the check."

Livvy eyed him suspiciously. Was that another dig at Horizon's tuition fee? It was difficult to tell when he looked so pleasantly obliging.

"All the forms are in my office, upstairs," she said, moving ahead of him.

The walk upstairs was silent, Livvy's only regret being that Jake chose to walk behind her instead of by her side. She was painfully conscious of each swing of her skirt as she climbed, and of the aqua eyes fastened so intently on the modest display.

On entering her office, Livvy went directly to her desk, collected registration forms, medical releases, and questionnaires, and held them out to him. As he began perusing them, she laid the folder she had carried throughout the tour onto her desk and went to the window.

Soon. He would be gone soon, and maybe she could finish out the afternoon in normal, everyday routine. It would be a blessing.

"I don't have the information you require."

His brusque statement brought her head around and

she sent him an inquiring glance. With a grim smile he said, "I have no idea what their toilet habits are, much less the words they use to indicate a need to use the toilet. As for nap habits, allergies, special fears, tension releases —that's all Greek to me."

"We can discover most of those things once Mellie and Bret are with us," she assured him. "Knowing beforehand just makes their first few days here as problem-free as possible."

He sighed in frustration. "I wish I did know."

The turbulence in his aqua eyes touched off a spark of sympathy. Livvy suggested helpfully, "Perhaps if you contacted your ex-wife, she could supply some of the answers."

Like a thundercrack, his palms slapped against the desk top, causing her to jump. His tone impatient, he demanded, "What in hell has she to do with this situation?"

Livvy's back went ramrod straight. She was fed up with his erratic mood swings. First he was insulting, then civil, then friendly, then angry. Would the real Jake Masters please stand up? She eyed him coldly and said, "As their mother, I assume she'll know something of their habits."

After a surprised moment, he yelled, "Don't those glasses help you to see?"

Tense and angry, she said, "See what?"

Something must have come through in her voice, despite her effort to make it calm and level. He yelled a little less fiercely, "Have I frightened you?"

"I'm not frightened!"

"Okay, you're not frightened," he agreed instantly, doing yet another of his quick about-faces of mood. The underlying indulgence in his deep voice made it clear he didn't believe her, that he thought her statement so much bravado. He moved to her side, took her by the shoulders, and said earnestly, "God, I'm sorry. You're trembling like a leaf." He smiled a little, trying to reassure her. "My bark's much worse than my bite, you know. I wouldn't harm you."

Which was a lie. His closeness, the gentle movements of his fingers over her slim shoulders, were the most harmful things he'd done so far. In dismay, Livvy felt her anger subside under an alarming new feeling.

"When you gathered up the papers from my folder, didn't you look at any of them?" he asked quietly.

She was affected by the pervading scent of his clean male body. "I looked at the pictures. Mellie and Bret are very beautiful children," she said in a shallow tone, and watched his eyes widen perceptibly. Her answer had surprised him.

A soft rumble of laughter started in his chest and broke warmly over her upturned face. He had an attractive laugh, Livvy thought, finding its timbre pleasantly soft and deep. Amusement put creases in his cheeks to soften the bold lines of his face. Intent on the transformation, Livvy did nothing to prevent his hand from reaching out to gently remove her glasses.

She blinked rapidly, focused with difficulty, and complained unsteadily, "Without my glasses, I get dizzy."

"Then close your eyes, Olivia, because I can't give them back just yet," he said in husky amusement, slipping the glasses into his coat pocket. Very gently, he aligned her body to his from chest to thigh, and his hands moved over her back. His fingers lightly explored each individual rib, then tactilely counted the shivers skipping up her backbone. "The dizziness seems to be spreading to your spine," he murmured, sounding pleased.

"Mr. Masters, this is—"

"Jake."

"Jake, this is totally insane."

"No, it isn't." He breathed the words near her temple. His lips edged down the delicate hollow of her cheek and swerved slowly to the corner of her mouth. "This is with

53

all my faculties honed sharply and soberly. And because I like a woman who tries to emulate Olive Oyl, can't see past the nose on her face, and thinks all the little Swee' Peas are beautiful."

With the utmost care his mouth took insistent possession of hers, applying the lightest pressure to part her lips and boldly secure a deeper claim. His taste was sweet, his probing tongue gentle, and Livvy fought an intense and silent battle between apprehension and the insidious pleasure curling up from her midsection. Her bones seemed to liquefy, taking the decision from her mind, and she melted against him. The kiss was brief in duration, but very warm, very expert, very intimate. Dimly, Livvy was aware not only of her acceptance of it but of her participation in it; for one electric moment her lips and tongue joining his willingly.

When he drew back, his breathing was thick, and she was scarcely breathing at all. She stood still under his hands as he found her glasses and pushed them gently into place on her nose.

Very soberly, he told her, "Thank you, Olivia, for not going for your mop. I would have hated fighting you for that second chance to touch you."

With her eyesight back to normal Livvy saw the return of her common sense. Despite the solemnity of his voice, Jake was looking confident and amused and knowing, studying her like the shark he was to determine whether or not the new fish he had circled was enough for a meal or two or just a taste. *Oh, damn.* She had just welcomed the kiss of a man who held her in contempt, called her Olive Oyl, and obviously came on to anything in skirts. The final skirmish was his. Had he won the war? With effort, Livvy drew her cool defenses around her, retreating with flags flying.

She said distantly, "It's getting late. Unless you've changed your mind about enrolling your son and daughter, could we settle this now?"

The pause before he spoke was electric with a new tension. His eyes narrowed and his mouth developed curling edges. He said slowly, "You should have studied more than the pictures. You're lacking some very vital information."

"What information?"

Instead of answering he removed his checkbook from his inside coat pocket and went over to her desk to make it out. She watched as he scrawled his signature and jotted a quick notation on one of the enrollment forms. Then he tossed the pen on her desk and straightened.

"It's settled, Olivia, except for one question."

"Yes?"

"Don't look so uneasy. I just want to know why you're so willing to have my—son and daughter—under your care when you want nothing to do with me."

She knew a moment of pure panic followed by pangs of conscience. He didn't know and she couldn't tell him. "I don't see that the two have anything to do with each other. I told you before that I don't lump parents and children in the same category."

"So you did." His mouth twisted a little, and he said mockingly, "I feel compelled to dispute your logic. And to wonder why you're so determined to dislike me. I don't return the feeling, you know. I've been irritated with you once or twice, but you disturb me in other ways, too."

His eyes made his meaning clear, warmly scanning her slim figure. Her body flushed with heat, but she said coolly enough, "I doubt I'm the only one to do so."

Thick chestnut eyebrows formed a crooked line over the bright aqua of his eyes. "I confess you're not the first woman to manage it," he said, grinning wickedly.

Livvy agreed wholeheartedly. At his age and with his ingrained sensuality, the women in his past were probably countless. And in his present there was Michelle, with sexy garments and a throaty voice. Livvy knew for certain she wouldn't be added to the list.

With a pointed glance at her watch she said, "It's rather late. The children are expecting me."

Jake accepted the dismissal with a shrug. He collected his checkbook, inclined his head mockingly, and said, "All right, we'll go into it some other time. I'll see you in a couple of weeks." His long strides took him to the door, where he turned and said, "I'll leave the folder with you. Except for the pictures, all the papers are photocopies." He grinned rather strangely, as if enjoying some inner joke. "You might want to give them some attention in the next two weeks."

Livvy watched his broad shoulders swing through the door, and breathed a tired little sigh when she heard his footsteps descending the stairs.

She went to her desk, picked up the check and enrollment forms, and gasped softly when she saw the amount of the check. It easily covered three months' tuition for both children. Studying the bold slash of his signature, she decided that Jacob Steven Masters was as unpredictable as he was formidable. He had criticized Horizon's tuition fee more than once, and then written a check that would stagger most checking accounts.

Her pensive glance fell to the enrollment forms, and she read the brief note he had penned. *Olive—I'm not who you think I am.* It was signed *Brutus.*

Cryptic or facetious? she wondered, and felt a grin tugging at the corners of her mouth. He certainly was amusingly mysterious!

She opened the folder, curious. Deciding the beginning was a logical place to start looking for clues to solve a mystery, she found the birth certificates. A quick scan of each enlightened her as to full names and ages. Bret Daniel and Melanie Sue Masters were ages three and four respectively. She studied the two documents more carefully, discovering times and places of birth, even birth

56

weights and lengths. Then she saw it, and she groaned aloud at her slowness of perception.

I'm not who you think I am, he had written. No, he wasn't the children's father. Under mother and father on the birth certificates, she read: Susan Patrick Masters and Daniel Nathan Masters.

Her fingers flew through the remaining papers in the folder to find other documents—the legalities Jake had spoken of. And more. There were even copies of month-old newspaper clippings detailing the tragic boating accident off the coast of California in which Susan and Daniel had lost their lives.

The man with the strange grin and the stranger sense of humor was Mellie and Bret's uncle and legal guardian. Or would be within two weeks.

Poor Mellie and Bret.

CHAPTER THREE

Rain beat softly against the roof, mingling with the sounds of water gurgling down the bathtub drain and the sink tap's steady trickle as Livvy brushed her teeth. Another sound joined the liquid symphony, and Livvy paused, her head cocked to the side, listening. A heavy-handed and persistent tapping rose above the other sounds. She quickly rinsed her mouth and toothbrush, and turned off the faucet. The Little Yellow House wasn't equipped with a doorbell, sporting an old-fashioned door knocker instead. Someone was at the front door.

She grabbed her glasses from the bathroom counter, shoving them onto her nose before snatching her fleecy robe from the hook by the towel rack. She hurried out to the living room, air whispering against her nude, dampened body and making her shiver. As she neared the door she pushed her arms inside the robe's sleeves.

She called hesitantly, "Who is it?"

"Jake Masters, Olivia. I'd like to see you."

A hot, uneasy current went through her damp body and a warning steam seemed to rise about her. For the last ten days she had tried, with reasonable success, to push him and his young wards from her thoughts. Seeing him again wasn't conducive to a peaceful state of mind.

"At this hour of the night?" she stalled.

Through the door she heard a quick, surprised laugh; then a very dry "It's only eight thirty, Olivia."

So it was. Livvy frowned, her thoughts flying to another excuse. "I'm not dressed for visitors."

His response came immediately and in an impatient tone. "Unless you're in your birthday suit, would you mind opening the door? It's cold and raining out here and I'm getting damned uncomfortable!" There was a pause before he said less sharply, "I need to talk to you."

Had he changed his mind about enrolling Mellie and Bret at Horizon House? Had he come to tell her so? Livvy's troubled gaze darted to the framed picture on the small lamp table at the end of the sofa, then to the coffee table where the Masters folder lay unopened, as it had for the past ten days. After that first night when she'd compared the photograph of Bret Masters to the one of her son and had read the file, she hadn't touched it again.

She acquiesced reluctantly. "Give me a moment to slip into something."

And to slip something out of sight, she thought unhappily, belting her robe securely as she walked toward the lamp table. Feeling furtive and devious, she slid Jamie's photograph under the sofa and, in a miserable whisper, misquoted, "Oh, what a tangled web I'm weaving."

Immediately she bristled to her own defense. She hadn't deceived. She just hadn't confessed her life story to a complete stranger. Nor did she intend to.

She opened the door with a scowl and a brusque "What do you want?" that sent Jake's eyebrows climbing up his forehead.

"I don't think you're ready to hear," he said ironically, thrusting damp curls off his forehead as he stepped inside. "For the moment this nice, dry indoor atmosphere will suffice."

Livvy closed the door on the miserable November weather and stared at her visitor. His curling hair was misted with tiny droplets of rain, and the short-sleeved sweat shirt he wore was darkened in damp spots across his chest and shoulders. Faded jeans faithfully hugged his hips and thighs, delineating each male sinew down to the dampened edges of denim brushing against equally wet sneakers. He shivered a little, and goosebumps broke out along his forearms.

"You're cold and wet!"

Her exclamation sounded more concerned than she'd intended it to, and Jake smiled disarmingly. "You're right, Olivia. Would it be an imposition to ask for a towel?"

Curiously opaque, his aqua gaze made her uncomfortably aware that she wasn't fully dressed. Inclining her head in assent, she moved away from the door and preceded him toward the back of the house.

"There are towels in the bathroom, through here," she said when they entered the tiny, darkened hall. She stopped by her open bedroom door, turned on its light to illuminate the hallway, and pointed down the hall. "It's the last room. There are clean towels in the linen cabinet behind the door."

His eyes went past her to the chastely turned-down single bed, and for a moment he paused indecisively. Then he said, "Thanks, Olivia," and walked to the bathroom, shutting himself inside.

For long seconds Livvy was unmoving, staring down the dimly lit hallway. Jake Masters was the only man to have entered her bathroom since she'd bought Horizon House and The Little Yellow House a year before. She felt oddly unsettled.

She entered her room and gave the door a nudge with the heel of her bare foot to shut it. Then she quickly took jeans and a sweater from her closet and tossed them onto her bed. Modest cotton panties were found in a dresser drawer, and she loosed the tie of her robe and pulled them on. She shrugged out of the robe, let it fall to the floor, and reached toward the bed for the sweater. Bent slightly forward, her fingers outstretched, she froze when a brisk knock on the door sent it flying back against the inner wall.

Framed in the doorway, a towel draped around his neck and falling onto his bare chest, was Jake, looking as stunned as Livvy felt. She watched his eyes slip from her face and throat, then linger on her small, upthrusting breasts. One of his eyebrows rose in a curious, almost infinitesimal movement as his gaze proceeded down, discovering her one garment—the chaste cotton panties. Lower still, his glance missed not one inch of pale flesh along her slim thighs and long legs.

His gaze came up like a startled jack-in-the-box and collided with her paralyzed one. He broke the silence, saying slowly, "I don't suppose I should read too much into this."

The trace of huskiness in his voice shattered Livvy's immobility. In a flash she snatched the sweater up and held it, shieldlike, to her bare torso. "What are you doing in here?" she croaked accusingly.

"I couldn't find you in the living room or kitchen so I went searching. Your door wasn't shut completely. I did knock."

"You're *undressed!*" The fact clearly shocked her.

He leaned a negligent shoulder against the doorframe and crossed his arms over his wide chest. He said easily, "My shirt was damp and I took it off, Olivia. It's hanging over your shower rod, drying. *You're* undressed."

The slightly stressed quality of his last two words was frankly challenging, asking if she'd deliberately left her door ajar. Her eyes flashed indignation and her back straightened.

With more poise than she felt, she said coolly, "If you'll leave, I'll finish dressing."

Jake's mouth twisted briefly. "I thought the cheesecake was too good to be true." His shoulders moved in a lazy shrug and his eyes glinted. He came away from the doorframe, saying meditatively, "I've never tried diet cheese-cake, but it looks tasty enough." Then he turned down the hallway, his taunting grin lingering in his wake.

Diet cheesecake. Oh, hell's bells! Olive Oyl and diet cheesecake. The man was *so* good for her ego!

Her rigid posture relaxed and she sighed ruefully. Well, at least diet cheesecake was a better analogy than any he could have come up with had she been totally nude. The accident and subsequent surgery had left their constant reminders scored into her lower belly. She doubted Jake would have found anything amusing about pink and white scars crisscrossing her flesh as if it were a road map.

She rushed through her dressing and entered the living room with a determined jaw, steady eyes, and a stomach full of butterflies to remind her of her recent embarrass-ment. And found Jake imperturbably seated on the sofa, bent over the coffee table, the folder on his niece and nephew opened out for study beneath his gaze.

He looked up at her, not a bit self-conscious about the sense of intimacy his bare chest lent to her small living room. He leaned comfortably back, subjecting her to a detached appraisal, and she became acutely aware of what he was seeing. Her toes were bare and curled into the thick carpeting, and she wrapped her arms around her waist. The jeans she wore were old and snug, the sweater warm and frayed a little with wear. Her hair was held by combs on top of her head, and there was nothing tidy about the way loose tendrils had escaped to wisp softly around her neck and the delicate outline of her face.

"Legs," he said after a contemplative silence, as if that summarized her whole appearance.

"Two of them," she agreed, a little stiffly.

"Long, endless legs," he continued, his eyes measuring their slim length in the worn denim.

"They help me to walk."

One of his eyebrows lifted. "You're not used to being told how sexy long legs look in tight jeans?" His smile was tantalizingly wicked. He hadn't forgotten how they looked *out* of tight jeans. "I, for one, can't let long legs go unremarked upon."

Was that a sincere compliment or just teasing flattery because he was male and she was female and he had recently seen more of her than the jeans and sweater showed?

"Did you come here to pass judgment on my legs?"

He drawled with provocative humor, "I passed judgment on your legs the first time I laid eyes on you. I was just passing the thought on to you."

"Thank you!"

His eyes glittered at her snappy retort. He nodded benevolently and murmured, "You're welcome." His gaze swept to the opened folder and back to her. "You haven't deposited my check."

"No."

"Why not?"

"For one thing, it's way too much. All my other clients pay monthly, sometimes on a weekly basis. I don't hold them to long-range tuition commitments. They're always free to make other arrangements for their children if they're dissatisfied with Horizon House." Her shoulders moved in an uneasy shrug. "I was giving you the same option."

"Why would I change my mind?"

Because, she thought a little hysterically, *you might decide your nephew is better off in the care of someone a little more detached than I could ever be.*

Feeling increasingly disquieted under his questioning regard, Livvy moved to the chair facing the sofa and sat on its edge. "You don't know me, Jake," she pointed out reasonably. "And you don't know Horizon House. It stands to reason you might find something about us that displeases you."

He leaned forward, his forearms braced on his knees and his hands hanging loosely between. "I told you when we first talked that I'd investigated all the day-care possibilities in the area. I'm satisfied yours is the best, and I consider you completely trustworthy." A hint of impatience crept into his eyes when her mouth turned down. He said sardonically, "I don't have any reservations, but you seem to. Do you still dislike me?"

"No, of course not," she retorted instantly, and knew she wasn't lying. She didn't dislike him. Her uneasiness of him was only partly due to the situation with Bret. It was the man himself—virile, confident, playing flirting games with her.

He leaned back and spread his arms along the back of the sofa, and she suddenly found herself trying not to look at his chest. It seemed unfair that he was so relaxed and she was so tensely aware of the brown hair curling over bronzed sinew and arrowing down his flat midsection. She trained her eyes meticulously on his face and realized he was studying her, his gaze speculative.

"How long have you owned Horizon House?"

"Almost a year."

"Did you work for another day-care center before that?"

The pause was fractional. "No."

He waited for her to expand on the answer and, when she didn't, one corner of his mouth quirked. Very dryly, he asked, "What *did* you do before you started Horizon House?"

She moved restlessly in her chair, saw his glance sharpen, and quickly curled her legs under her, keeping her hands still in her lap. "I worked for a large insurance company for several years as assistant head of personnel." After that came maternity leave that extended into three beautiful years with Jamie. "It was a very ordinary job," she said, smiling faintly.

"What made you decide to start a child-care center?"

She averted her gaze, ill at ease with his questions, her mouth an impatient line. "Did you come here tonight to delve into my professional background?"

"Hey, hold on!" he said, the soft laughter in his voice bringing her eyes to his face. "I'm interested, not suspicious."

Of course he was. Lord, she was becoming paranoid. She drew a deep breath and made herself relax. She said quietly, "I've always liked children. I started Horizon House because . . . I needed a change." *Because my life was so empty after Jamie died, because surrogate mothering was the closest I could ever come to the real thing.* Jake's brows were drawn together in puzzlement and she quickly forestalled further questions. "Would you like something to drink?"

"A cup of coffee would be nice, Olivia."

"I don't have coffee, only diet soft drinks," she said, and felt a niggle of irritation when his eyes moved over her thin frame and his expression became ironic. She knew where the conversation would lead.

"You're not one of those females who's forever on a diet and afraid to gain an ounce, are you?"

His tone was disapproving and, remembering his appreciation of Glory's lush curves, Livvy was certain he thought model-thin women ridiculous.

Mentally counting to ten, she said patiently, "Not all diets are weight-reducing ones. I exclude sugar and caffeine from my diet because it's healthier, and I don't include sugar or caffeine in the menus for Horizon's children."

"No candy for special treats? No ice cream and homemade brownies as rewards for being good little kids?"

He was teasing her, and her soft mouth quirked at the corners in the beginnings of a grin. "As trite as this may sound, being good is its own reward. The children are served fruit and fruit juices for snacks, and when they're good I tell them so."

"And when they're bad?"

Her grin broke freely across her face. "I tell them how to be better."

He laughed, a soft, warm, relaxed sound. "I can't argue with the logic of such a reasonable woman. Maybe it's time I tried a diet soda."

Livvy left her chair, saying over her shoulder, "There's milk and both tomato and pineapple juice in the refrigerator. You're welcome to either of those if you prefer."

"I prefer the diet stuff," Jake said gravely, following her out to the kitchen.

George lay in his favorite spot on the floor in front of the refrigerator, and as Livvy removed two cans of diet cola and pulled the tabs, Jake stooped down to inspect the sleeping dog. His fingers gently scratched between George's ears, the soft petting creating a ripple of contentment in the dog's fur.

Jake grinned, looked up at her, and asked, "Your watchdog?"

Surveying the lethargic basset hound, Livvy smiled softly. George was low on energy and high on affection. Brad had presented him as an awkward puppy on their first anniversary, coaxing her into mothering it instead of having the child she wanted. *Children complicate things, Liv. This little guy needs love and so do I. Let's wait,* he'd said. And they had waited, almost too long. Their marriage had been on the verge of falling apart when she discovered she was pregnant with Jamie.

"George is a very old friend," she told Jake. "And too lazy to be a watchdog. He seldom has the energy to do more than sleep and eat and occasionally cuddle in my lap."

"Nice work if you can get it," Jake murmured, his eyes narrowing in appreciation as his glance trailed up her length.

Rising, he took the soft drink she handed him and smiled at her over the rim. He drank it all quickly, as if he considered the drink more medicinal than flavorsome, something to be taken rather than savored. Livvy swallowed her quick amusement along with her sip of soda. To each his own, and despite his assertion, Jake did not prefer diet drinks.

Holding the empty can out in front of him, he read the label. "No sugar, no caffeine," he said. "What do you do for stimulation?"

She gave him a brief, cool look and said, "A typical day at Horizon House provides all the stimulation I need. Being with over twenty energetic children has a very vitalizing effect." She understood Jake's game; she just wasn't playing.

Jake smiled, saying nothing, but his eyes communicated—an amused acceptance of her verbal sidestepping, a provocative promise that he played to win. Livvy held his gaze as steadily as she could and breathed more freely when his eyes left hers to study her small kitchen done in shades of melon and white. A small recipe clip standing on the counter received most of his attention. Made of wood, it had a scripted *L* painted on its base.

"*L* for Livvy, not *O* for Olivia," he murmured, his significant look reminding her that she'd specifically told him to call her Olivia.

He wanted an invitation to use the less formal version of her name, she realized, and was prevented from issuing it when George suddenly flopped his head onto her bare foot, demanding attention. She bent down, captured the dog's sad face in her palms, and gently shook his head. Her quick glance upward saw the movement of Jake's chest as he took a long, resigned breath, then his crooked smile.

"While you're here, would you mind signing the medical release forms? In case of accident or illness Horizon House needs your authorization to get emergency medical treatment for Mellie and Bret."

Jake's wry expression registered her deliberate change

of topic to the impersonal. A lazy flex of his wide shoulders agreed to her suggestion, at the same time setting forth an interesting display of rippling, well-toned muscle Livvy found difficult to ignore. If she was diet cheesecake, her guest was definitely a lean chunk of beefcake. Frowning slightly in exasperation at the admiring tenor of her thoughts, she stood and led the way back to the living room.

After he affixed his signature to the proper forms, Jake studied the forced way she smiled her thanks, and faint question marks curled into his brows. He said slowly, "Maybe I'd better get my sweat shirt and leave now. You look tired, Olivia."

Her tension couldn't be credited to fatigue, and she had a feeling Jake realized that, but she didn't contradict him. The sooner he left, the sooner she could relax again. He must have read something of her thoughts in her expression because his gaze sharpened analytically before he left the room.

When he came back, she was waiting politely by the door. He came toward her, his mouth a wry line. "I leave for California tomorrow to collect Mellie and Bret. They're staying with friends of Dan and Sue's right now."

"I'm sorry about your brother and sister-in-law," Livvy said quietly. "The children are very fortunate to have you to take over for their parents."

"You think so?" His eyes were smiling. "Well, by tomorrow night I'll be a daddy legally and technically, if not by biological fact. Not the conventional way to become a parent, but who knows? I might get to like it and start from scratch next time."

"Some people find adoption so rewarding, they don't feel a need to have children the conventional way."

Oh, God, *why* had she said that? *Because,* she drummed relentlessly into her head, *you just had to see his reaction, didn't you?*

And his reaction was a soft, incredulous laugh. "Oh, no, Olivia. As much as I want Mellie and Bret, I reserve the right to do some things for myself." His hand went to the doorknob, but he didn't turn it. His gaze swept over her, amused, speculative, frankly masculine. "I like you, Olivia Waring. I know the feeling isn't entirely reciprocated, but I'm hoping things will change with time and exposure. You'll find that when it comes to something I want, I can be a very patient man." His hand came up to her face, his fingers adhering warmly to her jaw. His eyes were a brilliant aqua blue, making silent promises. He continued softly, "Just in case it matters, I don't beat women and children, I'm reasonably young, and I have all my working parts. I'm also adaptable to changes in life-style, habit, and diet. That sugar-free cola wasn't bad. Before long I hope to sample the diet cheesecake."

In a light, warming caress his fingers traced her jawline to the slight point of her chin, and Livvy involuntarily trembled. Her mind was swamped with the context of his little speech, her eyes searching his face to discover how seriously he meant it. All conjecture ceased the moment his mouth swooped to brush hers in a gentle salute. He raised his head and murmured her name, and she made a tentative movement away from him, her heart catapulting into her throat.

Again he said softly, "Olivia," with warm amusement in his tone. He reached for her and drew her tightly into his embrace. His lips came down on hers, and he kissed her the second time with an urgent but patient persistence. By almost imperceptible degrees Livvy relaxed, slowly becoming distracted from the reservations she held, steadily warming to the bold exploration of her mouth by his. She leaned quietly and pliantly into the increasing heat of his body, and felt the quickened thud of his heartbeat against her breast.

His mouth glided hotly to her neck, moving down the backswept invitation of her throat, his tongue testing the pulsebeat at its base with teasing little thrusts. One of his hands shaped her shoulder in caressing fingers while the other went to her waist, gently kneading and turning her sideways so that her hip and shoulder rested against his flat belly and hard chest.

A quiver went through her when his mouth nuzzled a place beneath her sweater into the soft curve of her neck and shoulder. She moved her head in a slight, negative shake, and he murmured something in answer, a low reassurance. Boldly, his hand pushed beneath her sweater, his palm finding and gently claiming her small breast. When his fingers discovered and lightly exploited the hardening peak, her world did a crazy cartwheel and her hands clutched his forearm in an effort to steady the wild spin of her senses.

With a soft groan his mouth came back to hers, prising her lips apart with an urgent, twisting pressure. His forehead bumped against her glasses, knocking them askew, but neither of them seemed to notice as the kiss lengthened and deepened.

After a moment he lifted his head and spoke. But his whispered words, thick and inarticulate, were lost below the tumultuous riot of blood rushing to her brain, and Livvy murmured a soft "What?"

In answer his fingers moved from her breast and lowered to the silken flesh of her waist. His mouth found hers again, gentle and coaxing, and his hand moved to her hipbone, pressing her firmly to his uncompromising maleness, then across to flatten upon her lower belly.

Like a firecracker ignited, Livvy exploded out of his arms, falling back against the wall by the door. Her reaction to his touch upon her stomach was instinctively rejecting, the force of it appallingly unexpected by both of them. Her fingers jerked her glasses into place, then covered the lower half of her face, her eyes huge and distressed above them. She watched Jake take a harsh, irregular breath, saw the tensing spring of his body, and half expected him to pounce on her.

Instead, after a long tense moment, he controlled the frustration his darkly flushed countenance portrayed, and eyed her with a touch of irony. A little thickly, he drawled, "That was very effective, Olivia, but a simple no would have done."

Through her fingers she mumbled inadequately. "You mustn't keep kissing me!"

Something flared briefly in his eyes and he said, "My pardons, Olive. I forgot for a moment you're a maiden lady and might be offended by my unbridled passions. I'll try to show more restraint next time."

It was a good thing her fingers were already covering her face, Livvy discovered. Otherwise, Jake would have seen the quick, undisciplined grin his words produced. With effort she controlled it and brought her hands down from her face. Despite her insistence on keeping their relationship impersonal, he was getting to her. He was sexy and humorous and, yes, charming in his own distinctly individual way. Jake Masters was as potent as wine, and she'd have to remember she had a low tolerance for heady spirits.

She said, "I just . . . thought it should end."

"So I gathered," he murmured, but he was slowly smiling.

There was a warm, gentle quality to his smile that affected Livvy as readily as a toasty fireplace on a winter's night. A soporific heat spread through her and the last of her tension melted away. Her expression softened and the corners of her mouth curved upward in response.

Brilliant and audacious, his aqua gaze burned over her countenance. "I consider that smile a penetration of my control, pretty woman. You do understand that I'm more than ready to shelve restraint and reciprocate, don't you?"

His tone was so softly indulgent that it took a moment

71

to realize what he'd said—and the deliberate intimacy of his choice of words. Assuming cool equanimity with a hot, glowing complexion was difficult, but Livvy managed a slight lift of her slim nose. Striving to sound lightly ironic, she said, "You make it impossible to misunderstand." And watched his eyes glitter appreciation for her feeble attempt to show casual unconcern.

He sighed gravely. "That's good. I strive to be open and honest." He reached for the doorknob and twisted it open. Before he left, he touched her heated cheek and winked, promising, "I'll see you Monday morning, early."

Standing in the lighted doorway, Livvy watched him lope across the wet yard to his car, his broad shoulders hunched against the continuing patter of cold rain. Moments later his Mercedes purred to life and pulled away from the curb, its engine a distant hum before she closed the door and locked it.

Moving away from the door, she breathed confusion into her lungs and expelled dismay, muttering aloud, "What have I gotten myself into?"

Almost immediately her worried features fell into lines of disgruntlement. It wasn't so much what she'd gotten herself into as what was mushrooming about her, heedless of her efforts to keep it under control.

Turning out the living room and kitchen lights, she then made her way to the bedroom, releasing some of her frustration with the length and force of her stride.

"Damn, damn, damn," she cursed softly under her breath, plopping down on the edge of the bed and falling back to stare up at the ceiling.

Why couldn't Jake Masters be an ordinary man with ordinary children and bring an ordinary situation to her door? Why did he have to be sexy and funny and warm? Why did his nephew have to look so much like Jamie? And why did the damnably honest man have to consider Horizon's owner so utterly trustworthy? She was dreading Monday morning as she never had dreaded a single day since opening Horizon's doors.

She had begun Horizon House with a cautious belief in second chances and a definite need to be around children, using proceeds from an insurance policy never intended for her advantage. Without Brad's approval she had insured Jamie's life soon after his birth. It had been meant as an investment for her son's future—a college education, perhaps, or maybe a means to start his own business. She'd wanted security for Jamie and had known it was left to her to see any plans to fruition. Brad made no plans for anyone's future, not even his own. He spent money with a careless disregard for any contingency. Like a beautiful, spoiled little boy, he indulged himself endlessly—the newest sports cars, a country club membership, a snazzy catamaran he sailed on the local lakes with smiling panache. When Jamie died, Livvy had hated the insurance money, horrified by what it represented. She put it in the bank and tried to forget it. How could she *profit* by her son's death? Eventually her irrational guilt and horror of the money were put into perspective. When she planned the day-care center, "Jamie's money" bought the needed property and financed the first few months until her business grew and stabilized. Horizon House became a gift—a special one from her son. She found love there, and new meaning to her life.

Now, with the impending arrival of the Masters children and their uncle's looming and persistent presence, the center suddenly seemed an albatross about her neck, weighting her down and trapping her in a situation she found dismaying. Every time Jake opened his mouth and used words like *truth* and *honesty* and *trustworthy* and *open,* she felt as apprehensive as an arrested criminal contemplating the scales of justice.

And why, she wondered defensively, would she feel blameworthy about anything? She hadn't asked for Jake

Masters' patronage. She had done her best to discourage it.

Did you really? Is that why you proudly showed him through Horizon House and offered nothing more meaty than cryptic warnings about your suitability as caregiver to his niece and nephew?

Well, she hadn't been looking for a replacement for Jamie. Fate had dropped that little number in her lap, and she had come to terms with the insanity of looking at one child and seeing another.

So you've kept Jake's folder close at hand just to prove how sane and unselfish and perfectly removed from the situation you are, have you?

By no means had she wanted Jake to be attracted to her. She had kept herself cool and aloof.

How? By melting into his arms each time he touches you?

Annoyed, she went to the cheval mirror standing in one corner of the room. Truth wasn't always a simple case of black and white, and was often neither pretty nor easy to accept.

Ruthlessly she stripped away her clothing and stood nude before the mirror, staring at her reflection. The intersection of pinkish, puckering lines on her lower stomach was starkly visible and, as Jake had done, she flattened her hand across it. Then, very lightly, her fingers traced each individual scar, tactilely reading one more page from her book of truths. She had let Jake believe it was his boldness, not her self-consciousness, that had taken her so forcefully out of his arms.

Deliberately using the latest appellation Jake had given her, she whispered disgustedly, "Pretty woman, the honest-to-God truth is that you're scared stiff." She had run into a confident, attractive, teasing man whose legs might be long enough to hurdle the self-protective barriers she'd erected during the last eighteen months.

When her hand dropped back to her side, her eyes were clouded with agitation.

Calm down! she told herself. So far, nothing disastrous had happened. Jake had kissed her a few times, intimated an interest in her as a woman. He was probably interested in several women. She remembered Michelle. An entire weekend lay ahead of her in which to regain her equilibrium, to erect her aloof facade.

CHAPTER FOUR

Livvy stooped down beside the low table in the art center, tucked the swing of her hair behind her ear, and examined the finished crayon drawing her young pupil Mindy so proudly displayed.

"It's the manster," the little cherub announced serenely in her high-pitched Texas twang.

Manster as in monster? Livvy wondered, knowing she would have to tread carefully until she received concrete evidence that her suspicion was correct. Often the drawings of preschoolers were understood only by the artists. A wise adult skirted away from the question "What is it?" for the more discreet "Will you tell me about it?" Already that morning, submerged in confused personal thoughts, she had nearly bruised the fragile ego of a budding artist by mistaking his chicken for a cat. Fortunately the little artist had been too busy hamming it up, pantomiming helpful hints as to the subject of his drawing, to be hurt by her mistake. Mischievously he had offered clue after clue until one finally penetrated Livvy's inner absorption. It had been impossible to misconstrue —either consciously or unconsciously—his flapping his elbows like wings and the "cluck-cluck" sounds he made. Warmly she had praised not only his art but his acting. And had flailed herself for not paying more attention to her job and less to the personal dilemma she faced.

Meeting Bret Masters was a daunting prospect. A part of her dreaded it even while another part of her recognized the flutters periodically attacking the region of her heart as the twinges of expectancy they were. Regardless of how many times her logical self said it was unwise to consider comparing one child to the memories of another, her emotional self was quick to retort, *How can you not?* Just as, how could she not have thoughts of Bret lead to thoughts of Jake?

For a few minutes Friday night, while his hands had been touching her and his mouth coaxing hers, she had forgotten his nephew's resemblance to her son; she had forgotten her marriage and its disappointments; she had forgotten the pain that came from emotional involvement. She had been thinking solely of Jake, of the way he made her feel, of his warmth and vitality slowly filling an emptiness and promising to do so much more.

And those thoughts were dangerous ones that she couldn't allow to continue. There were too many risks involved; Jake's discovery of Jamie and his resemblance to Bret was only one. With a little luck she could play the hand fate had dealt her and no one but her would be affected. A touch of despairing humor crept into her thoughts. *I hope I have a poker face.*

Mindy's uncertain "Don't you like him?" broke into Livvy's troubled musings. She arranged her pensively set facial muscles into a warm, reassuring smile and quickly nodded.

Mindy's "manster" was crookedly etched in black crayon and consisted of a squat, misshapen body, a large head, and weblike hands extending from the body without benefit of arms. The face featured a long line of upcurving mouth, no nose, and four round eyes—two blue and two brown, one pair set above the other in a forehead that led to a hairless pate. There were no ears and no neck.

Detecting no anger or fear in her small student's features, Livvy assayed gently, "He looks to be a nice fellow."

A tranquil nod transformed Mindy's initial uncertainty. "He's good. Mansters are s'posed to be good, my mommy says. They don't like being bad."

Livvy made a mental note to congratulate Mindy's mother. If the woman was dealing with her daughter's fear of monsters, she had chosen a positive approach. "Why don't you tell me more about him?" she invited, smiling.

"His voice is big. Bigger than my daddy's."

Easily translating *big* to mean *deep,* Livvy commented, "You've made him smile. Does he like to laugh?"

Mindy cocked her head to the side, considering. "He laughs sometimes, but mostly he talks and sings."

A singing monster? With effort Livvy controlled the urge to chuckle and asked, "Do you like him?"

"He likes boys and girls."

Which, in the language of a four-year-old, meant that Mindy liked him. Livvy's smile broadened; she was liking the manster more and more herself. Her finger lightly traced the face in the drawing. Hoping to elicit an explanation of why Mindy had given him four eyes, she complimented warmly, "He has very nice eyes."

This time Mindy's nod was an adamant up-and-down agreement. She leaned closer to Livvy. "The brown ones are his. The blue ones belong to Jesus," she confided in a whisper, adding wisely, "the manster said Jesus gives everybody his eyes to see with."

Surprise kept Livvy momentarily silent. It seemed Mindy's monster was not only good, he was blessed. Wondering if the child was again quoting her mother or had come up with the theory on her own, she asked curiously, "Do your mommy and daddy know he said that?"

The answer came quickly and with a touch of asperity. "Of course! We go to Sunday school every Sunday, then to Big Church. The manster pats my head and tells me I'm a good girl. He shakes my daddy's hand."

Sudden enlightenment put a twinkle of amused delight in Livvy's eyes. Oh, what a Texas twang could do to some words! The "manster" wasn't a monster but a minister.

"Can I take the picture home with me?" Mindy asked hopefully. "I want to show it to the manster."

"Certainly you can," Livvy agreed promptly. "The minister will love it!" He was bound to. A lot of love and inspired thought had gone into it.

When Mindy giggled her pleasure, Livvy gave in to the amusement bubbling inside her, laughing warmly with the child.

In a more relaxed frame of mind Livvy inspected the last few drawings; then, with the help of the children, she put away the art supplies and straightened the chairs under the tables. When Jenny Clarke arrived, exuding vigor and youthful confidence after her early class at a local college, the entire group had moved to the lunchroom for a snack. Jenny found them happily sampling juicy orange segments, their faces and fingers sticky, their moods ranging from grins to giggles. Good spirits were contagious.

"What a happy group!" the young woman exclaimed, her smiling gaze skimming to each youngster before settling on her employer. She eyed the rainbow of crayon marks decorating Livvy's white coverall jacket, and commented drolly, "I see there was an art session this morning."

Livvy smiled around the finger she was licking free of a trickle of orange juice. "You'll have to look through the pictures, Jenny. Some of them are quite . . . uh . . . inspiring." Her eyes twinkled in reminiscence as she assumed a singularly pious expression.

"Inspiring, huh? Somehow I sense an anecdote," Jenny said, her eyes sparkling with anticipation. She had a keen, dry wit and a heart like so much mush. She was easily amused and just as easily touched. The cute and often endearing episodes involving the children were ambrosia to her. "Remind me to talk with you later," she said.

A high screech of pain at a nearby table drew both women's startled attention. A small boy tumbled out of his chair, wailing pitifully as he threw himself at Jenny's jeaned legs. She knelt down, gathered him into her arms, and murmured soft words of comfort while he sobbed out his hurt against her chest. Finally running down, he sniffled and drew back, mumbling tragically, "I bi' my ton'." His adult sympathizers looked back in incomprehension, so he stuck out the injured part for them to inspect the tiny cut and the almost nonexistent smudge of blood on the end of his bitten tongue. New oohs and aahs of compassion came his way. Livvy produced a dampened paper towel and mopped up his tearstained face. The wounded three-year-old smiled stoically and clung to Jenny's neck.

Around the little fellow's strangling hug, Jenny grinned. "I'm going to have a dozen of these!" she announced with smug enthusiasm. Then, on another thought, she exclaimed, "Oh, I almost forgot! Glory was finishing a phone call when I came in. I'm to tell you that the fresh sweet peas will be delivered soon by the man with the spinach." She shrugged a little in puzzlement and asked, "Are we having groceries delivered now?"

Funny, *funny* Glory had taken Jake's little joke a step further, Livvy realized, not amused at having him cast as Popeye to her Olive. In answer to her young employee's curious gaze she smiled faintly and said, "We're getting new students this morning. Can you take over here?"

Jenny's easy nod sent Livvy out of the lunchroom. In the hallway that led upstairs she discarded her coverall jacket and laid it over the banister. Without conscious direction her fingers checked the buttons on the cuffs of her long-sleeved turquoise blouse, then ran lightly up the tiny pleats that ribbed its front. She unbuttoned the top two buttons at her throat, frowned, then rebuttoned them, absently smoothing the soft, rounded collar. The trim gray skirt she wore was fashionably cut and had four small pleats at the waist to ensure freedom of movement. Her shoes were gray pumps with open toes, a delicate scalloped edging, and one-inch heels. The entire outfit was less casual than her normal wash and wear attire. She had dressed with more in mind than Horizon's demanding physical activity.

Standing in front of her mirror that morning, she had thought she looked nice. Attractive and womanly in an unobtrusive way. A woman a child would be drawn to. A woman a child would instinctively trust. She had left her hair down, the ends curled under slightly to skim her shoulders and soften the outline of her face. Her makeup was understated, her jewelry the tiny gold studs adorning her earlobes and the slim watch on her wrist. Her whole appearance had been planned to make a favorable impression.

Why, then, did she suddenly feel so uncertain . . . so vulnerable? As if she looked too soft and too feminine.

A pair of gleaming aqua eyes floated into her mind's vision, mocking her confusion. The echo of a baritone voice calling her "pretty woman" resounded in her brain, suffusing her with agitation.

Snap out of it! she told herself. *It's too late for second thoughts now!* Her mouth firmed in a deliberate attempt to drive away the vulnerability and, with a shallow, corrugated sigh, she moved toward the door leading into the entrance alcove.

The soft click of Glory's typewriter muffled her footsteps, but Glory saw her approach from the corner of her eye. Her fingers ceased their movement on the typewriter keys and she swiveled in her chair.

A beaming smile lit her face as she took in Livvy's appearance. "That coverall jacket hid some good stuff. You look great!"

"Too dressy?" Livvy asked charily.

"Not on your life! The man will appreciate the effort."

Livvy's mouth turned down. That's what she was afraid of, knowing Jake would need discouraging, not encouraging. "The idea was to have the Masters *children* appreciate the effort. I want them to like Horizon House and me."

"Since when hasn't a child immediately liked you?"

Avoiding Glory's amused eyes, Livvy glanced down at her watch. "It's after ten," she murmured.

"Don't worry, they should be here soon. Although when Jake called, there was so much screaming in the background, I might have misunderstood his exact words."

"Screaming?" A vague note of censure had crept into Livvy's voice.

"Yep. Bloodcurdling howls. Jake sounded very distracted."

"Was one of the children hurt, do you think?"

"I believe Jake was the one hurt. I heard him threaten to beat the next one who bit his thumb."

"Oh, no!" Livvy whispered, then more sharply, "He wouldn't!"

Glory laughed and advised, "Don't look so horrified. His niece and nephew will undoubtedly arrive unscathed."

Not as willing to see the humor in the situation as Glory was, Livvy said, "You can't be sure of that."

"I trust my instincts," Glory returned easily, adding speculatively, "and I'm more objective than you are."

"What do you mean?"

Glory's sigh was rife with exasperation. "I mean, darling friend," she began mockingly, "that Jake Masters seems to upset you and I think we both know why." She held up a silencing hand when Livvy started to speak. "Don't deny it! You've been skittish for the past two weeks. Each time I mention any member of the Masters family, you shy away, suddenly finding yourself too busy to talk."

"It's not because I'm battling feelings for Jake! It's—" Livvy began, only to curtail her tongue abruptly. *It's because of Bret,* she'd almost said. Her chin lost its defensive tilt and her gaze skittered away from Glory's intent one.

How could she explain that in her eyes Bret Masters was Jamie's twin image? She couldn't. Not without conveying that seeing him, holding him, was becoming an urgent longing. Not without revealing the guilt and confusion that relentlessly followed on the heels of that desire. So she'd kept the information to herself, trying not to think about it. Thinking about it all the time.

Self-despair darkened Livvy's brown eyes to a cloudy ebony. A wry truth brought a bittersweet curve to her lips. In a matter of minutes Bret Masters would arrive and Glory would see him. All her skittishness—her edginess—would be explained.

"Livvy, what is it?" Glory asked quietly. "You look so . . . I don't know . . ." She spread her hands lamely, her eyes concerned. "Saddened, I guess."

With difficulty Livvy shook away the personal demons that bedeviled her and resolutely garnered her composure. She managed a teasing smile. "I'm a little wound up, I suppose. You know Mondays are always hectic."

Glory's eyes flashed a quick doubt, but she didn't pursue the subject. Her gaze went past Livvy and she whistled softly through her teeth. "Brace yourself. From the looks of it, we're about to receive the next installment in the Masters family quarrel."

The spacious entrance alcove suddenly gave Livvy an overwhelming feeling of closeness that was nearly claustrophobic. Her fingers slipped inside her collar, easing it away from her tightened throat. She breathed shallowly. At the sound of the door opening behind her, she slowly glanced over her shoulder. Jake walked inside. Alone.

The effect of the unexpected respite was staggering, and she tightly gripped the edge of Glory's desk.

Jake's face was like a thundercloud, the grooves running from his nose to his mouth drawn in grim severity, his lips compressed into a hard, forbidding line. Beneath scowling eyebrows his eyes glittered sharp irritation, and his curling hair was tousled as if impatient fingers had combed through it more than once. The jacket of his dark-gray well-tailored suit fit smoothly across his broad shoulders, but the tie knotted at the neck of his blue shirt was a little askew. Had he tied it with one hand, or had he jerked it away from his throat in a moment of anger? There was a small wet area, somewhat crinkled, on the otherwise perfect crease of his right trouser leg just above the knee. As he neared them, his thumb, wrapped in a bandage, stroked soothingly across it.

At the corner of Glory's desk he stopped and said, "Good morning!" his voice a low, abrupt growl.

Livvy and Glory chorused subdued return greetings, one's expression disquieted, the other's inquiring. There were no small figures trailing behind him. Acutely aware that Glory was settling back in her chair, somehow making herself an observer rather than a participant, Livvy half turned from her position facing her friend and faced Jake instead.

She stated the obvious. Was it relief or disappointment that put the edge of accusation in her soft voice? "Your niece and nephew aren't with you."

At her sharp tone Jake's mouth twisted ironically. "Would you sue me for breach of contract if I told you Horizon House is presently in disfavor?"

"I would refund your check for tuition. I told you, you're free to change your mind."

Exasperation vied with cynicism in his expression. "Well, hold on to the money, Olivia. I haven't changed my mind and I've a feeling you're going to earn it."

He stepped nearer, within touching distance, so close,

in fact, that Glory no longer had to flick her gaze back and forth like a spectator at a tennis match in order to gauge their expressions. Jake's gaze went over Livvy's features, reacquainting himself with the color of her hair, the texture of her skin, the shape of her mouth. His jaw flexed, adding to his look of aggression. He said gruffly, "You look different with your hair out of that crazy little ball."

The crazy little ball was the topknot she'd worn the other times he'd seen her. Had he just complimented her? She wondered. She doubted. She studied him.

Thickly fringed by reddish-brown lashes, his eyes were unbelievably blue against the bronze of his complexion. They glittered. Disapproval or appreciation? Above his cleft chin his unsmiling mouth was uncompromisingly male, his lips firmly molded, vaguely sensual. Unbidden, the remembered feel of his mouth upon hers, warm and alive and incredibly stirring, tingled its way from her nerve center. She felt her cheeks heat with her thoughts and looked away, wetting her lips nervously.

"Thank you," she said, her voice brittle, then wondered why she had thanked him. Her expression cool and assured, she looked back at him.

Jake had turned his attention to Glory and his expression was no longer difficult to read. It was clearly flirtatious.

"I don't suppose you've dumped your husband since I saw you last?" he ventured hopefully, his eyebrows waggling suggestively.

Livvy frowned.

Her eyes amused, Glory shook her head. "No, I'll keep him a while longer."

"Pity," Jake murmured regretfully.

Their little exchange shot through Livvy like a purging medication. She asked coldly, "Where are Mellie and Bret?"

His aqua gaze made a detour to the glassed entrance

doors before coming back to her, sharp with irritation. He answered shortly, "Outside. In the car."

"You left them in the car! They're probably frightened to death!" The dismay in her expression was matched by the anxiety in her voice.

"Anything that can put a little healthy fear into those two has my complete blessing," Jake muttered, not in jest.

Livvy gaped at him. Then she looked past him, through the glass doors and at the Mercedes parked at curbside. In the passenger seat two small bodies were huddled together. "Oh, the poor darlings are holding each other," she whispered, touched by their obvious solidarity.

"The *poor darlings*"—Jake mimicked her term, a testy edge in his voice—"are probably plotting insurrection. Their first two power plays only spilled a little of my blood. They're aiming for my complete subjugation to their will."

Livvy stared at him, finding her impatience with his insensitivity increasing. Couldn't he understand the fear that drove his children to rebellion? He was a stranger to them. "It's negligence to leave two preschoolers in a car by themselves."

Jake didn't appreciate her tone of cool reproach. His brows lowered, as did his voice. "If they're my two preschoolers, I'll leave them anywhere I damned well please!" he said in a muted growl. Then, oblivious to the watching, very interested Glory, his hand reached out and caught Livvy's nape, bringing her surprised face within an inch of his darkly frowning one. "I'm the *daddy* now, remember? Friday night you thought that was something admirable. Don't change your mind just because you automatically sympathize with short people!" The sarcasm in his voice held an underlying note of grievance that widened Livvy's eyes. He sounded hurt by her criticism. "And another thing," he continued, his tone aggressive, his breath a hot blast against her face. *"I'm* the head of my family. No pint-size hellions are going to undermine my authority. And no nearsighted schoolteacher is going to slap my wrists verbally when she disapproves of my parenting methods."

They were nose to nose, the moist heat of their combined breaths beginning to rise. Livvy muttered tightly, "You're fogging my glasses."

Seconds passed before the fingers at her nape eased their pressure—moments of absolute silence broken when Jake said heavily, "Ah, hell, I've upset you again, haven't I?"

Unable to see anything through her clouded lenses, Livvy blinked, her brow furrowing in a scowl that had little to do with poor eyesight. She heard Jake's regretful sigh when he released her, then felt his touch near her temple when he removed her glasses. She gasped a little in surprise and heard Glory snicker under the skillful guise of a sneeze. How wonderful to have an audience witnessing the little contretemps between her and Jake! And how nice to be able to entertain that audience so easily! She would kill Glory later, Livvy decided disgruntledly.

Before she could focus on the room, her glasses were back in place, wiped free of condensation. Jake was eyeing her warily. "I'm sorry, Olivia," he said. "I've had a lousy morning and it's made me an irritable bas—" He broke off the word on a wince, looked chagrined, and started again. "I'm a foul-tempered son of a gun this morning, and I apologize if I offended you." Evidently contrition wasn't Jake's long suit. His lips twitched a little and his eyes filled with blue sparks. "Just in case I gave you the wrong impression, I'm kind of partial to nearsighted schoolteachers."

Across the short distance that separated them, Livvy ignored his teasing and stared at him levelly. She was still nettled and trying to control it. Her gaze dropped and she studied the toes of her shoes. Couldn't she find a neutral ground on which to meet him? Something between attacking his methods and agreeing with them? She raised her eyes. "I'm sorry too. I was concerned for the children's safety, but I had no right to interfere in your family matters."

Jake frowned, opened his mouth as if he wanted to contradict her, then abruptly shut it. She watched him run his fingers through his chestnut curls and sigh again before fixing her with a rueful stare.

"I have the car keys in my pocket and I've been able to keep half an eye on the car. Unless they've used their tenacious little teeth on the upholstery in the last few minutes, no harm has been done." He held up his bandaged thumb and tapped a lightly fisted hand near the dampened spot on his pants leg. "Bret bites," he said in succinct explanation.

"He's just frightened, Jake. He's not used to you."

Jake grimaced and shook his head ruefully. "Yeah, well," he muttered on a soft explosion of breath, his mouth a wry line. "His fright has drawn my blood twice this morning. His sister screeches like a little shrew, and when I tell her to cool it, the boy sinks his teeth into me." His sober gaze went to the glassed doors and the view beyond. "They were wary of me from the beginning, but the promise of a plane ride seemed to perk them up a little. They were relatively manageable until we left the airport last night to drive home. Since then it's all been downhill. They hate my apartment, the food I provide, and me—not necessarily in that order." He paused, took a deep breath, and summed up the situation in clipped sentences. "They don't want to be enrolled at Horizon House. They don't want to live with me. They don't want anything I have to offer. They want to go back to California and live with Dan and Sue's friends."

Livvy's understanding grew to compassion—for Bret and Mellie, orphaned and taken away from the only security they knew, and for Jake, frustrated by their hostility. Hesitantly she asked, "Would you mind if I talked to them?"

Jake's slow grin was endearingly lopsided. "Right now, Olivia, I'm batting zero. Maybe your professional objectivity will have some sway with my little fugitives from reason. Just be careful," he warned. "They're armed and dangerous."

Livvy had averted her face at his mention of objectivity, but she met his gaze and smiled a little in answer to his humor.

Glory spoke up for the first time since she and Jake had exchanged brief, teasing words. "Don't worry, Jake. Livvy has a way of disarming most everyone. She makes child's play of trouble." Her words were for Jake, their underlying meaning for Livvy. Her earlier concern had been rerouted, not forgotten.

With a glancing, preoccupied smile Livvy left them. Her insides aquiver, she made her way outdoors. The November air was crisp and cool and she drew in great gulps of it, trying to slow her galloping heartbeat. She squeezed her eyes momentarily shut, then opened them and started down the walk. If Mellie and Bret were frightened and defiant, she would need a clear head and an uncluttered heart to deal with them.

When she reached the Mercedes, her eyes, naturally enough, fell to Bret first. Her heart turned over. His picture hadn't lied, and she allowed herself a moment to cherish his small, beloved features before her gaze widened discreetly to encompass his sister. Neither child did more than blink in reaction to her presence. On knees threatening to buckle, Livvy knelt down beside the car, unmindful of what the brittle drying grass was doing to her panty hose.

It took a great deal of self-control to smile naturally and say, "Hi. I'm Livvy."

They stared back at her mutely, assessing her as thoroughly as she assessed them.

Knowing she needed time to regain her wandering equilibrium before looking at Bret too closely, Livvy studied Mellie first. As she examined the girl's thin, impassive features, she found herself missing the perky mischief she had seen in the photo. Mellie's blue eyes were shuttered against emotion, her mouth thinned only slightly in distrust. Her long brown hair needed combing, and her clothes had a careless, thrown-together appearance that practically shouted Mellie's uninterest in making a favorable impression. Her jeans were fairly crisp, but the leg warmers over them were drooping at the ankles and caught under the heels of her shoes. Her cotton top was wrinkled at the hem where she had twisted it into a knot and untwisted it, and the buttons down its front were mismatched to their buttonholes, creating a lopsided image. Livvy's heart responded to the anguish behind the child's dishevelment, and it must have shown in her expression because Mellie frowned and looked away.

Double jeopardy of Livvy's heart occurred when she detailed Bret's appearance. His chubby legs were covered by neat khaki pants, but his shoes were untied. His pullover top was splotched with the obvious and heedless fall of teardrops. Indeed, his eyes were suspiciously pink-rimmed, the blond lashes spiked with the moist residue of recent distress. His lips quivered and his cheeks worked spasmodically as he sucked industriously on a thumb. Torn by conflicting emotions, Livvy studied the anxious pattern of mouth and thumb. She drew an instinctive comparison. Jamie had never sucked his thumb. He had been more apt to angle his chin and put on a brave, big-boy front when he was distressed. Under her intent regard, Bret's chubby hand crept into his sister's thin fingers; and Mellie, betraying a protective instinct Livvy found unbearably touching, edged her brother's sturdy little body behind her slight one.

She told Livvy flatly, "We don't like you."

"That's a shame," Livvy replied, her smile unwavering. "I like both of you. And I think you'll find Horizon House is a very nice place. We have lots of toys and other children to play with."

The thumb popped out of Bret's mouth long enough for him to ask, "Does Popeye live here?"

Out of the mouths of babes! Livvy thought ruefully, and answered, "No, just me and three other ladies and lots of nice kids."

"Uncle Jake lied!" Mellie announced with a scornful toss of her head. "He said Olive Oyl lived at Horizon House."

"Uncle Jake lied," Bret echoed in a mumble around his thumb. Then, with the saddest eyes Livvy had ever seen, he confessed, "I bit him. Two times. He yelled at Mellie."

Livvy decided not to address the issue. She said instead, "Why don't you two come out here with me so we can get acquainted. I like boys and girls."

A sly look entered Mellie's eyes. "Bret might bite you. He hates grown-ups."

In a quick aside to his sister, Bret said earnestly, "I don't hate *her*, Mellie."

Mellie frowned, temporarily thwarted. Then her chin came up and she reminded her brother severely, "We don't like school."

"We don't like school," Bret parroted faithfully, but his melancholy expression said his heart wasn't in the agreement. He worked his thumb with more energy, unconsciously working his way farther into Livvy's heart.

"Horizon House is a lovely school," she told them persuasively. "On days like today, when the sun is shining, we all play outside in the back courtyard. There are swings and slides and sandboxes." An inner glow spread throughout her when both children looked intrigued. But Mellie was a tough nut to crack, her interest changing rapidly to resentment.

"Uncle Jake is mean and he lies and he growls like a big bear!" she charged heatedly, looking away from the gentle concern in Livvy's eyes. She flinched a little before setting her mouth in a defiant line.

Livvy said quietly, "When I was a little girl, I had a big stuffed teddy bear with button eyes and a red felt tongue. He kept me company every night in bed. The only time he ever growled was when I forgot to cuddle him. Maybe Uncle Jake is like my teddy bear. Maybe he growled because you and Bret forgot to cuddle him."

For a moment Mellie looked ready to relent; then she said, "Uncle Jake wouldn't let us bring all our toys on the airplane, and he lost Sammy."

The crimes against Jake were mounting. Livvy asked carefully, "Who's Sammy?"

"Bret's giraffe," came the bitter answer, while Bret's mouth drooped in a mournful little pout. "Bret sleeps with Sammy, and Uncle Jake wouldn't go back to the airplane to find him. Bret cried and cried."

Livvy was torn between amusement and sympathy. Evidently the tragic loss of Sammy was the unscalable wall between Jake and his new family. Jake had said things had gone downhill after they'd left the airport. She offered helpfully, "We have a giraffe inside Horizon House. Bret could borrow him until Sammy gets found." Or until his loss wasn't such a tender sore.

A conferring glance passed between the two children. Mellie asked cautiously, "What's his name?"

The stuffed giraffe was old and washable and had received a lot of handling. The stuffing in his neck had collapsed with age and wear, so that his head constantly hung down to his chest. He looked rather timid. "His name is Bashful," Livvy invented, not too originally. "He's a little shy around people."

Mellie considered. Bret looked hopeful. Livvy held her breath. The verdict came reluctantly. "Okay," Mellie decreed slowly while Bret smiled, sans thumb, managing to look more like Jamie than ever.

Livvy was getting used to the strange reactions of her heart. Bret's smile encouraged it to rise and do a tiny flip-flop near her throat. As matter-of-factly as thickened speech would permit, she said, "You two hop out of the car and we'll go get Bashful now."

The soft click of the door release announced their compliance. Without rising, Livvy scooted back to accommodate the opening of the car door. The brittle grass snagged both knees of her panty hose, but she scarcely noticed. Willing her hands not to tremble, she extended them invitingly. When both were taken, she blinked a sudden burning from her eyes.

Mellie, watching her, leaned forward and whispered, "Bret won't really bite you."

"I know he won't," Livvy replied with a betraying catch in her voice that she covered with a smile.

Following his sister's every lead, Bret snuggled trustingly inside the circle of Livvy's arm. He, too, whispered. "You're nice."

"So are you," she whispered back, her smile soft with pleasure.

The urge to crush him against her was oddly missing. He felt sweet and lovable, but somehow not as familiar as she had expected him to feel. She found the same pleasure in giving Mellie's fingers a gentle, reassuring squeeze as she did in lightly caressing Bret's rounded cheek. The trusting smiles of both filled her soul with warmth. They needed affection. They had suffered losses she understood all too well. The adjustment to their new life would be difficult, and she felt a strong desire to help and protect them. Her heart slowly settled into a regular beat, and she felt the taut muscles of her body easing with relief. Everything was going to be all right. She might look at Bret and see Jamie, but she no longer feared confusing the two in her heart.

When she stood and turned, a child's hand in each of hers, she blanched under the force of a forgotten danger. Jake stood a few feet away from them, his narrow-eyed scrutiny fixed unwaveringly on her. A quiver ran up her spine and her heart boomed like a kettledrum. How much had he seen and heard? How much had she given away by her reaction to his children? The thought of having her private emotions on display unnerved her; she couldn't hold his unreadable gaze. Her eyes moved away from him . . . and found Glory standing just to the right and behind him. Glory's expression was easy to decipher. It held the knowledge of the resemblance between two small boys; it held understanding, a trace of worry; and, more importantly to Livvy, it held a lack of condemnation that was absolution.

It was Mellie who shattered the little frozen silence. Her voice crisp and sharp, she addressed her uncle. "Livvy has a giraffe for Bret, so we'll go to school now." Her shriveling glance accompanied her curt words.

"How very gracious of you," said her withered uncle dryly.

"Bret *needs* a giraffe," the child pointed out in another attempt to cut the man down to size.

Jake's glance returned to the slim woman standing between his two children. His eyes were brilliant and intent. "It looks like Bret will get what he needs, then," he said in a satiric tone.

Livvy felt her face stiffen. "It's a little cool out here. Shall we go inside?" she said, trying to sound practical and untroubled, her efforts producing another of Jake's curious, twisted half smiles.

In the entrance alcove Glory took over. After one probing glance that registered the strain beneath Livvy's outward confidence, she smiled brightly and began chattering with the children. She tied Bret's shoes, straightened Mellie's leg warmers and buttons, and produced a comb to untangle their hair. She directed comment after comment at Jake, including him so effortlessly that a temporary truce was established between him and his niece and nephew without their being aware of it. Livvy watched from her position by the door leading into the hallway, grateful for her friend's tact, more grateful for Glory's ability to dissemble. Under the smaller woman's happy direction, no one seemed aware of Livvy's continued tension.

"Okay, you two," Glory told the children when she had them groomed. "Let's go find Bashful and meet Jenny and the kids."

Mellie had a few reservations. Her eyes went to her uncle. "Are you staying with Livvy?"

Jake's eyes crinkled at the corners. "As much as the thought appeals, I'm afraid I have to go to work," he said. And became the recipient of two uncertain glances.

As the undoubted leader of the pair, Mellie expressed their fear. With just the tiniest quiver in her voice, she asked, "Are you coming back?"

Comprehension of their anxiety put a slight roughness in Jake's voice. "What do you think?"

Very seriously, Mellie offered an inducement. "I think if you come back, it's okay about not finding Sammy."

Jake crouched down, balancing on the balls of his feet. Equally serious, he said, "Baby, you just said the magic words. I'll be back."

Three feet of space separated the man from the girl. When Jake held out his hand in invitation, Mellie leaped the distance like a broad jumper, barreling into him, the surprise of her assault nearly knocking her uncle on his backside. He made a strangled sound—half chuckle, half something else—gained his balance, and gently spread his fingers over her small back to keep her close.

Surprisingly, Bret didn't ape his sister's actions. He hung back, casting a distressed look their way. Above Mellie's head Jake returned the look with a frown.

"What is it, hotshot?" he asked the boy a little impatiently. "Are you still sore at me?"

Bret shook his head, stuck his thumb inside his mouth, and mumbled miserably, "I bit you."

After a surprised moment Jake nodded and said slowly, "I haven't forgotten," the funny catch in his voice suggesting laughter, although his face was sober. "Tell you what, pal, we'll make a deal. You promise not to do it again, and we'll forget about the first two bites. How does that sound?"

Obviously it sounded good. Bret was nodding emphatic agreement as his sturdy little legs carried him toward the same secure haven his sister had found. Standing a moment later, Jake had a clinging child balanced in each arm. His face held a look of pleased discovery and there was a movement in his throat. Before he relinquished them to Glory's care, he told them huskily, "I'll be back at six o'clock on the dot."

The entire scene enacted by the Masters family tugged at Livvy's heartstrings, but seeing Jake's undisguised emotion touched her intensely. He cared deeply for his niece and nephew, she realized, despite the shaky start of his relationship with them.

Inevitably she found herself remembering that Brad's interest in Jamie had been limited to the times when Jamie was sunny and bright and a source of amusement because of his antics. She couldn't recall a single instance when her ex-husband had shown concern for his son's feelings as Jake had shown all morning for his niece's and nephew's. Nor could she remember hearing the same intense frustration in his voice or seeing the same depth of caring in his expression. Brad had avoided his son's unhappy times, his sorrows, his insecurities and fears. The realization brought with it a certain anguish. Jamie had deserved so much more.

"What are you thinking?"

Jake's quiet question sent Livvy's eyes to his face. He

looked tough and strong and very gentle at the same time. For a fleeting second she considered telling him, then squelched the desire before it could become definite need. She was a woman on her own, and Jake Masters was the last person to unburden herself to. Telling him about Brad would lead to questions about Jamie, which in turn . . . Oh, God, what a mess!

He was waiting for an answer, his eyes intent upon her features. She said hurriedly, "I'll call you if anything comes up with Mellie and Bret. Not that I expect any problems, of course, but I realize you'll feel better knowing we would reach you in case of any emergency. You can go on to work. There's no need to worry."

Jake looked anything but worried, his eyes amused by the startled embarrassment on her face following her rush of words. "Do you have my business number?"

"I can find it in the phone book," she said, her fingers twisting the buttons at her throat.

He leaned a shoulder against the doorframe, bringing his lean body very near to where she stood. "No need to do that, Olivia. I can give it to you now."

"Oh."

He took a note pad and pen from his inside breast pocket, scribbled his phone number, then something else, his eyes darkened in thought. He folded the small paper in half before handing it to her.

"Before I leave, I have something to say to you," he said.

Instantly on guard, Livvy stood very straight, her head tilted at a proud angle. "What is it?"

His eyes narrowed a little and he reached behind her to shut the door, creating a privacy Livvy found ominous, especially when he didn't move back. He placed his palms on either side of her head against the door, his elbows locked, and smiled faintly when she crowded back to keep some space between them.

"I appreciate your help with Mellie and Bret. I don't

think I could have gotten them inside on my own . . . not without using force, and I didn't want to do that."

Gratitude. Not suspicion. Relief and guilt flooded through her in equal parts. Rather sharply she said, "Don't thank me." *Not for doing something I was compelled to do,* she thought, and jerked her eyes to his face when he suddenly laughed.

"For some reason you don't trust me," he said softly, his amused eyes going over the rigid set of her shoulders, the tense cast of her features, the slight negative shake of her head. In a low, provoking drawl, he said, "Don't deny it, Olivia. I can tell you're thinking of the last time we were together. You're expecting me to pounce and ravish you, aren't you?"

"I'm not *expecting* it," she retorted, annoyed at being made to sound prim and old maidish and man-shy.

Without moving, he seemed to loom closer; she could feel the heat of his body, though he didn't touch her. A corresponding heat slowly uncurled in her midsection, radiating outward to all parts of her body. Wicked amusement put iridescent sparks in his eyes. "I told you I would use more restraint with you—that's a promise—but I must warn you that I won't give up on our relationship."

"We don't have a relationship. We hardly know each other," Livvy said calmly, and frowned a little when her peripheral vision glimpsed his palms inching in on her. She held her neck stiff, knowing the slightest movement of her head would put her hair against the backs of his hands.

"Hey!" he said, his expression too injured to be believable. "Every relationship has to start somewhere. We've met . . ." His eyes traced the swing of her hair from temple to jawline, then moved in warm admiration to the soft angle of her cheekbone. "We'll be seeing more of each other . . ." The aqua gaze claiming hers was a compelling promise. "And, as we do, you'll see that I'm right. Ours is definitely a relationship." He seemed fascinated by the mulish set of her mouth.

"I doubt it," she muttered, stubborn in the face of his amused persistence. She had spent years with Brad, always working on their relationship, only to be wounded time and again by his selfishness and his infidelities. Her marriage had ended in the aftermath of tragedy, but it had never been the close relationship she had sought.

Jake's gaze sobered as he studied her face, half shadowed by the downward tilt of her head. "Look at me," he insisted quietly, and once she had met his gaze she found it impossible to look away. "What are you afraid of?" he asked, a slight gruffness in his voice.

"I'm not afraid. I just view our . . . acquaintance differently than you do. I'll be caring for your children during the day, and naturally there will be times when we see each other, but that hardly constitutes a personal relationship."

"Maybe I can change your mind," he ventured huskily.

"I don't play flirting games."

"Is that what you think I'm doing?"

She shrugged, uncomfortable with the conversation.

"I can see you'll need some convincing of my sterling motives," he said dryly.

"Don't waste your time."

"I won't." He grinned, adding, "My idea of wasting time might be different from yours. Besides, I already have one advantage."

"What's that?"

"My little Swee' Peas."

Jolted by his words, her head jerked back, making a little thudding noise as it hit the door. She winced and swallowed the pain, her fingers coming up to investigate the damage to the back of her head. Jake's fingers joined hers, replaced them, carefully tunneling through her hair to stroke soothingly over her abused scalp. His touch was incredibly gentle, but Livvy was too distracted by what he'd said to appreciate it.

She asked unevenly, "What did you mean?"

"About my Swee' Peas?" At her nod his fingers glided through the silken length of her hair to fall upon her shoulder. He smiled and said, "Somehow I doubt that you greet each new child with the same tenderness and concern you showed my two today. Oh, I'm not accusing you of callousness with the other children, but Mellie and Bret got to you, didn't they?"

"They were frightened," she retorted with a defensive sharpness. Then more calmly: "I wanted them to feel welcome here."

His eyes assessed her, mercilessly detailing the defensive cast of her gaze and her unsmiling mouth. "You're lying," he said softly. "There was something special about the way you looked at them—as if they were an anxiously awaited gift. Your friend saw it too. She was very startled when she first saw you with Mellie and Bret."

In a desperate attempt to sound lightly scoffing, Livvy said, "You're exaggerating." But she knew that he wasn't. He was right on target, only he didn't realize exactly what the target was.

"I'm not accusing you of nefarious intent," he said around a sloping grin. "Just for the record, though, I should warn you it's a package deal. My particular little Swee' Peas are two members of a threesome that includes Brutus. You take them, you take me. Simple mathematics."

His tone mocked seriousness and the laughter in his eyes freed the last of Livvy's tension. He was teasing. Only teasing. The man was a flirt, and she was his present target. She felt her mouth tug upward in response and a sparkle lit her brown eyes. His reasoning had encouraged her sense of humor out of hiding.

"That's not mathematics, that's—"

"Blackmail!" Jake supplied with such obvious relish that she glared at him in laughing reproach.

Male confidence hovered above her, enveloped her in its silken snare. The need to challenge him, to bring him down a peg, drove her to say primly, "Blackmail is useless. I can't be bribed."

His eyes glinted and both his hands came back to the door beside her head, his lean body the fourth side of the trap, standing just a heartbeat from hers. "Not even if I sweeten it with a little persuasion?" he murmured, husky intent in his voice.

There was just enough time to rue her challenge before his mouth met hers in gentle aggression, his tongue a sweet invader, pressing firmly for entry . . . and receiving it as her lips parted on a yielding sigh. His hands came away from the door to shape her face and shoulders, then moved to her waist, urging her fully against him. A nameless yearning flowed through her. She became supple in his arms, instinctively seeking his strength, her fingers finding the muscled cords of his neck and staying to caress. Her mouth asked what her mind couldn't—to be cherished, for surcease from emptiness. His lips and tongue answered willingly, their tender giving filling her with delight.

He drew back after a moment, the slight tremor in his fingers pressing into her waist telling of his restraint. He ran a gentle knuckle down her cheek, smiling and whispering, "Have I told you how much I like you, pretty woman?"

Her heart slowly ceased its rioting beat and she smiled back, slightly shaking her head no.

But he had. With laughter and lightness and teasing. He admired her neat and tidy appearance. He liked a woman who thought the little Swee' Peas were beautiful. He was partial to nearsighted schoolteachers. He called her "pretty woman."

"No?" He made the word a husky rebuke, and she relented, saying softly, "Perhaps you have."

Repeating the promise he had given Mellie and Bret, he murmured, "I'll be back at six o'clock—on the dot," the deepness of his voice making it sound like a lover's intent.

When he had gone, Livvy unfolded the notepaper on which he'd written his business phone number. It contained a small message, as well. As she scanned it, she felt laughter bubble inside her. Without salutation, it read: *Call me anytime, for any reason. Call me paranoid, if you like, but let me call you Livvy soon. A man could go crazy being the only one not given that privilege.*

Livvy folded the note carefully, her smile thoughtful. The man was a charmer, and a dangerous one, at that. Somehow he'd sensed she was more susceptible to teasing persuasion than to aggressive coercion. He'd discovered her need for lightness and laughter.

She frowned a little, suddenly filled with a vague uneasiness. She'd have to watch out or he'd discover her other needs. Elusive needs she refused to put names to. The ones that gnawed relentlessly at her soul—late at night and when she was alone.

While Horizon's children took their afternoon nap, Horizon's mistress used the unencumbered hour to prepare the next day's lunch. Macaroni casserole was a favorite with the children and also relatively simple to prepare in advance, as were all Horizon's meals. Elaborate menus took time Livvy couldn't spare from her busy schedule, and the little ones fared well on simple, nutritious foods.

Glory joined her as she was covering the grated cheese with plastic wrap and setting it inside the refrigerator alongside the casserole dishes filled with macaroni in cream sauce. With a faintly subdued smile the smaller woman pushed the froth of blond curls from her forehead and said, "Do you want to talk?"

"What about?" Livvy was deliberately obtuse, turning to the sink to wash the grater and saucepans. She knew Glory deserved a complete rundown of the situation with Bret, but she had hoped for more time to think it through before discussing it.

Glory hoisted herself onto the counter beside the sink and gave Livvy an encouraging smile. "Jake mentioned that there were photos of the children in the file he left with you that first day. It explained why you've been so uneasy the past two weeks."

Livvy rolled back the cuffs of her sleeves, swished her fingers in the dishwater, and collected her thoughts. Her face averted, she dried her fingers on a paper towel and said, "It was difficult to explain, Glory. I was stunned when I first saw Bret's picture. I think I've been a little dazed ever since. I couldn't talk about it."

Glory's small hand reached out and covered Livvy's tense fingers curled into a fist around the wadded paper towel. Her eyes were soft with understanding. "It's okay, you know. I haven't come in here to disown our friendship because you didn't confide in me."

A little shakily, Livvy laughed and gave the other woman a quick hug. "I never thought you would," she said, pulling back. "But I had to work it out on my own."

For a moment Glory seemed indecisive about saying more; then, quietly resolute, she said, "Livvy, I know Jamie's death was awful for you, but Bret Masters isn't—"

"I know he isn't," Livvy interrupted soberly, her eyes reflective. "He's an adorable little boy, but once you get past the shock of his physical resemblance to Jamie, there are so many differences." She smiled faintly. "Actually, Mellie is more like Jamie than Bret is. You remember how Jamie used to lead his playmates in all their activities. How he used to angle his little chin when he was hurt or just being stubborn? Mellie does that. Bret . . . doesn't. He's like a little shadow to his sister. He echoes her words and lets her make all the decisions."

Concern drove Glory to emphasize, "Still, it will be difficult to look at Bret and not see Jamie."

"I can handle it," Livvy said with conviction, believing it. "I worried at first that I wouldn't be able to, but I know I can. Besides, I have to, don't I?" she added quietly. "Mellie and Bret have suffered enough recently without my turning away from them just as they're beginning to trust in me."

There was a short silence. Glory looked straight into Livvy's eyes, a very steady look that accepted her claim and yet questioned. "It's obvious Jake knows nothing about Jamie. When are you going to tell him?"

After a fractional pause, Livvy stated evenly, "There's no need to tell him anything. My past is my business."

"Do you think that's fair?"

"I won't let it affect his nephew."

"Of course you won't!" Glory was mildly astonished. "I meant, fair to your relationship with Jake."

"There is no *relationship*," Livvy declared firmly, thinking the word overused lately. The small upward tilt of her chin was not lost on her friend.

"What about Friday night when you thought his being a daddy was something admirable?" Glory quizzed insinuatively.

Livvy suddenly began scrubbing the pan she had used to cook the macaroni, her head bent to the task. "Oh, he dropped by my house . . . and signed the medical release forms he'd failed to sign the day he registered Mellie and Bret. He didn't stay long," she explained lightly. And unwillingly remembered events of that evening with startling clarity. Jake had appeared, unexpectedly, with the cold November rain. And stayed to heat her conscience with his probing questions, to warm her body with his stirring caresses. Disquiet made her voice sharp.

"I admired his taking responsibility for his niece and nephew. A lot of men do much less for their own children. But there's nothing between Jake and me."

Glory looked faintly skeptical, but she shrugged and said, "The way he looks at you, I thought there might be something in the works for you two."

"How does he look at me?" she asked before she realized how eager she sounded.

Glory's innocent expression did little to conceal her quick amusement as she saw the heat slowly tinting her friend's complexion. "Oh, like he'd love to gather you up and spirit you away, but he's afraid to startle you by moving too swiftly," she explained softly.

"*Glory!*" Livvy was shocked, trying to scowl away the other woman's words. They reminded her too forcefully of Jake's promise to use restraint with her. More calmly, she accused, "You've got a vivid imagination!"

One of Glory's shoulders moved nonchalantly, shrugging away the accusation. "There's nothing wrong with Jake looking at you the way he does," she pointed out. "It's very complimentary if you think about it."

"Good grief!" Livvy muttered in disgust, adding scoffingly, "He flirts with you, he *looks* at me, and he's got a girl friend named Michelle."

"He told me Michelle works for him."

Irony put a high arch in one of Livvy's brows. "That's how Brad explained his first two girl friends. I believed him till I saw him watching the *second* little secretary at a Christmas party. After that I learned all the signs and could tell which woman was his current interest. If I had to judge, I'd say Jake is more interested in you than in me. He wants to know if you've dumped your husband. He calls me a nearsighted schoolteacher."

"Are you afraid Jake is the type to play around?"

Livvy shook her head in a dismissive little gesture, meaning it didn't matter one way or another. She almost laughed. Despite the ironic parallel she'd drawn a moment before, she was beginning to fear just the opposite. She'd know how to turn him out of her thoughts if she truly believed him a womanizer.

"There's something about him I trust," Glory said sagely. "I'm not fooled easily. He's an honest man and he won't mislead you."

Glory sat there, looking at her with her blue eyes wide, waiting to hear a response. But Livvy was tired of the conversation. It had been a long day and she didn't want to examine her emotions any longer. So she grinned and quipped, "No wonder Paul loves you. You're cute when you're clairvoyant."

After an inelegant sigh, Glory grumbled, "And you're exasperating when you refuse to see what's right before your eyes!" She lithely hopped off the counter and headed for the door, adding slyly over her shoulder, "No wonder Jake calls you a nearsighted schoolteacher." She laughed when she heard a pan clatter onto the counter top.

Nearsighted? Perhaps. Certainly cautious. Livvy finished the dishes in moody thought. Was caution synonymous with hindsight? Her years with Brad had taught her well. She viewed man-woman relationships more warily than she used to. Jake's interest in her was flattering. She couldn't help a certain response. But deeper relationships brought vulnerability. She wasn't ready to risk being hurt again.

Yet, when Jake arrived at six o'clock—on the dot, as he'd promised—she found herself answering his teasing glance from his watch to her with a reckless little grin of amusement. With his tie unknotted, his shirt unbuttoned at the throat, his smile crooked, and his eyes laughing, he really was irresistible.

Mellie greeted him with a belligerent inquiry, the day's separation having given her time to put up her guard. "Did you get milk and breakfast crunchies? Bret likes cereal."

On cue, Bret promptly repeated the statement, and

Jake's face held a resigned look. Going down on his haunches before the pair, he drawled, "Well, if it isn't Miss Mellie Misgiving and her bosom buddy Bret. Do you suppose you two could save the grumbles until after you've greeted a hardworking uncle?"

The alliterative titles did the trick. Both children walked into his arms, repeating their new names through a bevy of giggles. Livvy suddenly felt light and happy, watching the trio with her eyes sparkling.

Holding a child's hand in each of his, Jake stood and came toward her. His aqua eyes went over her, caressing her features, quickening her pulse. "My phone was silent today. I stayed in my office for hours, slowly going crazy when it didn't ring," he told her, reminding her of his note.

He wore such a martyred expression that she smiled and said, "I refuse to be the cause of anyone's paranoia." And felt her heart thud erratically when warm pleasure filled his eyes.

"You've got a kind heart, Livvy Waring," he said slowly, his tongue rolling the shortened version of her name into a warm caress. Most humbly, he added, "I plan to take advantage of that."

CHAPTER FIVE

During the month of November, Livvy fought a frustrating and intense battle with herself. She wasn't ready to take a step toward emotional involvement with anyone. Cool reasoning told her to put a guard on her feelings, to protect herself against future heartache. Yet there was a nagging within her, subtle and indefinable, that evaded the rigorous discipline of her logic and helplessly responded to the potent enticement of Jake Masters.

Though she wondered at his motives—light flirtation? serious seduction?—she nevertheless felt something unfolding within her, answering the open interest he showed in her. Other than the mothering she gave Horizon's children, she had denied womanly needs of heart and soul and body for almost two years. Longer than that, really. Her last years with Brad had been sterile of anything remotely connected with adult affection. Against her will, those repressed needs instinctively sought sustenance from a wide male smile, a warm aqua gaze, a deep, compelling laugh that somehow caressed and cherished as it teased. Twice a day, five days a week, without touching her or using physical persuasion, Jake subtly cast his net, while Livvy floundered on the seas of attraction, floating ever nearer the bait.

Two times that month she found support for the logic of staying free of involvement. Once, when Brad contacted her. If ever she needed a reminder to be wary of relationships, her ex-husband provided it.

Very unwelcome, very unsettling, Brad's phone call came to The Little Yellow House on a night in mid-November. He wanted to see her again. At his most persuasive, he told her he missed her, that she was still his special lady, reminding her how much they had once meant to each other. Livvy answered each inducement with a cool, impassive reply, refusing to see him. After a while an edge crept into Brad's smooth voice, like a sharp needle piercing satin cloth.

"The divorce hasn't bothered you, has it, Liv? You've made a new life for yourself."

"I had no choice. There was nothing left of my old life," she said dispassionately, while each muscle in her body tensed and braced itself against the ordeal of talking to him.

Brad changed the subject; or, rather, detoured it. Sighing moodily, he said, "You've always been so controlled, never letting anything touch you. That's why I never knew where I stood with you. I wanted you to love me. I don't believe you ever did."

This was old territory—Brad wanting to be reassured he was adored. An aching tiredness seeped into Livvy's bones. She said, "I loved you once, a very long time ago." When she was young and he had seemed a golden man whose physical beauty and craving for the joys of life had seemed ideal. Only later had she discovered that his beauty was mirror-deep and that his pursuit of pleasure left hapless victims by the wayside, stranded in the mire of his selfishness. More to herself than to him, she murmured, "If you hadn't divorced me, I might have clung to our marriage out of habit or duty." *Duty to what?* she jeered inwardly. *The sanctity of our marriage?* And almost laughed at the incongruity of the thought.

Brad's tone turned conciliatory. "I may have acted hastily, baby, but I knew as soon as you were well, you'd want to be free. Jamie was the main reason you stayed with me. When the accident took him and left you sterile, I knew you wouldn't want to be reminded of the losses every time you looked at me."

The theory afforded Brad a protective screen, obliterating his guilt. He did believe his motive for divorcing her had been altruistic. She couldn't and wouldn't argue with the element of truth in his reasoning. Those last years, her belief that Jamie deserved two parents had kept her in a marriage that was nothing but a legal shell.

Like a needle stuck in the scratched groove of a record, Brad came back to his original point. "And I was right. You didn't waste any time making a new life for yourself." His tone was aggrieved. He seemed to be annoyed that she wasn't hiding in some dark corner, nursing wounds that wouldn't heal. "Why bother with a bunch of kids who'll never belong to you? Surely you don't feel for them what you did for Jamie. You let Jamie take precedence over everyone else, even your husband."

The accusation was so typically self-absorbed, it should have made her laugh. But when Brad spoke so carelessly of his son, she felt sickened. She took a deep, controlling breath before saying, "You never did understand how much children mean to me."

Brad laughed, a short, derisive sound that held a touch of bafflement. "I understood, all right. Kids, always kids. You were nagging me for kids the year after we married. You were never satisfied with just me."

"The same could be said of you with more accuracy," she countered coldly. "I wasn't the one who cheated on our marriage."

His voice dropped to a soothing softness. "Emotionally, I was always faithful to you, baby. You should have realized that. Sometimes a man just can't help himself."

Livvy smiled ironically. It had been a long time since that particular excuse had held any water with her. His own pleasure was the motivating force in all his actions,

110

and he excused his shortcomings with self-deceiving rationalization. Promiscuity in marriage was excused by delegating it to the male sex drive. No premeditation in sexual infidelity, therefore no serious misdeed.

"Are you seeing anyone now, Liv?"

The question irritated her. "It ceased to be your concern, Brad, when you divorced me. My life is my own."

"So you are seeing someone!" he exclaimed softly, and laughed. "Well, it obviously hasn't led to the bedroom yet. Either that, or the man is as nearsighted as you are."

The scorpion's sting. Livvy flinched involuntarily, her hand flattening over her stomach. With the utmost care, she replaced the receiver in its cradle. She had listened to more than she should have.

And she spent the rest of the night wondering if another man could possibly overlook her physical imperfections. Brad had sown his mischief well.

The next day she told Glory about the call, leaving out the more vicious details. She asked her not to put through any calls from Brad should he try to contact her at Horizon House.

After a quick scan of Livvy's strained features, Glory made her own assessment of the damage Brad had done, and said aggressively, "You've got it! Can I tell him what I think of him when he calls?"

Livvy smiled faintly. "I doubt it would do much good. Brad hears only what he wants to hear. He always has."

"But it might do me good," Glory retorted around a malicious smile. "Nothing would give me greater pleasure than to knock him right on his hedonistic, narcissistic backside with a few well-chosen words!"

Vengeful Glory. Loyal, sweet, ready-to-do-battle-for-a-friend Glory. Livvy hugged her, laughing.

In the days immediately following Brad's phone call, Livvy found it easy to keep a cool distance between herself and Jake. Her bitter experience shunned romance, spurned any male-female relationship, even the most innocuous. But Jake was persistent, she had to give him that. He always accepted the little setbacks with a twisted half smile, mocking himself, perhaps. He didn't give up. In fact, his teasing attentions seemed to escalate, and Livvy found herself once again caught in the undertow of his appeal. She allowed herself a certain enjoyment from his attention while holding back enough to keep things on a casually friendly basis.

November had almost left the calendar when Livvy's caution and cool logic received another outside boost. The Masters children were the last to leave one Tuesday evening in late November, and it wasn't Jake who came to fetch them.

The stunning, green-eyed brunette who walked inside Horizon's entrance alcove was a complete stranger. Her flawless complexion, impressive proportions, and wide-eyed sexiness were enough to give any woman pause for thought. Her throaty contralto voice played upon Livvy's memory, and thought didn't pause, it rioted.

Flashing a brilliant million-watt smile, the woman announced cheerfully, "I've come to get Jake's kids."

Blinking against the toothy brightness, Livvy said politely, "No one but Mr. Masters is authorized to pick up his children."

"Oh, it's okay. Jake is working late and asked me to get them," the brunette explained, adding in an easy, friendly manner, "I'm Michelle."

The identification was superfluous; Livvy had guessed who she was. "I'm afraid it's impossible. It's against our rules to let the children leave with anyone the parents haven't specified to take them."

There was a brief, nonplussed silence before Michelle said, "Oh, I get it! You think I'm one of those child stealers." She laughed, a throaty, unaffected sound that practically wrote music on the air. Livvy suppressed a wince. Michelle's green eyes went very wide and reassuring. She said earnestly, "I'm not, honest. Call Jake and he'll confirm I'm not a baby snatcher."

Although Horizon House rigidly enforced pickup rules, the possibility of Michelle being a kidnapper wasn't the reason for Livvy's stilted responses. She felt petty, since the woman seemed very nice. Too nice, in truth, and a long list of other superlatives, too open and friendly among them. But was that a crime? Livvy's rigidity tumbled. She smiled and said, "I'm sorry, but I have to be sure."

"No problem," Michelle said with another big smile that placed beautiful accents along her perfect cheekbones. She flicked long, tapered fingers in an understanding gesture. "Listen, if I had kids as sweet as Jake's two, I'd want them well protected. You're only doing your job, and Jake appreciates conscientiousness."

What else does he appreciate? Livvy thought cattily, remembering red satin and black lace. Then she silently cursed her bent toward the malicious. Was it Michelle's fault if Jake Masters spread his charm at random? When the woman turned to chat with Mellie and Bret, Livvy picked up the phone on Glory's desk, dialing a number she'd never called but that came to mind instantly. *Oh, blast!*

Jake answered after the first ring, his voice brusque and preoccupied until she identified herself. Then male intrigue colored his tones as he said softly, "This is unexpected, Livvy. Did you want me for something?"

For the life of her, Livvy couldn't help the accelerated tempo of her heartbeat. She allowed a moment for it to steady before asking coolly, "Did you send someone for Mellie and Bret?"

There was a surprised silence. "Didn't she arrive?"

Livvy turned her back on the interested green-eyed glance Michelle was sending her way and spoke low and tightly into the receiver. "Yes, but you failed to let me know. It's against our policy to release the children to anyone but the parents unless otherwise specified."

She heard Jake's heavily released breath before he said dryly, "It's okay, Livvy. Michelle is there under my instruction. Didn't she tell you that?" When she didn't immediately respond, he drawled provokingly, "Perhaps her description would convince you everything is on the up and up. She's about five six and has brown hair, green eyes, and the biggest—"

"That's her!" Livvy intervened quickly in whispered, aghast tones, uncomfortable prickles running over her flesh. She didn't want to hear Jake listing Michelle's big . . . whatevers . . . in his description.

"Smile," Jake finished as if she hadn't spoken. "She's very friendly." And the undercurrent of laughter in his voice sent Livvy's nails jabbing sharply into her palms. He did so *enjoy* a little joke at the expense of her sensibilities!

A moment passed before she said coolly, "After today, anyone who comes after Mellie and Bret will have to be authorized in writing to do so. I'll give you the forms tomorrow."

All laughter absent from his voice, Jake said quietly, "I should have called and let you know Michelle was coming after the kids. I'm sorry you were caused any worry, Livvy."

Damn him! Why did he have to sound so contrite? So genuinely concerned that he'd been the cause of her disturbance? Confused, Livvy murmured a quiet "That's all right" and quickly hung up. When she turned from the desk, Michelle had a child's hand in each of hers and both eyes on Livvy. Squaring her shoulders, Livvy went to her and said, "Jake verified you. I'm sorry you had to wait."

Michelle shrugged her understanding—a sensual movement defining each hill and valley of her beautiful body. And smiled—the *biggest* smile. She said, "Mellie

114

and Bret trust me, you know. They've been around me several times. You don't have to worry that they'll be uncomfortable with me."

"No, of course not!" Livvy murmured quickly, turning to get the children's jackets, her action hiding an odd flush of disconcertion. Had she been so obviously disapproving?

When the children were in their jackets and the three of them were ready to leave, Michelle paused, eyeing Livvy with frank speculation. "I've heard a lot about you."

I've heard almost nothing about you. Livvy smiled politely and said, "Have you?"

Michelle laughed, unselfconsciously admitting, "I have an insatiable curiosity. What Jake didn't volunteer, I dug out of him."

Vaguely uneasy that the two of them had discussed her, Livvy adroitly turned the course of the conversation. She asked pleasantly, "Do you and Jake know each other well?"

"I met him seven years ago, the day he hired me as his office manager. That was when Masters and Mackensie was a fledgling in the freight-hauling business. Jake and Mac were running most of the deliveries themselves and they needed someone to man the home front and pull in more customers." Her grin was decidedly wicked. "Not that Mac thought I was the *man* for the job."

"Mac is Jake's partner?"

Michelle nodded, and her smile had a reflective quality. "He nearly burst an artery when Jake hired me. In Mac's mind, if a woman is attractive, she's brainless. I am not brainless."

No, she wasn't, Livvy realized. There was intelligence in Michelle's beautiful green eyes and a sense of humor behind her lovely smile. "You've obviously proven your worth, or you wouldn't still be with them."

"It wasn't easy, with Mac's prejudice, but Jake was a doll from the beginning, giving me all kinds of support."

I'll bet. Livvy's smile almost cracked her face.

With a glance down at the children, Michelle said ruefully, "I should be getting home. I promised Jake I'd feed these two, and if he calls my place and finds me not there, he'll be worried."

Livvy stooped down to hug the children and, when she stood, found herself the recipient of another of Michelle's speculative summing-ups. The brunette said, "You know, Jake is really a terrific guy. He has a bit of a devil in him, and he teases unmercifully at times. And he's human, he gets impatient and angry like anyone else. But he's a darling, with a warm heart and a generous soul, and I love him." She winked. "You'll see. When you get to know him better, you'll be as crazy about him as I am."

And Michelle's parting smile was as big as all outdoors.

Livvy smiled wan confusion in return. Had she just received the go-ahead or the warning?

A few days later, on Friday morning, the Mercedes was parked at curbside when Livvy unlocked Horizon's doors at 7:00 A.M. Jake carried a sleepy-eyed and thumb-pacified Bret up the walk, while Mellie raced ahead to complain, "Uncle Jake is mean. He wouldn't let Bret sleep."

Livvy gently smoothed the girl's silky hair. Mellie and her uncle didn't see eye to eye in all instances, and the child was quick to use her brother's name, as if to give her complaints more weight.

Livvy said quietly, "He'll be okay, darling. He can take a nap if he's too sleepy."

Bret practically fell from his uncle's arms into Livvy's waiting ones, yawning hugely, his small face still flushed with sleep. He smiled drowsily and whispered against her neck, "I love you, Livvy."

The kick in her chest dismayed her. Even after a month, it was sometimes very hard. Snuggling him against her shoulder, Livvy helped him out of his light-weight jacket and whispered back, "I love you too."

Jake had overheard, of course, and his expression went from surprised to inscrutable as he took the jacket from her and hung it on a peg inside the entrance doors. His eyes followed his niece's meandering progress to the un-occupied desk.

"Where's Glory?" he asked Livvy.

"She doesn't arrive until eight thirty. She sees her chil-dren off to school before coming in."

His brows rose a fraction. "She has school-age chil-dren?"

Moving her hand caressingly over Bret's back, Livvy smiled a little and nodded. "Ages nine and ten. Both girls and the apples of their father's eye. You seem surprised."

"Frankly, I am. She looks like a child herself."

"Yes, doesn't she," Livvy murmured, a shade of irony in her voice. She was remembering Jake's very male, very adult, admiration of her friend's ripe figure.

Jake grinned, a straightforward, untroubled grin that deflected her irony. "She's small," he said.

"Yes, *isn't* she." The irony was more pronounced. Mentally comparing bra sizes with the other woman, Livvy knew who was small and who wasn't.

For a moment Jake studied her face, a half smile curv-ing his lips. He seemed to read her thoughts, because his eyes glinted and he said, "Perhaps short is a more appro-priate term than small."

"A pocket Venus, I believe is the term."

Jake nodded absently, his eyes going over her. "You two are very different," he murmured, then gave a strange, uncomfortable start and amended quickly, "You're tall and she's short."

Livvy had to bite the inside of her cheek to keep from

laughing. He looked so worried. "Mutt and Jeff?" she suggested helpfully. "Olive Oyl and Blondie?"

"*No!*" burst from him so forcefully that Bret's head came up from Livvy's shoulder. The boy scowled a sleepy reproach to the room in general before dropping his head again.

Mellie, ever the protector, muttered, "It's not nice to yell and not let kids sleep," and scooted her thin body back in Glory's chair, swinging her feet and sending her uncle a censuring glance.

Jake turned an intimidating glare on the little sprite. She stared back belligerently. He said sardonically, "I can always count on you, Mellie, to point out my mistakes."

"You *do* yell."

"You *do* keep reminding me."

"You're mean!"

"You're sweet!"

"I am not!"

"No, you're a little nag, and if you weren't my niece, I'd marry you. You'd make a perfect wife."

Mellie wriggled in her chair, ducked her head, and tried to smother her giggle. She peeped up a second later, and there was mischief in her eyes. "I'm too little to get married. You're silly," she said so coyly that Jake looked curiously nonplussed. He had expected more truculence, not playful teasing.

The finale of their little verbal exchange was too much for Livvy. She struggled valiantly against a laugh, her muffled sound making her the recipient of Jake's narrowed aqua gaze.

"You find it amusing, do you?" he said in low, threatening tones. He came closer, standing in front of her, and his expression was forbidding except for the telltale glint in his eyes. "If we didn't have an audience," he muttered in a dark undertone Mellie couldn't hear, "I'd tell you a thing or two."

Knowing it was all a game, knowing too that Jake could do little with his children present, Livvy felt a little reckless. "Don't let that stop you," she murmured tauntingly.

He leaned toward her, his face very near, his eyes gleaming. "You're fantastic, pretty woman," he drawled softly. "You're tall and I like not having to bend my head to see your face. You've got the biggest eyes behind those schoolmarm glasses and I love it when they widen like they're doing now." His voice dropped lower; his gaze fell to her mouth. "And your mouth is soft. I remember how it feels under mine—sweet, just a little apprehensive, but very warm and responsive." There was wicked laughter in his eyes, but also something else, and Livvy wondered if he could see the crazy pulsebeat at her throat. His eyes dropped to where Bret's hand had fallen innocently against her breast. "You have small, perfectly formed—"

Livvy jerked back a step, her heart skipping a beat. "You've told me more than a thing or two," she said in crisp tones.

Soft laughter rumbled up from Jake's chest, but he said nothing, silently regarding her flushed features.

Livvy didn't look away. "You're a wicked flirt," she said accusingly. But her eyes held reluctant amusement. He had taken up her challenge and neatly turned the tables on her.

"You keep using that word," he muttered, and for a moment his face wore a look of hard impatience. Then his expression lightened and he said dryly, "There's a difference between indiscriminate flirting and a scrupulous campaign."

"Scrupulous?" she questioned in mild mockery. His tactics had been wickedly underhanded. And there was still the spectre of Michelle to consider.

"Selective, then," he amended easily. "I'm not the big bad wolf you make me out to be."

119

The rakish slant of his mouth negated his words, and Livvy eyed him dubiously. "If you say so."

"You don't believe me, do you?" He looked wounded. "You could hurt my feelings with these constant doubts. If you'd relent a little, come to my apartment one night, have dinner with us, you'd see I'm just an ordinary man —a family man. You might even like me."

Her retreat was immediate and physical, though she didn't move. Her eyes became aloof and unreadable. The lingering curve of amusement on her mouth evened out to a cool, polite line. At Bret's back, her fingers flexed nervously, once, then stilled. She glanced down at the child and said, "He's fallen asleep again. I should lay him down before the other children start arriving."

There was a knowing glint in Jake's eyes, but he didn't press the point. He reached out and ran a long finger over the back of Bret's hand where it lay against her breast. Then he smiled and moved away to say good-bye to his niece. Long after he'd left, Livvy felt the tingling in her breast where he hadn't touched her, where she felt as if he had.

The Masters children were the last to leave again that evening, and Livvy was ready to close up for the weekend when Jake arrived. She helped him bundle his niece and nephew inside their lightweight jackets, then grabbed her purse and thick sweater and followed them out, locking Horizon's doors behind her. The walk home was a short one, even though she would take the more circuitous route around the block instead of the shortcut through Horizon's courtyard.

At Jake's car, Bret's hand found hers and tugged her down. " 'Night, Livvy; love you," he whispered as he had that morning, his little voice carrying on the deepening twilight's cool breeze.

Livvy smiled softly and kissed his cheek. " 'Night, Bret; I love you too." She turned immediately to tickle

Mellie's ribs gently, saying, "Have a nice weekend, darling."

She stood and backed away as the two youngsters clambered inside the car. Jake shut the door softly behind them, turning to Livvy. In the thick twilight it was difficult to read his expression, but she felt the intentness of his glance. She adjusted the shoulder strap of her purse and stuffed her hands inside her sweater pockets, waiting for him to speak.

"You've made a conquest of my nephew. That's twice today he's told you he loves you," Jake said, his words quiet, meant only for her ears.

She stepped closer, sensing he didn't want the children to hear their conversation. Meeting his shadowed gaze, she said, "He's very affectionate. Do you object?"

His mouth turned down at one corner. In dry, satiric tones he said, "I'm as jealous as hell."

"You needn't be," she said quietly. "Bret follows his sister's lead, and Mellie accepted me that first day. You're the central figure in their lives, but, contrarily, their trust in you will come slower."

"That wasn't quite what I meant," he said, still in that same ironic way. Then, more seriously, he sighed and said, "But you're right. I think they correlate Dan's and Sue's deaths with desertion. They expect me to leave them too. It's frustrating to fight something like that."

"Give it time, Jake."

"I will," he said, and slowly smiled. His eyes made a significant top-to-toe appraisal of her as he added, "I'm a patient man."

Her glance slid away from him to the two small noses pressed against the car window, their breaths creating a foggy condensation against the glass. Livvy's soft laughter teased the uncomfortable silence, and she met Jake's gaze. "I think even you, Uncle Jake, would have to admit you've definitely caught their interest."

Jake's breath came out on a laughing sigh, misting the

cool air. He turned his head toward the little faces watching so avidly. Barely moving his lips, he murmured, "Do you have any idea what it's like to have your every action witnessed and assessed by two judges who barely come up to your knee?"

Livvy saw the amused twitch of his lips and ventured softly, "Wonderful?"

"Yes," he admitted thoughtfully. "In a crazy sort of way, it's wonderful." His eyes met hers. "It's also scary as hell. I went into this with all the confidence of a fool, positive all it took to raise two children was a little organizational know-how and enough money to keep them fed and clothed. I got disabused of that theory the first night. All it took was Mellie's glare of angry defiance as she yelled she hated me and Bret's look of fright as he clung to his sister. That surprised me, you see," he confided with a grimace. "I was supposed to be their hero, rescuing them from an orphaned existence and magnanimously taking them into my home." He laughed suddenly. "I haven't earned my cape and Superman costume, but I'm working on it. I've already left bachelorhood behind on the quest for family ties. I'll make a close-knit group out of my little family yet."

At that moment Jake seemed a hero to Livvy. An imperfect, human hero who made mistakes and admitted them, who respected the importance of love and family and relationships. She smiled, very softly, very admiringly. "Yes, you will," she agreed.

With glinting eyes and a smile that bordered on arrogant, he said, "You know why? Because I have this exceptional ability to adapt to change and know what I want. I'm a wonderful, persistent, straightforward, unbeatable son of a gun."

"A rare man indeed," she praised in properly impressed tones, falling victim to his teasing charm.

He nodded smugly. "Correct."

"And a modest one."

"Absolutely," he agreed with a complete lack of that very trait.

"And so self-effacing," she extolled dryly, finding inordinate pleasure in teasing him.

"Come to my apartment tomorrow and talk me out of my shyness over lunch," he invited suddenly in suggestive tones that jerked Livvy's pulse out of kilter.

In the fractional pause before she spoke, Livvy dug her fists farther into her sweater pockets and drew a shallow, stabilizing breath. "Sorry, I can't. Tomorrow I have a prior appointment with the leaves in Horizon's courtyard."

Jake didn't try to change her mind. He gave her an unnervingly knowing smile and said, "Get in the car and I'll drive you home."

"I only live around the block," she said, stepping back.

"I know, but I'll drive you anyway. You shouldn't walk alone at night."

Livvy eyed the small Mercedes and shook her head firmly. "No. There's very little room in your car, and crowding so many people in with the driver is dangerous."

"You only live around the block," he repeated in amused exasperation. "Hardly time for an accident."

But Livvy knew that short drives weren't always safe, that suburban streets claimed victims as easily as highways did. Her mind recoiled in horror from the recurring sound of screeching tires and metal crunching against metal, from a small boy's terrified cry. She backed away from Jake, from painful memory, saying sharply, "No, I'll walk." Turning quickly, she called over her shoulder, "Thanks anyway, Jake." As she walked, she heard him breathe her name in a puzzled way that lengthened her strides.

The Mercedes hummed to life behind her. Its headlights beamed on; its tires slowly crunched forward on the pavement. All the way to The Little Yellow House, her path was illuminated, her route followed. She was being tracked by a wonderful, persistent, straightforward, unbeatable son of a gun.

And, damn it all, she couldn't stem the warm feeling of pleasure it gave her.

The Saturday morning temperature was in the upper forties, the sun was bright, and there was just enough breeze to invigorate the senses and energize the spirit. Horizon's courtyard was covered in oak and pecan leaves and the occasional maple or sycamore leaf blown in from neighboring yards. The brown and gold and gray carpet rustled under Livvy's steps as she made the first stroke of her rake across the lawn. It was a beautiful day for working outdoors.

Scarcely half an hour later, Livvy stopped raking, surprised by the arrival of visitors. Surprised and inordinately pleased when she saw who they were. Her heart swelled with delight.

Bret and Mellie were wearing hooded warm-up suits in Smurf blue and hot pink, their cheeks rosy and their smiles wide with excitement. Their greetings were exuberant as they bounded through the gate that separated The Little Yellow House from Horizon's courtyard. Amid hugs and laughter they talked animatedly, filling her in on the recent happenings in their young lives.

They had slept in Uncle Jake's big bed with him, and he *snored* and grew whiskers during the night. And they watched him shave them off and he tried to kiss them with soap all over his face. Uncle Jake wanted biscuits for breakfast, but when Bret spilled the milk, the can of biscuits *'sploded* and the biscuits went *everywhere*. Then Mellie bumped his knee with the skillet and Uncle Jake dropped the eggs. And his face was so *funny* when he saw the mess on the floor. But Uncle Jake didn't yell. He rubbed his eyes and said "Let's go get doughnuts." Doughnuts were yummy, 'specially the ones with chocolate and little candies on top. Coffee was yucky, but Uncle Jake liked it and he got them milk. Uncle Jake said they were going to help Livvy rake leaves. Could they play on the swings and slides too?

When they finally ran out of chatter and raced off, whooping their way to the swing sets, Livvy's face was animated with the pleasure engendered by their disclosures. For a moment she watched their energized feet toss leaves into the air to drift slowly back to earth, then her eyes squinted up into the glare of the sun. She sent Jake a broad smile. He was leaning against a rake he'd brought with him, and the sunlight placed an unlikely halo about his breeze-tossed chestnut curls. His humor drove creases into his lean cheeks, and his eyes were as brilliant as the Texas sky.

"This is a nice surprise. I didn't expect help with the yard work," she told him, rising and dusting her jeans and warm twill shirt free of twigs and leaves.

Jake grinned and shook his rake. "I'm a man, strong and chivalrous. It's my duty to see that Horizon's mistress doesn't wear her delicate self out working in the yard. She's to save her strength for the Monday-through-Friday demands of some very important people."

Her eyes looked him over. His sweat shirt was a garish shade of orange and was emblazoned UNCLES ARE PEOPLE TOO in obnoxious neon letters. A pair of gray sweat pants hung from his lean waist, baggily disguising the muscle and sinew of his thighs and legs. On his feet were the disreputable running shoes he'd worn to her house weeks before. But with Jake it was a case of the man making the clothes instead of vice versa. He looked virile and alive and incredibly sexy, and Livvy's pulses did a quick double-time beat of purely sensual pleasure.

She pointed to the front of his sweat shirt. "Your motto?"

He nodded solemnly. "My special shirt. When I wear

125

it, I'm invincible. You just find a place to sit and relax. I'll whip this yard into shape in no time."

Livvy smiled. "It's a big yard. You might need help. I'm a woman, strong and unselfish," she said, playing on his description of himself. "And I've got muscle tone that surpasses that of most adult males."

"Is that so?" He sounded suitably impressed, but his laughing eyes went over her slim form in a summing up that doubted her assertion. "Remind me to investigate that sometime."

"You'll see," Livvy said smugly, bending to pick up her discarded rake. When she straightened, she found glowing eyes investigating at will. From ankle to hip, her legs received male approval, and the snug fit of her jeans across her trim hips seemed to be worthy of an extra moment's consideration. She brought his eyes up by saying challengingly, "Would you like to test my muscle tone against yours?" And scurried back when he took a step nearer, his eyes wickedly intent. She said sharply, "I meant a contest of stamina!"

His face fell. "Oh."

"We could divide the yard in half and whoever rakes the most leaves in an hour will be declared the winner."

He looked at her for a long, considering moment. "What does the winner get?"

She knew his intent and smiled serenely. "The satisfaction—"

"Good idea!"

"Of winning," she finished as if he hadn't spoken.

"That, too."

Her brown eyes reproached him, but their gleam of amusement made his crinkle at the corners. Businesslike, she laid out the game plan. "If we stack our leaves side by side, it will be easier to judge the winner. You take the right side of the yard and I'll take the left and we'll put the leaves dead center."

His glance went to the heap of leaves already stacked

126

on the left side of the yard, and he said ironically, "I like a woman who plays fair and square."

With a pang of guilt Livvy glanced at the sizable mound of leaves she'd already amassed. She almost laughed. She'd forgotten they were on the left side of the yard. "That itty-bitty pile?" she asked in scoffing tones.

One corner of Jake's mouth curled upward. "That *itty-bitty* pile would fill a few leaf bags."

She became gracious, if sweetly jeering. "We'll split them in half, then, if you feel cheated."

He leaned toward her and his eyes were brilliant, roaming her animated features with approval. "I never felt less cheated in my life," he said huskily. His finger brushed down her cheek, went beneath her chin, lifted it . . .

"Aren't we gonna rake leaves?" asked Mellie from somewhere near Jake's knee, shattering the moment.

Jake sighed and drew back, looking down at his niece and nephew. He smiled crookedly. "Sure, choose up sides. Livvy and I are having a contest. If she rakes more leaves than I do, she gets to win. If I rake more . . ." His words trailed off. Both children were moving to Livvy's side. "Traitors!" he muttered, but he was smiling.

At first the two children scooped up tiny handfuls of leaves, usually right in the path of Livvy's rake, their intent good, their accomplishment little, their loyal hovering more detrimental than helpful. Then Livvy instructed them to load up the play wagons from the sandboxes. They enthusiastically complied, and Livvy smiled. Jake's accumulation of leaves was mounting fast, and with the children better occupied, hers would stay just larger than his.

Eventually, Bret tired of helping and plopped himself down between the mounds of leaves. He popped his thumb inside his mouth, looking inconsolably lonely. The languishing glances he sent Livvy's way added to his forlorn appeal. She paused once or twice to give him a quick cuddle, her heart not able to ignore him as she watched in dismay as Jake used his rake like a vacuum, sweeping area after area clear of leaves.

The first time her rake intruded into Jake's leaves was really an accident. She had tossed it down in order to tie Bret's shoes and receive his smacking kiss of thanks. When she picked it up again, dragging it over the ground, a healthy portion of Jake's leaves came away in it. Mild guilt struck her, but instant rationalization chased it away. Jake did have an advantage, working alone. Biting her lip against a grin, she quickly added them to her accumulation.

The second time it happened wasn't exactly premeditated, but it wasn't an accident either. Bret and Mellie had deserted her for the more interesting pastime of cavorting in and around the playhouse, and her collection of leaves was a meager companion to Jake's. Besides, she reasoned disgruntledly, a man who whistled while he worked and turned smug grins her way deserved a little setback. She neatly swiped two large rakefuls and quickly tidied the area between the two stacks, smothering her pang of conscience with an exhilarated grin.

After that it became a matter of timing. Jake worked swiftly and methodically, going to the far reaches of his side of the yard to meticulously pick up every leaf. All she had to do was wait for his loping strides to take him far enough away so that her tactics weren't detectable. At one point, peeking up from the careful tidying and shaping of her growing pile, she saw his puzzled eyes on the two stacks. But when his gaze swung to her, she adroitly averted her face, raking energetically.

When the hour was up, Jake's half of the yard was raked clean. Livvy's was not quite so uncluttered, but her stack of leaves was noticeably larger. They met in the center and inspected them.

Trying not to sound too triumphant, Livvy said modestly, "It looks like I won."

"Yes, it certainly looks that way," Jake agreed slowly, but with unmistakable irony.

She kept her innocent expression. After all, he couldn't *prove* any foul play. Graciously, she offered, "Maybe my teensy head start gave me an advantage. You really should have taken half."

"Maybe so." His eyes had narrowed, the hard suspicion more pronounced, causing her a moment of alarm.

"And the kids helped me," she added quickly. "That gave me two advantages."

His eyes swept over the two sides of the yard, making inevitable comparisons. "You're very generous."

She pushed her luck. Very admiringly she said, "You know, in a contest of physical stamina with a woman, most men let their egos clutter the issue. I'm glad you're not hung up on all that macho supremacy." She shrugged uneasily under his hard-eyed scrutiny and gestured toward the leaves. "Facts are facts."

He murmured, "Funny how the female mind works— facts and fantasy all jumbled up." He took an ominous step nearer.

Livvy took a cautious one back, her shoes crunching into the scattering of leaves at the edge of one pile. She smiled nervously. "I told you I had better muscle tone than most men. It's something a lot of people find hard to believe."

His sudden smile sent her heart thumping crazily. His hand came up, his finger gently tugging a strand of her hair. "And who would believe that behind those large, honest eyes of yours is the conscience of a cheater."

"Jake! What an awful thing to say!" She knocked his hand away. Her eyes reproached him as she mildly taunted, "What's the matter? Are you a sore loser?"

"No, you're a terrible liar," he stated softly, adding, "and the only satisfaction a cheater deserves is swift and unmerciful punishment." The retribution in his eyes had her feinting quickly to the right.

He was there, steely-eyed and determined, and she stumbled back, unexpectedly measuring her length in the leaves, her legs and arms sprawled, her mouth rounded in gasping surprise. With a low, wicked laugh, Jake dived in after her, falling on top of her but very careful not to crush her with his weight, catching himself on his forearms and looking down at her with gleaming eyes.

"What are you doing!" she yelped breathlessly; then, with laughter predominant: "Get off me, you idiot!"

"Nothing doing!" he breathed softly. "I have to make sure you don't get away." An undercurrent in his voice made it sound as if he meant something deeper than whether or not she stayed to face her punishment.

And suddenly it wasn't a game to Livvy, and the laughter inside her died. She watched his eyes darken to a smoky turquoise and knew he was feeling the awareness of his body upon hers; she felt it too. Their thighs touched, their hips were in perfect alignment, and her small breasts just brushed his chest with each shallow breath she took. He removed her glasses, folding them in his palm, and his other hand came up to shape her neck in caressing fingers, his thumb gently positioning her jaw.

"Let me up, Jake," she said, sounding shaky rather than commanding, and he smiled faintly.

His voice low and husky, and still with a trace of amusement, he whispered, "Don't be nervous, pretty woman. This can't possibly hurt."

In the next instant his mouth was on hers and there was no amusement in his kiss. Shatteringly intimate, it expressed a pent-up desire, a burning urgency, that shot through Livvy like a fiery draft. Every nerve in her body sizzled to life. He maneuvered his arms beneath her, and the weight of his body, hard and warm, pressed her down into the bed of leaves. Livvy felt his heat searing into her, melting her beneath him, and she moaned a soft, indistinct protest against his mouth.

He broke the kiss, the moist expulsion of his uneven

breath creating a heady vapor she inhaled deep into her lungs. He smiled down at her, squeezing her gently in a reassuring hug. "Has the punishment been too brutal?" he whispered.

"No." The word came out reluctantly. Then, with a touch of mischief, she asked, *"Are* you punishing me?"

His laugh was soft and low and very sexy. His eyes were dark embers, showering her with blue sparks. His hard thighs pressed against the cradle of her hips. "Punishing myself, I think," he said.

He was a man, fully roused, and she said shakily, "Maybe you'd better let me up, then . . ."

He was shaking his head. "I can stand the pain."

When his lips came back to hers, they were gentle, so incredibly gentle, the tender ravishment of his tongue seducing her reason and her senses. She could feel her body's response to the persuasive lovemaking, her breasts growing hard, her thighs quivering and relaxing beneath his, her hands coming up to glide over his shoulders and stroke the lean sinew of his back through his sweat shirt.

His muscles tensed beneath her fingertips and a sound of pleasure rolled from his throat to be muffled against her jawline. Soft, ardent kisses nuzzled into the hollow of her neck and shoulder. One of his arms came from under her and he shifted slightly, his hand finding the collar of her shirt, his fingers dipping inside to flirt lazily with the silken strap of her bra. He stroked her shoulder lightly before his touch found the top swell of her breast, then lower. Livvy felt her nipple tighten against his caress, heard his indrawn breath of satisfaction, then twisted her head to find his mouth.

Her eyes closed against the sunlight, against thought; in her sense-shattered state she would have welcomed the gentle lovemaking forever. It felt right and unthreatening and she hadn't the will to stop it.

He raised his head, saying thickly, "Come home with me."

More by rote than by certainty, she breathed weakly, "I can't."

"Yes, you can," he growled immediately, repeating more quietly, "yes, you can, and you will."

And he kissed her again, a long, drugging kiss that anesthetized protest. His mouth took full satisfaction from hers, his tongue chasing hers, demanding capitulation, devastatingly sure and sensual . . .

The lilt of childish voices nearby intruded into their sensory world and Jake rolled away, his breathing coming in short, hard gusts, while Livvy lay there dazed and shivering, suddenly deprived of his warmth. A moment later something plopped onto her stomach, and she heard the rustle of leaves as Jake jackknifed to his feet and disappeared.

In slow motion her fingers touched her stomach, found her glasses, and put them on. She rose to a sitting position, heard Jake's deep voice mingle with the higher ones of his niece and nephew. Then Mellie and Bret were scrambling onto the pile of leaves, laughing and falling upon her, gaily inviting her to come home with them for supper. Jake was standing at the edge of the leaves, watching her, daring her to deny his children. And his mocking eyes were filled with unabashed chicanery that amused Livvy even while she sent him a dire look of reproach.

"Please, Livvy," Mellie begged earnestly. "You've never seen where we live. And Uncle Jake says we can have spaghetti for supper."

"Please, Livvy," Bret echoed, his blue eyes, so like Jamie's, enchantingly pleading. "I like s'ketti."

Livvy playfully tickled his round stomach, making him chuckle. "You like a lot of foods, you little conniver," she teased him. Her eyes went from one small, hopeful face to the other. She sighed, hugging each child close. "All right. I can't refuse such a yummy supper."

But the glance she sent Jake said supper was *all* she was accepting.

He smiled, unperturbed. "First we finish the yard work, then we go home and make spaghetti," Jake said matter-of-factly. He grinned as he offered Livvy a hand up. "I'll let you help with the spaghetti sauce."

"No, I'll finish the yard by myself," Livvy corrected. "You've done more than enough already. You take the kids on home, and I'll come later. What time is dinner? Seven? Eight?"

The way his mouth firmed and his brows lowered, she expected an argument. But after a moment he said, "Seven. And timing is important with pasta, so don't be late."

133

CHAPTER SIX

Livvy was five minutes early. Jake greeted her as if she were thirty minutes late, a hint of an anxious scowl on his face, which faded when he drew her inside his apartment and closed the door.

"I was beginning to wonder if I'd see you tonight," he said, hanging her coat in the entry closet.

"You said seven o'clock and it's scarcely that now," Livvy responded on a note of surprise. She glanced past the foyer into a large split-level den and kitchen. "Where are Mellie and Bret?"

"Putting away their toys." He stood before her, looking tall and lean in tan cords and a light blue polo shirt that accented the color of his eyes. His long fingers grasped her shoulders lightly. "I figure I've got about two minutes before they learn you're here," he said, his intense, glowing eyes appraising her.

Her rose-colored soft wool dress had wide raglan sleeves that fell just below her elbows. The loose-fitting bodice, softly gathered skirt, and belted waist hinted demurely of the slender woman beneath. The neck opening was high, slit straight across from shoulder to shoulder, and his fingers found the rim of ivory flesh exposed to his gaze. Beneath his light, stroking touch she stirred a little, and his grip tightened fractionally.

"Don't move, Livvy. Not much can happen in a couple

of minutes' time. Before we're interrupted, I need your cooperation in a little memory development," Jake told her, the huskiness in his voice flooding over her like warm summer rain.

"If things develop, you'll remember my cooperation?" she teased as she felt herself drawn closer. She saw the slow nod of his head as his smiling mouth descended the short distance to hers.

As kisses went, it was gentle and undemanding, yet it created a tiny sensory storm inside her. Her hands went to his lean waist and her mouth moved softly beneath his. He drew back slightly and murmured against her lips, "Just as sweet as I remembered." Then, moist and enticing, his tongue traced her lips from corner to corner before gently delving inside the parted welcome of her mouth. His second kiss stoked fires, incited a sensual receptiveness, weakened inhibitions and her knees. Her slim body flowed against the lean, hard length of his.

When the tender adhesion of their mouths was reluctantly severed, he smiled, saying softly, "Would you think less of me if I admitted this is one moment I miss my bachelor existence?"

She stepped out of his light embrace just as Mellie and Bret rounded the hallway corner. As she knelt to receive their lovingly exuberant greetings, her sparkling glance lifted to Jake. The broadest grin stretched his wide mouth, and she felt something jerk inside her chest. Grinning back at him, she wondered how much longer she could hold out.

The main area of Jake's apartment was done in shades of blue and oatmeal with bright turquoise and warm coffee accents. Contemporary furnishings filled the spacious den, and as they stepped up into the kitchen, shiny copper appointments gleamed a gracious welcome. At an island bar, four place settings were laid out in readiness for the meal. Four padded barstools stood sentinel, two adjusted to sit higher than the others. A piquant spaghetti sauce, redolent with thyme and oregano, simmered in a copper pot atop a burner, while the aroma of warm bread and herb butter floated enticingly into the air.

Everything looked well ordered and smelled delicious. Standing near the stove, Livvy said admiringly, "I'm impressed. You definitely get my vote for homemaker of the month."

Accepting her praise with a cocky brow and a solemn nod, Jake said, "With my organizational expertise, I ought to be a household necessity."

Smiling at his smugness, Livvy inwardly agreed. Every household deserved at least one Jake Masters. For a month she had observed the way he handled what might have been an insurmountable situation for many people, the way he shifted from bachelor to parent with determination and gritty patience. And Mellie and Bret kept her informed about the things she didn't see. Through their candid disclosures she learned when he went to the grocery store and what he bought; when he cooked and how often he took advantage of take-out restaurants. She knew his brand of toothpaste, his grouchy disposition before morning coffee, and his penchant for orderliness. Each family argument had been reenacted for her—Mellie had a flair for drama—and she'd heard how he growled, the way he stood with his hands on his hips, and the fierce faces he made. She even knew the times when his niece and nephew cried out during the night for their parents, and how Jake dried their tears with the strong comfort of his arms.

"We helped cook dinner," Mellie told her proudly, beaming up a gamine grin. "Bret shook the salad dressing and only spilled a little. And I mixed the butter and put it on the bread, 'cept I ran out of butter and Uncle Jake showed me how to find some on the bread already fixed."

On the pretext of leaning around Livvy to stir the spaghetti sauce, Jake whispered laughingly near her ear, "If you get the slice of bread with half a pound of butter on it, don't blame me."

Then he moved back and scooped a child in each arm, carrying them, laughing, to their barstools.

Through the salad course, conversation was light and mostly the chatter of Mellie and Bret. When the spaghetti and French bread were placed before them, the children dug in with relish, talking only sporadically. Jake set glasses of milk before his niece and nephew, and glasses of dry Chianti before himself and Livvy.

Into the relaxed ambience of the meal, Bret innocently dropped a tiny bombshell. "I like 'Chelle," he said out of the blue. "She laughs a lot."

A warning prickle ran from Livvy's nape to the top of her scalp, but she smiled and agreed easily, "Michelle is very nice."

Looking unbelievably cherubic with spaghetti sauce spread from ear to ear and a napkin stained the same tomato-orange tucked into the collar of his shirt, Bret continued, "'Chelle calls me beautiful boy and Uncle Jake calls 'Chelle *gor-geous.*" He separated the word, emphasizing both syllables as he sent an anticipatory glance his uncle's way, obviously expecting approval.

Slow to come was Jake's crooked smile. "You have a great memory, pal," he praised his nephew in a voice riddled with humor.

No denial, Livvy noticed. But then, Michelle *was* gorgeous, Bret was beautiful, and she was suddenly wondering why she was sitting in the Masters kitchen. By all the standards she had set for herself, she should have discovered Michelle's position in Jake's life before accepting his dinner invitation. *Ah, well, it wasn't too late.* With a determined glint in her eyes, she started to venture a probing inquiry. Mellie forestalled her.

"You know what, Livvy?" the girl mumbled around a mouth stuffed full of spaghetti.

"What?" Livvy smiled, enjoying the child's pixie-eyed appeal.

Prudently, Mellie reached for her glass, washing down her food with a long drink of milk before answering. "Michelle has a bird. A miner," she said, smiling impishly beneath a white mustache.

"A mynah," Jake corrected. Using his own napkin, he reached across the bar and gently wiped his niece's upper lip free of milk.

When her uncle drew back, Mellie's elfin features were puckishly bright, her small nose caught in an adorable wrinkle. "The miner talks! Guess what it says, Livvy!" she said, then with barely suppressed excitement supplied the answer. "It says 'Hit the sheets, big guy!' and 'I've got the hots!' "

Both children fell into fits of giggles, finding the phrases enormously funny, while Jake looked briefly pained and Livvy murmured satirically, "Clever bird."

"Decorum wasn't part of the mynah's education," Jake muttered, managing to sound suitably disapproving. But the effect was ruined by the spark of laughter in his eyes as he bent his attention to his meal. Evidently he enjoyed the mynah's bawdy sense of humor.

And the bird's gorgeous owner, Livvy added to herself. Her fork went round and round on her plate, absently twirling strands of spaghetti. Her thoughts made similar circles. Suspicion. Disappointment. Trust. Suspicion.

Trying to sound casual, she said, "Michelle is a very close friend, isn't she?"

Jake nodded easy agreement.

Mellie said, "She's nice."

Bret announced happily, "We play fish kisses," pursing his lips and sucking in his chubby, spaghetti-stained cheeks to demonstrate.

A sudden vision of Jake's widely carved lips puckered to receive Michelle's ripe, moist ones drove Livvy to ask with unseemly haste, "Who plays fish kisses?"

"Me and Mellie and 'Chelle," the boy explained, slurping a long spaghetti noodle inside his mouth before mumbling, "Uncle Jake didn't know how. 'Chelle teached him."

Poor *dumb* Uncle Jake! Her voice saccharine and whispery soft, Livvy asked him, "Were you a fast learner?"

Jake's lazy, untroubled smile as he bit into a crusty end of French bread nettled her further. Winking, he confided, "I catch on to some things faster than I do others."

I'll bet! Livvy thought acidly, dropping her gaze from his. Becoming "the other woman" was her last ambition. The distinction held too many humiliating reminders of her marriage to Brad—his initial pleas for forgiveness, his explanations that the other woman meant nothing to him, his rationalization that sexual infidelity wasn't the same as emotional faithlessness.

"Afraid of my culinary efforts?"

The low, teasing query brought her gaze up. Jake was eyeing her tense features quizzically. She smiled brightly and said, "Not at all."

"It's safe, Livvy. I make it a policy not to poison the woman I'm planning to seduce."

The faint trace of complacency in his voice was maddening. It sent her gaze downward again. Her eyes were beginning to feel like those of a jack-in-the-box. Up, down; up, down. Irritated with herself, with Jake, with the entire situation, she wound a bite-size portion of spaghetti around her fork and calmly ate it. She flashed him a cool smile. "You're an excellent cook, the spaghetti is delicious, but I never overindulge . . . in anything," she said with just enough significance to bring swift annoyance to his eyes.

"Ahhh, a woman of controlled appetites," he drawled benignly after a moment. Then he advised levelly, "You might as well give in, you know. I'll find a way to tempt you."

In the silence that followed, Livvy was torn between an

139

unwilling amusement and an urgent desire to disrupt his self-assurance. She put down her fork, brought her elbows to the top of the bar on either side of her plate, and folded her hands beneath her chin. Very confidently she stated, "I resist temptation."

"I'm aware of that," Jake said through a grin that verged on ferocious.

Apparently finished with his meal, he pushed his plate aside; hooking an arm over the back of his barstool, he surveyed her face and the upper half of her slender form, as if searching for a chink in the armor of her self-control. A slight inclination of his head indicated his niece and nephew. "Sometimes a reluctant appetite can be whetted with the most unusual delicacies," he commented, reminding her that she was sitting across from him because of Mellie and Bret's coercive powers.

She countered coolly, "Are you the type of man content with subterfuge?" She meant more than his using the children as bait.

His sudden grin was wolfish. "Desperate men use desperate means."

A grim little smile curved her lips. She said, "You're not desperate, Jake." Just greedy, like Brad, perhaps like all men, needing more than one woman to satisfy their sexual egos.

A muscle danced along his jaw and there was a shark-like intensity to his smile that reminded Livvy of their first meeting. He was angry, she realized, though he was keeping it in check. He drawled slowly, "Lady, I'm desperate, all right. You just refuse to recognize it."

She brought her hands down to her lap, clenching them together. "I recognize more than you think!" she said in a brittle, driven way that lowered his brows into a definite scowl.

After a telltale pause in which Jake controlled the exasperation claiming his features, he said, "You're not all sugar and spice, are you? You have a tendency to prickle

140

at the oddest moments." His eyebrows were sharp question marks above eyes glinting with an inquisitor's fervor.

Again, Mellie changed the course of the conversation. In a subdued voice that relayed her awareness of the adult tensions, she piped tentatively, "Mac calls me sugar and spice."

Shelving her irritation, Livvy turned to the child beside her and smiled reassuringly. "Mac's right, darling," she said quietly.

Mellie's worried little countenance brightened and she asked, "Is Mac Michelle's daddy?"

There was a dumbfounded silence before Livvy's glance flew back to Jake. On his face was a vaguely arrested look and his brows were drawn slightly together, but she couldn't read his expression. "Is Michelle married?" she asked.

"Nope."

"Engaged?"

"Nope."

"Oh." Feeling a little stupid, she chewed her bottom lip. Children often referred to husbands and wives as daddies and mommies. It had been a natural assumption —or had it been hope?

"Mac's my partner," Jake threw out laconically.

"Yes, I know."

"Do you?" Still that same offhand tone, but his eyes were brilliant and intense, tracking her face with its guarded eyes and unsmiling mouth. "He's also a very good friend."

"As close a friend as Michelle?" she felt compelled to ask, and watched the slightest of twitches catch the corner of his mouth.

"Yes, I consider them both good friends," he said, then added informatively, "In different ways, of course. I never shared the cab of a truck with Michelle and I never received a fish kiss from Mac."

Livvy eyed him stonily. Jake wore a vaguely pleased

expression that indicated he was enjoying himself—while she was tense and uneasy. The vast dissimilarities between their moods antagonized her.

Much as she had done before, Jake sat forward, his elbows on the counter top, his index fingers steepled and tapping against his cleft chin. "Michelle is open, outgoing, and easy to know and like. She's generous to a fault, giving away her time and caring as easily as she does her smiles," he told her, watching the quick, irritated toss of her head with admiring eyes, his gaze tracking the sheen of dark hair as it brushed her shoulders. "Mac, on the other hand, is a man of few words, almost taciturn. He's a loyal, supportive friend, but hard to get to know. And he's not nearly as generous as Michelle. Mac has definite limitations on what he'll share, even with a friend. There's one thing he guards to the extent of possessiveness."

He seemed to be waiting for her to comment, so she did, with a cool politeness that bordered on uninterest. "And that is?"

His answer came very softly, very significantly. "His woman. Mac loans her out for fish kisses and smiles, but that's as far as his sharing of her goes."

It took a moment for it to sink in, and Livvy's expression went from cool uninterest to surprise to overwhelming relief, all in the space of seconds. Michelle and Mac, not married, not engaged, but definitely a couple. She bent her gaze to her hands clenched tightly in her lap, and watched her fingers slowly uncurl. Elation took root somewhere in her chest, alleviating the constriction in her lungs. Then it surged upward in tickling butterfly leaps, so that when it formed a grin on her lips, a little hiccup of mirth gave it voice. Sparkling and penny-bright, her brown eyes slowly met Jake's waiting gaze.

"You look pleased, Livvy. Do I take it you approve of my friendship with Mac and Michelle? Or are you happy about the relationship between them?" His eyes were laughing and there was a gleam in them that was totally new. His relieved expression told her he'd been worried a little, but that her previous anger had been explained to his immense satisfaction.

Her cheeks grew warm, but she didn't avert her face. "You like to tease, don't you?" she accused, unable to keep the ebullience out of her voice.

"A little, I guess," Jake admitted, unabashed. "Mostly I like to get things out in the open. I prefer having suspicions voiced instead of insinuated."

"I asked," she was miffed into replying.

"You think so?" He gave an ironic little laugh. "Perhaps obliquely, but you never came right out with it, did you? Try the direct approach next time. You'll find I won't lie to you."

Point taken. Livvy went back to her meal. Her appetite had returned.

The large den included a fireplace. Jake lighted it soon after supper, though the apartment was centrally heated and needed no extra warmth. His smile was only slightly mocking as he told her, "They say a fire has a hypnotic effect on some people, loosening their tongues and their inhibitions."

Mellie and Bret were tugging at her hands, chattering about showing her their toys. Over the din Livvy retorted, "They also say if you play with fire, you get burned," as she let herself be led toward the hallway.

Laughing, Jake called after her, "When the kids wind up their part of the evening, I'm going to tell you everything you always wanted to know about me but were too shy to ask."

Was he referring to her misconception about Michelle? Or was he planning a little question-and-answer exchange? If the latter, he'd discover true confessions weren't her forte.

An hour later the children were in bed for the night, and Jake dimmed the lights in the den before guiding

Livvy to a comfortable sofa facing the fireplace. He seated her at one end and stood in front of her, bent forward slightly with his hands braced on the arm and the back of the sofa. Pressing discreetly back, she stared into his intent aqua eyes.

Very quietly, he instructed, "Look into the fire, Olivia, and relax. Let all the tension seep out of you and let your mind become totally receptive. You're going to hear all about me. You're going to lose all your fears and doubts and suspicions."

Her mouth quirked a little, but she managed a scoffing tone, saying, "Hypnotism doesn't work on me," and wondering if the firelight or her imagination was putting those glowing, sparkling, incandescent flames in his eyes. They teased her, toasted her, scorched her. Would moving away put her out of the proverbial frying pan and into the fire? She sat very still.

"Doubter," Jake muttered, laughing a little, his finger flicking the end of her nose. He moved back, saying, "I'll get us something to drink."

Wine or something stronger? A fiery brandy, perhaps, to further the mood created by the fireplace and the warmth in his eyes? Livvy relaxed back into the cushions of the sofa, not finding the situation too alarming. Her eyes were half closed when Jake came back, and as she lifted her heavy lids, she saw him standing before her with a steaming cup in his hand. The aroma of rich coffee drifted to her nose, making it twitch.

"I don't drink—"

"This is decaffeinated," he interrupted, offering it to her. "I'm not out to corrupt your principles." His roguish smile made mincemeat of his statement, and she grinned as she accepted the cup.

Leaving space between them, Jake sat in the cleft of two cushions. He took his coffee from the table in front of the sofa, and his first swallow brought forth a gusty sigh of appreciation.

Watching him, Livvy asked suspiciously, "Is yours decaffeinated too?"

For a moment he looked uncomfortable. Then he said, "You're too damned smart. No, mine's not decaffeinated. It's the full, unaltered brew, and I'm addicted to it." His tone was both defensive and aggressive, and he thrust out his chin as he added defiantly, "I put a spoonful of sugar in it." His eyes were laughing.

Over her cup Livvy's eyes sparkled. With condescending sweetness she said, "I don't force my diet or my principles on anyone. If you want to ruin your health with sugar and caffeine, that's your business."

After a wry grunt of a laugh, Jake indulged in another satisfying swallow of his health-ruining brew and leaned contentedly back into the sofa cushions, stretching his long legs under the coffee table. The hand holding his cup rested atop his flat belly, and his eyelids were at half-mast as he stared into the fire.

"I got addicted to coffee that first year Mac and I teamed up," he told her, smiling a little. "We used to drink gallons of it to stay awake, afraid if we slept, an opportunity would pass us by, I guess. We were struggling to compete against the large freight lines and needed any job, no matter how trivial or disgusting."

Livvy thought his choice of adjectives amusing. "Disgusting?" she said, laughing.

He grinned. "We weren't proud. We couldn't afford to be. We'd haul anything that was legal and brought in some money." His nose wrinkled and he drawled, "There ain't nothing smells more disgusting than a truckful of squawking chickens after a long haul."

Livvy laughed, and Jake continued speaking of the lean years of Masters and Mackensie in an amusing way that kept her smiling. He made their struggles into funny anecdotes instead of the hard, backbreaking, and frustrating work it must have been. He and Mac had saved money by living in the same converted garage that housed their only truck, putting all their profits back into the business.

"Mac was, and still is, the guts behind the operation. He had been driving for a major freight line and wanted to be his own boss. He needed a partner and chose me. I was just a kid with a college degree in business management and a lot of energy and drive. Mac had the truck, the savvy, the contacts, and a taciturn way of summing up people and possibilities. Only once since I've known him has he been completely wrong about a person."

"Michelle?"

He gave her a surprised look and said, "That can't be woman's intuition."

Livvy grinned. "Michelle mentioned that when you hired her, Mac didn't think she was the man for the job."

His eyes narrowed and he said slowly, "Michelle likes to talk. Did she say anything else?"

"She thinks you're a terrific guy and she's crazy about you."

"She didn't explain about her and Mac?"

Sensing accusation, Livvy replied tartly, "If she had, I'd hardly have made the mistake I did about your relationship with her."

"And you thought I was as *crazy about her* as she was about me, that I was just having a little fun on the side with you." He sounded disgusted.

"Naturally." Still defensive.

"And, *naturally,* it didn't occur to you that Michelle and I were just friends."

Livvy bristled more under the mocking chastisement. Her chin came up and she said coolly, "The first time I talked to you on the phone, Michelle interrupted you. I distinctly remember overhearing something about sexy black lace and red satin."

After an astounded silence, Jake burst out laughing. "God, no wonder you've been so hard-nosed about not trusting me." He grinned and explained, "Mac is reluctant to shop for women's things. He doesn't trust his taste, and he's like a bull in a china shop outside the realm of Masters and Mackensie. On Michelle's birthday, in front of me, he stuffed a wad of money in her hand and told her to buy something pretty. His lack of sensitivity hurt her a little, and I advised her to make it something expensive and sexy, adding a pointed remark to Mac about a gorgeous woman deserving only the best. Mac scowled at my humor, got a little red about the neck, but still didn't go out and do the shopping himself. Michelle took it a step further. She bought the most outrageous little bit of black lace she could find, wrapped it inside red satin sheets, and opened it in front of the entire office, cooing sweetly that Mac was very generous and had excellent taste. He got the message."

Livvy laughed, but her eyes were sympathetic. "Poor Mac."

After draining the last of his coffee, Jake leaned across and planted a hard kiss on her surprised mouth. He said huskily, "Poor *Jake,* suffering all this time because of Mac's stupid mistakes. I may kill that hulking s.o.b. Monday morning." He took her cup from her fingers. "I'll get us more coffee."

When he came back with the refills, Livvy had slipped off her shoes, drawn her legs up under her, and settled comfortably into the corner of the sofa. Jake handed her cup to her before easing his lanky frame into the same relaxed position as before, his head resting on the back of the sofa.

"Now, about the women in my life," he began insinuatively, turning his head to look at her. His eyes held a teasing glitter as they slipped over the graceful lines of her rose wool dress from the high neckline to the hem modestly pulled over her knees. Livvy regarded him with cool, almost wary speculation, and he grinned, saying, "I'll segment them into past, present, and future, and I'll leave out the prurient details."

147

His humor was contagious and she smiled. "You're very considerate."

He nodded complacently, accepting the praise. "My ex-wife should be a good start on the past. No sense going all the way back to my teen-age years," he said. "I met Denise the year after I teamed up with Mac. She was the greatest-looking thing in a bikini I'd ever seen. I was twenty-three and knew exactly what qualities to look for in a woman." A self-mocking smile quirked the corners of his mouth. "I don't think Denise and I spoke more than a dozen words those first few weeks, and then it was too late, we were married. Communication and personality traits were second runners to . . ." He paused, searching for a polite way to phrase it.

"The hot blood of youth?" Livvy suggested in a low murmur. Jake might be leaving out prurient details, but the picture he drew was very clear.

"Well put," Jake said dryly, his mouth twitching a little. "I was young, hot-blooded, and ambitious. Denise was young, passionate, and beautiful. We wrapped up physical attraction with ribbons of romance and called it love." His tone was introspective, not bitter, as if the only ghosts haunting his past were the foolish mistakes of youth.

Still, Livvy felt a sharp disquiet. Her dark hair moved against her neck and shoulders as she cocked her head to the side. She said earnestly, "Jake, it isn't necessary to tell me this."

With intent eyes he studied her worried face. His tone consciously reassuring, he said, "It's not all that tragic, Livvy, not in a personal sense. The only tragedy was the easy way Denise and I went into a marriage destined to be a divorce statistic." He smiled a little. "We probably should have had an affair, but she wanted a ring and I wanted her." The shrug of his wide shoulders conveyed acceptance of things that couldn't be changed. Then devilment looked out of his eyes as he leaned closer. "What about you, Livvy? Have you always been an independent lady, shunning involvement and refusing to consider sharing your life with one of us males?"

He'd hit the bull's-eye, but she could tell Jake didn't realize it; he was too relaxed, too amused. She just couldn't emulate his openness in discussing the past. Maybe if she knew him better. Maybe if her life with Brad wasn't still an open wound. Maybe it if didn't all lead back to Jamie. She heard herself murmur facetiously, "George has lived with me for years."

Jake laughed softly. "George is a lucky dog," he said, grinning crookedly at his pun. Observing the faint tinge of color in her cheeks, his eyes taunted her modesty.

But it was equivocation that made her feel miserable under the wavering smile she gave him. She said evenly, "George is a very faithful companion."

After a moment Jake again eased back into the cushions, his eyes on the fire. "It took about a year of marriage for me to notice signs of Denise's restlessness. I was seldom home, working late hours hustling for business, and she had a lot of time to brood and think and be dissatisfied. She started going out in the evenings, to movies with girl friends, she told me, because she was bored. I suggested, man-like, that she needed kids to give her something to do. She screeched, not without cause, that I could barely support her, much less kids, and that she wanted more—excitement and fun and pretty things— before she tied herself to children." Jake drank deeply from his cup, his expression reflective.

"Anyway, Mac and I began making money. Denise and I celebrated with a shopping spree. She looked great behind the wheel of a new little Trans Am. I hustled a little harder to make the payments."

"But?"

A rueful expression altered his face. "But it was just a stopgap measure in the marriage, dragging it out a while longer. Neither of us put much effort into the relationship. Denise spent more time away from home; I concentrated on Masters and Mackensie instead of Masters and Masters, and a few months later I found out there was another man who thought she looked great in a bikini."

"Oh."

"Oh," Jake echoed dryly. "She left in the Trans Am and I received divorce papers in the mail a week later. And, after a year or so of damning all women as cheats and liars, I realized Denise was smarter than me. She'd known our relationship was too one-dimensional to last, and had gone about dissolving it. I saw her a couple of years ago. She was still beautiful, had three children, and was very happy. I envied her."

"Did you?"

"I was feeling restless and dissatisfied with my own life at the time, and I envied her contentment," he explained, smiling. "I told myself it was irrational. Masters and Mackensie was a success. I had material comforts and pride in my accomplishments. And, other than the loyalty I owed Mac, I was free of any personal obligations. I scoffed away the feelings, working a little harder, playing a little harder. Then Dan and Sue died, and I inherited two little people who showed me what I'd been missing." He turned the most beautiful smile to her. "At first I thought it was the call of duty that appealed to me, or the challenge of raising two children. Now I wonder if some repressed fathering instinct wasn't there all along, waiting for an opportunity to show itself." Suddenly he looked uneasy, as if afraid he had sounded pretentious. His lips twisted with self-mockery. "I think you know what I'm saying. Children obviously enrich your world. And you chose your role, whereas mine fell into my lap. The way you give your heart to children, I'm surprised you've never had any of your own."

All the breath stilled in her body and for a moment a cloying panic seized her. In slow motion she turned her gaze toward the fire, bent her head over her cup, allowing the swing of her hair to provide a protective screen. What better opportunity would there be to explain about Jamie? her conscience directed. But she said nothing, trapped inside a sickening silence, her stomach churning.

Her side vision saw Jake lean forward to place his empty cup on the coffee table. Then he reached across and took her hand, bringing it to the cushion between them. Idly playing with her fingers, he said, "The next segment is the present." His tone was riddled with laughter, as if he thought her silence a ploy to keep a personal distance between them. He was half right. "At the moment the only female in my life is my niece. Naturally, Mellie can't fill all my needs, so there's a vacancy open for the right woman." He slanted a glinting gaze her way. "Interested?"

After half a heartbeat, Livvy managed to send him the same sideways glance. "Of course I'm *interested,*" she said lightly, playing the game because it was easier than dealing with her thoughts. "You will keep me posted if someone applies to fill the vacancy, won't you?" Her smile was serene.

Without missing a beat, Jake said, "As to cohabitation, I've got some great habits to team up with. I'm neat, I know my way around the kitchen, and I'm handy in other rooms as well." He paused and added, "I'll be thirty-three soon."

"When?"

He turned a guileless face to her. "When do you and I cohabitate?"

"When is your *birthday!*" she corrected instantly, her bravado slipping a little.

Jake grinned, unperturbed. "February eighth. I'll be thirty-three."

Livvy smiled faintly, said nothing, and blew softly into her cooling coffee, studying the swirling ripples she had created.

Jake eyed her for a probing moment, saw a vague

frown drawing her brows together, and said, "How old are you, Olivia?"

"I'll be thirty-three the thirtieth of this month. I was born a whole year before you," she said with a touch of teasing condescension, but really, it bugged her a little.

"You were born less than two months before me," Jake corrected dryly, adding, "I like older women."

"Thanks!"

"You're welcome," he murmured lazily, the wicked delight in his eyes registering her pique. "Let's see, what else should I tell you? I used to smoke and quit. I used to be a heavy beer drinker and quit. I used to see a different woman every night and quit."

"And now you're a saint."

He winked. "Now I don't want lung cancer, heart disease, a beer belly, or—"

"Sex," she supplied, straight-faced.

"Indiscriminate sex," he amended, laughing and gently squeezing her fingers. Then, with an almost solemn expression, he went back to his summary. "You should know my tastes run to Merle Haggard music, women who wear glasses and run day-care centers, and Neil Simon plays. I'm partial to a good steak, an occasional glass of wine, and deliciously slim wedges of cheesecake." He brought her hand up, bent his head to kiss her knuckles, and watched her reaction through eyes heavily fringed by reddish-brown lashes.

Livvy tried her best to remain expressionless, but her pulse had gone out of kilter again and, very casually, she removed her fingers from his grasp, using both her hands to hold her cup. Oh, he was a teasing, smooth devil, lumping her neatly between a singer and a playwright, then negligently adding that bit about cheesecake. She smiled—her polite, you-haven't-said-a-thing-to-impress-me smile, while her gaze traced his oh-so-innocent face and wickedly laughing eyes. She struggled with a rising trepidation. He was just too appealing, and she was wary of her growing response to him.

Jake shifted his position, his legs stretched toward her now, his arm laid over the back of the sofa. "You ready to hear about the future now?"

Glancing at her watch, Livvy said lightly, "Not tonight. It's getting late and I really should leave."

As she started to rise, Jake leaned forward and caught her arm, holding her back. He shook his head. "It's barely ten o'clock, Livvy, not late for a weekend. Stay with me a while longer. The future is the interesting part and you don't want to miss it." His voice was a low, coaxing drawl, but his gaze was intent and determined, and she realized all his teasing hid a very real purpose.

Her retreat came instantly; she felt vaguely threatened. She leaned forward to lay her cup on the table. "Some stories are better told in serial form," she said with a touch of cool detachment that erected a wall between them.

"Don't do that," Jake muttered gruffly, his face suddenly harsh and annoyed.

"Don't do what?"

"Don't pull back from me. Don't hide inside that polite indifference where I can't reach you. It bugs me."

Inside the grasp of his long fingers, her arm moved a little, trying to gain release. When he wouldn't let go, she said tightly, "I enjoyed the meal and the company, and I appreciated your help with the leaves today, but—"

"But don't try to make something more of it, is that it?" The hot flare of temper in his eyes startled her.

"I didn't say that," she said quietly and, she hoped, soothingly, but under his condemning stare she became defensive. "I told you I don't play flirting games."

His fingers tightened on her arm, and his expression turned mocking. "You've been playing flirting games all day, smiling and teasing and driving me crazy." He jerked her closer so suddenly that her hands flew up to

153

his chest to prevent a headlong tumble into his lap. He took her shoulders, shaking her a little. "And I liked it. I like you, damn it, but I'm tired of watching you retreat every time I try to get near you."

"Then don't try," she said mulishly, feeling as if he had backed her into a corner. She had liked it too. Almost too much, and it frightened her.

He shook her again, very gently, and muttered, "God, you stubborn, intractable woman!" Beneath her fingertips his chest rose and fell on an irregular sigh, and he said, "I can't stop trying. Don't you realize you're in my head?"

"I'm not!" she whispered forcefully, staring at him with eyes that were dark and dismayed by the implication of his words.

"You are. You have been for a long time."

His quiet statements had the effect of wildly aimed bullets, sending her panic ricocheting back to her, embedding itself in her heart. She pushed her hands against his chest, saying unsteadily, "I've got to leave."

"No."

"Yes!"

"No!"

Something unreadable glittered in his eyes, and his mouth crushed down on hers, stilling her next protest. She fought to free herself, twisting her head and digging her nails into his shirt to encounter the hard, inflexible muscle beneath, while he hungrily took the long, merciless, draining kiss from her mouth. Almost immediately his mouth turned devastatingly gentle and supplicating, as if Jake regretted the brief violence. She stopped resisting, going supple against him, her mouth giving him the soft response he wanted. His fingertips skimmed down her cheek and neck, then trailed to the wide edge of her sleeve. Very lightly he caressed the receptive flesh on the underside of her arm. Sensory delight quivered in the wake of his touch. He lifted his head finally, and gave a whispered little laugh.

"You're always so sweet and amenable when I kiss you," he said huskily.

Chagrined by the truth, Livvy mumbled disgruntledly, "It's a weakness I'm fighting."

Laughing again, he said with soft irony, "Yes, I know."

She pushed out of his arms, self-consciously patting her hair into place and adjusting her glasses. His hands came up and bracketed her face, his assessing eyes noting the faint color in her cheeks, the cloudiness in her eyes. "Look, it's nothing to run away from," he said persuasively. "I like being with you, and you enjoy it too, when you let yourself. Today proved that."

"Jake, I think—"

"You think too much," he murmured softly, interrupting her. "I don't know what you're afraid of, but I'm not going to force you into anything you don't want. We'll take it slowly, I promise."

She searched his face, saw the sincerity, the banked desire, and something that destroyed all fear, perhaps all reasoning. Why did he have to look so caring and gentle?

"I'm not sure what I'm getting into," she murmured at last.

It was capitulation, and he knew it. Triumph glinted in his eyes, but his voice was soothingly mild when he said, "Nothing bad, pretty woman. Just pretend I'm one of Horizon's children and you'll find me easy to accept."

A quirking smile trembled to her lips. "Oh, well, in that case, I've no need to fear the big seduction, have I?"

He laughed, hugging her under his arm, his fingers gently tipping her head back against his shoulder. Against her mouth, he murmured, "There isn't going to be a big seduction. When it happens, it will be mutual give-and-take. It's called lovemaking."

He kissed her again, several times, with a deep, tender urgency expressing warmth and pleasure and desire, while his hands moved over her in gentle exploration. Her arms slid around him. Accepting his controlled ardor, she thought: A little light romancing? Where was the harm in that, as long as serious emotions didn't become entangled?

Through her dress, his palm searched out her breast, and she sighed, enjoying the caress, welcoming the pleasure of his touch. Yet, when his hand moved to her midriff, then lower, he must have felt the sharp contraction of her stomach muscles, that unmistakable, entirely involuntary recoil, because he moved his hand to her slender waist and raised his head.

His rough sigh of resignation blew against her face. "Okay, we'll move at your pace. But first we'll move off this sofa."

Her eyes were grateful. "Could I have a glass of water, do you think?"

"Is that the ladylike equivalent of a cold shower?" he muttered sardonically, standing and extending his hand to help her up. He was smiling broadly.

And so it began.

156

CHAPTER SEVEN

"Family dating" Jake called it with one of his crooked half smiles. The first two weeks of December he and Livvy saw each other often, always with Mellie and Bret in tow. The children thought it was super having their two favorite adults frequently together. Livvy enjoyed the companionship, the fun, and the comfort of advancing their relationship at an undemanding pace. Jake? Well, Jake merely moved with the flow, seeming to derive enormous pleasure just out of being with her. He wanted more, but he tempered his pursuit to warm teasing, discreet touches, and brief good-night embraces.

Eventually his unfailing restraint produced a chain reaction of guilt and defensiveness and irritation in Livvy.

Jake wasn't a boy and she wasn't a young maiden shying away from passion. Quite the contrary. She was very attracted to him, admitted it to herself, knew he knew it. She saw his frustration at times, but more often saw his calm air of waiting. *Guilt.* She squirmed silently under its weight.

Her life and body were her own. She would decide when to share one, and how and when to give the other and to whom. *Defensiveness.* It helped ease the guilt.

One evening in mid-December they drove toward downtown Fort Worth in Jake's new "family" car. He never mentioned her once-expressed aversion to traveling in his little Mercedes; he just calmly drove up for their first date in the modest Datsun with front and rear seats, commenting that it was a practical acquisition for a man with small children. But Livvy sensed that one reason he had bought the car was to counteract any excuse she might offer for not going out with him. She was silently and frankly appalled. What kind of man was Jake Masters? Considerate or practical? Giving or realistic? Undemanding or determined? A blasted underhanded man! she decided, who was all of the above and therefore likely to puncture a woman's last defense. She almost laughed. *You're running scared, Livvy, ole girl, or you wouldn't curse the very things that attract you to him!*

"Ooh, look, Livvy! Isn't it pretty?" Mellie exclaimed softly from the back seat, her starbright eyes fixed on the city skyline.

Livvy followed the child's gaze. Fort Worth's buildings at Christmastime were outlined with thousands of amber lights, making them appear from a distance like huge, glowing Christmas packages. Red candles, twenty stories tall, brightened the two Tandy Center towers. Mellie's enchantment was understandable.

"Fort Worth wrapped itself up for Christmas," Jake said softly, reaching across the seat to wrap Livvy's knee in the gentle squeeze of his fingers.

His hand went immediately back to the steering wheel, and she sighed. He was very demonstrative, often touching her, but always, *always* discreetly. Another plus for the man.

Jake parked the car near an area of the city historically renovated to turn-of-the-century ambience. Sundance Square, once a locale frequented by Butch Cassidy and the Sundance Kid, held a variety of shops, restaurants, and small businesses. Visitors and shoppers could browse while soaking up the atmosphere.

Swinging Bret onto his shoulders as Livvy took Mellie's hand, Jake grinned and said, "Shall we follow the brick road and see where it takes us?"

"Yellow brick road," Livvy murmured absently, her eyes on the display window of a gallery that featured American folk art.

Jake stopped in his tracks, looking down at the street. "Definitely not yellow," he said. "More red."

"It's not yellow, Livvy," Mellie chimed in, tugging at Livvy's arm to get her attention.

Livvy turned, saw the direction of their gazes, and said sheepishly, "Sorry, my mistake."

Jake grinned. "That's okay, Dorothy. Stick with me and we'll find our way together. Not to the Emerald City, but to a chunk of Cowtown."

Fort Worth was once noted for its extensive brick streets, most of which had been paved over through the years. Around Sundance Square the original brick road-surfaces had been restored. The foursome followed the wide sidewalks paralleling the streets to find brass ensembles and mimes, roving musicians and singers, entertaining the passersby. And before the evening was over, they enjoyed a carriage ride, the horses clip-clopping along the bricks. Bret shouted "Giddyup, giddyup!" like a real Texas buckaroo in his tiny designer jeans and nylon bomber jacket and suede loafers. His "Stetson" was a green ski cap, and his chaw of tobacco, a piece of sugarless gum that kept sticking to the thumb never far from his mouth. Jake winked at Livvy over the boy's head, encouraging softly, "You tell 'em, pardner!"

The next evening they dined at a modest family restaurant on the outskirts of the city. Over the main course of juicy burgers and fries, Jake, face utterly expressionless except for dancing eyes, asked mildly, "Who wants to help me find a Christmas tree tomorrow?"

"Me! Me!" was a chorus shouted in unison, Mellie's and Bret's excitement bringing them to their knees on the booth seat across from Jake and Livvy. A wide-eyed pixie, Mellie asked hopefully, "A big one, Uncle Jake? With an angel and lights and lots of orn'ments?"

"A big one, with all the trimmings," Jake agreed, smiling. "Do you suppose Livvy would help us choose it and decorate it?"

Another shouted chorus, this one "She will! She will!" nearly drowned out Livvy's "I'd love to." She was smiling broadly. When Jake's thigh pressed against hers, she reached down and gave it an absent pat, cherishing the appealing glow on the small faces across from her.

"I have to be at my office at eleven thirty tomorrow morning for a meeting with my terminal manager, but I should be free right after lunch," Jake said, popping a french fry into his mouth and chewing contentedly. Beneath the table, his hand covered Livvy's still on his thigh. Slightly startled, she jerked her hand back to her lap. His followed, brushing the hem of her skirt aside to fall gently to her knee.

Livvy grabbed up her hamburger, bit into it, wondering how long her hand had been on his thigh, wondering, too, how long Jake intended keeping his on her knee. The heat of his palm was pleasantly disturbing. The heat in her face was less so.

Jake spoke to his niece and nephew. "You two will have to come with me tomorrow and promise to behave while I meet with the man. After I get through, we'll hightail it to Livvy's and kidnap her for the day."

His white teeth closed around another french fry. His fingers closed round her knee, shaped bones, caressed kneecap, discovered the texture of her panty hose, registered the slight tensing of muscle under his touch. His exploration curved to the underside of her knee, stroking softly over her tendon and sending a current of electricity up her thigh.

The hamburger dropped to her plate; one of her hands dropped to her lap. Smiling, she dug her nails sharply into the back of his wrist. To the children she said brightly, "I'll be ready right after lunch." Turning to Jake, she whispered through clenched teeth, "Stop that!"

"You have a very touchable knee," he whispered back through a faintly roguish smile, but he removed his offending hand and laid it casually on the booth behind her.

Eyes unamused, Livvy went back to her hamburger.

One-handed, Jake brought his hamburger to his mouth, took a huge bite, and chewed appreciatively. He winked at his niece and nephew, murmuring, "Mmmmmmmm!"

Two-handed, Bret immediately tackled his hamburger in the same lusty fashion, his chubby cheeks soon stuffed, as if he were a squirrel storing nuts for winter. His murmur of appreciation was a distorted "Gmph-gmph!" as he concentrated on chewing and winking at the same time. Somewhere a muscle signal got waylaid. Both bright blue eyes screwed tightly shut and blinked open, casting an expectant gaze about the table.

His sister's giggle rewarded his antics. Grown-up laughter applauded his efforts.

Mellie asked hopefully, "Will there be presents under the Christmas tree?"

Remembering the puzzles and games she'd bought the week before, Livvy said, "I believe there will be. After all, what's a Christmas tree without *presents!*"

Accompanying her shriek was the abrupt forward jump of her body. She did a curious wriggle and buck; her eyes widened, then narrowed. She hadn't dislodged the warm masculine palm curved against her backside. The children giggled at the slapstick display, and Jake's glittering eyes showered her with an innocent look of concern.

"Why did you *yell?*" Mellie shouted through her laughter.

"I . . . uh . . . bit my tongue," Livvy croaked weakly, her smile thin. Where had she gotten the impression that Jake Masters was discreet with his touches? In the middle of a busy restaurant, for heaven's sake! Again her hand dropped beneath the level of the table, twisting back to find the one still molded to her backside. A brief duel of fingers ensued before the guilty ones were captured and duly punished in an unmerciful squeeze. Jake winced and Livvy said sweetly, "Things like that happen when you bite off more than you can chew."

"Your poor tongue," Jake drawled sympathetically, wisely rescuing his hand and bringing it back to the table. He flexed his fingers, his glittering eyes on her mouth. "Want me to kiss it better?"

Another round of giggles came from the children, undoubtedly as they envisioned Livvy with her "injured" tongue stuck out for their uncle's healing ministrations. Casting Jake a dire look, Livvy muttered under her breath, "You never give up, do you?"

"I'm like the mailman," Jake explained easily. "Neither rain nor sleet nor lack of encouragement can keep me from my deliveries."

"I got your message a long time ago," Livvy retorted. In spite of her offended dignity, she was struggling with a grin.

"Who's writing letters?" Mellie interjected curiously.

But Livvy and Jake were intent on each other. His aqua eyes were seducing her to compliance. "You haven't replied yet," he reminded her softly.

So she hadn't. And with good, sound, cowardly reason. Smiling brightly, Livvy said evasively, "Maybe I'm a terrible correspondent."

"Uncle Jake, did you give Livvy a letter?"

"You're not a bad correspondent, pretty woman, just a reluctant one. On short postscripts you do great, expressing yourself warmly. It's the body of the letter you have trouble committing yourself to." He winked. "I've no doubt you can express yourself eloquently once you set your mind to it."

"Uncle Jake! Why do you and Livvy write letters?"

"You said we'd move at my pace," Livvy reminded him, trying not to look guilty, managing to look defensive, hiding her irritation.

"Snail," he accused softly, a lazy grin stretching his mouth.

Livvy found his myriad smiles impossible to resist. With a giddy surge of pleasure, she wondered if kissing the cleft in his chin would be too rapid a move for a snail.

Loudly, matter-of-factly, Bret announced, "Mellie's mad."

The adults tore their gazes apart and sent questioning glances across the table. Mellie sat back in the seat, her arms crossed over her thin chest, her bottom lip thrust out. Her eyes were glaring reproach.

"What's your problem, Miss Mellie Misgiving?" Jake asked, his eyes laughing and genuinely puzzled by his sprite's obvious temper.

"I asked and asked who's writing letters! I asked a hundred times! You and Livvy just kept talking!"

Eyes continuing to twinkle, Jake said easily, "Sometimes Livvy and I have things to say that are just between the two of us."

"Why?" she asked, her bottom lip still thrust out and sulky.

For a moment Jake looked out of his depth. Then he said, "Because she's my friend and we enjoy talking together."

"Why?"

"Because we like each other."

"Why?"

"Because she's sweet and I'm sweet on her!"

"Why?" Her bottom lip was back in place now and her eyes were clearly mischievous.

"Because that's the way it is!" Jake muttered in a muted growl.

Impish blue eyes sparkled into exasperated aqua ones.

And suddenly both Jake and his niece were laughing. He reached across and tweaked her nose, but wisely changed the subject, asking, "Who wants dessert?"

Mellie and Bret chose their favorite, ice cream. Livvy requested a bowl of unsweetened strawberries. And Jake, all innocence and charm, told the waitress, "Cheesecake for me, please, but just a slim wedge. I'm on a restricted intake of sweets."

Livvy eyed him askance and sighed. What could a woman do with a man whose humor was teasing and double-edged and funny and unfailing? Join him, she supposed.

The next day Jake and the children arrived shortly after the noon hour. Bret, blond curls hidden beneath his green ski cap, went straight into Livvy's arms, his thumb removed from his rosy mouth long enough to plant a smacking kiss on her smooth cheek and whisper his usual loud "I love you, Livvy."

Just as secretively, she whispered back, "I love you, too, Bret." Then she gathered Mellie under her other arm for the same greeting.

Mellie, rosy-cheeked, a pert little red knit cap on her shining brown head, wrinkled her nose comically and announced, "Uncle Jake called us Christmas elves. I'm the red pixie and Bret's the green sprite."

Laughing, Livvy hugged them again before glancing up at Jake. "I like your Christmas elves," she said.

He smiled. "Yes, I know you do." His gaze encompassed the loving embrace enfolding his children and became speculative. "Maybe I should shrink myself about three feet. That seems to be where all the action is."

"You're a man of action?" She pretended slight surprise. "I thought you were the man of patience," she teased him.

"One doesn't cancel out the other."

"Oh?" She was well aware of the provocation in that one syllable.

Jake didn't miss it either. His eyes glinted wicked humor. "I'd be glad to demonstrate if you'd like."

"I'll take your word for it," she said instantly.

His eyes laughed at her quick retreat. "I thought you might."

She smiled. "I'm almost ready. I just need shoes and a coat."

"And a little more nerve."

She didn't answer him, releasing the children to go to her bedroom. As she stepped into casual pumps, she heard the phone ringing. Grabbing her coat and the paper sack that held wrapped presents, she rushed out of the room. Jake was bringing the phone to his ear as she entered the living room. After a brisk "Hello" his eyes found Livvy, glinted over her in a frowning question. Then he silently handed her the phone. He didn't move away, didn't answer her quick smile of thanks as he took the sack and her coat, didn't take his eyes off her.

"Hello?"

"Who answered your phone?" her ex-husband said by way of greeting.

"Brad." She made his name a flat acknowledgment, her fingers hovering above the base of the desk phone before finally tapping irritably against the plastic. To hang up on him would probably elicit more questions than holding a brief conversation. She turned slightly and bent her head, her hair swinging forward to shield her expression from Jake's steady scrutiny. She spoke quietly into the receiver. "What is it this time?"

"Baby, that sounded cold, and there are too many years between us for you to pretend indifference to me."

Same song, thousandth verse. The world revolved around Brad. Sighing, Livvy said, "You think so?"

Brad's voice became cajoling. "I thought we'd go out tonight, Liv, have dinner, maybe go dancing. I haven't danced with you in ages. We used to be great together on the dance floor."

"I can't." *I don't want to.* "I have other plans."

"With the man who answered your phone?"

"Yes."

There was a pause before Brad said, "I found some pictures taken that week we spent on Padre Island. Most of them are of Jamie, and I know you'll like them. Why don't you cancel your plans, and I'll bring them by?"

She was tempted. Not to cancel her plans; but for a moment she was tempted to say yes, she wanted the pictures. However, seeing Brad again canceled out the desire for additional pictures of her son. She said, "No, I don't think that would be a good idea."

"Don't you want them?"

"Don't you?" *Say you do, Brad. Give me that much. Say you want visual reminders of how your son sweetly embraced the sand and sun and life.*

She didn't realize she was holding her breath until Brad said casually, "I wasn't the one who took pictures of him from the day he was born. You were."

She released the breath on another sigh, suddenly very tired of trying to find traces of fatherly sentimentality in Brad. "Look, I'm in a hurry. I can't talk to you any longer."

"Afraid your *lover* will be jealous?" Brad said, laughing softly, reminding her of their last conversation.

Not this time, Brad. She managed a light, contented tone. "Not at all. There's no reason he would."

"He is your lover, then?" He was still fairly assured she had no lover.

"Why, of course," she said, as if she thought his doubt slightly naive.

"I don't believe you!"

Again lightly, with a touch of condescending amusement, she said, "Of course you don't."

"You're lying!"

"Whatever you say," she agreed, borrowing one of his soft laughs that had the underlying sting. Then she trilled sweetly, "Bye now," and replaced the receiver in its cradle. A victorious smile was spreading across her face. That felt good! She felt good! Almost gaily, she turned to Mellie and Bret.

Extending her hands, she said, "I'll bet Christmas elves can pick the best, most beautiful tree ever." Her beaming smile included Jake. "Don't you agree?"

She could see the tension in him, the questions, and her smile turned softly appealing. *Please don't ask. Please accept that it has nothing to do with you.*

It seemed an eternity, though only brief seconds passed, before Jake's half smile appeared and he said quietly, "I'm sure you're right."

After that, the day was a kaleidoscope of impressions and sensations, and somewhere along the way Livvy made a decision. She was halfway there already and it wasn't a difficult one, just a quiet surrendering toward Jake. . . .

Jake—who laughed at his niece's and nephew's enthusiasm, then cast her a look over their heads so frankly sensual she was rocked on her toes.

Jake—who inspected every tree in three lots before finding the perfect specimen, tall and symmetrical, then adroitly convinced the children it was their choice, sharing a twinkling, conspiratorial smile with her as Mellie and Bret proudly claimed it theirs.

Jake—who strung twinkle lights on the tree, his baritone voice singing a Merle Haggard tune about "making it through December" and looking down at her from his stepladder to blast her with such burningly possessive eyes she nearly dropped the box of glass ornaments she held.

Jake—who harmonized shared laughter, family closeness, and tender caring, who was warmth and fun and passion.

When the tree was decorated, they all stood back to admire their handiwork, their faces glowing. The queenly fir wore raiments of twinkle lights and shiny-bright ornaments. A regal beauty, she was crowned by a glitter-and-braid angel, and the hem of her skirt was heavily adorned by ornaments placed where little hands could reach. Small oohs and ahhs and cries of "bee-*yoo*-tiful" paid her tribute. Exchanged winks and smiles over little heads echoed the praise.

At Mellie's pleading suggestion, Jake agreed to serve the evening meal in front of the tree. To Livvy, it couldn't have seemed more romantic. Instead of candlelight casting a soft glow, there were twinkle lights and a fireplace for flickering illumination. Instead of wine to relax the senses, there were four fat goblets of milk to intoxicate the spirit. Instead of violin strings playing soft refrains, there were Gene Autry's renditions of "Rudolph, the Red-Nosed Reindeer" and "Santa Claus Is Comin' to Town" providing mood music. Instead of quiet whispers and intimate conversation, there was high-pitched, excited chatter and low, indulgent responses.

Thoroughly seduced by the day and the family and the man, Livvy sat on the floor with a paper plate of takeout chicken and potato salad balanced on her lap. And each time her gaze met, and was held, by a brilliant aqua one, she felt a warm glow of pleasure and a quickening heartbeat.

Together, she and Jake tucked Mellie and Bret in bed, and side by side they walked back to the den. The caressing weight of Jake's hand on her nape beneath her hair added an intimacy Livvy had no wish to dispel.

He led her to the fireplace. Then he was holding her closely, kissing her softly, parting her lips with the gentle pressure of his as he tipped back her head to his shoulder, his fingers caressing the arch of her throat.

He raised his head and his eyes held a speculative, almost reckless glitter. But his smile was slow and lazy, and he asked huskily, "Have you enjoyed yourself today?"

"Yes."

"No regrets? No wish that you'd made other plans?"

Her head tilted back as she studied his expression. Curious? Teasing? Taunting? "No, of course not," she said finally, faintly surprised that he needed to ask.

"Just checking," he murmured, his smile slightly mocking. "And the kiss just now, did you enjoy that?"

She smiled. "I enjoyed it."

"I guess the next question is how much," he said, offering enticement with the coaxing caress of his voice.

His arms tightened about her and his mouth made a leisurely journey to hers, kissing her with a deliberate sensuality that induced a like response. Her mouth moved eagerly under his, and she answered each slow thrust, each gentle nudge, each teasing swirl of his tongue with one of her own.

At the corner of her mouth he breathed, "How much?" Faint laughter underlined the question, as if he already knew the answer, and for a brief moment his mouth took on a vaguely jeering twist.

"The first one or the last one?" she teased, looping her arms about his neck, encouraging his normal half smile into place.

"Both."

Her voice going husky and low, Livvy murmured, "Very much."

"And the man kissing you?" Jake prompted, then crushed her answer to silence under another ardent kiss, his hands moving over her back, warm, compelling, aligning her body to his in a possessive embrace. His jeaned thighs pressed to her jeaned thighs, and the buttons of his shirt stamped her skin beneath the soft wool of her loose sweater.

"I like the man," she confessed when she could, her

voice a trifle uneven. Before he could ask, she added softly, "Very much."

Smiling, Jake suddenly swung her off her feet and brought her down on the carpet before the fire. Half gasping, half laughing, she twisted in his arms, evading the intimate entrapment of her body by his. Jake indulged the mild resistance, pressing his entire length alongside hers, his lean, muscled body radiating heat and strength and purpose. His hand went beneath her loose sweater, teasing her smooth midriff, stroking slowly upward until his fingers brushed the underside of her breast. Her indrawn breath was very soft, very expectant, and very audible in the room's quietness. She met the intensity of his gaze with a soft and curious regard, wondering what lurked behind the faint mockery of his expression.

"You like my touching you," he murmured quietly.

It was more statement than question, yet she answered him. "Yes," she said in a throaty whisper. She sensed more than teasing seduction in his unrelenting inquiry and, with wary amusement, added, "Are all these questions important?"

"Not the questions, pretty woman, the answers," he said in a voice gone gruff around the edges. "I like answers."

Teasing, flirting, his lips played with hers, slightly parted so that their breaths mingled, moist and warm and heady. She sighed, and he smiled against her mouth. Then he took her glasses and gently shoved them across the carpet away from them. A second later his body slid over hers, and there was a difference in him, a measure of grim determination as his legs parted hers and his hard, aroused body blanketed hers, dominating her senses. His mouth slanted across hers in a kiss that was somehow both supplicating and aggressive. His hand between them moved onto her breast with the same mixture of entreaty and imperative demand, enclosing it in a sensual caress that elicited her soft moan of pleasure.

A desire-induced lethargy enervated her body, and her hands rose slowly to the front of his shirt. Buttons were undone, one by one, unhurriedly, and her fingers enmeshed in the springy hair covering his warm flesh. Her fingertips caressingly investigated texture and heat, sinew and bone, from his shoulders to his lean waist, while Jake grew tense and his breath quickened.

His mouth moved down to her throat as he urged roughly, "Tell me you want me."

A languid sigh escaped her. She closed her eyes and her body moved in a convenient arch to his continued caress at her breasts, encouraging the teasing of their tautening peaks. She was telling him, only not with words. She had lost all concept of the questioning game he played. She was responding to the needs brought to life by the lure of his kiss, the persuasion of his hands, the seductive weight of his body.

"Tell me," he insisted, his voice throbbing huskily at the curve of her neck.

A thrilling heat pulsed through her veins, and she moved her mouth to his ear, whispering the admission on a soft, yielding sigh. "I want you, Jake."

Her breath in his ear sent a trembling shudder down his spine, and he took her mouth in another searing kiss, burning a demand, scorching a promise. Then he raised his head, his glinting eyes holding hers.

"How much?" he asked very softly around a smile that was wide and determined and utterly ruthless.

She stared up at him, her eyes suddenly clouding with confusion. Where was the gentleness, the teasing, the tenderness? In his eyes was a faint hostility she couldn't define. Lines of tension made his expression grimly forbidding despite his smile, and a pulse hammered at his temple. Desire had changed from warmth to anger in a flash.

Shaken, she whispered unsteadily, "Jake . . . ?"

But he ignored the plea in her voice. Tangling his fingers in her hair, he held her head immobile while he kissed her again, mercilessly, draining the protest from her. When he tore his mouth from hers, he muttered thickly, "Answer me, Livvy. Tell me how much you want me. Tell me I'm the only man you want."

Pushing against his shoulders, her body arching in a desperate attempt to escape the dominance of his, she choked, "Why are you forcing admissions?"

Almost negligently he captured her hands, bringing them down to the carpet on either side of her head. With the weight of his body he stilled her twisting struggle, subduing her resistance beneath his superior strength. And through it all, he continued to smile. That horrible, sharklike smile that turned her blood cool and her eyes wary.

"Why are you fighting, Livvy? You know you respond to me. Is it so difficult to admit how much?"

Under force it was. She couldn't and she wouldn't. What his gentle, teasing passion had induced, his anger destroyed. Panting, breathless, she stared up at him. Tension made her voice scratchy as she whispered, "Let me up. I'm not answering any more questions."

Eyes glinting, he taunted softly, "Why? Because I'm not the man you want? Or because I'm not the only man you want? Which is it?"

Her expression became incredulous. *Only* man! What other man . . ." Her words trailed off as she suddenly recalled her ex-husband's phone call. "Brad!" she gasped weakly.

Jake's mouth compressed, and he abruptly rolled away from her. He lay on his back beside her, an arm thrown across his eyes, his chest rising and falling harshly until he controlled his anger and his breathing became quietly rhythmic. His hand fell away from his face. "Who is Brad?" he asked finally in a flat monotone.

Everything was falling into place. Jake's questions, his demands, his desire, and his anger. Jake, who was open

172

and honest and direct, had played an underhanded game, subjecting her to a teasing, merciless seduction while expertly wringing admissions from her. The police department ought to hire him! Livvy thought.

Tersely, she answered his question. "Brad is my ex-husband!"

There was a dumbfounded silence before Jake muttered, *"Ex-husband!* I thought . . . !" He clipped off the words, his mouth a grim line.

Exhaustion and resentment seeped through Livvy in equal measure, and she lay looking up at the ceiling. After a moment she laughed, a slightly testy little explosion containing no mirth. "What did you think, Jake? That I was leading you on while conducting a secret love affair with another man? Why didn't you ask? You're the man who prefers to have suspicions voiced instead of insinuated!" Sarcasm coated her whispery tone. She was fast becoming furious.

Jake lay as still as she; he, too, gazing up at the ceiling. There was a yard of floor space separating their bodies, more than that in the air between them. Very tightly, he said, "I've been asking for the last few minutes!"

"No, you've been playing a game!" she retorted just as tightly. "Do I like your kisses? Do I like your touch? Do I like you? You didn't want answers! You wanted admissions of guilt!"

Neither of them moved, and his heavy sigh floated above them like a malevolent cloud of distrust. "All right, I was suspicious and angry, and I admit it. But it was a shock learning there was another man, especially when you didn't offer to explain who he was. You've always drawn back from my lovemaking as if you're nervous of sex or don't have much experience with men. Your side of the phone conversation sounded intimate. You laughed and flirted with him." His voice had gone a little gruff, accusation intermingling with the explanation. "When you hung up, your face was glowing like you'd just received your fondest wish."

Livvy had developed selective hearing, and she latched onto one word with fuming annoyance. *"Experience!* Did you think I was some old-maid schoolteacher who'd never known a man? I'm almost thirty-three, Jake. Surely *experience,* or my *lack* of it, was a pretty farfetched theory!" Her words were brittle, underlined with resentment, and even on her back, her chin came up a notch. She added goadingly, "Of course, if you're looking for *innocence,* you've obviously been looking in the wrong place!"

Jake turned his head to stare at her, noting the angle of her chin, the cross of her arms over her chest, the tight set of her soft mouth. He laughed suddenly, his baritone voice low and amused. "I wasn't looking for innocence, Livvy. I was looking for the woman who keeps hiding from me, the one who'll respond to me without drawing back."

"I am *not* hiding!" she retorted, sending him a withering glance; then, turning her eyes away from him, she looked up at the ceiling. She firmly buried the tiny seed of guilt brought about by his words, adding with cool hauteur, "And I responded to you tonight until I realized you were playing your grim little game."

After a moment, he asked quietly, "How long since your divorce?"

"Almost two years," Livvy told the ceiling.

"Were you married long?" Jake asked.

"Nearly twelve years."

"Twelve!" he breathed, as if she'd said one hundred and twelve. He was clearly astounded.

Livvy turned her head, watched his expression do a rapid-fire change from astonished to thoughtful to grim. She goaded coolly, "An even *dozen,* minus a few months. Too much *experience* for your taste?"

Their eyes met. Hard accusation glared out of his eyes.

"You're still in love with him, aren't you? That's why you've never mentioned him!"

With a short, incredulous, fed-up little laugh, Livvy went back to glaring up at the ceiling. Then, less tersely than before, she admitted, "No, I don't love Brad. He killed my love long before the divorce."

"Then why all the secrecy?"

"It's not secrecy, Jake, if I don't discuss my life as easily as you do yours. Brad is in my past where he belongs. I don't like talking about him." From the corner of her eye she caught a quick flash of white as Jake's tanned face was split by a sudden grin. Bully for his miraculous mood changes!

"Okay, it's not secrecy." His voice held chagrin and resignation and a hint of grim humor. He reached across and touched her arm. "Will you accept my apology for behaving like a jealous idiot tonight?" When her arm remained tense beneath his fingers, he dropped his hand and said heavily, "When I heard you talking to him today, I thought . . . Well, you know what I thought."

It was Livvy's turn to sigh. Her anger was diminishing. She sat up, drew her knees to her chest, and rested her cheek on them. She looked at Jake, blinked, and sighed again. "Where are my glasses?"

Jake rolled away, then came back, closer to her now, raised on one elbow beside her as he handed her the glasses. She put them on, hugged her arms about her knees, and again laid her cheek upon them.

"I was nineteen when I met Brad, and he was twenty-six. He seemed so positive about everything he did and said, I credited him with maturity." Her voice was scratchy and low. She didn't like talking about her marriage, but she didn't want Brad to come between her and Jake, not now or ever again. "Brad is totally self-absorbed. He loves himself, fun and the good times, life on his terms, in that order. What I thought was maturity was selfish determination to have and do the things that please him." She closed her eyes briefly, coming to a difficult part. "Perfection is important to him . . . physical perfection. The first time I fell short of the mark was when my nearsightedness forced me to get glasses. He wanted me to wear contact lenses. I balked and . . ." Here she paused again, and let out a long breath as if searching for words.

Tell him now, her inner voice directed. *Tell him about your major physical imperfection. Tell him now.* When Jake said nothing to interrupt, she heard herself continue thinly, "Brad's very good-looking and he likes surrounding himself with beautiful people, most of whom are women. His infidelities were numerous, and he excused them as the sex drive of a normal, healthy male. He claimed he was never unfaithful to me emotionally because he loved me and the other women meant nothing to him. I believed it the first time or two."

She stopped talking, wondering what Jake was thinking. He had been so still, so quiet, while she talked; his eyes were solemn as they studied her. He was dear to her and she sensed his compassion and she knew his strength. And more than anything she wanted to throw herself in his arms and forget the past in the beauty of his embrace. She shifted a little, placing her chin rather than her cheek on her knees, staring not at Jake but unseeingly across the room at the Christmas tree.

"Brad is a beautiful, selfish, spoiled little boy who never grew up. He's forty years old now, and he's never realized there are other people with needs and emotions and goals. He's like one of Horizon's children, only not as lovable once you get past the surface charm and good looks. He has never been able to handle any kind of stress, and he continuously refused to cope with marital difficulties." There was a rawness in the back of her throat. She had to clear her voice before she finished very quietly, her voice faintly hoarse, "At a crucial point in

176

our marriage he ran, evading the problems by divorcing himself from them."

The silence that followed lasted only briefly. Jake broke it, asking huskily, "Does he want you back?"

Livvy shook her head. "No, I don't think so. I hadn't heard from him in eighteen months when he called this last October. Since then he's called twice more. I really don't know why. He may be indulging a momentary whim of nostalgia, or perhaps he just wants to be reassured that I won't forget him. Brad needs a lot of reassurance."

"And do you reassure him?"

Livvy grinned suddenly, a totally malicious little grin that drove away the clouds of the past and put wicked laughter in her eyes. "It seemed to bother him today that you might be my lover. I told him you were." Her grin widened. "No, I don't reassure him."

Reaching up, Jake traced the line of her jaw with one fingertip. His eyes were gentle, edged slightly with worry. "Have I blown it with you?"

The slow shake of her head was as sober as her quiet "No."

A lazy smile curved his mouth. He drawled hopefully, "I get a second chance, then, despite my blunders?"

She smiled. "You didn't lose your first chance. We were both at fault for what happened tonight."

His aqua eyes regarded her intensely, questioningly, before he asked quietly, "Will you stay with me tonight?" He didn't miss her quick indrawn breath, her shaky sigh, the way she tried to keep her smile, or the way it wavered. Loosely grasping one of her arms, he tugged until she unfolded and came toppling onto his chest. He was very gentle. Pushing her hair behind her ears, he framed her face in his palms. "I'd like very much to become your lover," he told her softly. "For real, not just pretend."

Earlier, Livvy would have given herself gladly; now she held back. Memories of Brad had underlined her doubts about her shortcomings. Her eyes clouded with indecision as she stared down at his face. It was in his eyes—that he wouldn't force the issue, that he wanted her very much. Her expression cleared with resolve. One more night. Just one more night to garner all her courage.

Bracing herself by her forearms on his bare chest, she asked lightly, "Do you suppose you could find a baby-sitter for Mellie and Bret?"

One of his brows rose a fraction. "Tonight?"

"No, tomorrow night," she said, smiling, reaching up to trace his arched, questioning brow.

The whorls of her ears received his light attentive touch, her earlobes his gentle caress. Jake asked curiously, "What did you have in mind?"

"You once mentioned that you were partial to a good steak."

"That wasn't all I mentioned being partial to," he reminded her very softly, tender amusement back in his eyes.

She ignored the amusement and concentrated on the tenderness. "I owe you dinner. If you'll come to my house tomorrow night, I'll fix you a nice steak."

"Anything else?"

"Salad, baked potato, anything you like."

"You."

She drew a deep breath, found an insouciant smile, and said, "Okay," her voice only slightly husky.

"You mean that? A night alone, just the two of us, starting with steak and ending with you?"

He said it teasingly, but his eyes were dark and smoky, and his voice was slightly thick, and she said, in a similar way, "You got it."

Jake closed his eyes and breathed a heartfelt sigh. "The answer to all my prayers!" he murmured fervently.

When his eyes opened, they were glittering with wicked humor, and Livvy's were clouded a little.

Through a shaky laugh, she said, "I hope you won't be disappointed."

And confidently, not understanding the basis of her fears, he winked and hugged her, saying, "I can guarantee there's no chance of that."

Then his mouth was on hers in the softest, most promising kiss he'd ever given her.

CHAPTER EIGHT

"Seductress, a.k.a. scaredy-cat!" The title and alias came from Livvy on a little huff of self-derision.

For the third time her stiff fingers rummaged through the small wooden box that held her jewelry, and at last found the delicate amethyst earrings she was searching for. She quickly pushed one through her earlobe, snapping the back in place. The other slipped from a grasp that seemed to be all thumbs.

Uttering a mild "Hell's bells!" she dropped down on her knees, running her fingers over the plush pile of the carpet until she found it. Sitting back on her heels, she put it on, then pressed cold fingers hard against her midriff, trying to still the riotous flutterings in her stomach.

Did other women feel giddy and rattled before their lovers came to them the first time? Or was nervousness the exclusive condition of a thirty-two-year-old divorcee whose only past lover was her ex-husband? Her mouth turned down ruefully. "Your *experience* in these matters boggles the brain!" she muttered, emphasizing the word that had offended her the evening before.

A voice echoed out of the past. *Ever heard of sexual liberation, Liv?*—Brad at his most sullen, hostilely attacking what he termed her inhibitions and lack of sexual initiative.

In reality, her mechanical responses on that occasion

had been rooted in the other problems in their marriage. Brad's cheating, his hedonistic approach to life, which forbade any consideration but his pleasure of the moment, had killed her desire for him and her love and respect. Where once she had welcomed his lovemaking with joy, by that time she had simply endured it. Odd, how the mind controls the emotions.

How long ago had that been? At least six years. When Brad learned she was pregnant with Jamie, he turned to his other women exclusively. To Livvy, he turned for reassurance. "You'll love the baby more than me," he had charged, and it had been more than a sullen gripe. It had been a very real fear, based on his need to be number one. Then, too, he had feared lasting physical changes from her pregnancy. The possibility of stretch marks and sagging breasts scared him, and he would look at her stomach as if she nurtured a cancerous growth instead of his child. In panic, he even worried that his own fitness might be impaired somehow by the process of procreation. He began working out in a gym three nights a week, making certain fatherhood didn't betray his lithe, muscular body the way maternity swelled hers.

And the paradox was his pride in Jamie. Or was it a paradox? With the arrival of his son, Brad accepted fatherhood as a miracle of rebirth, one he had performed single-handedly. To Brad, looking at Jamie was like looking into a miraculous time-warped mirror. Physically they were so alike, both blond and blue-eyed and even-featured.

Shaking away the disturbing memories, Livvy got up and walked to the cheval mirror and stared at her reflection. Her long, flowing hostess caftan was a deep violet in color, a shimmery drape in design, its only pattern in the horizontal grain of the cloth. Falling from her shoulders to the floor in one smooth line, it highlighted here, shrouded there, promised one minute and evaded the next. Like herself? She had promised herself tonight and, if possible, would cloak the giving in darkness. The thought of stretch marks had been abhorrent to Brad. The reality of lines scored and crisscrossed into her flesh was what she was offering Jake.

Nervously her fingers fluffed her dark hair over her shoulders. The use of a curling iron had given it soft, full body, and it framed her face like an ebony cloud. The caftan's color made her brown eyes seem darker, her ivory skin more translucent, and she suddenly saw herself as a lovely, desirable woman. She smiled a little, reassured. Jake wanted her, but his desire was a tempered emotion that gave her hope. He had enormous control, usually letting her set the pace of their lovemaking. And tonight she would orchestrate it with special consideration to lighting and mood—a civilized consummation precluding extensive body explorations and unwelcome discoveries. And when Jake left tonight, he would be satisfied. She'd see to it . . . somehow.

"And all that from a woman with butterflies in her stomach!" she muttered, turning away from the mirror and stalking out of the bedroom.

In the kitchen she checked the oven temperature, then placed foil-wrapped potatoes inside. At the refrigerator, she removed washed and prepared salad vegetables, smiling smugly at the steaks marinating in a covered dish. Every adult male enjoyed a good steak, and the way to a man's . . .

Her arms full of plastic-wrapped vegetables, she stood stock-still in the center of the kitchen. No, absolutely not! Syrupy Valentine wishes had no place in her relationship with Jake. What was it Glory had suggested weeks before? A consenting adult relationship that included fun and companionship. She'd concentrate on that. Fun and companionship tossed into a physical liaison. Mixed with a touch of caring, the heavy dressing of love could be eliminated and replaced by the spices of lightness and laughter.

Ruefully she wondered whether she was creating a salad or planning an affair. Making a salad, her prosaic mind told her, sending her to the counter with her armload of vegetables.

"Don't lose your head. Keep it light and easy," she reminded herself aloud, and was answered by the thwack-thwack of George's tail as it hit the tiled floor. Over her shoulder she told the sad-eyed basset hound, "I'm having company tonight, George. Male company, and he's coming for more than dinner. What do you think of that? Think I can handle it with casual panache?"

The dog buried his nose between his front paws, his eyes drooping slowly shut, and Livvy muttered reproachfully, "Thanks for the vote of confidence!"

From the cabinet she took down a bowl for mixing the salad. Then, as an idea struck her, she ran to the living room and inserted a tape into the cassette player. The upbeat sounds of a current rock group floated into the room. She hummed along, her shoulders squared and her eyes bright as she returned to the kitchen, praising her ingenuity. That's the ticket! Mood music, upbeat, happy, carefree!

She was just adding the finishing touches to the salad when the thump of the door knocker announced Jake's arrival. Her knife clattered to the counter top and her humming ended on a little moan of panic. So much for being happy-go-lucky! She quickly rinsed her fingers under the faucet, dried them on a paper towel, and hurried to the living room. Her heart was jerking in her chest like an out-of-sync pendulum.

When she opened the door, a big, friendly smile—one Michelle would have envied—gave her cheerful "Hi! You're early!" more pizzazz. At least, that was her intention.

If Jake saw overbright eyes, or skittishness in her shiver as she shut the door on the cold December night,

183

or a tremble in the fingers taking his coat, he was gentlemanly enough not to comment. Smiling, he reached out to snag her wrist. "Hi, yourself," he drawled softly.

"I'll just put your coat in here," she said, gesturing vaguely toward the living room with the hand he held. She felt his fingers test her nervously beating pulse and wisely twisted her hand from his grasp.

Turning from the pursuit of his eyes, she went to the living room, draping his coat over the back of the sofa. When his hands fell lightly to her shoulders, she jumped about a foot and whirled to face him. Immediately, Jake leaned forward and braced his hands along the back of the sofa. Without touching her, his arms on either side of her provided an effective cage.

His eyes moved from the uncertain flicker of hers to the agitated shimmer of cloth covering her breasts. "Purple's my favorite color," he said.

Aqua's mine, she thought, caught by the warmth glowing in his eyes. She drew a quick, stabilizing breath, caught the neckline of her caftan in her fingertips, and retorted lightly, "I'll have you know, this is wild violet."

"Like I said, wild violet is my favorite color."

Briefly studying the material in her grasp, she mused, "When it catches the light, it's almost amethyst."

Jake nodded solemnly. "My next favorite color, amethyst."

Her tension relaxing under his teasing charm, she laughed and demanded, "Name a color you don't like."

"Any color you're not wearing."

Cocking her head to the side, she said, "Ah, I'm beginning to understand."

Jake winked, his smile approving. "I like a woman who catches on quickly."

Trying to sound lightly flirtatious, Livvy retorted, "You just like women."

All of a sudden his mouth lost its teasing curve and the corners drifted down into a solemn line. He studied her, his gaze moving over her hair, her mouth, her nose, and settling on her wide brown eyes behind the glasses. "Only the ones with soft brown eyes and glasses, wearing purple/wild violet/amethyst," he said quietly.

Feelings rioted through her, and they weren't the light, easy emotions she had promised herself. When he said things like that, it was difficult not to add thoughts of love to the ones of lovemaking. For a moment panic shone out of her eyes, and in that moment Jake's face became a mask, inscrutable, incomprehensible.

"Would you like a drink?" she asked.

"Sure, why not," he said easily, moving his hands from the sofa and dropping them to his sides as he straightened in front of her.

"Wine? Caffeine-free lemon soda? Carrot juice?"

"You're kidding. Carrot juice?"

Livvy nodded, smiling at his startled look.

"I didn't know anyone really drank that stuff. I thought grocers just left it on their shelves to give the stock boys something to dust."

She studied the blue in his eyes and said softly, "And I was certain you drank it by the gallons. How else did you get those beautiful healthy-looking eyes?"

The compliment surprised him, but as he stared at her, catching the teasing twinkle in her eyes, he said slowly, "You better watch yourself. Turning a man's head is like twisting the tiger's tail."

"Dangerous?"

A predatory gleam lit his eyes. "You betcha!"

"I could find myself in a precarious position?" she asked, deliberately injecting wistfulness into her tone, surprising him again. She heard the quick, indrawn breath he took, saw his eyes narrow over her, and smiled at him with beguiling innocence.

His mouth quirked and he said, "You're very brave suddenly. Have you been nipping at the wine?"

"Not a drop," she was able to say honestly, fluttering

her eyelashes and hoping the effect wasn't lost because of her glasses.

It wasn't. Jake moved closer, his eyes amused, brilliantly appreciative, and boldly masculine. "You're not by any chance trying to find out if I'm a tiger, are you, Livvy?"

Stepping slightly to the side, she let her gaze travel down his length. The outline of his tightly muscled buttocks was defined by the snug fit of his dark, beltless slacks. Keeping her eyes on his hips, she said blithely, "I don't see a tail."

Her smugness lasted until Jake turned and she found herself staring at the crotch of his slacks. Three shades of scarlet washed into her face before her eyes flew to Jake's. "You did that on purpose!" she croaked accusingly.

"I assure you it was quite involuntary, Olivia," he said, his thickened tone underlining what her eyes had already noted.

"I meant, you set out to embarrass me," she mumbled uncomfortably, having trouble holding Jake's level stare that reminded her she had started the flirting. She said, "I should put on the steaks."

He stepped closer. "Should you?"

Not deliberately this time, but warily, her eyelashes fluttered down. "The potatoes are almost done and timing is important for a well-prepared steak."

His hands came up and bracketed her face, his thumbs tracing the delicate hollows of her cheekbones. "You're not feeling so brave right now, are you?"

His eyes were laughing wickedly, and she suddenly wanted to hit him. Instead, she obeyed an impulse older than time. She lifted her face the inch or so needed and placed her lips on his. His hands tightened on her face and his whispered "Damn!" held no amusement whatsoever. Hot and moist, his tongue thrust through the token barrier of her lips, his mouth slanting across hers. His kiss was deep and tender, savoring rather than rapacious,

186

and when he drew back, his eyes smoldered in turmoil between gentlemanly intent and male inclination.

"We could skip the steaks," the gentleman suggested huskily. Then the male stated bluntly, "I'd rather have you."

On wobbly legs Livvy backed away from him. Rather breathily she said, "I promised you a steak dinner."

"And a night with you."

"Steak first."

"Coward."

Her soft laughter floated behind her as she turned and led the way to the kitchen. The mood was set midway between light and ardent. Livvy wasn't displeased.

The meal was interspersed with the same ingredients. Livvy chattered lightly about inconsequential matters. Jake smiled agreeably as his aqua eyes burned over her features. Livvy was a gracious hostess, solicitously offering food and wine. Jake was a genial guest, accepting her offerings while his eyes hungered for more.

"How did you leave Mellie and Bret?" she asked when they were halfway through their steaks.

"Excited. They were looking forward to Michelle's spoiling."

"You're not worried they'll miss you tonight?"

Jake shrugged, cutting another bite of steak. "We've come far in the last month or so. I think they trust me enough now to know I'll be back for them."

"Don't be surprised if they're a little cranky when you pick them up tonight. Children do that when they're left with baby-sitters, even ones they like." Noticing his glass was only half full, she reached for the wine to replenish it. Glancing at him questioningly, the wine bottle aloft, she found herself impaled by his intent, brilliant stare.

He said, "I'm not picking them up until tomorrow afternoon at Horizon House. Michelle promised to take them in for me tomorrow morning before coming to work."

A new tension gripped Livvy and a moment passed before she responded slowly, "I see." Suddenly aware that she was still holding up the wine bottle, she thrust it toward him, asking, "More wine?"

Jake inclined his head, his glittering eyes watching the extreme care she used to top his glass and place the wine back on the table. "Anything wrong, Livvy?"

"Not a thing," she lied around a brilliant smile.

Wineglass in hand, Jake leaned back in his chair. His scrutiny was piercing. "You're lying," he said mildly, bringing the glass to his lips.

The tiny movement of her slim shoulders was vague annoyance for his pursuit of the subject. "I'm surprised you want to leave Mellie and Bret overnight," she equivocated, earning one of Jake's twisted half smiles.

"I *want* to be your lover tonight. You know that."

Did he ever beat around the bush? Livvy wondered irritably. She said coolly, "Yes, I know. I just didn't think it would take all night." And felt very foolish indeed when a trace of surprise mingled with the devilment in Jake's eyes.

"Didn't you, Livvy?"

Holding his gaze became impossible. She dropped her eyes to the table, raised her fingers to the distressed pulse at her temple, and spent a moment wondering how an intelligent woman could talk herself into a corner of idiocy. Of course Jake intended to spend the night! Hadn't she already convinced herself he would be an unhurried, controlled lover? He wasn't apt to eat her steak, ravish her body, and hurry on his merry way! The damnable truth was, she hadn't given the time element much thought.

Jake's laughter started as an abrupt guffaw, quickly escalated to hearty chuckling, and was soon reverberating throughout the kitchen. George stirred a little from his position in front of the refrigerator; Livvy squirmed a little in her chair. Through drooping lids the dog eyed the humans censoriously; through narrowed eyes Livvy flashed Jake a look of reproach. When his laughter had subsided, Jake leaned forward and grabbed her hand, squeezing it gently.

Grinning, he said, "You're priceless, Olive. So bold one minute, such a puritan the next."

"And such a source of amusement," Livvy added tartly to his summation, but the beginnings of a grin were pulling up the corners of her mouth. She had, indeed, swung on a par with the cartoon character he dubbed her. She suddenly wondered if he realized how new to such encounters she was. One husband/lover, one marriage, one failure. "I hate to send you into convulsions again, Jake, but this is the first . . ." She gestured vaguely with her free hand and gave a little hic of a laugh. "What I'm trying to say is . . ."

"I know what you're trying to say."

"You do?"

"I do."

He said it with the solemnness of a vow, and Livvy sighed, returning the pressure of his fingers before drawing her hand away. It was a moment before he asked quietly, "Are you worried that tonight will result in pregnancy?"

Her head was bent, her hair falling forward to shield her expression. "No," she said so softly he couldn't have heard. In a stronger voice she said, "No, there's no fear of that."

"You're protected, then?"

Ironclad protection. I don't have the equipment to make babies, she thought bitterly. Aloud she said, "It's taken care of." She couldn't look at him, and again there was silence.

They finished the meal in that same taut silence, and the strain of it brought back several of Livvy's reservations. Like plucked petals from a daisy, her thoughts fell one by one. Could she? Could she not. Would she? Would she not. Should she? Should she not.

When they stood from the table and Jake offered to help with the dishes, Livvy shooed him out of the kitchen, saying, "Go call Michelle and check on Mellie and Bret. Use the phone in the living room."

Jake ran a thumb over her lips, his eyes questioning. "Join me soon?"

She nodded, smiling, and as soon as she was alone almost burst into tears. So far tonight she had made a fool of herself twice, and she was dreading the final confrontation. Would that, too, end in embarrassment? Or humiliation?

With nervous energy she cleaned the kitchen and, once she had expended it, a measure of calm enveloped her. When she snapped off the lights and walked to the living room, she was quietly resolute.

Jake was on the sofa, lounging back with his eyes closed and his hands behind his head. The cuffs of his light blue oxford shirt were unbuttoned and turned back, and he'd taken off his shoes, propping his feet on the coffee table. He looked completely relaxed, maybe asleep, with an upward curve to his wide mouth that suggested his thoughts were pleasant. Or was it his dreams? She stood at the end of the sofa, watching him, and when she moved toward him, her caftan made a silken rustle. Jake's eyes slitted open, blazed over her.

"Come here," he said huskily, his baritone voice low and inviting.

For a brief moment she hesitated, then bent a knee to the sofa. "Are Mellie and Bret all right?" she asked.

He nodded and reached for her, pulling her to a half-reclining position across his lap. "They're fine, but I don't want to talk about them. You promised this night to me, and I'm selfish," he told her, and though his lips curved upward, his eyes were serious.

Then his hands were at the back of her head, pulling

190

her hard to his mouth, and there was no gentleness and no restraint in his kiss. Like a man starved, he took famished possession of her mouth. Behind closed eyelids Livvy saw the end of his waiting, the termination of her indecision, and she pushed her fingers through his burnished curls and held on for dear life. Sounds of frustrated passion came from low in his throat, and he tore his mouth from hers, burying it in the curve of her neck, his deep breaths coming in gusts against her skin.

"*Hell*, pretty woman!" he ground out, raising his head to look at her. "The last twenty-four hours have been the longest in my life."

In an effort to counteract the debilitating tremors running through her, Livvy laughed, a soft, throaty sound that was more than shaky. "They have seemed rather long," she agreed.

Removing her glasses, Jake kept his arm about her as he bent forward and laid them on the coffee table. When he leaned back, one of his hands cupped the side of her neck, the other her shoulder. "I have a confession to make," he said huskily, his lips toying with the tiny amethyst at her earlobe.

"What's that?"

"I hardly tasted that beautiful steak you served me." His mouth moved to hers, taking quick, teasing tastes. "I kept thinking of how you tasted and savored your memory instead."

At the opened neck of his shirt, her fingers caressed his throat. "You did justice to the meal, so I'd have to say you're very polite . . ." she breathed, sighing shakily when he laughed softly and strung ardent kisses from her chin to the base of her jawline.

His hand worked between them, releasing the buttons of his shirt. Drawing her hand down, he pressed it firmly against his bare chest over the thud of his heart. Then he was stroking her side, from thigh to breast, barely touching her while he whispered, "As much as I like this pretty purple thing, I'd rather touch your skin."

Through the silken fabric of her caftan his palm covered one breast, just lying there, neither demanding nor taking, while the mist of their combined breaths thickened the air and their thoughts were shot with a charge of sensual electricity.

Thoughts swiftly became action when Jake abruptly pulled her beneath him, smothering her involuntary cry of surprise with the hungry pressure of his mouth. His teeth nipped at her lips, eliciting a gasp from her, gaining entry for the deep, ravenous plunge of his tongue. His body was rock-hard and tense above her, and his hips moved compellingly against hers. When the silken touch of her fingers edged between them, pulling one side of his shirt free of his slacks, he sucked in a hard, quick breath and jerked slightly, tearing his mouth from hers.

"Livvy." His voice was thick and impelled. "Let's go to the bedroom."

A weak "The sofa . . ." was all she could manage, wanting to tell him it became a queen-size bed, which was more comfortable than the single one in her bedroom.

But he whispered, "No," and kissed her again, driving the thought from her brain. He moved off the sofa, pulling her up beside him, his arms encircling her, his mouth on hers, unrelenting, placing devastating kisses over her face as he backed her out of the living room.

Twice more she tried to speak, no longer sure what she wanted to say. Each time, Jake silenced her with his mouth and it ceased to matter. Whatever she had to tell him could wait.

He kept his arms about her until they reached the bedroom, then he stood back to remove his socks and pull his shirt completely free of his slacks. Then his hands were at the back of her neck, his fingers lifting her hair out of the way.

He drew her zipper down, sliding the caftan off her shoulders. It fell to her waist, where her hands caught and held it. His eyes feasted avidly over her small, pale breasts with their dusky pink centers, and his trembling fingers reached out to take them into his palms.

"I don't think I've ever needed anyone as much as I need you at this moment," he told her, his low, resonant tones, impeding her heartbeat. "Since the night I stood in your bedroom doorway and found you undressed, I've kept the memory of you like this. I knew we'd make love one day."

His hands slid to her waist and gently exerted pressure to bring her to his chest, the soft points of her breasts cushioning into the brown hair beneath his opened shirt. Through the layers of caftan his long fingers grasped her hips, pulling her into the cradle of his thighs. His mouth met hers for a scorching moment, then coasted to the silken hollow of her neck and shoulder on a questing foray that hungered and tasted and appeased.

She arched against him, whispering, "The lights . . . ?"

But he shook his head and said, "Help me undress." His desire-thickened voice slurred the words together.

With but a gentle push of her fingers and his accommodating shrug, the soft oxford shirt slid off his shoulders and arms and drifted to the floor. Her fingers combed through the mass of brown curls that arrowed to his waist, sending quivers of delight racing over his flesh. She felt them and her hands grew more confident. As she worked at the unfamiliar beltless waistband of his slacks, his mouth repeatedly brushed hers, the distracting little kisses making her fingers clumsy. His deftly helped. Mingling with the sound of their impaired breathing were the hiss of his zipper and the whoosh of his pants as they fell to the floor.

Jake moved back, dropping his hands away from her

and kicking out of his slacks. Without the support of his hands, her caftan drifted into a silken puddle at her feet.

Her modest white cotton panties were an odd contrast to his dark, skimpy briefs, and she saw him register the comparison. Glinting and curious, his eyes inspected the lack of frills or lace on her undergarment, and she knew a moment of unease.

She should tell him, now, before they went any further.

Then her eyes drifted over him, down the broad expanse of naked chest, over his flat belly, then lower, and thoughts of confession and explanation fled. His masculinity was boldly detailed by the straining briefs and his blatant need of her suspended her breath and her inhibitions. She took his hands in hers and, backing, led him to the bed while his gleaming, desire-laden eyes held hers prisoner. When her calves met the edge of the bed, she sat down, tugging at his hand to urge him down beside her.

Instead he knelt on the carpet before her, his hands grasping her waist, the stretch of his long fingers reaching to her spine and arching her toward him. His face buried in the satin of her midriff. His mouth pressed hot kisses from her waist to the underside of her breasts, sending shivers of expectation cascading throughout her system. As if compelled, her hands came up to his shoulders, her fingers gliding over smooth skin and bunched sinew, the heat of him sending a fiery current from her fingertips to her spine. She cried out softly when his mouth took one of her breasts and tenderly fed upon it, his tongue savoring, his teeth nibbling. His kneading fingers moved over her back and hips, and when his head oscillated to her other breast, it surged readily to his mouth. Her fingers twined in his chestnut curls to hold him to her.

Again she urged him to the bed, pulling his head up and saying unevenly, "Turn out the lights and come to me, Jake. I don't want to wait any longer."

"Don't you, love?" he asked in a husky, pleased voice.

His eyes ensnared hers, watching her helpless reaction when his fingers surrounded her distended nipples and investigated the moisture left by his mouth. The darkening of her irises, the heavy drooping of her eyelids, brought from his throat a low, exultant sound. But still he made no move to join her on the bed, whispering hoarsely, "We've got all night. There's no need to rush."

But there was a need. One Livvy couldn't completely forget. One that had to do with lighted rooms and unspoken disclosures. "Jake, I—"

With an index finger over her lips he shushed her, whispering, "Just relax and enjoy the loving."

Nothing was happening as she'd planned. She had lost control of the lovemaking—if she'd ever had it—and the moment had progressed beyond the point where she could unemotionally prepare him for the sight of her scarred stomach. She was torn, wanting to explain, wanting to enjoy the loving as he'd suggested. She almost managed to do the latter.

His continuing explorations of her shoulders and breasts and waist were devastatingly sensual, almost mind-destroying. He was drawing pleasure to the fullest, unhurried, unselfish, rendering her insensible. Yet, when his thumbs hooked inside the soft elastic waistband of her panties, edging them down, she lost her love-drugged lethargy and reacted with instinctive recoil. Her hands flew to his, tugging at them desperately, but he was intent on his purpose, his determined fingers easily resisting her frantic efforts.

He murmured thickly, "No, pretty woman, let me. . . ."

His use of the endearment only added to her panic. Her body twisted violently, her shoulder knocking against his and throwing him off-balance. Not expecting such strong resistance, Jake uttered a low, startled growl and sprawled back, his arms flying as he measured his length on the floor.

In horrified slow motion Livvy's knees hit the carpet beside him, her arms wrapped about her middle. Her eyes, wide and distraught, watched as he came up by his elbows, his expression slightly dazed. There was a long hesitation, seconds stretching interminably, while his eyes registered and misread her half-bent, defensive position. Then a blaze of angry contempt looked out of his eyes and he jackknifed to a sitting position, the muscles in his neck and shoulders rigidly strained. His mouth was a hostile line.

"You have the most unusual ways of telling a man no, Livvy, and your timing is lousy," he said roughly.

In conciliation, she said unsteadily, "I'm sorry."

"Are you?" Lowered brows lent a hard edge to the question, and his eyes were merciless, raking her nudity. It wasn't the scrutiny of a lover, and Livvy's hands fluttered up to cover her breasts, her act of modesty producing one of Jake's grimmer half smiles. "Is covering yourself meant to quell my interest or quicken it?" he asked. "I find you intriguingly sexy in your prim underwear and with your hands chastely covering your breasts. I get this powerful urge to strip everything away and find out what's underneath, what goes on in that head of yours."

"Jake, you don't understand. I—"

"Tell me something I will understand," he demanded, skewering her with the fierceness of his gaze. "Did you intend making love with me tonight? Or was it another of your little advance-and-retreat ploys designed to drive me crazy?"

"No!" Then, taking umbrage at his accusations, she protested indignantly, "You know that's not true! I—"

"How?" He aggressively drilled the word at her, interrupting again. "You were married a few years. Tell me how your husband made love to you without undressing you, without touching you below the waist. You go a little berserk each time I try. Did you tease him, let him go so far and then turn him away, the way you do me? Is that why he turned to other women? Why he finally divorced you?"

Her stricken expression wiped the savage contempt from Jake's face, and he slowly came to his knees in front of her. "I'm sorry," he muttered, but she kept herself very still, her eyes a dark wound in her pale, averted face. His hands came up, hovered near her shoulders, then dropped to his sides, clenching into fists. "Livvy, listen to me," he implored quietly. "What I said was lousy and unfair. It was my frustration talking."

Embroiled in a mixture of pain and self-contempt, Livvy scarcely heard him. The bid to gain the joy of his lovemaking without the horror of his knowing had been a foolish, unrealistic, cowardly plan, producing nothing but disappointment and anger and injurious complications. Her tensed muscles went limp and she sagged to a sitting position, drawing her knees to her chest and wrapping her arms about her legs.

"My stomach is scarred, Jake. I didn't want you to see."

The flat, unemotional confession produced nothing but a dumbfounded silence. Livvy shivered, not looking at him. After a moment her peripheral vision saw him move away, and seconds later his shirt was dropped over her shoulders, his hands briefly lingering at her chin as he drew it about her.

Going down on his haunches before her, he asked, "Scarred how?"

She looked at him with a faint smile and said, "Enough that I wear prim underwear and go a little berserk when you try to touch me there."

A frown drew deep lines into his forehead. He said quietly, "I meant, how did it happen."

He looked strong and caring, a little sobered by her disclosure, and Livvy wanted to brush her fingers over his furrowed brow and take the gravity from his eyes. She knew the explanations he deserved, but she knew too how the complete truth would only tear him from her world. She pushed her arms inside the sleeves of his shirt and began buttoning the front.

"Almost two years ago I was in a car accident . . . a bad one. There were injuries that needed sewing up, others requiring emergency surgery." A brief look of anguish flickered in her eyes and her fingers faltered on the middle button of the shirt. What were external scars, really, compared to the tormented tearing of her soul?

"Was your husband with you then?" Jake's voice had gone gruff and deep.

"He wasn't in the accident, but we were still married when it happened." A shaky, slightly twisted smile came to her lips. "Brad never could handle any kind of stress. While I was in the hospital, he flew to Mexico for a divorce. It was just as well. There was no longer anything to keep our marriage together."

The haunting darkness of her eyes made her smile incongruous, and Jake stared at her, his face a contrast of tense angles and compassionate eyes. After a wordless moment he stood and moved away. Without her glasses Livvy couldn't define his movements, seeing only blurs of color and hearing soft sounds. When he came back, standing with his bare feet braced slightly apart on the carpet, she saw that he had donned his slacks. She silently mourned the destruction of an evening that had begun with such hope.

When he spoke, his voice was softly gruff. "Have you changed your mind about letting me stay the night with you?"

Surprised, she looked up at him. "You still want to?"

He extended a hand to help her up, his eyes half amused. "I've never stopped wanting to. I care about you, Livvy, and a few scars aren't going to chase me away." The disturbed flicker in her eyes betrayed her inner fear, obliterating the beginnings of Jake's smile. His fingers tightened around her wrist. Scowling ferociously, he exploded with the impatience he was capable of but seldom showed her. "You've credited me with *his* reactions all along, haven't you? That's why you've been so reluctant to become involved with me! You were expecting me to run from you like *he* did! I don't want perfection, damn it, just trust! You keep your secret fears inside a mouth zipped like a clam when a little honesty about what you're feeling would give me a chance to understand what's going on in your head!"

Bristling under his new attack, she retorted blisteringly, "Clams don't have zippers!" Her voice was an agitated whisper, falling slightly short of the strong feeling she wanted to convey.

Jake's nasty smirk told her what he thought of her brilliant defense. Once she had wrenched out of his grasp and whirled about, Livvy's slender back told him what she thought of having to defend herself.

She knew all about his honesty, and all about the truths she still kept from him. At the moment she was damning both to oblivion. She was sick of his probing, disgusted with the way she had handled the entire evening, and thoroughly chagrined as a result. *Where's your sweet, uncomplicated little affair now, Livvy Waring?*

When his arms wrapped around her from behind, pressing her back against him, she struggled feebly, irritated with him, angry with herself. Holding her firmly, Jake subdued her annoyed shrugs and agitated twists, grunting a little laugh at her flimsy resistance. She stilled and fumed.

In a voice wispy with vexation, she said, "What's your definition of honesty, Jake? Must I give up details of my past to you and tell you my private thoughts in order to be honest?"

His muscles of tempered steel accepted the defensive sharpness of her shoulder blades, and his chest rose as he drew a deep, controlling breath. When he released it, slowly, wisps of her dark hair were blown crazily askew. Bending his head, he laid his cheek alongside hers.

"Okay, I'm pushing and you don't like it," he said huskily, then admitted heavily, "You've a right to your privacy. Just don't let it come between us."

When she remained stiffly unyielding, Jake resorted to subversive tactics. His lips nuzzled against her temple and forehead. Keeping an arm securely about her waist, he raised a hand, combing through her hair and lifting it away from her neck. Warm and tantalizing, his kisses ran over her nape and shoulders. Against her midriff, his fingers became caressing; against her buttocks, his thighs pressed firmly.

"Livvy," he whispered, his voice compelling. "Don't resist me anymore tonight. I want to be with you."

Blood flowed through her veins on a warm, yielding tide. A fine tremor ran her length, the ebb of resistance. "You mean sexually," she said, her bid for cool scorn smothered under her breathlessness.

She felt his smile against her skin, heard the catch of amusement in his voice. "Yes, though making love with you isn't the only way I want to be with you," he said.

Her term had been "sexually." Jake had said "making love with you." The difference annihilated the last of her defensiveness. A smile bloomed slowly across her face, a pleased glow entered her eyes. When his nose nudged her cheek, urging her to turn, she twisted her head, meeting the ardent kiss waiting for her.

"I'd like you to stay," she said in a husky voice.

The heat of his breath dried the moisture of his kiss from her lips as he breathed "Thank you" very gravely. His eyes held a triumphant sparkle.

I'm putty in his hands, she thought in self-disgust. *A caress or two and all anger self-destructs.* Her lips briefly cherished one corner of his wide mouth. "My bed wasn't meant to sleep two, but the sofa in the living room opens out to a queen-size mattress."

200

Jake turned her in his arms, resting his forehead against hers. Around a slow, self-mocking smile, he said, "I think you tried to tell me this when we were in the living room. My mind must have been on other things."

"Mind had little to do with it," she retorted, sweetly jeering, earning his quick hug and approving laugh.

Armed with sheets, pillows, and a blanket, they converted the sofa in the living room into a bed. Livvy gave the blanket a final tuck while Jake stepped back and unzipped his slacks, shedding them with no more self-consciousness than one of Horizon's two-year-olds. When he stripped away his briefs and stood nude, Livvy no longer drew the same parallel. With leanly muscled buttocks and manly contours, he was strongly made, symmetrically perfect, and totally beautiful. He must have felt her admiring stare, because his reaction was swift and very natural, just as it had been earlier in the evening, only then he had been dressed. Her eyes flew to his face.

Through a thick fringe of burnished lashes, his eyes sparked, and she sensed he knew what was going through her head. Though faintly embarrassed for staring, she kept his gaze levelly, going only one shade of pink this time. Without a word Jake moved onto the bed, pulling the sheet to his waist over upraised knees, his wide shoulders propped against the pillows.

Livvy headed for the far side of the bed, stumbling a little as she turned the corner, and hoping Jake would think it was eagerness to bed him that had her tripping over her own feet. Crawling gingerly between the sheets, she arranged them neatly at her waist before folding her hands in her lap. She smiled serene self-assurance.

A moment later she uttered a muffled, high-pitched sound—much like the whine of a distraught pup—and flew out of bed. In a flurry of long, pale legs she darted to the wall switch, dousing the lights. Illumination was confined to the dim glow of a wall lamp just inside the front door. Back in bed, she again meticulously arranged the covers, again half sat with her shoulders on the pillow, again folded her hands in her lap. There was a yard of space between her and Jake, and though she nurtured it valiantly, her confident smile had slipped a notch.

Complete silence reigned for a full two minutes. Then, huskily ironic, Jake said, "Isn't this cozy?"

Dry-mouthed, Livvy muttered, "Yes."

The rustle of movement from his side of the bed sent her glance his way. He had scooted down to lie on his back, his glittering eyes fixed on the ceiling, his mouth twitching. Livvy swung her attention to the knot she was twisting in a fold of the sheet. Drat! So much for cool aplomb!

Quiet, mattress-shaking chuckles started just before Jake reached out and hauled her to his side. Her slender body absorbed his soft laughter, and she found herself smiling—at his contagious humor, at her lack of bedroom panache.

Propped on his elbow beside her, his arm across her waist, he gave her a smile like warm sunshine. "You make me happy," he said.

"Well, heaven knows I *amuse* you," she said in a long-suffering way, but her eyes were sparkling.

"That, too," he agreed, not a bit guilty for laughing. "But you make me feel good inside. I enjoy looking at you, touching you, being with you."

She stared into his eyes, enchanted. His compliments were never lavish, but they were sincerely given and very sweet. They affected her much more readily than being told she was gorgeous or beautiful or exciting. Speaking from the heart, she said huskily, "You're a very nice person, Jake. I've never known any man like you."

In his eyes was the knowledge that she'd never known any man but her husband to compare him with, but he said nothing. Bringing one of her hands to his mouth, he kissed each knuckle, smiling at her.

Livvy wound his chestnut curls around her fingers. Using his term, she asked huskily, "Will you make love with me now?" And watched desire kindle to life in his smiling eyes.

"I was searching for the nerve to broach that very subject," Jake admitted, while his entire body radiated anything but a lack of confidence and his face was etched by lines of bold self-assurance.

His aqua eyes held her brown ones captive as his palm stroked her breasts. Her pulse quickened with tingling excitement when his fingers caressed and coaxed her nipples to aching life. Unfaltering, his gaze went from her face to her breasts to her stomach.

In the need to read each nuance of his reaction, Livvy fleetingly missed the clearer focus of her glasses. She squinted and peered and saw nothing in his face but the tenderness of a lover. He laid his hand flat on her stomach, absorbing the tremors of her flesh with his palm and fingertips before tracing individual lines and gently grasping her hipbone. Then the entirety of her slender length came under his heated inspection. A muscle rippled in his jaw, and his eyes coming back to hers were starkly passionate, evoking sensual stirrings in her blood.

"You worried about the wrong things with the wrong man," he told her, and his low voice was vibrating with a need to convince her of his feelings. "Your body houses you, Livvy, and you're what I want. I find you very lovely."

Tears sprang to her eyes, and she wiped them away with the back of her hand, smiling shakily and whispering, "Oh, Jake."

He kissed her deeply then, while his hands roamed her body in tender, seeking caresses. Lost in the pleasure of his recent words, Livvy received his kiss, his touch, through a warm, peaceful glow. When his mouth moved down the arch of her throat, an unexpected sigh escaped her. Jake laughed softly at the velvet cleft of her breasts.

Her eyes opened, her limited vision encompassing two

broad shoulders and a downbent head burnished with thick curls. His mouth moved onto her breasts, kissing them with teasing slowness, cherishing them with moist applications of his lips and tongue. His knee nudged between hers, and their legs tangled. The friction of his crisp body hair was a delight to her naked legs, but this time it was Jake who sighed, in husky gratification.

Bracing his hands on either side of her shoulders, he looked down at her. "You feel good," he said in a raspy whisper.

"So do you," she whispered back.

Her arms came up and locked about his neck. Using that leverage, she pulled herself up and against him, her breasts teasing into the hair on his chest. Her tongue lightly traced his lips, entered his mouth to explore the warmth and taste of him, her tender ardor evoking his soft groan of pleasure.

At what point Jake took control of the kiss, she couldn't have said. She only knew his burning lips, his mouth hungering for the full taste of hers, and beneath the fiery, ravenous onslaught her head fell back and she felt feverish. Her arms clung and his trembled, and they drifted slowly back to the bed.

His hand smoothed down her lithe body and glided to her inner thighs. His intimate caress was bold in its execution, gentle in his regard for her. Beneath his touch she trembled, heat shuddering through her veins, and he smiled, as if the giving of pleasure was the source of his own.

Heightened needs drove her hands to his chest. Her fingers curled into brown hair, stroked lovingly down to his flat belly. She watched the glow of his gaze became a blaze as her touch grew more confident, and when her fingers closed around him, his eyes clenched tightly shut and his body tautened in every muscle.

Murmuring thick, urgent words of need and desire, he moved above her, pressing his length to hers. The heat of him branded her from shoulder to toes, the spurring need in him burned into her soft belly, creating a corresponding fire in the center of her being. Hungrily his mouth moved upon hers, his kiss fierce as his knees urged hers to part.

"Jake . . ." she whispered; and again "Jake . . ."

Sliding his hands beneath her hips, he raised her gently, slowly. Both caught their breath in rapt anticipation. And incredibly, through the dim shadows surrounding the bed, she saw the smile commingling with the desire in his expression, and she surged joyously upward, welcoming his possession.

His hoarse gasp, her soft moan, uttered their pleasure in the union, then guiding hands and soft murmurs became a language each understood. Her senses swam deliriously as he set a slow drive toward rapture, his body hot, his cadence strong, his movement stroking her to the edge of fulfillment. He was both the perimeter and the center of her universe, and she strained to him, meeting his ardor, matching it.

His breathing was harsh and ragged, and when he felt the first tightening convulsion of her body, he thickly whispered her name. Impassioned kisses burned her brow and temple and he breathed, low and feverishly, "I love you, Livvy, I love you," over and over again.

She heard and yet she didn't hear; it was all part of the unthinking, unreasoning ecstasy of the moment. Her world catapulted, rocketing upward on an explosion of riotous sensation, her soft cry calling out to him. His final surge was a racking shudder as he fell with her, his arms crushing her close.

They were enveloped in the peaceful aura of exquisite inertia, and it was long moments before Jake raised himself by his forearms and pushed the dampened wisps of ebony silk off her face. Through the deep shadows she squinted to see the contentment in his eyes, the quiet joy, the tender laughter.

He murmured softly, "Yum-yum."

Her quick, surprised laugh made his eyes crinkle at the corners. "Yum-yum?" she repeated, laying her hand along his jaw, her fingers caressing.

Turning his head, he placed a hard kiss in her palm and nodded once, emphatically. "Diet cheesecake is the tastiest, most fulfilling dish this man has ever known."

Her brown eyes went liquid with pleasure, though she tried to look stern. "You're a tease," she accused.

Laughing softly, he untangled himself from her. He drew her to his side, tucking her head on his arm, her back to his stomach, and pulled the covers around them.

Drowsiness soon followed contentment, and there was but one uneasy moment for Livvy. Jake's words spoken in the height of passion came back to her and she struggled with the voice of reality. *It couldn't happen.* By his own admission Jake was a family man. He loved his niece and nephew, wanted children of his own. What had she to offer?

The last thing she heard before sleep overcame her was so prosaic it was reassuring. It brought a smile to her lips.

With his voice slurred with sleepiness, Jake murmured, "Livvy, I'm lousy in the mornings without coffee. If I grumble, just ignore me."

CHAPTER NINE

The morning after. Livvy found the phrase as heady as any intoxicating elixir, her senses burgeoning with happiness. Completely dressed in navy wool skirt and loosely ribbed cream sweater, she sat in a chair facing the sofa bed, her stockinged feet curled under her. A steaming mug of coffee was in her hands, and her eyes were aglow. It was barely 6:00 A.M. and she was watching her lover come slowly out of the depths of slumber.

As she knew, Jake's natural body heat was somewhere near toasty. Insulation in The Little Yellow House was minimal, the room slightly cool, yet he slept with the sheet drawn barely to his waist. Sometime during the night he had kicked the blanket to her side of the bed, one long, bare foot escaping even the sheet. Lying on his back, a sinewy arm thrown across the upper half of his face in defense of the lamp she'd turned on just moments before, he drew the first wakening breath deep into his lungs. His bare chest expanded. His nose twitched, catching the scent of the coffee, and he mumbled something incomprehensible, barely moving his lips. With a lithe stretch his back arched and his hand searched toward the far side of the bed. He found nothing but cool, rumpled sheets. With startling suddenness, he jackknifed to a sitting position, every muscle in his body tensed. Open and alert, his eyes darted about the room; found her.

His taut shoulder and neck muscles slowly unbunched, and his chest moved, releasing a held-in breath. The tense lines on either side of his mouth disappeared. Alarm left his aqua eyes; they became warm and glowing, staring straight into hers.

"Good morning," she said, a buoyant catch in her voice. She was enchanted by the multitude of emotions his eyes could express.

Jake mumbled something that might have been a return greeting, but his deep voice was gruff with sleep, and Livvy heard only a low rumble of sound. She smiled, liking his sleepy uttering.

For a moment nothing else was said. Faint color washed into her cheeks when his eyes became heavy-lidded and sensual, traveling over her slim, huddled form and lingering here and there.

Lifting the cup and saucer for his inspection, she said, "I brought you coffee." The words came out husky and uneven, and she cleared her throat. "It's not decaffeinated. It's the real stuff. I went to the store for it while you were sleeping." An inner alarm had wakened her at five o'clock. She had showered and dressed, then driven to an all-night grocery store, smiling and humming all the way. "You sleep like a log. You never stirred when I left or when I came back. I had to turn on the lamp to waken you." Still, Jake said nothing, and her mouth curved into a quirking smile as she added, "Mellie was right, you do snore. The coffee is to ensure you don't grumble as well."

No answering amusement came to his face. It was as if he hadn't heard her. He leaned back, propping his shoulders against the sofa back and cupping his hands behind his head. His eyes were slumberous and lazy, and he studied her with a leisurely thoroughness. His pure male sensuality sent a tremor of response curling through Livvy's midsection. Although his smiles and his teasing were the things she liked best about him, she found herself seduced by this new graphic silence.

Smiling, a trifle breathless, she said, "Do you want it?"

A slight inclination of his head expressed his agreement. Or was it invitation? Livvy uncurled her long legs and stood, stepping the short distance to the bed while Jake's eyes burned over her smiling face. He took the cup and saucer from her hand and drank deeply. A heavy lassitude kept her unmoving, yet she felt energized by the torrid vigor of his gaze. How he kept from blistering his tongue with the hot coffee, she didn't know, but the cup was soon empty and he was leaning over the edge of the bed to set it on the floor by her feet. As he straightened, his hands caught the backs of her knees, jerking her toward him.

In surprise she yelped, "Jake!" her hands flying to his wide shoulders to prevent a headlong topple onto the bed.

With a strength born of purpose, he lifted her, her knees touching the bed beside his hips as he buried his face in her midsection. His breath was hot, scorching her flesh through the knit of her sweater. His hands were bold, stroking the backs of her thighs beneath her skirt to knead her buttocks.

Twining his sleep-tousled chestnut curls around her fingers, she again said, "Jake . . ." her voice breathy and slightly laced with humor. Then another "Jake!" came out on a note of alarm. Her body was suddenly in a dizzying leap.

Guided by his hands on her hips, she tumbled over him, laughing, panting a little as she landed on her back beside him. With a lithe twist Jake freed himself of the sheet and sprawled his thigh heavily across hers. His nudity while she was fully dressed should have seemed out of place. It wasn't.

Her eyes went down their lengths, admiring his hard male symmetry—the wide chest and flat belly and manly thighs, the brown hair that arrowed to a certain point and then spread again less thickly, the flow and taper and elongation of muscle, the tint of bronze and fade of tan. She heard his breath quicken and her eyes went back to his face.

Her smile was siren-soft, her expression deliciously wicked. Teasing laughter threaded her voice as she chided, "I've compromised my principles this morning, buying a whole pound of caffeinated coffee and brewing it in the same pot that was virgin-free of caffeine until this morning. I thought the least I would get in return was a simple 'good morning.' I even entertained ideas of indulging in a little conversation before we go to work." Behind her glasses, her lashes were a provocative sweep through which her eyes sparkled invitingly. "I'm a morning person. I wake up alert and ready to tackle the day. I enjoy communicating with someone else. Ask George."

With a low groan his mouth fell to hers, hot and hungry. He tasted of warm, sweetened coffee and impatient male demand, and Livvy savored both flavors, blending them with her own rising need, her arms wrapped about his shoulders. With fumbling urgency his hands worked at her clothes. With steadier and more careful fingers, she helped him strip them away. Almost frenzied, his hands and mouth ran over the parts of her as they were revealed, tasting, ravishing, instilling a similar delirium in her. Remembering the delicious rapture of his controlled lovemaking of the night before, she tried to slow him down, drawing his mouth to hers again and again, seeking soft kisses that became deep, hasty tastes when his seeking mouth roamed elsewhere. Too soon, it seemed, he rolled above her, his rock-hard thighs wedging between the pliant yielding of hers.

Somehow she was still smiling, although her breath rattled in short spurts from her lungs and her voice was a husky whisper. "If you don't speak to me soon, Jake, I'll think you're not a morning person like myself."

Without a word, he surged deep within her, the power that merged them communicating a message Livvy understood perfectly. His breath was like a cyclone in her ear as his mouth ravished her neck and throat. His movements whirled them both into the eye of the storm. He was utterly lost in her, she in him, and they swirled together through a mist where no words were needed.

She lay enervated, totally spent, beneath the repleted weight of his body. He raised his head from the curve of her neck and looked down at her through eyes still glazed with the residue of passion.

His voice was dark and low when he finally spoke. "We're both morning persons," he said. "I don't think I've ever been so eloquent this early in the day."

Her glasses were somewhere in the midst of her discarded clothing, but she squinted up at him and noted the corners of his eyes crinkling with laughter. It was then she experienced another swift, devastating high, not unlike the ecstasy her body had just known. Only this time it was her heart and soul that soared upward. Laughing delightedly, she threw her arms about his neck and covered his smiling face with wet, soppy kisses.

Two days before Christmas she was still floating on the same high. Her world was full. In her entire life she had never been the recipient of so much fun and laughter and passion as Jake gifted her with unstintingly. She spent all her free time with the Masters family and all her thoughts on Jake.

It was inevitable that Glory would notice the change and comment on it. She cornered Livvy in the storeroom one afternoon while Horizon's children were napping under the watchful supervision of Jenny and Lillian. Livvy was singing a soft, off-key version of a Christmas carol as she took stock of the cleaning supplies. Between phrases, a grin kept trying to break through. Jake had left just minutes before, after joining Horizon's group for lunch.

"You have a lot of holiday spirit," Glory remarked.

" 'Tis the season to be jolly," Livvy quipped gaily, counting the packages of paper towels and adding them to her list of supplies needed.

"There seems to be an outbreak of good cheer," Glory said drolly. "Jake was grinning like he'd been into the eggnog when he left a few minutes ago."

The color of poinsettia bloomed into Livvy's cheeks. "Do you approve?" she asked, smiling.

"Wholeheartedly," her friend agreed instantly, but her return smile had a quality of reserve about it. She hesitated before asking quietly, "Have you told him everything?"

A dousing with cold water couldn't have drowned Livvy's warm mood more effectively. But her smile wavered only momentarily, and she played dumb. "About what?" she asked, pretending a great absorption in how neatly she aligned bottles of disinfectant cleaner beside containers of liquid hand soap.

A multitude of expressions crossed Glory's face—the ones a mother bestows on a beloved child who has seriously erred. Exasperation, disappointment, chastisement, love. "You're making a mistake," she said finally.

No longer pretending not to understand, Livvy retorted, "I don't think it's a mistake." Her chin jutted out as she took stock of the supply of toilet paper.

"You're afraid to tell him, aren't you?"

Clever Glory, cutting straight to the core of the matter. "He knows about the accident and Brad," Livvy said evasively.

"But not about Jamie and not about your being unable to have children," Glory guessed all too easily, a worried frown puckering her forehead.

"Why go into those things with Jake?" Livvy asked stubbornly. "They have nothing to do with our relationship." Her chin angled higher, then dropped a little when Glory sighed and gently shook her blond head. Livvy managed a light laugh. "Glory, you're a worrier. Jake's happy; I'm happy. Why spoil the present with things better left in the past?"

"As long as the past doesn't mess up the present, you're doing fine. But what about the future?" Glory said, a spark of challenge in her gaze. "Do you know what Jake told me once? He was watching you one evening as you got his children ready to leave. You were laughing at something Mellie said and had your arm around Bret and your face was lit up like a Christmas tree. Jake turned to me and remarked that children were certainly a novel way to seduce a woman. Then he grinned rakishly and boldly confided that he liked being able to tempt a woman with something she wanted and had never had. And I just stood there like an idiot, my mouth gaping open, knowing you hadn't told him."

Livvy looked away, biting her lip. "You're reading too much into what he said. Jake's a tease and, of course, he's glad I like his niece and nephew. We spend a lot of our time with them. It would be awkward if I didn't enjoy being with them." Her words were logical, her tone convincing, yet it all felt like weak rationalization under Glory's level blue-eyed stare.

"Men don't go around wanting to offer a woman their children unless they've been thinking of how the two together would enrich their lives," Glory said. "And I don't believe Jake was referring only to his niece and nephew when he spoke of children."

"Now you're romanticizing!" Livvy said sharply. The pain that accompanied thoughts of Jake's future children was a fierce reminder of her own limitations. "Jake and I like each other and enjoy being together, but that's as far as it goes. We have fun and companionship and a certain affection for each other. A couple of months ago you were advising just such an arrangement for me. You said I needed to find a man I could enjoy being with. Well, I did, and I'm not going to ruin what we have with hurtful memories and unpleasant confessions."

"You're in love with him. That love deserves your honesty."

Livvy's fingers gripped the edge of a shelf so tightly they hurt. She couldn't deny it, but she made a bid for a smile, appealing to her friend. "Glory, don't do this to me. For heaven's sake, smile for my happiness, don't chide me for keeping private matters private."

"Oh, Livvy, I'm sorry," Glory exclaimed softly with instant remorse. She slipped her arm around her friend's slender waist and used the fingers of her other hand to push up the corners of her own mouth already stretching into a grin. "See this? This is definitely a smile—on the biggest mouth in town." When she moved back, her expression was that of a contrite pixie. "Forgive me for raining on your parade. That wasn't my intention."

Knowing her friend's motive had been concern, Livvy smiled at her, admitting, "I was being overly sensitive. This thing with Jake is very new. I'm not ready to test it too rigorously. Maybe someday I'll tell him everything, but not now."

After Glory left the storeroom, Livvy leaned her forehead against one of the shelves. A tired, uncertain sigh escaped her. Why must the past creep in and cloud something as new and bright and perfect as her affair with Jake? She wouldn't let it. She couldn't. Not as long as Jake enjoyed being with her, not as long as her world was colored by laughter and teasing and the gentle regard of a loving man.

She spent Christmas Eve with the Masters family, dining on turkey and dressing, and helping the bright-eyed Mellie and Bret hang their stockings. Later, when the two were in bed dreaming fitfully of elves and reindeer and chimneys, she helped Jake fill their stockings with fruit and nuts. Together they laid out Santa's surprises beneath the Christmas tree, whispering and laughing in low tones, like conspirators, as they imagined the reaction the next morning. There was only one shaky moment in the entire evening. Jake didn't want her to leave. As always when he suggested she stay overnight with him, she declined. Kissing the scowl from his face and the argument from his mouth, she promised to return the next afternoon.

Driving home that night, she felt the pain rip through her. Waking by Jake's side on Christmas morning, witnessing Mellie's and Bret's excitement when they discovered what Santa had left them—those things smacked too much of "family" and to her were the equivalent of chasing rainbows. And her sense of propriety would not allow her to sleep with Jake under the same roof as Mellie and Bret. She was having an affair with Jake, not indulging ideas of permanence. He valued family ties and loving homes. What had she to offer a man who so obviously deserved children of his own and a caring woman to give them to him?

On Christmas Day her face was wreathed by pleasure and laughter as Mellie and Bret enthusiastically showed her their cache of gifts. Her happiness took on a new dimension when she unwrapped Jake's gift to her. The beautiful little locket on a fragile gold chain was inscribed *To Olive* on the back and held miniature snapshots of Mellie and Bret. Reading the accompanying card, she was touched to tears, delighted to smiles.

I took the liberty of putting my little Swee' Peas inside, he had written.

There was a wealth of satisfaction in Jake's expression as he witnessed her pleasure with his gift. Yet the next day when he mentioned her upcoming birthday, she quickly forestalled any elaborate planning, and his lingering satisfaction became glowering frustration. Her insistence that the only birthday gift she would accept was the pleasure of having him and his children spend the day

215

with her drew his brows together in impatience and made his jaw bulge with irritation. Again she soothed away his bad mood with the warm offering of her mouth.

The weather was abominable the Sunday of her birthday, cold and misty, and they stayed indoors at The Little Yellow House, lazing about and playing games with the children. Livvy's laughter came often throughout the day, soft and content and spontaneous. Jake gave her the gift of his teasing and affection. As the afternoon wore on, the children were encouraged to nap on Livvy's bed by Jake's promise of ice cream before bedtime.

Walking back to the living room after tucking them in, Livvy said, "Would you like some coffee?"

Before she could detour to the kitchen, Jake had her in his arms near the window overlooking the front yard. "I'd rather have a birthday wish," he said.

"I thought birthday wishes were for the person having the birthday," she murmured, teasing his wide mouth with soft, tickling strokes of her fingertip, knowing by the sparkle in his eyes that she was going to enjoy his wish.

His teeth nipped her finger as he reminded her, "So are presents, but this is a birthday without presents. Why not break tradition further by having wishes for the well-wisher?"

A quick smile touched Livvy's mouth. He was still irritated. She kissed the cleft in his chin. "What wish did you have in mind?"

His eyes cut briefly to the sofa. "I wish Michelle and Mac weren't busy so they could baby-sit, and the sofa was made up, and we were lying there together, and—"

"Wait!" she exclaimed, laughing. "That's already three wishes!"

"And you were under me and I was inside you and we were making love," he finished as if she hadn't spoken, his deep voice compellingly low and slightly thick.

His explicit wishes jerked her heart to her throat, sent blood pounding through her veins, and made her eyes huge circles that eclipsed her face. Color washed into her cheeks, and she croaked weakly, "Jake . . . !"

His eyes glinted laughingly into hers. "Was that reproach or encouragement?"

Livvy wasn't sure. Jake helped her decide. Holding her closer to his lean, sinewy frame, his body betraying his wishes, he kissed her deeply. Several times. Against her neck, in a half-humorous, half-passionate murmur, he said, "For two weeks I've been making beautiful love with a woman my own age, and I've got to confess that making love with an older woman sounds so damned intriguing, it's driving me crazy." Pushing her glasses to the top of her head, he began distributing hot kisses over her laughing features. Livvy had finally decided to encourage rather than reproach. At the corner of her mouth he said huskily, "I keep thinking of the vast experience a woman your age could bring to my bed."

With her arms wrapped loosely around his lean waist, she let her head fall back on her neck and smiled at him mischievously. "So much maturity would probably . . ." Her voice broke. His hands were under her sweater, holding her breasts. Weak and breathy, she continued stoically, "Probably be too much for a younger man to handle."

His palms tested the weight of her breasts. "Not too much. There's barely a handful between these two, and I can hack that." His smile was smug.

"Oh!" She pretended outrage, grabbing his hands and trying to prise them away. "If you don't like my apples, don't—"

"Apples?" Jake hooted softly, spoiling her outrage. Wicked laughter was in his eyes, tenderness in his hands. "Pretty woman, apples these ain't! Little plums maybe," he said consideringly after he'd investigated their shape and size more thoroughly and watched the helpless darkening of her eyes. "Perfect little plums, ripe and firm and sweet and delicious."

His mouth met hers for another mind-destroying moment, and his hands moved to her spine, one between her shoulder blades and the other low on the small of her back, holding her tight, making the kiss a meeting of thighs and hips and breasts and mouths.

When his head lifted slowly, hers dropped to his shoulder. She felt his chin rest on her bent head, felt the slow regulation of their breathing, the gradual ebb of their thundering heartbeats. Then his chin moved slightly as he shifted his gaze to the window.

"Someone's here," he said quietly. "Were you expecting anyone?"

Livvy's head came up and she squinted out the window at the car approaching her driveway. "No," she answered, standing still while Jake lowered her glasses to her nose. She looked more closely. The car came to a halt behind the Datsun, its driver getting out. His thick blond hair and the confident angle of his head identified him easily.

"Oh, no!" she whispered in dismay, and the gentle pressure of Jake's fingers along her jaw brought her distressed eyes to his.

"Who is it?" he asked, trying to read the answer in the pale oval of her face.

"It's Brad!" With her lower lip crushed between her teeth, she stared at Jake, then whispered a distraught "He knows I don't want to see him. I don't understand why he's here."

"Shall I get rid of him?" Jake asked, his caressing finger running lightly across her bottom lip, persuading her teeth to let go.

Despite his gentle touch, his eyes glinted something hard and cold, and she knew he would like nothing better than to send Brad on his way before he ever cleared the door. In that instant Livvy composed herself. The last thing she wanted was a confrontation between Jake and

218

Brad. When he dropped his arms, she said quietly, "No, I'll do it. It would be better if I saw him alone."

Jake hesitated, his eyes reluctant and faintly questioning. Then slowly he walked to the kitchen, shutting the door behind him. Livvy opened the front door on Brad's first knock.

Although Brad squared his shoulders and took a moment to straighten the collar of his overcoat against the cold December mist, he spoke confidently, "Hi, baby. Surprised to see me?"

"What are you doing here, Brad?" she asked, keeping her voice low and under tight control. One of her hands braced against the doorframe, the other on the doorknob, her stance meant to discourage him from entering the house.

Undaunted by the chill of her welcome, Brad leaned forward and smiled cajolingly into her eyes. "Visiting you, Liv. I decided it was time I saw for myself if you were all right. You look great, by the way, healthier than I expected and very beautiful still." He studied her, then his hands came up as if to touch her. Livvy stepped back as quickly as she could, and he took advantage of the opportunity to move inside the house, closing the door behind him.

"What do you want?" she asked.

Instead of answering, he asked a question of his own. "When did you get the little Datsun?"

Ignoring that, she said, "You can't stay."

"Come on, Liv, that's no way to talk. I'm your husband."

"Not any longer." She said it without inflection, neither angry nor hurt. Her only emotions were slight amazement that she had lived with this stranger for so many years and a vague wariness that he might cause a scene.

He extended a hand in supplication. "Look, I know you're still hurt because I left you, but—"

"Hurt?" Her face grew rigid with amused contempt. "I was hurt almost two years ago, but not by you."

He understood her reference to the death of their son. She watched his handsome face fall into defensive lines before he said, "I suffered the same loss, Liv. You don't know how I felt."

"That's true. You didn't stay around for me to find out."

"Listen, let me explain—"

"It's too late for explanations, Brad. We're divorced. It's over."

"It doesn't have to be over, Liv. Don't you see? I acted hastily before, without thinking it through, but I started realizing recently that now we could have a better marriage. It would be just the two of us again. Before, you were never satisfied with just me, but the way you are now, no outside interferences would come between us."

Livvy stared at him in disgust. Outside interferences? His son? The possibility of any children at all? "I want you to leave, Brad. We have nothing to talk about."

The cold finality of her tone triggered his anger. Reaching out, he tried to slip his fingers about her arm, but she lithely twisted away, evading him. He scowled and said accusingly, "It's that other man you're seeing, isn't it? He's why you won't listen to me."

Smiling grimly and keeping her voice low and contemptuous, she said, *"You're* why."

Overlooking the insult, Brad suddenly smiled and said confidently, "We were together a long time, and you never left me, baby. You still belong to me. Whoever this other man is, your future's not with him."

The truth of that hurt more than Brad would ever know. "Perhaps not," she said coolly. "But not because I belong with you. If you think I have any feelings left for you, Brad, you're wrong."

He grabbed for her again, this time catching her arm before she could move out of his reach. "Damn it, be reasonable! You knew I'd come back for you!" he said angrily, his sullen eyes boring into her utterly fed-up ones before his gaze suddenly shifted.

Livvy saw surprise mingle with the anger in his expression, and followed the direction of his gaze. Jake leaned quietly against the kitchen doorframe, his thumbs hooked through the belt loops of his jeans, his expression grim. A flexing muscle in his jaw betrayed the tight rein he held on his anger. He neither moved nor spoke, and his very stillness threw out threatening vibrations. Livvy felt them, realized Brad felt them, too, when his fingers tightened on her arm.

"Who are you?" Brad demanded belligerently.

"The man who's advising you to let her go," Jake answered quietly around a wide smile, and Livvy felt her stomach begin to churn.

She knew Brad well enough to remember that he never tossed out or accepted physical challenges. He was a good two inches taller than Jake, and his body was lean and muscular, but he wouldn't risk bruising it. It wasn't his style. He preferred the safer and deadlier combat of words. She felt the fingers on her arm relax, then slowly fall away.

"Please leave, Brad," she said stiffly, her nerves corralled inside a rickety fence of control. She had too much at stake, and Brad could ruin it all with a careless word, a negligent disclosure.

Answering Livvy, Brad kept his eyes on Jake. "You were never rude, baby. Introduce me to your friend and tell him who I am. Tell him how much of a past we share."

"He knows who you are," Livvy said, hoping to forestall any revelations about the past. She added flatly, "And we never shared anything, Brad."

Brad opened his mouth to speak, but whatever he would have said was lost in the commotion of Mellie and Bret's entrance. Bright-eyed and rosy from their naps, the two tumbled into the room, slowing their headlong dash when they caught sight of the stranger with their uncle and Livvy.

Livvy watched Brad's gaze skim dismissingly over Mellie then narrow on Bret; watched the momentary shock before his lips curled into a nasty smile. Her heart thudded painfully and she wrapped her arms about her chest, instinctively protecting herself from the inevitable blows.

"Whose kids? His?" Brad sneered, jerking his head toward Jake. He laughed unpleasantly. "You haven't changed a bit, Liv. There's still only one thing you're interested in. Does this sucker know you're using him?"

Antagonism flashed from Jake's eyes before he knelt down beside his children. In low, quiet tones he instructed them to go to the kitchen and play with George, reminding them the dog was old and couldn't withstand anything too energetic.

Very seriously they promised to be careful. Mellie's "George doesn't care if we sit on him if we don't jump up and down and pull his ears, Uncle Jake" was echoed by Bret's thumb-muffled "Won't pull his ears, Uncle Jake."

Waiting until he closed the door behind them to come to his feet, Jake skewered Brad with a hard-eyed glare. "You'd better leave, Waring, before I'm forced to throw you out," he advised grimly.

There was a tense moment while Brad made eye contact with Livvy, seeing something in hers that brought a malicious glitter to his. Then he shrugged and moved toward the door. With his hand on the doorknob, he turned to look at Jake standing slightly in front of Livvy now, his lean body a barrier between her and trouble.

"Ask her," Brad advised quietly. "Ask her what really broke up our marriage. Ask her what she always wanted more than me, more than the good times, more than anything I could give her."

222

"You've said enough," Jake said warningly, his stance tensing.

"All right, buddy, it's your life." Brad shrugged in resignation. But he wasn't through, not by a long shot. Opening the door and turning his collar up against the cold mist, he directed one more glance to Livvy, laughing softly when she involuntarily winced. Then, very quietly, he told Jake, "If you want to mess up your future by tying it to hers, that's your business. But you'd better ask yourself if you can settle for being second best, because that's all you'll ever be with her. Second best. I should know. I tried for eight years before I accidentally stumbled onto the one thing she wanted above all else. Ask her how much that boy of yours looks like a ghost from the past. Ask her about Jamie."

Jake didn't give the game away. His facial expression didn't change except for a faint narrowing of his eyes. It was Livvy—going pale and breathing shallowly, the anguish in her eyes unmistakable—who handed Brad his final victory. His soft, stinging laughter cruelly speeded her heart to her toes. He was exacting revenge for her rejection of him. Oh, yes, Brad fought with words, and he fought dirty.

Around a mouth curled in triumph, Brad said softly, "Look at her. It's written all over her face. She's using you, like she used me."

The door closed behind him with a subdued click that was as stingingly soft as the deadly cruelty of Brad's laugh and voice and words. Livvy's heart echoed the sound, thudding a painful beat. Jake was staring at her, noting her pallor, the shock of her expression, the truth mirrored in her eyes.

"You have something to tell me," he said. Not a muscle in his body moved, and the hard, flat inflection of his voice made the statement a demand.

"Yes," she whispered, her hand at her throat.

"What he said was true, then?" His face was unread-

223

able, his eyes dark and opaque. A furious pulse beat at his temple.

They were standing only a yard apart, but Livvy felt a chasm opening between them, widening so rapidly she doubted her ability to breach the gap. She swallowed and said ineptly, "Brad was trying to hurt me."

"That doesn't answer the question!" Jake rapped out, and she saw the deep, frightening anger in his eyes and turned away, going to the back of the sofa.

Her fingers dug into the plush cushions as she searched her distraught mind for a simple explanation for a complicated situation. "Brad . . . never wanted children," she began jerkily. "I did. You heard him. My pregnancy was unplanned, but . . ." Her words faltered. *But it was the best thing that ever happened to me. But it produced Jamie, without whom I would have been totally empty.*

"Go on!" came the low, implacable command from behind her.

Very softly she said, "Jamie . . . my son . . . was a very beautiful child, sweet and intelligent and dear. I loved him with all my heart."

"Your son died."

His cold words held no sympathy, only bleak acknowledgment, and Livvy closed her eyes, wondering if the fabric of their relationship was torn beyond repair. The man speaking to her now was a hard, forbidding stranger. She said painfully, "Jamie died almost two years ago . . . in the car accident I told you about."

"But you failed to mention a son, didn't you, Livvy?"

Her head bowed a little under his harsh censure, and she whispered, "It's difficult to talk about his death."

"You find it difficult to talk to me about many things. Your accident. Your marriage. Your child. Your husband. Did he divorce you because you kept so much of yourself from him too? Second best, I believe he said." Jake's voice was grim and condemning, then laced with scornful amusement when he muttered, "And obviously no hope of moving to the winning position."

Swiveling her head, she looked at him. For a moment she watched the muscles working in his jaw as he ground his teeth together, the utter contempt on his face, and she inwardly quailed. Then her slender neck stretched, her chin going up. "You listened to Brad. Won't you listen to me now?" she asked, her voice a low plea.

Jake drew a quick, hard breath and his lips curled a little. "Let's hear the part about your son looking like Bret."

His cynical invitation ignored the entreaty in her eyes, sending her gaze away from him. Her chest ached and her throat felt raw. She admitted thickly, "They could have been twins."

"Where's a picture of him? I've been in this house many times, in every room, and I've yet to see a picture of this child you loved with all your heart."

The grating mockery in his voice didn't doubt her love for Jamie; it accused her of duplicity. Knowing she was condemning herself further, she went to the commode table at one end of the sofa and opened a drawer. Removing the framed photograph, she carried it to Jake. He took it, inspecting it with cold, expressionless eyes, his mouth twisting bitterly as he handed it back to her. Almost protectively she clutched it to her chest, earning his look of disgust.

"Obviously you didn't intend for me to know," he gritted out. "Were you hoping to replace that child"—like a rapier, his eyes flicked to the framed picture she held—"with mine? Was that the plan? Go through me to get Bret? What were you hoping for? A quick marriage and then later custody of Bret?"

Impatient with the ridiculous details he supplied as her "plan," Livvy shook her head vehemently. "Jake, please, there was no plan," she protested urgently. "Don't you understand? When I first saw Bret's picture, I was stunned, but you and I were strangers. I couldn't tell you this, not then."

Her explanation fell on deaf ears. Jake suddenly thrust his hands in his pockets as if he couldn't trust himself not to use them to display the cold violence of his expression. He said roughly, "But we weren't strangers long, so that excuse no longer holds. What did you do, Livvy? Sense my attraction to you and then feed it so skillfully that I thought I was doing all the running?"

"I didn't!" she cried incredulously, her temper surfacing at his continued insistence of her scheming. "I discouraged you in every way! I didn't want to be involved with you, with anyone!"

As if she hadn't spoken, he said grimly, "It was all very subtle, wasn't it? And like a lovesick fool I fell for it. When I think of the gentle way, the damned careful way I waited and courted you, fearing I'd make some wrong move and scare you away, I want to . . ." He didn't finish the thought aloud, letting his eyes go over her, hard, disgusted, accusing. "Tell me something. Did you ever see me? *Me.* Not just a link to Bret or to a dead child, but *me?*"

He was rigid with anger and wounded pride and Livvy's shoulders slumped as she stepped back from him. "Oh, God, Jake, don't do this," she said unsteadily. "I should have told you about Jamie, but you're so wrong about why I didn't."

His eyes bored into hers before he abruptly turned around, running his hands through his springy chestnut hair. Then, just as suddenly as he'd swung away from her, he swung back, grinding out, "I'm not wrong about the lies, Livvy!"

Barely above a whisper, she said, "That's not fair. I didn't lie to you."

"You lied by omission!" He hurled the words at her, scowling, his face as hard as steel and just as unbending. "You lied when you took my money to get Bret into

Horizon House. You lied every time you kissed me, let me touch you. If nothing else, you lied in the beginning by keeping information from me I had a right to know. Did you sense I wouldn't trust my children with a woman whose need to relive the past overrode her professionalism?"

Livvy knew he was hurt and, for that reason, was trying to hurt her. He was successful. That last deadly accusation, drawled with such amused contempt, went through her like a well-aimed bullet. But, remembering the longing and guilt and uncertainty she had felt those first weeks, she lost her will to defend herself. It was futile to argue against Jake's reasoning when it aligned so faithfully with what she had once feared. There had been a time when she'd doubted her own objectivity where Bret was concerned. Jake was wrong in many ways, but not all. And her silence? Her secrecy? What had once seemed imperative measures to guard her privacy now seemed a house of cards to be tumbled. And tumble it had, with Brad's help, until it lay about her feet in shattered dreams, leaving her naked and vulnerable under Jake's bitterness and contempt. She turned away from him.

But he followed, grabbing her shoulders in hard fingers and swinging her around. "You didn't answer me a moment ago," he bit out with cold hostility. "When you looked at me, did you see me?" Loosing one of her shoulders, he gripped the edge of the picture frame. "Or did you see nothing but this?"

Thinking he meant to jerk Jamie's picture from her grasp, Livvy held it tighter. And caused the very action she wanted to prevent. Eyes glinting violence, Jake stripped it from her hands and rashly tossed it aside.

Horrified, Livvy watched the glass and wood frame hurl through the air to the sofa. Skidding the length of the cushions, it crashed against the far arm and bounded to the floor. There was a muffled, splintering sound as the glass shattered on impact with the carpeted floor, then a dumbfounded silence in which only their dissonant breathing could be heard.

Twisting out of his grasp, Livvy ran to the front of the sofa, kneeling down, her face ashen.

Like the slight distortion of a fitted jigsaw puzzle, Jamie's picture behind the broken glass appeared made up of several spliced sections. As she drew away the larger pieces of glass, a spray of crystals fell heedlessly to her thighs and the carpet around her. Jamie's image emerged, a long, jagged tear running from his eye to his chin. Livvy's mouth moved and her chin wobbled, yet her eyes were so dry she had trouble blinking. Her fingers brushed lightly across the surface of the photograph, sweeping away particles of glass. One sharp-edged fragment lightly slashed her index finger and tiny drops of blood fell to the photograph. A slight shudder rippled through her as she watched the miniature scarlet pool gather, then separate into striated lines along the glossy surface of her son's dimpled cheek.

Jake came down on his haunches beside her, his hands on his knees. One of his hands lifted, as if to offer a comforting touch, then fell away, and she could tell by the quick clench of his jaw that Jake regretted the momentary softening. He said flatly, "I'm sorry it broke."

"It doesn't matter," she said, her voice as dead as her eyes. "I have other pictures of him."

Jake's brows met above his nose in a dark glower. He opened his mouth to say something else, then clamped his lips together as Mellie and Bret suddenly burst into the room, coming to a stumbling halt when they saw their uncle and Livvy on the floor.

"Uncle Jake was yelling," Mellie said sharply, her eyes on Livvy's strained face.

Though it was feeble, Livvy found a smile of reassurance for the girl. She held up her finger with its tiny smear of blood. "He was . . . warning me to be careful.

228

I cut my finger on some broken glass, but it's nothing to worry about, darling."

Mellie nodded, appeased, and said judiciously, "Accidents are horrible. I fell down and hurt my knee once, and Uncle Jake kissed it better."

And who will kiss me better?

Bret's blue eyes filled with sympathetic tears and he thrust his thumb inside a trembling mouth, mumbling uncertainly, "Do it hurt?"

Like hell. "A little, darling, but a bandage will fix it," she said, mustering a cheerful smile.

The tears disappeared as if by magic, the thumb came out, and Bret whispered loudly, "I love you, Livvy."

Aware of the cynical downturn of Jake's mouth, Livvy said quietly, "I love you, too, Bret."

Standing, Jake laid a hand on each small head. "You two get back in the kitchen while I clean up the broken glass. I don't want you hurt."

Double meaning? *I don't want you near the woman who cheats and lies and uses people?* Her voice quiet but firm, Livvy said, "No, I'll clean up the glass. The children were promised an ice cream and it will be their suppertime soon."

The dark, shooting look Jake sent her said he wasn't through with her. But Livvy had heard more than she could stand. When the children started yipping excitedly for ice cream, she turned the photograph facedown on the carpet and went to the bedroom to collect their coats. When she came back, Jake took them from her grasp, subtly insinuating himself between her and his children as he hunkered down to help Mellie and Bret with zippers and ties. The effect was as though he had turned his back on a stranger, casually excluded an outsider from the family circle. And perhaps he had.

Hands behind her back, Livvy watched him smile and tease his niece and nephew about what flavor of ice cream they would choose. She wanted to hug the children, to hold them. She wanted to tell Jake she was sorry, that she hadn't meant to hurt anyone, that she cared deeply for all three of them and mostly for him. She wanted to touch him and bring back the warmth to his eyes. But each time he glanced her way, his face was tightly controlled and his eyes were cold and remote, and she knew he wouldn't listen to anything she said. So she stood and watched and nearly broke down when the children hugged her legs and chirped innocently, "Happy birthday, Livvy. See you tomorrow."

Her beseeching eyes collided with Jake's distant, implacable ones, and her heart lurched. She knew she wouldn't see them tomorrow. Almost defiantly, she bent down and scooped each child under an arm, hugging them to her and trying not to hold them too desperately. She managed to tickle Bret's fat tummy and tease him about eating too much chocolate ice cream. And she gave Mellie's perky nose a little tweak, reminding her to be careful of ice-cream mustaches. Her heart told them a silent good-bye.

When they had gone, she went about the task of picking up the larger pieces of glass, of vacuuming the floor free of the smaller particles. Jamie's photograph was unsalvageable, but she put it back inside the drawer that had held it for two months. She bathed, brushed her teeth, got ready for bed, all her movements mechanical. Before the sun had set, she had made up the sofa in the living room and crawled between the sheets. She stared at the empty pillow next to her.

And the desolation grew inside her and the silence welled up around her. She curled herself into a tight ball, weeping for all she had lost and all the pain she had caused.

CHAPTER TEN

The Interest Center was cacophonous. Little voices called and chimed and chortled. A push-toy clack-clacked across the indoor-outdoor carpet, its driver pretending to mow the lawn and adding his *choo-kata, choo-kata* idling noises as he paused by each obstacle and turned his mower. Busy hands stacked blocks and then tumbled them, the wooden squares thud-thudding as they fell, squeals of dismay and/or delight punctuating each thud. Small plastic cars were hummed or *varoom-varoomed* upon flat surfaces. Sniffs and sneezes expressed the outbreak of the flu season. An occasional "Livvy, look!" or "Guess what, Livvy?" or "Do you like it, Livvy?" was shouted for attention or effect or approval. It was a normal afternoon at Horizon House.

Lillian Chester rocked a tiny sleepyhead in a corner chair, the drowsy tot pressed against her grandmotherly bosom as she sang, of all things, a current Michael Jackson hit in a gentle, scratchy voice. Jenny Clarke sat on the floor, helping two toddlers decide which shapes fit inside which slots of a learning toy, her delighted laughter when her young charges proved proficient to the task joining the other sounds.

Livvy was used to the noise. It buzzed about her head unnoticed. She smiled and approved and listened, occasionally grabbing a tissue to wipe a runny nose, or, with a gentle palm, checking foreheads for fevers. All the activity was familiar activity. She saw it, felt it, breathed it, and participated in it. She was moving from one side of the room to the other when her peripheral vision caught something out of the ordinary. She glanced toward the door. Jake stood there motionless, regarding her with quiet interest.

She was lateral to him in the middle of the room, her head turned toward him, all noise and movement in the Interest Center fading beneath the terrible, thundering upheaval in her chest. It had been over two weeks since their quarrel, since she'd seen or heard from him. On two occasions she'd called his home, hoping to find him less angry and therefore more receptive to explanations. There had been no answer either time. After a week she'd mustered the courage to call his office. An employee, not the throaty-voiced Michelle, had informed her that Mr. Masters was on vacation, but she hadn't volunteered where he was or when he was expected back. Livvy had murmured something polite and had hung up, not leaving her name or a message.

Now her eyes searched his face, looking for anger, not finding it, looking for the old familiar warmth, not finding that either. His expression was alert, his face slightly fatigued, as if he'd spent his vacation extending himself instead of unwinding. His eyes, she realized, were busy detailing her appearance—her stillness, her unsmiling mouth, her hands clenched into fists inside the pockets of the white coverall jacket she wore over casual skirt and blouse.

Walking toward him and stopping a yard away from him, she said solemnly, "Hello, Jake."

"I'd like to talk to you alone, Livvy, if you can be spared here." A slight inclination of his head indicated the activity behind her. His eyes never left her face.

Something about him, not a hardness, exactly, but a determination, filled her with trepidation. Mellie and

Bret weren't with him, nor had they attended Horizon House since before her birthday. Did Jake intend the final cut in their relationship? Nodding jerkily, she left his side to have a quiet word with Jenny. When she walked back to him, she said, "We can go to my office."

The fact that he made no attempt to touch her added to her disquiet. She remembered his touches—casual, intimate, affectionate, unfailing. Inside she was in a turmoil, though she walked slightly ahead of him with her head high and her body in graceful stride. It seemed there were a thousand questions on the tip of her tongue.

Where have you been? Why are you here? How are Mellie and Bret? Have you come to withdraw them from Horizon House? Will you let me explain that I meant no harm? Do you still hate me, Jake, because I failed to be all you wanted and expected?

She led him into her office without voicing a single question. Immediately, she went behind her desk, instinctively using its sturdy width as a protective barrier against whatever he had to say.

The silence grew heavy as Jake took the seat opposite her desk and studied her through grave eyes. She could feel a tension about him as powerful as the one gripping her. She was ready to burst out with one of the questions plaguing her when he finally spoke.

"I've been out of town for a couple of weeks," he said.

"I know," she murmured. When his glance sharpened, she added, "Not where you were, but I knew you weren't at home. I called your office and they told me you were on vacation."

Jake had settled back in the chair, one ankle over the opposite knee, his trouser leg hitched up over a dark sock, his foot moving in time with the drumming of his fingers on his thigh. It was the classic pose of the polite but restless male. Even his other hand added to the overall impression, long fingers alternately scraping over his chin or pinching the cleft together. And such obvious restiveness compounded Livvy's uneasiness. He had something to say, and she wished he would get it said. Her poise couldn't stand much more strain.

"Vacation," he repeated finally, as if the word was misleading. "I took the kids to California, let them visit their old friends. They had a great time, and I had a few days alone." His finger rubbed across his lips. "Dan and Sue left some property near Carmel. Some of their friends have been watching it for me. It has a small house near the beach. I stayed there, walking the beaches, enjoying the solitude. Everything was quiet, no hustle and bustle, just sand and sea air and sunsets and surf." He paused. As if impatient with himself, he suddenly shook his head and muttered, "I did a lot of thinking, Livvy. About us."

"So did I," she admitted quietly. Every night since her birthday. About what she'd lost. About Jake's unreasonableness and about his justification. About all the pain she had caused. Dropping her gaze from his intense stare, she reached for a pencil on her desk, taking it by both ends and twirling it nervously.

"I didn't like my thoughts," Jake said slowly. "Or the length of time it took me to work them out and decide what I needed to do."

The pencil snapped in two.

For a horrified second Livvy thought she might burst into tears. Recovery came on a deeply drawn breath, and she opened the top drawer of her desk, sweeping the broken pencil pieces inside. She stuffed her hands into her lap, pushing them between her knees, squeezing her knees so tightly together her hands hurt.

Looking anywhere but at his face, she said, "You've paid tuition through January, and since"—she swallowed—"since Mellie and Bret weren't here this month, you're due a refund." Her glance skittered to his face, saw his expression, and skated quickly away, not wanting to interpret the look in his eyes. Relief? Anxiety? Shock? Puzzlement? She said brightly to the top of her desk, "That's

Horizon's policy. None of our clients pay for the days their children are on vacation or have to drop out unexpectedly or miss because of illness."

"Business can't be too lucrative during the flu season," he murmured.

It was almost teasing. Livvy looked up. Though his voice had been slightly husky, there was a faint half smile hovering about his mouth. Rallying some of that same normality, Livvy made a weak attempt at return humor.

"Well, it's not the money we care about, it's the . . ." She stopped herself midsentence. Her love of children was the tender sore between them.

She jumped up suddenly and went to the far corner of the room, coming back with a plastic drawstring shopping bag. She laid it on the desk in front of Jake. "This is . . . I found some things at my house. Mellie's new puzzle and Bret's windup radio. They'll want them."

Jake stared up at her, his eyes searching into hers, and she crammed her hands back inside her coverall pockets, her nails torturing her palms. She swallowed again, mumbled "The check!" and practically leaped behind her desk, scrambling through the top drawer for the checkbook and a pen, her head bent.

In an oddly thickened tone, Jake said, "The money isn't important, Livvy."

Her head jerked up, her face stretched by overwidened eyes and an earnest desire to somehow make amends. "But it's yours! Honest, Jake, I'd refund it to anyone under the circumstances!"

He jumped up then, as she had done moments before, so forcefully that his chair flew back and crashed to the floor. A dark flush rode high across his cheekbones and he leaned against the desktop, bringing them in closer range than they'd been in two weeks. A rampant pulse worked at his temple and there was a harsh set to his features. He seemed to radiate a heat she couldn't define. Not anger, but something powerful. After a tense moment, he straightened, turning away to slowly bring the chair upright.

While he did, Livvy grabbed her checkbook, scribbled fast and furiously, her normally legible handwriting so much hen-scratching. When he turned to face her, she had pushed the check to the far side of the desk, next to the plastic shopping bag that held the toys. She was holding the ballpoint pen in a damp fist.

She said brightly, "There! I didn't cheat anyone this time!"

And Jake whispered tautly, "Oh, *God!*" His aqua eyes were scrunched tightly shut.

His reaction had the effect of a well-aimed broadside. Livvy simply crumpled back into her chair, all her brittle effort at normality deflating like a punctured balloon. Her shoulders sagged and she whispered, "I'm sorry, Jake. I'm making a hash of this too."

"Livvy, don't," he muttered, his tone hushed, strained.

"No." Her voice shook, as did her head. "I want to apologize for the foolish way I've handled everything."

Somber-faced, in that same quiet rasp Jake said, "Don't forget to blame the biggest fool."

"Oh. Brad." Her tone was weakly dismissive, her trembling fingers fluttering in her lap before she laced them tightly together. "Brad was only a catalyst. He wanted to hurt me, but if I'd told you about Jamie, he couldn't have said anything to hurt anyone."

"God knows Brad Waring is a fool, but I meant me," he said quietly.

"But you didn't do anything, Jake. You only reacted to the bombshell that was dropped in your lap that day."

Grimacing, Jake muttered, "That wasn't reaction. That was destructive self-indulgence."

Rounding the corner of her desk, he went down on one knee before her chair. He took her clasped hands, cupping them gently between his on her thighs, warming her cold fingers with his touch, warming her spirit with the

236

blazing look shining out of his eyes. The hope that unfolded within her began to burgeon.

"They say the guilty party always yells loudest and longest," Jake murmured, smiling a little. "Hasn't it occurred to you, pretty woman, that I found it too easy to believe that jerk's accusations about your using me?"

"Brad was very convincing."

"Not really. I'd heard your disgust with him and I knew he was retaliating. But he hit a little close to my own doubts and guilt when he talked about ulterior motives. From the beginning I knew how you felt about Mellie and Bret." His twisted smile mocked himself. "While I was struggling to win your smile, you opened up your heart to them. I wanted you in my life, so I deliberately dangled them under your nose like tempting bait. I even thought I was clever doing it. It's taken me two weeks to realize that while my motives were honest, my methods weren't. And to realize that your secrecy about your son hid a very tender hurt."

Her hands jerked inside his, but he held on securely; his clasp had the same determined gentleness that looked out of his eyes.

Remembering one of his accusations that day, her voice wobbled a little as she said, "Jake, I didn't use you or Bret as a link to the past. I admit that when I first saw Bret's picture, I wanted to see him, to touch him, but I never wanted to use him as a replacement for my son. Jamie will always be inside me, but I accepted his death a long time ago."

"I know that."

"But you thought—"

"No." He shook his head. "I didn't think at all. I just exploded, and said a whole lot of things in anger I wish I hadn't said."

"You were hurt. I understood that."

"And it was still no excuse for some of the things I said," he muttered, his mouth a line of self-contempt, a look of bitter anguish in his eyes. "I think I had some crazy notion that if I said enough, I'd feel better. I didn't."

Her eyes traced his self-disgust and became softly beseeching. "Don't be too self-critical, Jake, please. The biggest mistakes weren't yours."

His hands trembled slightly as he pried hers apart, bringing them to his mouth and covering their palms with supplicating kisses. "Okay, we'll skip the part where I offer my abject apology for being a stupid, self-righteous, hypocritical jerk," he murmured, watching with relief the wavering smile that broke across her face.

"You're also funny and sweet and terribly determined to have the last say, aren't you?"

His serious eyes began to twinkle. "You don't know the half of it, pretty woman. Now that all your secrets have been uncovered, you'll hear more from me. Working blind hampered my style."

Behind the lenses of her glasses, her brown eyes blinked, luminous tears hovering on the rims. All her secrets? Except the one that would prevent their having a future together. When he spread her hands on either side of his face and held them there, the tears spilled over onto her cheeks.

"Jake, some things are—"

But he reached to cover her lips with his fingertips, halting her words. "Hush, Livvy. I don't give a damn if you never mention the past again. All I want is your honesty about your feelings for me."

Her hands fell from his face and went to her own, wiping the tears away. Eyes still glistening, she looked at him and then away. An awkward indecision held her in its grip. Honesty? She loved him. Too much to tell him. Too much to chance limiting his life by the restrictions of hers.

With another swipe at her cheeks, she muttered, "I'm a mess."

Nudging her chin with his fingers, Jake urged her gaze to him. His eyes were full of pleas and promises. "I will be a mess if I don't kiss you soon," he told her huskily.

Pulses suddenly humming, Livvy stared at him. She saw that he wouldn't take the kiss and that he needed the seal of her forgiveness. She needed it too. To be in his arms again, to forget their past conflict and their limited future in the present succor of his kiss was what she wanted above all else. Her heart quaked, her face crumpled, and she threw herself against him, her mouth finding his in a kiss that tasted of salt and forgiveness and relief, and that for her was seasoned by the bittersweet knowledge that she still hadn't told him all he was entitled to know.

His arms came about her, pulling her completely out of the chair and onto his lap as he sat back on the floor, clutching her to him as if she were his salvation. When he tore his mouth from hers, they were both gulping for air. He pressed her face against the front of his jacket over the hard thumping of his heart, burying his face in the glossy mass of her hair. With a husky sigh of relief he leaned back against her desk.

From the muffling folds of his jacket, she confessed shakily, "When I saw you in the Interest Center, I thought you'd come to withdraw Mellie and Bret. I thought you wanted to sever the last tie with me."

His mouth moved against her hair. There was a smile in his voice. "Even if I hadn't squared things with you, I couldn't have done that. Mellie and Bret would have given me hell. All they've talked about the last few days is seeing you again. Besides"—he pressed her fingers to the pulse at the base of his throat where his life's fluid pumped in a rhythmic flow to his heartbeat—"I think you must be in my blood, and I need my blood to survive. As it is, I've been suffering anemia for the last two weeks."

She gave a little hiccup of a laugh and raised her head.

Though smiling, she said seriously, almost anxiously, "I can't deny loving Mellie and Bret, Jake. But they're not the reason I became involved with you. I care about you . . . very much. You're a very special man."

His expression ranged from pleasure to brief torment to controlled acceptance. The difference between loving his children and caring about him had not gone unnoticed. After a moment he lifted a brow, and it was there —the light teasing, the ever-ready amusement. "My mother used to cuff me on the side of the head and tell me if I wanted a nice woman to think I was special, I'd have to eat my spinach. It must have paid off, Olive."

She smiled. Reaching up, she traced his brow, a gentle supplication in her touch. *Don't be hurt by me. Don't expect too much from me,* she longed to say. But all she said aloud was: "I've missed you."

He hugged her closer. "I like that husky sincerity in your voice. Makes me feel wanted. I also like cuddling on the floor by your desk. Makes me feel like a teen-ager again."

"You cuddled under desks when you were a teen-ager?"

"One of my first cuddles, as a matter of fact. I was thirteen and helping the teacher clean out her desk at the end of semester. She told me I was a darling boy when I rescued a file she'd dropped under the desk."

"You said *cuddling* on the floor by the desk."

"Well, she kind of reached down and tousled my hair. That qualifies as a cuddle."

"That qualifies as a lie or an evasion, I'm not sure which."

His eyes gleamed, but he didn't contradict her. He merely took another cuddle from her, hugging her closely and kissing her softly. Then he captured her hand, looked down at her watch, and said, "It's almost five thirty. How much longer before you'll be through here?"

With an "Oh, my gosh! I should be downstairs now!"

Livvy scrambled off his lap. Straightening her clothes, smoothing her hair, she headed for the door, paused, and looked back. Jake was right behind her. She said uncertainly, "Will you wait for me? I'd like you to come home with me, if you want to. If you can, I mean." She smiled a little as he arched a brow, adding unnecessarily, "If you'd like that too."

Winking, Jake drawled, "I want—I can—I like."

While Livvy closed Horizon's doors for the night, Jake went to get pizza. She rushed home, took the fastest bath on record, and was drying herself with a fluffy towel when the door knocker thudded his arrival. Like the sudden, unexpected sting of a bee, doubt attacked her. She wanted to be with Jake, and yet . . . *Stop analyzing! Enjoy what you can, while you can! Let tomorrow take care of tomorrow!* "Great philosophy!" she muttered in self-disgust, stuffing her arms inside her old bathrobe as she rushed out of the bathroom. She was securing the tie at her waist when she opened the front door.

Jake had two huge pizzas clutched in front of him, boxed and still steaming. They smelled deliciously of spicy tomato sauce and fragrant toppings. Her mouth watered as her brain told her body to seek sustenance. But her heart sought something else: Jake, tall and lean and very, very dear. His eyes reflected some of the inner turmoil she felt. Did he, too, wonder where they would go from here?

As he stepped inside, she gave him a smile that was a little strained around the edges, and said softly, "Hi!"

Jake's smile was a replica of hers. His gaze seared over her swiftly yet managed to detail her appearance—her hair twisted into a hasty knot on top of her head, her face freshly scrubbed, the old robe clinging here and there on dampened skin. Moving back to her face, his eyes locked with hers. His jaw clenched and he abruptly shoved the giant pizzas into her hands.

"You must like pizza," Livvy murmured, knowing as

he shrugged out of his coat and loosened his tie that pizza wasn't what he intended to have. Her pulses thrummed to life, blood beating in her ears.

Stuffing his tie inside his jacket pocket, Jake tossed his coat carelessly toward the sofa. He took back the pizzas, set them on the floor, then took her hands and led her into the living room.

"I like pizza," he finally agreed huskily as he slipped off the tie of her robe. With unsteady hands he slowly spread it open and found her breasts. "I like cold pizza."

Her arms went about his neck in a clinging loop, her face lifted for the first touch of his mouth. The restrained ardor she'd learned to expect from him was nonexistent. His kiss held a measure of desperation not dispelled during the last hour. Lithe and engulfing and impassioned, his arms came about her. Together they fell to the sofa, his body fitted to hers and pressing her deep into the cushions. Taking her glasses, he reached to set them on an end table, then tugged impatiently at his belt, his mouth locked to hers. The control that was normal in his lovemaking was a thin thread. She felt the urgency as his lips crushed hers and his fingers closed round her breasts in a demanding caress. Her senses scattered.

The turbulence in him touched a quickening deep within her, yet allowed no opportunity for expression beyond her soft moan and the softer cling of her arms. He stripped off his belt and her one undergarment. Wanting to feel his flesh against hers, she tried to unbutton his shirt, but was impeded by the tight crush of their bodies. Muttering something low and fierce, Jake removed it himself, jerking it off his arms, then letting it fall to the floor. The rest of his clothing quickly followed, stripped away with the same rough impatience.

Devouring, plundering, his mouth and hands roamed her willowy form. Her breasts were supple for his kisses, her thighs liquid under his touch. Where he rushed, she flowed, answering his demands with yielding pliancy. She

242

was like a leaf caught in a wild summer wind, drifting, falling, rising, drifting again. And Jake was the wind, hot and whirling out of control.

As if she was the tranquillity his febrile body sought, he took her with possessive fierceness. And his fierceness didn't ebb but went on and on, until hard shudders ripped violently through his body, absorbing the flood of pleasure drowning hers. They both fell to glorious completion.

Then he was cradling her head in his hands, pressing his forehead to hers. "Are you all right?" he rasped, his deep voice breathy and anxious.

More than all right. Beautifully fulfilled and totally spent. All Livvy could manage was a faint smile and a weak nod of her head.

He kissed her deeply before untangling himself from the exhausted cling of her slender limbs. With a gentle tug, he pulled her with him to the floor. She cried his name softly in half-laughing protest, and he silenced the small rebellion with his mouth. There was more he wanted from her. When he began showing her how to tap the reservoir of passion, she realized there was more she could give.

The urgency of his caresses hadn't faded, but now she sensed his need for more than compliance, felt her own need in the quivers of renewed pleasure racing through her body. Her hands glided over him, seeking, finding, her intimate caress rewarded by his husky groan. His labored breath beseeched her, compelled her, and she laid kisses at his throat, across his chest, and down to his flat belly. She heard the hoarse entreaty of her name, then felt herself turned to her back as he came over her. She wrapped herself around him, arching upward to meet the second union.

This time Jake allowed her the freedom he had denied her the first time, no longer just possessing her but wanting her possession. Forearms braced and trembling, he held himself above her, glorying in her rise and fall beneath him and her tightening convulsions around him. Fulfillment burst within them, hot and exquisite and simultaneous. And he let himself collapse upon her, burying his face in the warm, tender curve of her neck, murmuring thickly, "Sweet love . . ." as if he meant her and not the loving they'd shared.

Both their bodies rested, and for timeless moments nothing was said. They lay curled to each other, his hand gently stroking the curve of her from waist to thigh. An occasional sigh drifted above them.

Eventually, Jake broke the silence, his voice low and dusky. "The two things that make me a great lover are subtlety and finesse."

And the words were such a droll criticism of his first loss of control, laughter gulped up from Livvy's throat. "Absolutely," she agreed.

The short exchange expended their energy. Again the room fell to silence. No longer heated by passion's warmth, Livvy soon began to feel the coolness against her nudity. She shivered. Jake, still warm and toasty, said, "We'd better make up the bed and get you under the covers before you turn into an iceberg."

"You could always thaw me yourself," she murmured around a delicious little grin.

Though wicked laughter gleamed in his eyes, Jake managed a sigh of wistful regret. "I'm afraid my heater blew a fuse. Twice."

Stumbling slightly on passion-spent legs, he stood up and extended a hand to her. After making the bed and hustling her under the sheet and blanket, he leaned down to bestow a quick kiss on the tip of her cold nose. "I'll get the pillows."

He returned with pillows, pizzas, and diet sodas. Side by side—Livvy huddled beneath bedclothes pulled to her chin and invariably slipping, Jake lazy and warm beneath a sheet drawn to his waist—they shared their belated supper. Livvy ate cold pizza, shivered, drank even colder soda, shivered, occasionally flicked crumbs from the sheets or his bare chest, and shivered.

After about the thirtieth such vibration from her side of the bed, Jake paused in his contented chewing and offered, "Where's the thermostat control? I'll turn up the heater."

"It is turned up. It's a very old heating system," she informed him, sipping from the cold soda he held obligingly to her lips so she wouldn't have to take her arms out of the covers. She shivered again, then frowned slightly when Jake went happily back to his pizza. Affecting a pathetic stutter to accentuate her chilled state, she said, "P-pass me some m-more pizza, p-please."

With an ironic sidelong glance that said he wasn't impressed with her acting ability, Jake calmly selected a wedge of pizza from the box in his lap and handed it to her.

The same teeth-chattering stutter became forlornly polite. "Th-thank you, J-Jake."

Resigned, he slid closer, pressing his warm thigh to the coolness of hers. "You're welcome," he mumbled, his white teeth biting gustily into his sixth slice of pizza.

Still not satisfied, Livvy stuttered sweetly, "Y-you're so w-warm. M-must be nice to have s-such in-"—she shuddered violently and outrageously—"inner b-body heat. You could pro-probably sh-share some of it and n-never m-miss it."

"What do you do for warmth when I'm not here?" he asked, blithely reaching for another slice of pizza.

Disgruntled because he still sat there calmly eating pizza while she was freezing and practically begging for his warm arm around her, she lost her stutter and said tartly, "I have an electric blanket, if you must know. Twin-size. It fits my single bed, but not my queen-size sofa bed, or I'd go get it now so I could get warm. I usually wear socks and long flannel gowns." She flounced a little, further dislodging her cover. She shivered for real.

"I've never seen you wear them."

"You've never given me an opportunity to put them on."

"Oh, yeah."

He sounded so supremely smug, so extremely male, that Livvy sent a soft fist crashing into his chest. But her soft fist was clamped around the cold but juicy wedge of pizza Jake had handed her just moments before. Cheese and tomato sauce, bits of sausage and olive and onion, flakes of crust and one thin slice of pepperoni, smeared and embedded into the brown hair under her fist. She drew back her hand.

Livvy's eyes widened. Jake's narrowed. She bit her lip. He parted his on a disgusted sigh. A giggle escaped her. He formed a glower. Quickly deciding that amends needed to be made, she threw the remains of her pizza into the box on his lap. Braving chills and goosebumps, she let the covers fall away from her to lean across him for the box of tissues she kept on the table beside the sofa.

At a strategic moment his warm hand splayed between her shoulder blades and applied quick pressure. She fell, her breasts flattening against his chest. Cheese and tomato sauce, bits of sausage and olive and onion, flakes of crust and one thin slice of pepperoni, plastered between them. Another shiver rippled through her—this one utter, squirming revulsion—while his two warm hands finally shared their heat in brisk strokes along her back and shoulders.

Nose to nose with her, Jake asked solicitously, "Warmer now?" Brilliant with gratification, his eyes stared into her brown ones clouded with disgust.

Spacing the words for more effect, Livvy muttered, *"I'm—gonna—kill—you!"* But she almost kissed him instead when his warm chuckle rushed against her face.

Jerking away to kneel beside him, she looked down at

the mess on her chest. A succinct "Yuk!" broke from her lips. Her breasts were a palette—a spatter of tomato-orange, blobs of green and black and brown, two swirling puckers of dusky pink, all set against goosebumped ivory.

Jake absently reached for the box of tissues, grabbing a handful and swiping at his chest, while her chest drew his avid interest. When she thrust a hand toward him, silently and imperatively demanding a tissue, he shook his head. Sitting forward, he dispensed with pizza and sodas and tissues. Then, braced on one elbow beside her, he again splayed a hand between her shoulder blades, drawing her down toward the upward inevitability of his mouth.

He murmured huskily, "I told you I like cold pizza."

Much later they had bathed, the sheets had been changed, the lights were out. They lay together in the dark, nearly asleep. Livvy's thoughts were content, if thoughts they were. More impressions, drifting in and out of her dreamy consciousness.

It's going to work was the most prevalent impression. Or was it hope? Jake—content, undemanding, generous, warm, fun. Herself—satisfied, requiring only him and today. *It's going to work.* Sharing the present, enjoying the laughter, forgetting the tears. *It's going to work.* For as long as possible . . .

"Livvy?"

"Hmmm?"

"I have a great heating system in my apartment."

"Mmmm." She snuggled closer to the greatest heating system in The Little Yellow House.

"Livvy?"

"Hmmm?"

"Would you say we're compatible?"

"Uh-huh." Cautiously. Eyes wide open now in the dark, and instincts alert.

"If you moved in with me, you could be warm every night."

Silence.

He nudged her. "Did you hear me?"

"Yes." Very softly. It's *not* going to work.

"Well?"

"Winter won't last forever."

"Come on, pretty woman, I'm serious."

"What's wrong with the way things are now?"

"Finding baby-sitters, leaving the kids more often than I should, not being with you as often as I'd like to be."

Another silence.

"You've never stayed at my place. You've never slept in my bed." He sounded wistful, his voice low and poignant. "We've never made love anywhere but here."

"Oh, Jake." *Her* voice was now low and poignant, but not wistful. Saddened. "You know I couldn't stay at your apartment with the children there."

"Why not?"

"Children are very curious and very candid. Anything they see, they ask questions about and report to the nearest ear. I'd just as soon it doesn't get passed on to all and sundry that I've been seen in Uncle Jake's big bed."

His response was slow to come and reluctantly delivered. "I never thought of it that way. I suppose it could be a problem."

Livvy shifted onto her back beside him, snuggling the covers under her chin. Jake wasn't convinced. "Did you know Christie's mommy wraps her beautiful mane of natural wheat-colored hair inside plastic caps and purple-stained towels?" she asked.

"Christie who?" came his absent query.

"Dean's mommy takes little white pills to keep the stork monster away."

Without comment, in a preoccupied manner, Jake found her hand beneath the covers and drew circling patterns on the palm with his thumb.

"Steven's daddy puts on funny little underwear beneath his warm-up suit before he goes jogging."

"Funny little underwear?" was a vaguely amused echo from the pillow next to hers. Then, as it sank in, Jake groaned and said, "Kids tell you those things?"

"Me, and any other available listener."

Jake's sigh held an undercurrent of resignation. "I guess you're right," he said, tugging at the hand he held to bring her back to his side. His shoulder pillowed her head, his arm encircled her in a gentle hug. She shivered, and he murmured, "Cold?"

"A little." A lot. But not from the room's chill. Why *couldn't* it have worked?

He drew the covers securely around them, but kicked one of his feet free and kept one of his shoulders bare. He gave her another light hug, then a skimming caress along her upper arm with his fingertips. "Hey, forget I said anything about your moving in with me. I wasn't thinking about anything but how nice it would be to have you in my home."

Livvy chewed her lower lip. "Could we compromise?" she offered slowly. "As long as Michelle is baby-sitting, I'll come to your apartment more often, but I'll live here?"

Next to her, his whole body tensed. He seemed to be holding his breath. "You mean, you'll start staying overnight at my place?"

Her heart turned over at the cautious elation in his voice. Smiling broadly in the darkness, she said, "Yes, I'll stay the nights Michelle's willing to keep Mellie and Bret."

"Promise?"

"Promise."

A gusty sigh and a *big* hug! Livvy thought happily, *Maybe it's going to work!*

CHAPTER ELEVEN

The first night spent in Jake's apartment began with his locking the door after Michelle's departure with Mellie and Bret, and Livvy ambling to his bedroom. Sitting on the edge of the bed, she rummaged through her large shoulder bag for her travel alarm. After winding it and setting it for five thirty, she placed it on the bedside table.

Seconds later Jake entered the bedroom and went directly to the nightstand. Peering at the face of the clock, he groaned and muttered, "So early?" pointing to the alarm setting.

"I'll need an extra half hour in the morning to drive home and get dressed before opening Horizon's doors at seven," she explained, smiling up at him. "But I'll be very quiet and you'll never know when I leave."

"That's what I'm afraid of," he retorted, not altogether teasingly. He sat down beside her, slanting a curious glance at her soft, bulky bag. "I can't decide if that thing is a suitcase or a purse. What's in it?"

"Just my nightgown and toothbrush."

Faint intrigue brightened his expression as he delved inside the bag. A moment later he withdrew a thick bundle of flannel. His eyebrows rose and his mouth expressed a wry disbelief as he shook out the voluminous folds of her nightgown.

"Where are the thick insulated socks that go with this wisp of feminine frippery?" he asked dryly.

Laughing, Livvy offered generously, "I'll let you keep my feet warm."

A quick flick of his wrist relegated the nightgown to the end of the bed. Drawing her into his arms, Jake fell back across the bed and began nuzzling her neck. "Forget the gown," he instructed huskily. "I'll keep all of you warm."

"When you're not intent on pizza, you can do that rather nicely," she agreed as her lips sought his. "Does Michelle realize you'll be home tonight?"

"Yes." He slipped his tongue between her parted lips to touch hers. "I always let her know where I'll be when she's keeping the kids."

"Oh." She brushed her lips back and forth over the cleft in his chin. "Evidently the nature of our relationship isn't a big secret."

He raised his head, frowning as he looked down at her. "Did you expect it to be?"

"Not really." Smiling, she ran a finger over the lines in his forehead. "I sometimes find it difficult to realize my private life is open to public view."

"That's an exaggeration," he said mildly as he released the buttons of her blouse. Placing his hands under her arms, he scooted her farther onto the bed. Side by side, their bodies turned toward each other, they lay crossways on the king-size bed. "Michelle is a friend, Livvy. She won't be broadcasting our activities to anyone."

"I know . . ." Her voice trailed away as she concentrated on pulling his shirt from the waistband of his slacks.

He helped her with the task, then unbuttoned his shirt, placing her hands on his bare chest. "I think you worry too much." His warm laughter rushed into her ear with the gentle brush of his lips over her earlobe. "But if you're concerned that your reputation might be compromised, I'll marry you. Even day-care center owners are allowed husbands."

Everything within her stilled. She didn't move; for a moment she didn't breathe. Jake was looking down at her with eyes that laughed at her utter shock, that flickered with something else—disappointment?—at the edge of panic he saw in hers.

Softly jeering, he murmured, "Are you afraid of tying yourself to me or to marriage?"

From somewhere Livvy found a teasing retort, issuing it in a voice that was slightly strained and husky. "I tried marriage once. Lousy institution."

"When it's with the wrong partner," Jake amended mildly, but he didn't pursue the subject. He lowered his mouth to hers in a long, drugging kiss.

How much of his comments had been teasing and how much serious intent? Afraid of knowing, Livvy let his warm, consuming mouth drive conjecture from her brain. When he started to unzip her skirt, she pushed against his shoulders and, with determined lightness, said, "Now . . . about my gown . . ."

He laughed softly, shaking his head. "No. That thing will hamper my style. I want your first night here to be perfect, not a fight with folds of flannel."

When his mouth wandered to her neck, she nibbled his earlobe, saying throatily, "Maybe we can strike a bargain." At her breast his arousing fingers worked their magic, evoking her soft gasp of pleasure. She continued on a slightly uneven note. "I'll wear the gown tonight and you'll wear your charming public image forever."

Jake slowly lifted his head, his expression vaguely suspicious. "Why do I get the feeling you're blackmailing instead of bargaining?"

Smiling very innocently, Livvy toyed with an interesting swirl of brown hair on his chest. "Mellie and Bret are as candid and open as other preschoolers," she pointed out innocuously, but with a suggestive undertone that reminded him how preschoolers loved to talk.

Jake stared down at her, his brows bunching together in a forbidding scowl above his laughing eyes as he watched her sweet smile slowly take on the edges of a smirk. "Okay, out with it! What did those little spies report about me?"

Assuming a thoughtful mien, Livvy murmured, "Well, I knew about the caffeine long before you confessed your addiction. And, of course, all about your snoring and the way you growl in the mornings. Nothing too terribly shocking except . . ." She let her voice trail away as if reluctant to say more.

"Except?"

His prompting brought forth her doubtful look of concern. "You're sure you want to go into this? Wouldn't you rather concede the nightgown to me and save yourself embarrassment?"

His hands went to her rib cage, his fingers playing over the back ribs, his thumbs threatening the front ones in skimming tickles. "Spit it out! I'm a man! I can take it!"

Laughing, she tried to grab his torturing thumbs, but found that where her fingers pounced, his thumbs had just moved on. Gasping little shrieks escaped her as he discovered particularly sensitive areas along her rib cage.

Between spurts of laughter, she gulped out, "Jake . . . ! Don't . . . !"

Immediately relenting, he began to caress her, his fingers and thumbs soothing the areas they'd abused. But in a low and threatening voice he ordered, "Tell me!" and swung his body over hers. He kissed her fiercely while his hands moved to her breasts for a different torture—a subtle, sweet, mind-destroying torment. When she closed her eyes and sighed his name, he said again, "Tell me." His voice was thickened and slightly vague, as if he'd lost track of his original intent.

Her eyes fluttered open, soft and sultry. "Your habit of

showering with the bathroom door unlocked should be worth my nightgown, shouldn't it?" she whispered, her hands gliding beneath his shirt to spread along the muscles of his back and to keep him close.

"Not when it's a habit I broke the second day Mellie and Bret were with me," he replied smugly, his mouth slanted by a lopsided smile. His hands edged beneath her hips, lifting her, pressing her tightly to his aroused warmth. With a glittering, frankly sensual look, he said, "Pretty woman, you're lousy at blackmailing, but—"

"Bargaining!" she corrected quickly, trying not to laugh.

"You could try a different form of persuasion," he continued suggestively, adding on a soft, positive note: "Not that it would get you your nightgown, of course, but we might enjoy it." He laughed when her mouth twisted in resignation.

Their lips met in a deep, tender prelude, unhurried, savoring . . .

The strident ring of the phone shattered the moment. Mumbling something hoarse and indistinct that somehow managed aptly to convey his reluctance to acknowledge the interruption, Jake slowly pulled away from her. As he sat on the edge of the bed and reached for the phone, Livvy reached toward the end of the bed. While he spoke low and huskily into the receiver, she watched the ripple and bunch of his back muscles beneath his shirt that indicated how hard-won his composure was. The corners of her mouth curled into a decidedly wicked grin.

Moments later, when he finished the call and turned back, he smiled wryly at Livvy already wrapped in flannel and under the covers. But he no longer argued against her nightgown. He stood, shucked his clothes, and joined her on the bed. And found that folds of flannel hampered him not at all.

January sped from the calendar while Livvy's happiness quickened on a direct course with Jake's contentment. It *was* working. She now spent as many nights in his apartment as he did in The Little Yellow House. The pleasure in his eyes was renewed each time she came to him so willingly. Late nights and early mornings seemed to invigorate her; she glowed.

One morning in his apartment Jake awakened when she did, but was heavy-lidded and vaguely bleak as opposed to her bright-eyed animation. Watching her skitter around, dressing, hurrying, he remarked slowly, "You know, every time I see you rushing about to leave my apartment, I get the oddest feeling it's me you're leaving."

His mouth wore its familiar half smile, but his eyes were serious and held an unusual touch of anxiety that jerked her heartstrings. She went to him, eager to dispel the vulnerability in his eyes. Kissing him, she told him with husky sincerity, "I won't leave you, Jake, not as long as you still want me with you."

Against the soft parting of her mouth he murmured, "Forever?"

Such a simple word. Forever. Such a confoundingly impossible word. After that morning, Livvy spent every waking moment trying to shelter her fragile dream from the cold grip of reality. She would *make* it work.

With time, Livvy's anxiety ebbed. "Forever" became a once-mentioned but never-repeated threat to her happiness. She refused to allow it back into her consciousness, again falling victim to the dream of "today" she wanted so desperately to believe in.

She felt closer to Jake than she ever had to another human being. She had given him her body, her friendship, her caring. What she gave him next was a natural extension of her love. She found herself opening up her former silence about Jamie and Brad and her marriage, while Jake listened, his eyes encouraging her, filled with

255

tenderness and quiet concern and pleasure that she trusted him enough to tell him.

In bed one night, after she'd shared some of her memories of her son, Jake gathered her to his chest, saying quietly, "Jamie was a lucky little boy having you for a mother."

Against his neck, she whispered poignantly, "No, I was the lucky one."

Lifting her face for his inspection, he saw the controlled anguish, the quiet acceptance. "What you need, pretty woman," he said with a gentle smile, "is a houseful of Jamies and Mellies and Brets to mother."

Inside her chest her heart skipped a beat, then thudded an agonized one. Her guard came up in the form of a teasing grin and a light quip. "I have a Horizon Houseful."

"And that's enough for you?" His raised brow lent skepticism to the question.

She pushed out of his embrace, lying on her back beside him. "Yes," she said firmly. "It's enough. It's all I'll ever have."

He came up on his elbow beside her, eyeing her thoughtfully. "Why do you say that?" he asked quietly.

She shrugged, a little fretfully, wishing she'd chosen her words more carefully. She tried to change the subject. "Glory and Paul have invited us to their house next Friday night. Would you like to go?"

"Sure, why not?" Jake answered easily, but went immediately back to the topic he found more interesting. "You're afraid to give motherhood another chance to hurt you, aren't you?"

She turned her head on the pillow, facing away from him, her chin inching higher. "Glory said she's serving smoked turkey. Paul does wonders with turkey. He uses mesquite wood, I think, to give the meat that special, mouth-watering flavor."

Threading his fingers through her hair, Jake gently and

persistently turned her to face him. He stared at her defensive features and, on a breath of reluctant laughter, said, "You know, Olivia, besides being obstinate, you're a coward."

He wasn't teasing, despite the laughter, and she glared at him, hurt by his assessment but unable to contradict it. Yes, she was a coward. Not quite the way he thought, but a spineless, craven, yellow-bellied coward, running from the damn, damn, damnable reality of her life!

She persisted stubbornly in carrying on their double conversation. "Glory says her girls are excited about meeting Mellie and Bret. They're older, of course, but they're sweet and good with younger children."

He had seen the emotions chasing across her face and he wasn't pleased. "You lost one child, Livvy. It was tragic and you were hurt, but has it occurred to you just how quickly you sought other children? You give everything to Horizon's children except your vulnerability to pain."

"Glory says—"

His hand clamped over her mouth, smothering her words. "Damn it, listen to yourself! You won't even talk about it! Does it frighten you that much?" His voice was soft, but frustration was darkening his eyes and making his jawline tight.

Frightened? Yes, yes, yes! More so than ever. Jake's insistence on pursuing the subject of children had to mean it was important to him. Tugging his hand away from her mouth, she went back into his arms, holding him tight, burying her face against his chest.

"Don't quarrel with me, Jake. Please don't," she whispered desperately.

And he didn't. He held her, very closely, very gently, very quietly, but with a new restraint that said she had disappointed him.

And in the days that followed, he watched her searchingly, as if she were a puzzle he meant to solve, as if his

257

mind were busy seeking solutions, seeking answers, even while he smiled and talked and loved her. The irrational fear that he would discover she was sterile plagued her constantly. She wanted to tell him but always held back, fearing that the disclosure would promote the same reaction his learning about Jamie had done. He was bound to feel used if he learned she couldn't have children. Wouldn't he see their continuing relationship as her desperate attempt to mother his children? She couldn't bear losing him, not to the truth, not now, not yet.

Then one night Jake unknowingly introduced the beginning of the end of their affair. After a particularly tender session of lovemaking, he held her close, his chest to her back, and said very quietly into her hair, "I love you, Olivia." Moments passed while she made no response. She couldn't, her throat was locked. He gave a whispered little laugh, murmuring, "Did you hear me? I said I love you."

And tonelessly she said, "No, Jake, don't."

Turning her to face him, he frowned slightly at her impassive expression. "No, don't love you? Or no, don't tell you I love you? Or no, you don't love me in return?"

"No, don't confuse lovemaking with love," she said lamely.

"I haven't," he said, his voice low and deep. "I loved you long before I ever made love to you."

"That was lust for my sexy Olive Oyl body, Brutus," she corrected, trying to tease but failing miserably.

"I assure you it wasn't." He smiled faintly and amended his answer to: "Well, not altogether. Flannel and all, Olive, that body of yours does inspire my licentious instincts." His mouth straightened and he said very soberly, "I've waited a long time to tell you again. I did tell you once."

She remembered. The first time they'd made love. She whispered unhappily, "Oh, Jake . . ."

A painful softening came over his face, tearing at her

heart. "Okay, you're not ready to believe me yet. I'll wait and tell you again in the cold light of day. Maybe then you'll realize that the love I have for you is the real, abiding kind."

And he reached across her to snap off the bedside lamp.

Long after he had fallen asleep against her shoulder, Livvy's frightened thoughts whirled and escalated in her brain.

On a Saturday morning in early February, weak sunlight pushed anemically through the kitchen window at The Little Yellow House. Livvy's dream of sharing the present without worrying about the future was beginning its third week.

"I've been thinking," Jake said quietly as Livvy took her empty breakfast plate to the sink and came back with the coffee pot.

Filling his cup, she said, "What about?" and turned to replace the glass pot in the automatic coffee maker on the counter behind him.

"About us. About where we're headed."

There was an odd determination in his voice, and an awful choking dread began clutching at Livvy's stomach. She turned from the counter and said brightly, *"I'm* headed for the bathroom and a quick shower." Throwing a smile in his general direction, she breezed by his chair.

"Hold it!" he ordered softly, grabbing a handful of her bathrobe as she whizzed past him. Gently, inexorably, he tugged her back. With his bare foot, he nudged her chair from under the table. "Sit!" he said, releasing her robe.

She sank into the chair with her head lowered. She stared at her hands clasped in her lap, at the frayed edges of her bathrobe, at her sock-covered feet peeking out from the equally frayed hem. His dry laugh brought her head up.

"Try the window," he said mildly, too mildly.

"What?"

"If you can't look at me, try looking out the window. I'd like to know what you see out there."

As bidden, her gaze turned to the window. Quietly she described the bleak scene. "A winter morning—brown grass, bare trees, pale sunlight peeking through gray clouds."

"The cold light of day?"

She let her gaze meet his and, dry-mouthed, whispered, "Yes."

Making no attempt to touch her, except with the intensity of his gaze, Jake said the words quietly, his voice low and deep. "I love you, Livvy. I want to marry you."

Her heart somersaulted, then thudded painfully. It should have been a time for rejoicing, but she was trapped by circumstances that wouldn't let her embrace the joy. She stared at him, her heart's torment in her eyes. Reality had caught up with her, shattering her dream.

"I care about you, Jake. You know that, but—"

"You love me," he corrected flatly, his eyes bleak. "I don't know why you won't admit it in words, but I know you love me. I feel it in your touch. I see it in your eyes. I sense it in your moods."

She wanted to reach across the table and erase the pain and confusion on his face. She pushed her hands punishingly between her tightly clamped knees. "Marriage is a big step, Jake. We've only known each other a few months."

"Are you asking for a longer courtship?"

The words were sweetly old-fashioned, said with unbearable tenderness. The temptation to answer yes was very, very strong. And very, very wrong. Such a response would imply she could be persuaded, and she could not be.

"No," she said hollowly. "I'm not asking for a longer courtship."

There was a tension-fraught silence. Jake broke it by laughing unsteadily. "No, you're retreating again, aren't you, Olivia? You don't like handling serious emotions."

She floundered, trying to buy time. "Can't we continue the way we are, Jake?"

"With what? Our relationship? Our romance? Our entanglement? Our affair?"

"Affair, I guess," she mumbled unhappily.

He drew a short, hard breath, then let it out slowly. Very gently he said, "We've been having a *love* affair, Olivia. It leads to commitment and marriage and an abiding relationship."

The challenge in his tone was soft, but there nonetheless. Livvy sat there, feeling the bottom dropping out of her world, wondering how to prevent herself from falling through the void. Her eyes pleaded for help. "Marriage isn't the answer for every relationship, Jake."

Beneath his pullover sweater, his shoulder muscles bunched as he propped his elbows on the table, staring at her hard. "It is for this one. I love you and I want to share all my life with you, not just bits and pieces of it. What we have is worth building a future on. Don't deny it," he said, his voice raspy and intense. "Don't deny *us!*"

She stared at him without speaking, her chin inching higher, her mouth a straight, defensive line. She was denying them. She had to. And it hurt.

"God!" His head fell back to his shoulders, his eyes turned ceilingward as if appealing to the Supreme Deity. "Why did I fall in love with the one woman who's as stubborn as a mule, as blind as a bat, and as frightened as a rabbit?" His eyes came back to her, hard and accusing and hurt. "Would you tell me what you find frightening about sharing a closet with me? Or a bank account and credit cards? Or anything more than my bed? I'm honest. I don't cheat the IRS. I don't smoke, drink too much, or curse without provocation. I'm kind to animals and chil-

261

dren and old people. I provide a decent home for my niece and nephew."

"And you want to fill your home with more children," she said, swallowing heavily, her fingers twisting the ties of her robe into tight little braids.

There was an electric silence. Then Jake scrunched his eyes tightly shut and breathed shakily, "So that's it!" When he opened them again, his eyes were brilliant with relief. "You think I'll pressure you into having babies right away, don't you?"

The sorrow in her welled up as she stared at him wordlessly.

Jake came out of his chair, went down on his haunches before her, and took her hands in his. "Livvy, that part of it can wait until you feel more comfortable with it. And you will, you know," he said with quiet confidence. "You love children too much not to want your own again someday."

"I can't—" she began painfully, but he shushed her, gently squeezing her hands.

"Okay, you can't right now. I understand that." His eyes twinkled a little. "But when our grandchildren come along, I want to hear your apology when I say I told you so."

His gentle, sweet, assured, innocently incognizant smile sent the sorrow spilling from her eyes. She wrenched her hands from his grasp and covered her face, bumping her glasses askew. Tears seeped through her fingers as her shoulders shook with silent, wretched sobs.

With a husky groan Jake stood up and reached for her glasses, laying them on the tabletop before pulling her out of the chair and against him. While she wept, he held her, offering her the comfort of his mouth in her hair, the gentleness of his hands stroking her back, and the strength of his arms about her.

"Hush, Livvy, it's all right. I love you. I won't force you into anything. I won't ever do anything to hurt you."

Raising her tear-ravaged face, she looked at him and whispered unevenly, "You couldn't hurt me, Jake, but I might hurt you. More than I already have. And I love you too much for that. I can't—"

Her words were smothered under the sudden fierce pressure of his mouth, the breath squeezed from her lungs by the bone-crushing embrace of his arms. Then he covered her face with kisses, hard ones, elated ones, possessive ones, triumphant ones. And between them he said hoarsely, "I knew you loved me! You crazy, stubborn woman, I knew you loved me!" And again he crushed her mouth under his until she yielded limply against him, her head whirling, her tortured thoughts momentarily pacified under the warm solace of his mouth.

When he finally raised his head, her heart was thundering in her ears, and she said shakily, "Jake, I—"

"You love me," he interrupted firmly. "I won't listen to anything else."

"I love you." She whispered it, her voice a thread of sound, her eyes misty and her heart breaking at the incredible joy on his face. How could she hurt him with the truth? How could she not? But not now, not today . . .

He bracketed her face in hands that trembled, while his mouth cherished her temple, her forehead, her nose, then brushed hers. "Say it again," he instructed thickly.

"I love you," she complied weakly, hanging on to his neck by the clinging loop of her arms.

"Again!" he breathed at the pulse at her throat.

"I love you." Her words were clearer this time, but with an underlying note of despair.

His burning kiss rewarded her. "Now tell me you'll marry me, that together we'll work out our future."

For a moment she said nothing. Then, pushing out of his arms, she complained thinly, "I can't think when you're kissing me." He grinned and reached for her, and she backed away, imploring urgently, "Please, Jake, I've got to think. You must give me time to think, time to be alone." Her eyes pleaded as her inner voice jeered, *Atta way to go, Livvy! Evasive to the end!*

His reluctance was in every line of his tensing body, but as he stared at her pale face, saw the torment and the fear and the indecision, he jammed his hands inside his jeans pockets and said, "How long?"

"A few days, Jake. Please, just a few days," she requested quickly, her voice soft and wispy. And when his mouth tightened a little, she said, "You told me you're a patient man. Surely you can let me have a few days."

Jake sighed and it was back—the old amusement, the self-mocking half smile and raised brow. "Me and my big mouth," he muttered, adding, "okay, pretty woman, you've just bought yourself a few days."

A fragile smile came to her face. She knew her reprieve was only temporary. Somehow in the next few days she would have to muster her courage and find a way to tell him everything. Her heart felt like a solid lump of clay, just sitting in her chest, no longer thumping madly, no longer filled with hope.

CHAPTER TWELVE

On Sunday afternoon, after a weekend of troubled thought and indecision, Livvy came to the desperate conclusion that there was no easy way to tell Jake why she couldn't marry him. Only a less difficult way. Written words, sent by mail, might explain simply and unemotionally a very complicated and emotional situation. At least, that was the hope that spurred her to find pen and paper.

An hour later, staring down at the sheet of blue note paper she had just scribbled her name to, she tried to imagine Jake's reaction, then suddenly tried not to. She wasn't proud of the way she had let their relationship progress without warning Jake of its limitations. Following his initial disappointment was bound to be a bitter contempt for her cowardice and selfishness and near-deceit. Would the regret conveyed in her letter be enough to assuage some of the pain she'd caused?

My loving Jake, said the salutation, and she knew it was a meager way to express her regard for him. Tears formed and she blinked them away irritably, resolutely reading what she'd written.

Because of you the last few weeks have been the sweetest of my life. You've brought me love and warmth and caring, so undemandingly I loved you before I knew it. I wish

I could return all you've given in the way you want and deserve, but it's impossible. I can't marry you.

Irrevocably impossible. She dashed an impatient hand across her face, wiping away the tears that insisted on coming in streams. "Oh, damn, you crybaby!" she mumbled, snatching a tissue to dry her face and blow her nose. Sniffing, slightly more composed, she read on.

You had me pegged when you likened me to Olive Oyl. Her circumstances and mine are very similar. Swee' Pea was given to Olive. I like to believe Horizon's children are given to me. I know they're gifts I cherish—for themselves, and because they're the only children I'll ever have. I can't be the mother of your children, Jake. I'm sterile. Forgive me for not telling you sooner.

Forgive? Could he possibly forgive when her confession came so late? And yet . . . She took a deep breath, reading the unmistakable hope of her last words.

If you still want me, I'd like to be with you. I'll be your lover or anything else within my capabilities.

She had signed it *All my love, Livvy.* Would he understand how deeply she meant that? Would he read the overused words and realize they were much, much more than a trite, meaningless phrase?

Before she could change her mind, she folded the paper in half and slid it into an envelope. Finding a stamp, then her purse and coat, she left the house and drove to the nearest mailbox. He would get it in Monday's mail. Tomorrow's mail.

Feeling more dispirited than relieved, she drove home and did something she'd never even considered doing before. She couldn't take a chance on seeing Jake in the next few days, so she called Glory and arranged for her to take over the running of Horizon House for a week. Glory was cooperative, intuitive, concerned.

"You've been crying." She probed gently. "Is there any special message you want passed on to Jake tomorrow morning?"

"Just that I'll see him in a few days."

"Will he accept that?"

"Yes." On Monday morning he would. He would be thinking of the few days she had requested to consider his proposal.

"You've told him, haven't you?"

On a ragged sigh, Livvy admitted, "Yes."

"Surely he didn't take it so badly," Glory said in mild surprise.

Livvy drew a deep breath. "I don't know," she said hollowly. "He won't get the letter until tomorrow." And in the ensuing silence she sensed her friend's utter disbelief.

"Oh, Livvy! A letter?" Glory's soft remonstrance triggered Livvy's defensiveness.

"He wants to marry me, Glory," she said tightly. "He can hardly wait to see our *grandchildren* come along so he can tease me about my unnecessary fear of risking motherhood again. He was so damned eager and happy, I couldn't bear watching his expectancy turn to disappointment."

"And in the letter you refused his proposal because you can't have children," Glory concluded grimly. "Do you honestly believe Jake will accept your decision?"

"He'll have to," Livvy averred stubbornly, then added less rigidly, "I told him I'd be here if he still wants me."

"Oh, that's just peachy!" Glory exclaimed in blatant exasperation. "The man wants marriage, and you offer him an affair! I'm sure he'll be thrilled with your generous compromise!"

Glory was her friend, she meant well, but an anguish of resentment swept through Livvy at her words. "At least it's a compromise! When they take out the baby-making equipment, there's no compromise!" she erupted with bitter frustration. "They don't give it back with a pat on the head, saying, 'There, you're all whole again!

Go out and find a man who wants children and give him at least a dozen!' "

There was a subdued silence following her outburst, and Livvy immediately regretted her words. Just because she was miserable and wound as tight as a drum was no reason to spew angry words at Glory! She felt like crying again.

A few minutes passed before Glory said quietly, "A lot of women are barren. A lot of men are impotent. Children aren't the only reason a couple chooses to marry."

Point for Glory. But when one partner wanted children and the other was physically incapable of supplying them, the decision to marry was precarious at best and could lead to bitter disappointment.

Knowing she and Glory would never agree, Livvy released an unsteady laugh. "Glory, darling, when you get your girls raised to womanhood, will you give me some of the credit for helping you discover all the right values to pass on to them? You've had such a lot of practice instructing me."

"Are you calling me a mother?" Glory riposted immediately, knowing she was forgiven, her ready laugh ending the tension between them.

That evening Livvy began her vigil of waiting, sorting through her thoughts and emotions, mentally preparing for the next confrontation. There would be one. Jake was nothing if not persistent. He would contact her. She wanted him to.

On Monday evening the phone rang incessantly, and Livvy knew Jake had received her letter. But she didn't answer the phone. His spur-of-the-moment reaction wasn't what she wanted. She wanted him to think carefully through his options.

On Tuesday the phone rang all day. On Wednesday it was silent. Midway through Thursday the door knocker banged twice—hard, short, impatient raps.

On her way to the door she chanced a quick glance out

the window. No help there. It was impossible to gauge his mood. Jake had turned to face the street, and her fleeting appraisal saw only the back of his lean, business-suited frame and his chestnut curls blown into disarray by the cool February breeze. A nervous flutter rioted in her stomach, anticipation and dread vying for supremacy as she stepped to the door, half afraid to open it.

Another demanding thud, this one of knuckles rapping sharply on wood, sent her damp palms down the thighs of her jeans. Taking a deep breath, she opened the door—

—to be subjected to electric aqua eyes glittering a bold and possessive regard as they went over her, a gaze glinting with something akin to reckless purpose as it locked with hers; to be the recipient of a wide, slightly mocking grin; to answer it with a cautious smile.

She had expected to see anger, bitterness, contempt, hurt, disappointment. The lack of those emotions in his features sent relief coursing through her, while an indefinable anxiety gnawed insistently at the recesses of her consciousness.

"I accept," Jake said without preamble, shoving a small, flat gift-wrapped package into her hands as he stepped inside. When she accepted it uncertainly, he explained, "A present to seal your proposal."

"Proposal?" she echoed, head angled warily.

"Nothing respectable, pretty woman, so you needn't look so worried," he jeered softly, his eyes full of sizzling sparks and his grin now slightly wolfish. "You proposed remaining my lover or anything else I wanted."

The choices of her letter. The "anything else" had been meant to imply friend or companion. A warning bell sounded dimly in her mind, but she ignored it. He was here. He had obviously accepted that she couldn't marry him. She wouldn't question any overture that kept him with her.

Impulsively she leaned forward and kissed his cheek. "I love you, Jake," she said huskily as she drew back.

"Do you?" One brow rose in teasing mockery.

She nodded solemnly, her eyes drinking in his beloved features.

His slow smile prefaced an ironic observation. "That wasn't the kiss of a lover, Olivia," he pointed out in soft, drawling tones. "I've waited several days. I think I deserve a lover's kiss for my patience."

Encircling her with his arms, his hands found the tender curves of her buttocks and pulled her against him. With slow deliberation, using several mind-teasing seconds, he aligned her pelvis intimately with his. There was a lazy curve to his mouth as it slowly came down on hers. There was nothing at all lazy about his long, draining kiss. It rocked her on her toes and sent her arms looping about his neck to support her suddenly whirling senses. Expert, sensual, his mouth tasted of heat and hunger and raw need, slanting, clinging, devouring hers. Obstinately disregarding the pangs of unease that still hovered in the shadows of her mind, Livvy met his passion with the ardor he always instilled in her.

Raising his head, Jake murmured huskily, "Now that's a lover's kiss." And immediately took another from her upturned mouth, this one tinged with violence, crushing resistance from her unresisting lips, taking punitive toll of her passionate acceptance.

When he raised his head the second time, he was breathing hard, his glinting eyes tracing the fringe of uncertainty in her expression. His half smile appeared, slightly strained, and he brushed her swollen lips with a curiously gentle thumb, as if to erase the momentary savagery he had subjected them to.

"Lover is a very straightforward term, Olivia," he said while gently adjusting her glasses, which had slipped slightly sideways on her face during the last kiss. "I couldn't misconstrue it. But I'm confused about what else you were offering me. Were you agreeing to be my mistress?"

The last query was just short of a taunt, and sharpened her gaze over his face. "If that's what you want," she said slowly, deciding that the sparkle in his eyes was a teasing one.

Leaning forward, Jake placed a soft kiss at her temple, breathing laughingly, "I've never had a mistress before. You'll be my first."

"I've never been one," Livvy murmured, shivering a little as his lips brushed her ear. Teasing back, she said, "We'll learn together."

A quick, hard kiss dropped to her mouth before Jake moved back. After glancing at his watch, he sent her a rueful grin. "I'm pressed for time right now, but it shouldn't take too long to work out a few details, should it? At least we're starting even this time. You know what I want. I know what you're prepared to give."

"Jake . . . ?" Her soft voice asked questions, begged explanations. The anxiety she had tried to smother was back, edging into her relief. He wasn't serious, was he, behind his smiling countenance?

His grin widened as he turned her toward the kitchen with a familiar swat on her backside. "Go get me some coffee. I talk better with caffeine in my system."

A little confused by his half-teasing, half-taunting mood, she left him. Absently setting the small gift-wrapped parcel on the kitchen counter, she reached for the coffee canister and began spooning aromatic grounds into a paper filter.

Jake had not once mentioned her sterility, she realized uneasily as she poured water into the top of the automatic coffee maker and switched it on. Nor had he mentioned love. He seemed bent on some teasing game to label their relationship. As the coffee brewed, Livvy pondered. Less than a week before, Jake had proposed marriage, determinedly and lovingly. Now he was accepting her refusal without question. She found that odd and out of character for the persistent man she knew him to be.

Sighing, she found a cup and filled it with the hot brewed coffee. Perhaps grins and heavy-handed humor were Jake's way of sugarcoating a painful situation. Spooning sugar into his coffee, she found a smile, reassured by her reasoning. With both coffeecup and smile held steady, she left the kitchen.

As she entered the living room, her careful smile readjusted to accommodate a startled "Oh!" She came to a dead stop, every wary nerve in her body jangling to life. Not far from where she'd left Jake just minutes before, his discarded shoes lay on their sides, and not far from them, his socks. Her wide brown eyes leaped from item to item dropped in a trail on the floor toward an inevitable destination—jacket heaped carelessly, tie almost arrow-straight between jacket and shirt, then slacks with belt still through the loops, until finally dark navy briefs completed the path, like a period at the end of a sentence. Jake was pressed for time. Evidently he meant to make the most of it.

A swift, darting glance found the sofa cushions tossed in haphazard fashion at the end of the opened-out sofa mattress. Livvy did a quick mental reassessment of Jake's motives and said a forlorn farewell to the hope that he was sugarcoating. No, his latest action had all the earmarks of an overstaged burlesque. But to what purpose?

"Smells good! Does a mistress serve her lover coffee in bed?"

The low, mocking query jerked her eyes to the one place they'd refused thus far to go—the sofa and its occupant. He wore such a bland, totally guileless expression, she thought distrustfully before her gaze involuntarily sought the length of him.

Naked, of course. Totally naked. He hadn't even bothered drawing the sheet to his waist. Long and lean and boldly male, he was half sitting, half lying, one knee drawn up, his arm dropped lazily across it.

Coming slowly out of her immobility, Livvy took him

272

the coffee, with an effort keeping her eyes meticulously on his face. Her shock was very real, very disturbing, but some inner warning system told her not to show it. As Jake took the first sip of coffee and sighed appreciatively, Livvy wondered at his motive for stripping bare and sprawling like a lazy, waiting tiger on the bed that had known their tenderest moments. Not desire, she speculated, casting a quick, furtive glance at his sprawled body. Well, at least not overwhelming desire. She kept her face deliberately blank, conveying, she hoped, not one iota of the unrest she was experiencing.

After a moment Jake murmured approvingly, "Tight jeans," as his eyes made a tour of her long legs, flat stomach, and slender hips encased in the snug denim. He winked, reaching out to cup his palm over the back of her knee. "When it comes to mistresses, I'll have the one who looks greatest in tight jeans. I think I'll buy you a dozen pair and never let you wear another skirt." His voice was low and sexy as he added, "But I wouldn't mind if my mistress took them off right now and joined me here."

It was all Livvy could do to keep her gaze level with the teasing glitter of his and her knees from wobbling as his fingers began a bold caress up her inner thigh. To her mind, the term "mistress" was becoming gratingly overused.

More snappily than she'd intended, she said, "Are you certain you have time for your *mistress* right now? You said you were in a hurry."

Her slight sarcasm produced Jake's wide, white grin. "I'm going to enjoy making time for you, pretty mistress," he drawled, casually indulging in another sip of coffee before adding, "Did you open your present?"

In slow motion Livvy blinked, admitted "I forgot," and about-faced, heading for the kitchen at a steady march that bordered on militant. Jake's little theatrics weren't only overstaged, they were overacted! And she was putting two and two together fast! Since he'd walked into her house, he had given her one clue after another—"proposal," "respectable," "mistress," and now his insensitive striptease! In the kitchen, she snatched the frilly package from the counter, jerkily tearing open the wrapping.

Seconds later a thin little screech—somewhere between aghast and enraged—emanated from the kitchen, producing an echo from the living room in the form of a low rumble of satisfied masculine laughter. Steam seemed to envelop Livvy's head like a volcanic cloud. Her eyes narrowed as she glared at the two little wisps of scarlet spilling from the tissue paper of the opened present.

Mistress, huh! No self-respecting mistress would be caught dead wearing such ridiculous excuses for lingerie! They were pure provocation, six steps beyond skimpy, in her mind less risqué than obscene. Bra and panties, she supposed grimly. Minuscule cups and diminutive triangles, threadlike ribbons and see-through lace. Grabbing up the offensive garments, she stormed out of the kitchen. Jake's game had gone far enough!

Five feet nine inches of slim, trembling hauteur drew to a halt by the side of the bed. Her flashing brown eyes found its occupant. As if firmer handling might detonate them, tiny scarlet wisps dangled from the tips of her enraged fingers.

"I am not a Barbie doll!" Livvy announced in a tiny, dignified whisper.

In the next second two fragile missiles were hurled through the air toward the target of a bland, unblinking masculine face. Weightless, free-floating, the delicate projectiles fluttered to a stop, one draped across a glittering aqua eye, the other suspended from a bold nose to cover a wide mouth. Scarlet ribbons dripped in helter-skelter profusion from his ear and jaw, unfortunately doing little to disguise Jake's unperturbed expression. Livvy fumed.

Blowing softly, Jake dislodged the bit of fluff that decorated his mouth and nose. It drifted to his bare chest. A slight nod of his head sent the other piece gliding to the same destination. He covered them with a caressing hand, rubbing them through his chest hair as if the feel of them pleased him.

"Don't you like them?" he asked mildly.

"Of course I don't like them! I don't wear . . . those . . . those . . . !" She couldn't think of a bad enough description.

"Delectables," Jake supplied without batting an eye. "The saleswoman called them delectables. I understood they'd be a perfect gift for a mistress." He shrugged and tossed them aside. "Oh, well, get your clothes off and come here. I can always imagine you wearing them."

"It wouldn't take much imagination!" Livvy stated acidly.

A quick glitter, decidedly gratified, came to Jake's eyes. "Perhaps not," he conceded, grinning. "And besides, I think I can get my steam up without the enticement of the little delectables."

Gasping at his crudity, Livvy squawked, "Jake!"

Smiling benignly, he drank the last of his coffee and set the cup aside. Folding his hands behind his head, he eyed her temper-flushed features and flashing eyes, and murmured coaxingly, "Come on, Livvy. I don't have much time. I have some contract negotiations to get through this afternoon."

Her hands met her hips as she leaned forward and demanded tautly, "If you're in such a hurry, why did you come here and . . . and strip!"

In a voice so dark and liquid she almost missed the barbed insult, he suggested, "A quickie?"

She blinked and gasped anew. "Why are you being deliberately offensive?" she asked in a strangled voice.

"Offensive?" He rolled the syllables in his mouth as if tasting a new word in the English language. "I'm only trying to entice my lover who promised to be my mistress into bed with me. Why are you so huffy?"

"Huffy!" she huffed out on another enraged gasp.

"Huffy," he repeated, nodding judiciously. His eyes went to half-mast, pure male sensuality oozing from him as he said huskily, "Come here, pretty woman, time's running out and I really do need it."

"It!" Her voice had thinned to a horrified thread. She was thoroughly insulted. And hurt.

"It," Jake repeated levelly. "You know, the only thing you're prepared to give me. Your body. The use of it. Sex. It."

The understated contempt of his mildly spoken words dropped his last pretense of humor. As he stared at her, the faint hostility in his eyes sent Livvy back to plop weakly into the chair behind her, all her outrage deflated, all her fine, furious energy depleted.

"Jake, I've disappointed you again, I know," she said unsteadily, "but don't be like this, please."

"What makes you think you've disappointed me?" he asked curiously.

Her hands fluttered uselessly, dropped to her lap, and clenched tightly together. "The letter," she whispered miserably.

"Your *love* letter?" he qualified with deadly irony.

Nodding unhappily, Livvy watched him calmly swing his legs over the side of the bed and reach for the pants he had discarded. From the pocket he withdrew a slightly crumpled, but neatly refolded, blue paper. Her letter. Sitting there, naked, hard-eyed, he opened it. "This letter?"

Livvy could only nod again and wait for Jake to play out the drama he'd begun the moment he walked through her door.

"Why would this letter disappoint me?" he asked, scanning the contents thoughtfully. "It begins 'My loving Jake.' When I read that I thought I was getting an early Valentine." His mouth twisted bitterly, his face filled with remembered pain. His eyes dropped to the end of the page. "You signed it with all your love. How could *all* your love possibly disappoint me?" His voice was almost gentle, the dark sarcasm understated.

"Jake, don't—"

"Don't what? Don't read the letter? Too late, my love, I've already read it at least a dozen times," he said, still in that deadly pleasant voice. The paper in his hand shook a little from the tense tremor of his fingers. "Or do you mean don't read it aloud now? Why not? Surely, if you're brave enough to put your thoughts on paper, you're brave enough to hear what you've written."

Livvy stared at the starkness of his face, the accusation in his eyes. "The letter was an explanation, Jake. I'm not ashamed of writing it, only of waiting so long to tell you. I'm sorry it made you angry."

"Nothing so mild," he assured her easily. "I'm as close to furious as I've ever been."

Her heart was making skittish little advances to her throat. "I love you, Jake," she tried to say quietly, but her voice cracked and she had to clear it to repeat: "I love you, and I wanted you to understand why I couldn't marry you."

Jake surged to his feet, suddenly towering above her, his entire body trembling with suppressed rage. His face looking down at her was all taut lines and rigid angles.

In a low, tight voice, he said, "You wouldn't know love if it walked up to you and tried to take your hand! You're too busy running!"

Being told she didn't love him brought Livvy to her feet. Hands on hips, head angled forward, she whispered furiously, "That's not true!"

"Yes, it is!" he gritted through clenched teeth. "You've run from me every step of the way! Hell, I've worn out a dozen pairs of shoes chasing you! And you're always just beyond my reach, hiding in places I don't even know about! Come out of hiding, lady! Face what you're running from! It's not me, damn you, but your own fears!" He paused in his tirade, breathing hard, his hands clenched into fists at his sides, and his eyes stormy with fury.

"If I ran, it was because I've always known you and I had a limited future!" she defended herself vehemently. "I've always realized I could do nothing but hurt you!"

"Hurt! Hurt!" he raged, his voice an incensed growl. Suddenly his head was thrust forward, putting them nose to nose, his next words blasting the hot mist of his breath over her face. "Do you know how it hurts to love someone who gives it back in tiny, equivocal doses? Who won't trust you, won't confide in you, won't share with you?"

Startled by his charges, Livvy blinked and said more quietly, "I trust you."

"Enough to be my wife? Enough to realize I love you, not your ability to procreate?" Jake demanded, though he, too, was calmer, his fury diminishing to hard frustration.

In agitation his fingers combed through the hair on his chest. Livvy's eyes followed the movements, went lower, widened a little as she realized anew that he was naked. Jake's eyes followed the same path, blinked with the same realization.

"Hell!" he muttered, very distinctly, very flatly, bending down to retrieve his briefs and slacks.

As he put them on, Livvy turned away, confused, agitated, shaking her head and wrapping her arms about her waist. "You've never hidden your desire for children, Jake."

"I've never hidden my desire for *you*," he corrected grimly. She heard the slide of his zipper, then felt his hands come down on her shoulders, pulling her back against him so that her soft hair was against his cheek and jaw. "Children were never my foremost concern, Livvy, but they seemed to be important to you, and I was very eager to become all you wanted. Don't deny me now because I expressed something I thought would gain me you."

"But you would like children of your own," she insisted quietly, stubbornly. "I know you would."

In the following silence Jake's chest rose and fell at her back, his heavily released sigh redolent with patience. "It would be tempting to say no, Livvy, but I won't lie to you. I want children. *Our* children."

"Then you understand why—"

"No, I don't understand," he disagreed harshly, his fingers tightening on her shoulders. "I love you. You love me. I don't understand why the disappointment can't be shared. I don't understand why we can't work out the problem together."

"That's just it, Jake. It's my problem. I never intended it to be yours."

He turned her to face him, laying his palms alongside her cheeks to hold her face level, to make her look at the intentness of his expression, the sincerity in his eyes. "It's *our* problem. Loving is sharing."

Livvy was torn, wanting to believe, unable to give up all her doubts. Placing her hands over his on her face, she said, "But you could share your life with someone else, someone who could give you what I can't."

Jake said nothing for a moment, staring at her as if she'd suggested something obscene. Then his eyes shut tight and he took a long, jagged breath, releasing it to whisper very softly, "Ahhh, damn you!"

When his eyes opened, they were glistening, and the sight of his pain jerked her heart in her chest. With unsteady fingers she brushed the wetness from his lashes. "Jake, I wish—"

"So do I," he said gruffly. "I wish you would understand that I can't share with someone else what I've given you. My love is yours, Livvy. I can't take it back and give it to somebody else because it's more convenient. I don't want to." A painful softening came over his face, his mouth and eyes filling with gentle humor. "Since the day I fell on my back in Horizon's hallway, I've known you were mine. That discovery left me more winded than the fall. Sometimes I think I'm still catching my breath."

It was all there—the pain, the quiet conviction, the love, even the humor. She stared at his face, felt her doubts crumbling. "Jake, I've hurt you so much already. I can't bear being the cause of your future disappointment," she whispered urgently, needing one last reassurance.

He touched a finger to the rim of her glasses. "Pretty woman, you're not just nearsighted, you're blind. Mellie and Bret aren't faring too badly with me, and I love them. Hasn't it occurred to you that I'm a damned good adoptive father? And, God knows, Horizon House proves you'd be a good adoptive mother. Physical coupling isn't the only way to become parents. We already have two—and when we're ready, when our hearts tell us it's time, we'll get other children."

His words, uttered so gently, with such positive belief in the future, filled Livvy with a drowning exhilaration. They were the essence of the man, of his unqualified, unselfish love, and they banished her doubts forever. He was staring at her, waiting, watchful, hopeful, and a tremulous smile worked its way across her face. Her love surged in overwhelming swells to overflow from her eyes, blurring his image.

"Jake, why are you so good?" It was almost a complaint, issued in a joy-wracked whisper. "I think I could fight almost anything but your sweetness."

And he laughed, exultantly, knowing he had won. He kissed her once, hard, then looked at her with wicked eyes and a smug expression. "When a man goes after tender game, he doesn't bait the trap with rancid meat," he explained teasingly. Then, face sobering, he said deeply, "It will be a good marriage, Olivia. I know it will be."

"Yes," she whispered, for the first time as positive as he. "Oh, *yes!*" she repeated fervently, throwing her arms about his neck and seeking his mouth with hers.

Very gently, as if she were a fragile and precious gift he had coveted long and finally received, he removed her glasses, tossed them onto the chair she had vacated, and wrapped her in the careful embrace of his arms, his hands moving over her body in tender, intimate caresses. Edging toward the bed, they drifted onto it together, mouths clinging, sighing, mingling, hands searching, finding, giving in unhurried, loving touches.

When Livvy surfaced, her face was flushed, her lips soft and swollen, her eyes dilated, the salt of her joy long since kissed away. "I've never been able to resist you," she confessed, not altogether teasingly.

"That's because I drive an irresistible bargain," Jake said with easy understanding, driving her temperature a little higher as he sent warm hands under her loose sweater for the small swells of her breasts, the valley between, the twin crests.

In the midst of another softly adhesive communion of mouths, Livvy suddenly groaned as if in pain and bolted out of his arms. Kneeling beside him, she answered his look of concern with an unhappy "Your negotiations, Jake. We forgot all about them."

His grin was a flash of white in his tanned face. "Don't worry about it," he told her laughingly, reaching for her again.

But she eluded him, sitting back on her heels, holding his hands tightly in her lap. A suspicious gleam in his eyes had her squinting for a better look at his expression. She questioned slowly, "Have you forgotten the contract you're supposed to negotiate this afternoon?"

"Nope." Easily twisting his hands from hers, he gripped her wrists, tugging her back to his chest. "Come here and tell me when you'll marry me. That's the only detail we haven't worked out."

"You lied," Livvy accused softly, though she didn't resist when he snuggled her over his lean, hard body and trapped her legs with his.

"I didn't lie. Raise your arms," Jake murmured huskily, pulling up her sweater.

His removal of her sweater and bra was accommodated by her lithe twists and sensual contortions until all her upper torso wore was his heated gaze. Thickly uttered accolades expressed his pleasure in the sight of her. Gliding to her rib cage, gripping gently, his hands shifted her up his body. His mouth was hungry on her breasts, tasting, lingering, relishing, devouring.

Eyes closed, Livvy inhaled a blissful sigh deep into her lungs, trying to hang on to her whirling senses long enough to satisfy her curiosity. Her unsteady whisper asked, "If you didn't have business to conduct this afternoon, why did you say you had to leave?"

Silent, delirious moments passed while Jake continued to bathe her responsive flesh with the wet heat of his tongue. Near sanity's gate, Livvy forced his head up to meet her passion-clouded, questioning gaze.

The resignation in his sigh was barely noticeable, the thwarted desire in his voice a little more so. "I didn't say I had to leave, only that I was in a hurry, that I had some contract negotiations this afternoon. In case you haven't noticed, I've been"—his words broke, his breathing changing pace as Livvy wriggled down, brushing her mouth over his cleft chin and laying soft kisses on his bare shoulders and chest—"negotiating . . . for all I'm worth!" he finished on a jagged, pleasure-filled sigh.

Trying to keep up her end of the conversation, Livvy whispered in his ear, "You were awful, stripping bare and bringing me those detestables," she said, her voice low and throaty.

"De*lect*ables," Jake corrected in a quick burst of laughter.

As her teeth sank gently into his shoulder, she mumbled determinedly, "De*test*ables!"

When she glanced up, Jake was trying to look repentant and failing miserably in the attempt. His eyes were full of wicked sparks and his wide mouth was quivering at the edges. Reaching across the bed, he brought back a handful of scarlet and studied it consideringly.

"Michelle's black lace and red satin gave Mac food for thought. I figured a similar tactic might give you a thought or two," he explained sweetly around a placating smile.

No answering smile touched Livvy's mouth. "I *thought* you were deliberately insulting."

The wispy debatables quickly disappeared over the back of the sofa. Cradling her head, Jake brought her mouth down to his for a pacifying kiss. Very softly, but not without a measure of complacency, he said, "I was only trying to convince you to marry me, and I did, didn't I?"

"I guess so, since you've refused to make me your mistress," Livvy conceded grudgingly before her grin came splashing across her face. His bare rib cage became her playground. Her fingers danced and skittered its length, causing a tremor to course his body.

"When?" was a compelling request at her throat. "When will you make an honest man of me?"

"What's today?"

"Thursday."

Cherishing the corner of his mouth with the delicate applications of her tongue, she said, "I meant, what's the date?"

"February seventh." His tongue coaxed hers inside his mouth, kept it there for a greedy moment.

Her hands closing over his ears, she ended the kiss on a loud smack. "Good!" she uttered happily. "Tomorrow's your birthday. We can get married anytime after today."

"Nice birthday present," Jake reflected lazily. His

hands went between them, unsnapping, unzipping, tugging at her jeans. Laziness gave way to urgency as he instructed hoarsely, "Lift a little."

Instead of just lifting, Livvy sat up and quickly helped him dispose of their last garments. With teasing satisfaction she announced, "The marriage license will list us both the same age after today."

Jake grinned at her humor, though it was a slightly strained version of his usual wide expression of amusement. His body, his entire being, was suddenly, irrevocably intent on other matters. He pulled her to a silken sprawl atop him, kissing her deeply. "Thank you for accepting my proposal," he whispered softly.

Grasping the satiny curves of her hips, he lifted her and eased her slowly down upon him. Breath stilled in her throat before she gasped a soft, polite, slightly tardy "You're welcome." Then, looking down at him with eyes of love, she repeated, "You're welcome," the low and throaty utterance giving the words a different meaning, her feminine warmth giving his masculine strength a special welcome.

His gaze swept her slender body astride his, then wandered with joyful brilliance all over her face and hair. He smiled—the one she loved—that half smile expressing his utmost pleasure. At her thighs, his hands urged her to meet the compelling, rhythmic power of his body. His eyes locked with hers, ardent, loving, tender, passionate. He vowed huskily, "I love you, Olivia."

Giving herself up to the loving, Livvy knew his love was complete and many-faceted, a gift to her in all ways, and she quietly breathed against his lips, "And I love you, Jake."

LOOK FOR NEXT MONTH'S
CANDLELIGHT ECSTASY SUPREMES:

All-new

Candlelight Newsletter

An exceptional, *free* offer awaits readers of Dell's incomparable Candlelight Ecstasy and Supreme Romances.

Subscribe to our all-new CANDLELIGHT NEWSLETTER and you will receive—at absolutely no cost to you—exciting, exclusive information about today's finest romance novels and novelists. You'll be part of a select group to receive sneak previews of upcoming Candlelight Romances, well in advance of publication.

You'll also go behind the scenes to "meet" our Ecstasy and Supreme authors, learning firsthand where they get their ideas and how they made it to the top. News of author appearances and events will be detailed, as well. And contributions from the Candlelight editor will give you the inside scoop on how she makes her decisions about what to publish—and how *you* can try your hand at writing an Ecstasy or Supreme.

You'll find all this and more in Dell's CANDLELIGHT NEWSLETTER. And best of all, *it costs you nothing*. That's right! It's Dell's way of thanking our loyal Candlelight readers and of adding another dimension to your reading enjoyment.

Just fill out the coupon below, return it to us, and look forward to receiving the first of many CANDLELIGHT NEWSLETTERS—overflowing with the kind of excitement that only enhances our romances!

 DELL READERS SERVICE –Dept. B434A
P.O. BOX 1000, PINE BROOK, N.J. 07058

Name_____

Address_____

City_____

State_____ Zip_____

CANDLELIGHT
Ecstasy Supreme